PRAISE FOR WALKER PERCY'S NOVELS

"He is a beguiling, uniquely gifted novelist who deserves to be read in order and in full."

Newsweek

"Percy has a rare talent for making his people look and sound as though they were being seen and heard for the first time by anyone."

Time

"Mr. Percy's writing has a lyric quality. It is honest and can be bluntly humorous."

St. Louis Post-Dispatch

Also by Walker Percy:

Fiction
THE MOVIEGOER *
THE LAST GENTLEMAN *
LOVE IN THE RUINS *
LANCELOT *
THE THANATOS SYNDROME *

Nonfiction
THE MESSAGE IN THE BOTTLE
LOST IN THE COSMOS

* Published by Ivy Books

THE SECOND COMING

Walker Percy

IVY BOOKS • NEW YORK

Ivy Books
Published by Ballantine Books
Copyright © 1980 by Walker Percy

Library of Congress Catalog Card Number 80-12899

ISBN 0-8041-0542-1

This edition published by arrangement with Farrar, Straus and Giroux

Manufactured in the United States of America

First Ballantine Books Edition: January 1990

PART ONE

I

THE FIRST SIGN THAT SOMETHING HAD GONE WRONG MANI-
fested itself while he was playing golf.

Or rather it was the first time he admitted to himself that
something might be wrong.

For some time he had been feeling depressed without knowing why. In fact, he didn't even realize he was depressed. Rather
was it the world and life around him which seemed to grow
more senseless and farcical with each passing day.

Then two odd incidents occurred on the golf course.

Once he fell down in a bunker. There was no discernible
reason for his falling. One moment he was standing in the bunker with his sand-iron appraising the lie of his ball. The next he
was lying flat on the ground. Lying there, cheek pressed against
the earth, he noticed that things looked different from this un-
accustomed position. A strange bird flew past. A cumulus cloud
went towering thousands of feet into the air. Ordinarily he would
not have given the cloud a second glance. But as he gazed at it
from the bunker, it seemed to turn purple and gold at the bottom
while the top went boiling up higher and higher like the cloud
over Hiroshima. Another time, he sliced out-of-bounds, something he seldom did. As he searched for the ball deep in the
woods, another odd thing happened to him. He heard something
and the sound reminded him of an event that had happened a
long time ago. It was the most important event in his life, yet
he had managed until that moment to forget it.

Shortly afterwards, he became even more depressed. People

3

seemed more farcical than ever. More than once he shook his head and, smiling ironically, said to himself: This is not for me.

Then it was that it occurred to him that he might shoot himself.

First, it was only a thought that popped into his head.

Next, it was an idea which he entertained ironically.

Finally, it was a course of action which he took seriously and decided to carry out.

The lives of other people seemed even more farcical than his own. It astonished him that as farcical as most people's lives were, they generally gave no sign of it. Why was it that it was he not they who had decided to shoot himself? How did they manage to deceive themselves and even appear to live normally, work as usual, play golf, tell jokes, argue politics? Was he crazy or was it rather the case that other people went to any length to disguise from themselves the fact that their lives were farcical? He couldn't decide.

What is one to make of such a person?

To begin with: though it was probably the case that he was ill and that it was his illness—depression—which made the world seem farcical, it is impossible to prove the case.

On the one hand, he was depressed.

On the other hand, the world is in fact farcical.

Or at least it is possible to make the case that for some time now life has seemed to become more senseless, even demented, with each passing year.

True, most people he knew seemed reasonably sane and happy. They played golf, kept busy, drank, talked, laughed, went to church, appeared to enjoy themselves, and in general were both successful and generous. Their talk made a sort of sense. They cracked jokes.

On the other hand, perhaps it is possible, especially in strange times such as these, for an entire people, or at least a majority, to deceive themselves into believing that things are going well when in fact they are not, when things are in fact farcical. Most Romans worked and played as usual while Rome fell about their ears.

But surely it is fair to say that when a man becomes depressed, falls down in a sand trap, and decides to shoot himself, something has gone wrong with the man, not the world.

If one person is depressed for every ninety-nine who are not or who say they are not, who is to say that the depressed person

4

is right and the ninety-nine wrong, that they are deceiving themselves? Even if this were true, what good would it do to unde-
ceive the ninety-nine who have diverted themselves with a busy
round of work and play and so imagine themselves happy?

The argument is abstract and useless.

On the other hand, it is an undeniable fact that more people
than ever are depressed nowadays. At last count, the symptom
of depression outnumbered all other symptoms put together.
What if the proportion of undepressed to depressed people
changes from ninety-nine to one to fifty-fifty? Perhaps the argument will become less abstract.

At any rate and regardless of who was or who was not demented,
something odd did happen to him on the golf course.

It happened in fact on the day after he had received the local
Rotary's man-of-the-year award for service to the community.

He and his partner, Dr. Vance Battle, were one down and two
to go in the foursome. Number seventeen was a par-five medium-
long dogleg with a good view of Sourwood Mountain, curving
past a pond and a low ridge of red maples which in the brilliant
sunlight looked like a tongue of fire searing the cool green fairway. It was not a difficult hole. Par golf required only that you
hit two fair woods to clear the point of the ridge for an easy
straightaway pitch to the green. His drive was well hit and went
high in a strong following wind. It carried a good three hundred
yards. His partner gave him a wink. The other players looked
at each other. Though the ridge and the pond lay between him
and the green, he decided to go for the flag. The instant he hit
the ball with a three-wood, he knew it was all right. It drew
slightly, enough to give the distance and to grab and hold the
sloping green. Without seeing the ball, he knew he had a putt
for an eagle.

His partner, Dr. Vance Battle, who sat in the cart on the
outside of the dogleg waiting for his third shot, was watching.
Vance looked at the green, looked back at him, held his hands
apart as if he were measuring a fish, cocked his head, winked
again and, though it could not be heard, gave his cluck *tchk*.

He looked down at the glossy brown club head. We used to
call this club a spoon, he thought, not a three-wood. What do
you think? he once asked an ancient black caddy at Sea Island.
That's a *spoon* shot, the caddy said with a certain emphasis and

a rising cadence and handed him the club with the complex but clear sense of what a *spoon* could do.

Now you choose a numbered club from the back of an electric cart.

It was at that moment that he paused for several seconds, wood still held in both hands, fingers overlapped, and seemed to listen for something. He gazed up at the round one-eyed mountain, which seemed to gaze back with an ironical expression.

Certain "quasi-sensory" symptoms, as one doctor explained later, began to manifest themselves. There was a slight not unpleasant twisting sensation in his head. A pied weed at the edge of the rough gave off a faint but acrid smell which rose in his nostrils. The bright October sunlight went dark as an eclipse. The scene before his eyes seemed to change. It was not really a hallucination, he learned from another doctor, but an "association response" such as might be provoked by a lesion in the frontal lobe of the brain, the seat of memory.

The doctors did not agree on the nature of his illness or even if he had an illness.

Instead of the immaculate emerald fairway curving between the scarlet and gold hillsides of the Appalachians, he seemed to see something else. It was a scene from his youth, so insignificant a recollection that he had no reason to remember it then, let alone now thirty years later. Yet he seemed to see every detail as clearly as if the scene lay before him. Again the explanation of the neurologist was altogether reasonable. The brain registers and records every sensation, sight and sound and smell, it has ever received. If the neurones where such information is stored happen to be stimulated, jostled, pressed upon, any memory can be recaptured.

Nothing is really forgotten.

The smell of chalk dust on the first day of school, the feel of hot corduroy on your legs, the shape of the scab on the back of your hand, is still there if you have the means of getting at it.

Instead of the brilliant autumn-postcard Carolina mountains, he seemed to see a weedy stretch of railroad right-of-way, but no more than a wedge-shaped salient of weeds angling off between the railroad tracks and the back yards of Negro cabins. It was shaped like a bent triangle, the bend formed by the curve of tracks. Perhaps it was owned by the railroad or perhaps the utility company, because in one corner there was a small fenced and locked enclosure which contained an even smaller metal hut. Or perhaps it was owned by the city, because at the end of this narrow vista of weeds rose the town water tower. Or perhaps it belonged to no one, not even the Negroes, a parcel of leftover land which the surveyors had not noticed on their maps.

Only once in his life had he ever set foot on this nondescript sector of earth. It was shortly after he had seen Ethel Rosenblum. As he took the shortcut home after school, walking the railroad tracks which ran behind the football field, he saw Ethel Rosenblum practicing her cheerleading. She was in uniform, brief blue skirt flared to show gold panties. She was short, her hair was kinky, her face a bit pocked. But as if to make up for these defects, nature had endowed her with such beauty and grace of body, a dark satinity of skin, a sweet firm curve and compaction of limb as not easily to be believed. She was smart in algebra and history and English. They competed for four years. She won. She was valedictorian and he salutatorian. She could factor out equations after the whole class was stumped, stand at the blackboard, hip hiked out, one fist perched cheerleaderwise on her pelvis, the other small quick hand squinched on the chalk, and cancel out great $a^2 - b^2$ complexes *zip zip slash*, coming out at the end: $a/a = 1. 1 = 1!$ Unity!

No matter how ungainly the equation, ugly and unbalanced, clotted with complexes, radicals, fractions, *zip zip* under Ethel Rosenblum's quick sure hand and they factored out and canceled and came down to unity, symmetry, beauty.

Would not life itself prove so?

No, as it turned out.

They knew each other, had sat in the same class for four years. Not twenty words had passed between them.

Once in his life had he set foot on this unnamed unclaimed untenanted patch of weeds and that was when he saw Ethel Rosenblum and wanted her so bad he fell down. So keen was his sorrow at not having his arms around her, his fingers knotted in her kinked chalk-dusted hair, that he flung himself down in a litter of algebra books, ring binders, *Literature and Life*, down into the Johnson grass and goldenrod, onto the earth smelling of creosote and rabbit tobacco.

Ah, *that* was the smell of the pied weed on the golf course, the acrid smell of rabbit tobacco!

Ethel, why is the world so designed that our very smartness and closeness keep us apart? Is it an unspoken pact? Is it an accursed shyness? Ethel, let's me and you homestead this left-over land here and now, this non-place, this surveyor's inter-stice. Here's the place for us, the only place not Jew or Gentile, not black or white, not public or private.

Later a doctor raised the possibility of a small hemorrhage or arterial spasm near the brain's limbic system, seat of all desire, a location which would account for the sexual component of his disorder.

"What sexual component?" he asked. "Doc, that was Ethel Rosenblum and I was fifteen."

"Yeah, but you're talking about her now."

Now in the middle of this pretty Carolina fairway in the sweet high mountain air, as the sky darkened and the acrid smell of rabbit tobacco rose in his nostrils, he fell down again, but only for an instant. Or perhaps he only stumbled, for the next thing he knew, the electric cart hummed up behind him and there was Vance.

No, he did fall down, because he seemed to see and smell the multicolored granules of chemical fertilizer scattered in the bent Bermuda.

I wonder, he said to himself nose down in the bent Bermuda, what would my life have been like if I had had four years of Ethel Rosenblum instead of four years of a dream of Ethel Rosenblum—and the twenty words between us:

"How you doing, Ethel?"

"I'm doing fine, Will. How are you?"

"Fine. Did you have a good summer?"

"Fine. I didn't do a thing. Well—"

"Well, I'll see you, Ethel."

"Yeah, I'll see you, Will."

Ethel, give me your hand. I know a place.

On the other hand, how could his life have turned out better if things had fallen out otherwise between him and Ethel Rosenblum, for had he not succeeded in his life in every way one can imagine? The only sign of something wrong was that he was thinking about a girl (and a place) whom he had known in high school thirty years ago.

What if he and Ethel had followed their inclinations, assuming she was of like mind (and she might have been! On commencement day after she had given her valedictory and he his salutatory, he had taken her small hand in his and told her goodbye. She had held his hand for a second and shaken her head and said in a fond sorrowful exasperation: "Oh, Will—!"), and fallen down together in the Johnson grass or wherever, when-ever—what then? Would he have been better off? Would he have become more like the young people and not so young he saw in town who lay about at their ease, good-humored and content as cats but also somewhat slack-jawed and bemused, who looked as if they could be doing the same thing ten years from now and not discontented then either—would he have been better off? Who knows?

At least he probably would not be falling down on golf courses and recalling odd bits and pieces of the past.

Lately he remembered everything. His symptom, if it was a symptom, was the opposite of amnesia, a condition as far as I known unnamed by medical science.

Everything reminded him of something else.

A whiff of rabbit tobacco in North Carolina reminded him of Ethel Rosenblum and a patch of weeds in Mississippi.

An odd-shaped cloud in the blue Carolina sky reminded him of a missing tile in the Columbus Circle subway station, which marked the spot where he often stood to catch the Eighth Avenue Express to Macy's. The tile had been broken out except for a strip at the top, which left a grayish concrete area shaped like Utah.

Yes, he must have fallen down in the fairway, for now Vance had him by the arm in some kind of expert doctor's double grip which holds you erect without seeming to.

"That was quite a shot."

"Did you see the ball?"

"It's a gimme. I been meaning to talk to you."

"Okay. Talk."

"Not here. Come see me at my office."

"Why?"

"I think something is wrong with you."

"Why?"

"People don't fall down in the middle of the fairway."

"I was thinking of something."

"You thought of something and fell down."

"That's right."

"You been acting a little off your feed. You worried about anything?"

"No."

"Did those sleeping pills I gave you help?"

"Yes. No, I didn't take them."

"You haven't been with us for some time."

"Us?"

"Us. Your family, your friends."

"How's that?"

"You don't say anything. And what you say is strange."

"Such as?"

"You asked me if I remembered a movie actor named Ross Alexander. I said no. You let it go at that. Then you asked me if Groucho Marx was dead. Then you asked me if the tendency to suicide is inherited. Do you remember?"

"Yes. You didn't answer."

"I didn't know. Are you feeling depressed?"

"No."

"What were you thinking about a minute ago after you hit that three-wood?"

"I was thinking about a girl I once knew."

"Then I'll stop worrying about you."

"Let's putt out."

"Okay."

"No, wait." And again he went into one of his spells, a "petty-mall trance" his doctor friend called them. They were sitting in the cart. He sat perfectly still for perhaps five seconds, which was long enough for the doctor to smile uneasily, then frown and lean over the seat to touch him.

"What is it, Will?"

"I just realized a strange thing."

"What's that?"

"There are no Jews up here."

"Jews?"

"I've been living here for two years and have never seen a Jew. Arabs, but no Jews. When I used to come here in the summer years ago, there used to be Jews here. Isn't that strange?"

"I hadn't thought about it. Hm." Dr. Vance knitted his brow and pretended to think but his eyes never left the other's face. "Interesting! Maybe they've all gone to Washington, ha ha."

"Come to think of it, how many Jews are left in the state of North Carolina?"

"Left? Have they been leaving? I hadn't noticed. Hm." Again Dr. Vance frowned and appeared to be searching his memory.

10

"Think about it. Weren't there Jews here earlier? You're a native."

"Well, there was Dr. Weiss and Dutch Mandelbaum in high school who played tackle."

"They're not here now?"

"No."

"You see."

"See what?"

"You know, my wife, who was very religious, believed that the Jews are a sign."

"A sign of what?"

"A sign of God's plan working out."

"Is that so?" Vance's eyes strayed to his wristwatch. He pretended to brush off a fly.

"But what about the absence of Jews? The departure of Jews?" he asked, looking intently at the doctor until his eyes rose. "What is that a sign of?"

"I couldn't say." Vance looked thoughtful. "Hm."

It is not at all uncommon for persons suffering from certain psychoses and depressions of middle age to exhibit "ideas of reference," that is, all manner of odd and irrational notions about Jews, Bildebergers, gypsies, outer space, UFOs, international conspiracies, and whatnot. Needless to say, the Jews were and are not leaving North Carolina. In fact, the Jewish community in that state, though small, is flourishing. There were at the last census some twenty-five synagogues and temples, ten thousand Jews with a median income of $21,000 per family.

The foursome finished the round without further incident. He sank his putt, a ten-footer not a gimme, for an eagle three, won both the fifty-dollar Nassau and the press bet, some two hundred dollars in all, took much good-natured kidding from his friends while they drank and rolled poker dice in the locker-room bar, a cheerful place smelling of sweat, bourbon whiskey, and hemp carpeting and dominated by a photomural of Jack Nicklaus blasting out of a sand trap. In all respects he seemed quite himself, though a bit absentminded, but smiling and nodding as usual—so normal indeed that his doctor friend gave no further thought to his "petty-mall trances." After all, a golfer who cards a seventy-six can't be too sick.

Surely, though, all is not well with a man who falls down in the fairway, and finds himself overtaken by unaccountable memories, memories of extraordinary power and poignancy. But memories of what? Of the most insignificant events and places imaginable, of a patch of weeds in Mississippi, of a missing tile in a gloomy New York subway station, of a girl whom he had not thought of since leaving high school!

2

It was a fine Sunday morning. The foursome teed off early and finished before noon. He drove through town on Church Street. Churchgoers were emerging from the eleven-o'clock service. As they stood blinking and smiling in the brilliant sunlight, they seemed without exception well-dressed and prosperous, healthy and happy. He passed the following churches, some on the left, some on the right: the Christian Church, Church of Christ, Church of God, Church of God in Christ, Church of Christ in God, Assembly of God, Bethel Baptist Church, Independent Presbyterian Church, United Methodist Church, and Immaculate Heart of Mary Roman Catholic Church.

Two signs pointing down into the hollow read: African Methodist Episcopal Church, 4 blocks; Starlight Baptist Church, 8 blocks.

One sign pointing up to a pine grove on the ridge read: St. John o' the Woods Episcopal Church, 6 blocks.

He lived in the most Christian nation in the world, the U.S.A., in the most Christian part of that nation, the South, in the most Christian state in the South, North Carolina, in the most Christian town in North Carolina.

Once again he found himself in the pretty reds and yellows of the countryside. As he drove along a gorge, he suffered another spell. Again the brilliant sunlight grew dim. Light seemed to rise from the gorge. He slowed, turned on the radio, and tried to tune in a nonreligious program. He could not find one. In the corner of his eye a dark bird flew through the woods, keeping pace with him. He knew what to do.

Pulling off at an overlook, he took the Luger from the glove compartment of the Mercedes. As he stepped out, he caught sight of a shadowy stranger in the mirror fixed to the door. But he quickly saw that the stranger was himself. The reason the figure appeared strange was that it was reflected by two mirrors,

12

one the rearview mirror, the other the dark windowglass of the Mercedes door.

He smiled. Yes, that was it. With two mirrors it is possible to see oneself briefly as a man among men rather than a self sucking everything into itself—just as you can see the back of your head in a clothier's triple mirror.

He gazed down at the wrist of the hand holding the Luger. Light and air poured into the wrist. It was neither thick nor thin. Who can see his own wrist? It was not a wrist but The Wrist, part of the hole into which everything was sucked and drained out.

He fired five times into the gorge. The sound racketed quickly back and forth between vertical cliffs of rock. Firing the Luger, he discovered, helped knock him out of his "spells." But it did not work as well as before. He shot again, holding the Luger closer and firing past his face. The sound was louder and flatter; a wave of hot air slapped his cheek. The gun bucked, hurting his bent wrist. He held the muzzle against his temple. Yes, that is possible, he thought smiling, that is one way to cure the great suck of self, but then I wouldn't find out, would I? Find out what? Find out why things have come to such a pass and a man so sucked down into himself that it takes a gunshot to knock him out of the suck—or a glimpse in a double mirror. And I wouldn't find out about the Jews, why they came here in the first place and why they are leaving. Are the Jews a sign?

There at any rate stands Will Barrett on the edge of a gorge in old Carolina, a talented agreeable wealthy man living in as pleasant an environment as one can imagine and yet who is thinking of putting a bullet in his brain.

Fifteen minutes later he is sitting in his Mercedes in a five-car garage, sniffing the Luger and watching a cat lying in a swatch of sunlight under the rear bumper of his wife's Rolls-Royce Silver Cloud three spaces away. During the six months after his wife's death, the Silver Cloud had occupied its usual space on the clean concrete, tires inflated, not dripping a single drop of oil. Not once had he been able to bring himself to think what to do with it.

Beyond the big Rolls, almost hidden, crouched Yamaiuchi's little yellow Datsun.

Absently he held the barrel of the Luger to his nose, then to his temple, and turned his head to and fro against the cold metal of the gunsight.

Is it too much to wonder what he is doing there, this pleasant prosperous American, sitting in a $35,000 car and sniffing cordite from a Luger?

How, one might well ask, could Will Barrett have come to such a pass? Is it not a matter for astonishment that such a man, having succeeded in life and living in a lovely home with a lovely view, surrounded by good cheerful folk, family and friends, merry golfers, should now find himself on a beautiful Sunday morning sunk in fragrant German leather speculating about such things as the odd look of his wrist (his wrist was perfectly normal), the return of North Carolina Jews to the Holy Land (there was no such return), and looking for himself in mirrors like Count Dracula?

At any rate, within the space of the next three minutes there occurred two extraordinary events which, better than ten thousand words, will reveal both Barrett's peculiar state of mind and the peculiar times we live in.

First, as he sat in the Mercedes, Luger in hand, gazing at the cat nodding in the sunlight, there came to him with the force of a revelation the breakthrough he had been waiting for, the sudden vivid inkling of what had gone wrong, not just with himself but, as he saw it, with the whole modern age.

Then, as if this were not enough, there occurred two minutes later a wholly unexpected and shocking event which, however, far from jolting him out of his grandiose speculations about the "modern age," only served to confirm them. In a word, no sooner had he opened the Mercedes door and stepped out than a rifle shot was fired from the dense pine forest nearby, ricocheting with a hideous screech from the concrete floor at his foot to a *thunk* in the brick of the inner wall. A vicious buzzing bee stung his calf.

Later he remembered thinking even as he dove for cover: Was not the shot expected after all? Is this not in fact the very nature of the times, a kind of penultimate quiet, a minatory ordinariness of midafternoon, a concealed dread and expectation which, only after the shot is fired, we knew had been there all along?

Are we afraid quiet afternoons will be interrupted by gunfire? Or do we hope they will?

Was there ever a truly uneventful time, years of long afternoons when nothing happened and people were glad of it?

threatening

But first his "revelation." As he sat gazing at the cat, he saw all at once what had gone wrong, wrong with people, with him, not with the cat—saw it with the same smiling certitude with which Einstein is said to have hit upon his famous theory in the act of boarding a streetcar in Zurich.

There was the cat. Sitting there in the sun with its needs satisfied, for whom one place was the same as any other place as long as it was sunny—no nonsense about old haunted patches of weeds in Mississippi or a brand-new life in a brand-new place in Carolina—the cat was exactly a hundred percent cat, no more no less. As for Will Barrett, as for people nowadays—they were never a hundred percent themselves. They occupied a place uneasily and more or less successfully. More likely they were forty-seven percent themselves or rarely, as in the case of Einstein on the streetcar, three hundred percent. All too often these days they were two percent themselves, specters who hardly occupied a place at all. How can the great suck of self ever hope to be a fat cat dozing in the sun?

There was his diagnosis, then. A person nowadays is two percent himself. And to arrive at a diagnosis is already to have anticipated the cure: how to restore the ninety-eight percent?

Perhaps it is not necessary to say any more about Will Barrett's peculiar revelation, except to note that if it applied to anyone it applied to him and not to the good folk of Linwood, North Carolina, who, sitting in their sunny patios, did in fact seem happy as cats on this beautiful October Sunday.

At any rate, as he absently climbed out of the Mercedes, Luger forgotten but still in hand, he was musing over his discovery of this strange shortfall of the human condition and had no sooner reached the middle of the garage on his way to the interior door than *whangEEEEE* the concrete erupted, spat, stung his calf. There followed not in succession but all at once, it seemed, the sound of the shot, a sharp sting, and the solid *thunk* in the brick.

Then—and now occurred the most remarkable part of this odd episode—in the next instant he was transformed. It was as if the sting in his calf had been the injection of a powerful drug. Quicker than any drug, in the instant in fact of hearing and recognizing the gunshot, he was, as he expressed it, miraculously restored to himself. The cat of course had jumped four feet straight up and fled in terror, as any sensible animal would, reduced instantly to zero percentile of its well-being. But Barrett? The missing ninety-eight percent is magically restored! How? By the rifle shot! In the very same motion of lifting his stinging leg, he is diving for the floor, hitting the concrete in a roll, shoulder tucked, Luger cradled in his stomach. He rolls over at least three times, enough rolls anyhow to carry him under the high-slung 1956 Silver Cloud and against the far wall, where now he is feeling himself to be himself for the first time in years, flanked as he is by two adjoining walls, the Rolls above him as good as a pillbox affording a slot-shaped view of the sunny woods. And without his taking thought about it, the Luger is now held in both hands stretched out in front of him as steady as if it were propped on a sandbag.

Were terrorists after him? A kneecapping? Or just shooting up a rich man's house and Rolls? Or were they after his daughter Leslie, upstairs?

None of the above, as it turned out. In another minute he had caught sight of an oddly shaped peak of a red cap disappearing in the pines, not a deer hunter's cap but a Texaco or Conoco (he forgot which) mechanic's cap; he recognized the cap wearer and knew who fired the shot and why. It was Ewell McBee, a covite from the valley below, once his wife's family's gardener, who poached for deer in Barrett's ten thousand acres of mountainside.

No apocalyptic last-days irruption of terrorism then, no more than the annual unpleasantness with McBee. No, maybe a bit more: wasn't McBee saying in fact, maybe you'd better let me poach so I won't make the mistake of shooting up your garage?

He sighed: he'd rather an Italian terrorist than the complex negotiations with McBee (pay him a call? let him poach? call the sheriff? buy him a drink? shoot him?). At any rate, don't tell Leslie.

There he lay for some minutes, sighting down the Luger and speculating on the odd upsidedownness of the times, that on a beautiful Sunday in old Carolina, it takes a gunshot to restore a man to himself.

What man? How many men besides Will Barrett would have shared his feelings? How many men would have felt better for being shot at on a peaceful Sunday? Very few white folks and no niggers at all, as they say in old Carolina.

Even Barrett wondered. Why is it that I know perfectly well that it was Ewell McBee, that it was an accident, and that I am disappointed? How does it happen that this is what I do best and

a raking fire from a line of troops or guns

feel best doing, not hitting a three-wood on a green fairway but rolling away from gunfire and into a safe corner where I can look out without being seen and where I can't be enfiladed?— all with a secret coolness and even taking a satisfaction in it. This is better than—than what?

Very well, here I am and here it is at last, let them come. What have I to do with this Luger? I don't know, something. Why do I feel myself most myself here and not hitting a three-wood for an eagle on the back nine? What does my ease with gunfire portend? How is it that I know with certainty that everything is going to be settled in the end with a gun, with this gun, either with them or with me, but with this gun?

How could I know such a thing? How do I know that somehow it is going to come down to this, should come down to this, down to me and a gun and an enemy, that otherwise this quiet Sunday makes no sense?

Ewell McBee, it would turn out, had not of course meant to harm him or his house. At least not consciously. He was in fact poaching, had been circling to get upwind from a deer, had lost his sense of direction and got off a shot, which by the purest chance (surely) had gone ricocheting around the Barrett garage.

Strange to say, that made matters worse, to have to listen to Ewell apologize for shooting up his house. If there is an enemy, it is better to know who he is.

Ewell McBee, he reflected as he lay prone under the Rolls, was another example of the demented and farcical times we live in. Did the growing madness have something to do with the Jews pulling out? Who said we could get along without the Jews? Watch the Jews, their mysterious comings and goings and stayings! The Jews are a sign! When the Jews pull out, the Gentiles begin to act like the crazy Jutes and Celts and Angles and redneck Saxons they are. They go back to the woods. Here we are, retired from the cities and living deep in the Southern forests and growing nuttier by the hour. The Jews are gone, the blacks are leaving, and where are we? deep in the woods, socking little balls around the mountains, rattling ice in Tanqueray, riding $35,000 German cars, watching Billy Graham and the Steelers and M*A*S*H on 45-inch Jap TV.

So said Will Barrett.

Ewell McBee was one of them, a new Southerner and as nutty as a Jute. Ewell, who was exactly his own age, he had known as a boy when his father and mother spent the summers in Lin-

from Jutland, a peninsula of Denmark

wood. Ewell caddied for his father. A country boy who lived in a cove of the valley below, hence a covite, he went barefoot and shirtless and wore soft bib overalls smelling of Octagon soap. He was overgrown and strong and a bully. They used to neck-rassle, stand sweating and grunting, elbows crooked around necks until Ewell threw him down and sat on him for an hour, grinning and daring him to get up, thighs squeezing him, a heavy incubus smelling of sweet boiled cotton, Octagon soap and thick white white winter-white skin.

From Ewell's mother they got fresh eggs and country butter and from his father liquor, not white lightning but charcoal-cured light amber corn whiskey.

From Ewell he had first heard the word "pecker" and had seen an uncircumcised pecker, which he thought at first a pe-culiarity of country boys. To his even greater astonishment, Ewell showed him how to jerk off. A bully and a jerk-off Ewell was and remained.

Then Ewell had become the Peabodys' head gardener. Then he moved to town and became a businessman. As an ex-employee he figured he had a proprietary right to an occasional buck deer.

So Ewell had changed and yet not changed. Now if he had a drink with Ewell in a bar booth, Ewell might make a show of not letting him out, actually stand in his way daring him to get past, half joking, no not even half joking. "Boy, I want a piece of you. I could throw you down rat now."

"Well, I doubt if you could but right now let me out."

And Ewell would give way reluctantly, yielding to their middle-aged respectability and to Will Barrett's great Peabody wealth.

All that was left of the bullying was the poaching. "Hail fire, Will, I'm doing you a favor. You got so goddamn many deer in there they're chewing on the trees. Anyhow, what you going to do about it?" I'm sitting astride your ten-thousand-acre moun-tain like I sat on you, and how you going to get up?

When Ewell came up from the cove, he also came up in the world, operated a Texaco station, then owned a Conoco station, then five Exxon stations, then a movie theater. He shed bib overalls for the Jaymar Sansabelt slacks and short-sleeved white shirt of small-town businessmen, joined the C of C, ate lunch with Rotary at the Holiday Inn. But Twin Cinema had gone bust and Exxon cut back on gas and so now Ewell needed money and had a new proposition. Ewell wanted him to put up some money for the home-entertainment video-cassette business. He had a connection, a fellow in Miami who could supply him with any number of copies of any film at all, *Jaws I* and *II*, *Godfather I* and *II*, *Airport* of any year, you name it. More important, there was this whole new market for cassettes designed for motel and home bedroom viewing, but best of all he knew a young lady, a real professional, a recognized moviemaker, who made such movies right next door in Highlands, using as actors and actresses the college boys and girls who flock to resorts looking for summer jobs and are happy to work for minimum wage.

As if it weren't demented enough to go to Rotary lunch every Tuesday, where there might be a guest speaker on Encounter and Enrichment in Marriage, and hear Ewell tell him solemnly about the value of erotic movies in couples therapy—redneck Ewell come up out of the cove and talking about couples therapy! America is still on the move! A poor boy can still come up in the world. The South is rising again! As if this weren't enough, Ewell in the very act of making his pitch—"your hundred thou will buy you forty-nine percent; me and my potner, the little lady, got to keep fifty-one"—Ewell couldn't help coming at him again, shouldering him, hemming him up in a corner of the Holiday Inn Buccaneer Room! He didn't want to let him out! He wanted to neck-rassle! Throw him down! "You gon talk to my potner," said Ewell, eyeing him. "She'll fix you up with a little lady, her leading lady. We gon boogie at my villa tonight."

Lying under the Rolls, Luger still gripped in both hands, he gazed at an arc of sunlit pines. Was Ewell threatening him? Did he shoot up the garage as a warning: "Either you back my cassette business or—"? No, it was too simple. That would mean having a simple enemy. The world is crazier than that.

He smiled and nodded: I know why it is better to be shot at on a Sunday afternoon than not be shot at. Because it means maybe there *is* an enemy after all. If there is no enemy, then I am either mad or living in a madhouse.

Peace is only better than war if peace is not hell too. War being hell makes sense.

II

THE OCTOBER SUN WAS WARM ON HER BACK. HER HAIR WAS almost dry after the rain. Above the roof line of the village rose a mountain shaped like a head and covered by gold and scarlet trees except for two outcroppings of rock. One outcropping could be seen as an eye but the other outcropping was too close to the center to be seen as the other eye and too high and too far to one side to be seen as a nose. The wrong placement of the second outcropping caused her a slight unease, enough for her to tilt her head from time to time so that the outcroppings would line up either as eyes or as nose and eye.

Cars of tourists drove slowly up and down the street. It was the height of the red-leaf season. Some of the cars had four women passengers. A few had five. There were no cars with four or five men. The sidewalk was as thronged as a shopping mall, with women dressed in dresses as if they were going to a party, with older men in jackets and caps, with young people in jeans, with hikers carrying backpacks of brilliant blue or yellow or scarlet. A cloth banner with purple lettering *Go Wolves!* was strung high across the street.

Many cars had bumper stickers. Wasn't this something new?

One sticker on a truck read: DO IT IN A PICKUP. Do what? she wondered. Surely it didn't mean "doing it."

Another sticker read: I FOUND IT. Found what? she wondered.

Suddenly she gave a start and shuddered, then frowned as if she had remembered something.

She was sitting on a bench in the sun between The Wee Shoppe: Chockful of British Isle Authentics and The Happy

20

Hiker: Trail Gear and Camping Equipment. Next to The Wee Shoppe was a Gulf station with a clean rest room. There she had changed clothes, washed her face, and found a dirty plastic wallet-size Gulf calendar for 1979. How old was it? What year was it now? Across the street was a barbershop with two chairs, a man barber and a woman barber. Next to the barbershop was the Twin Cinema, an old frame movie theater cut in two. A movable sign on the sidewalk displayed posters of movies. The posters were old and tattered.

Her own clothes she had purchased earlier in the day from less expensive stores down the hill: new jeans stiff and blue, a gray Orlon man's work shirt size 14½ neck and 30-inch sleeves, a camouflage war-surplus jacket, thick white cotton tube socks, short lightweight moccasin-toed boots. Her feet felt good in the socks and boots.

Her clothes had cost $49.23. For $4.98 she had also purchased from an army-surplus store an Italian NATO knapsack which was made of khaki and was nothing like the iridescent nylon backpacks but small and lightweight, just big enough to hold the smallest sleeping bag she could find plus a few other items such as a Boy Scout knife, a Scripto pencil, a pocket notebook, a comb, a can of neat's-foot oil, a box of candles, and a small bag of food. Although there was a wine-and-cheese shop and a natural-food store down the street, she had gone to the supermarket and bought a wedge of American cheese and a small loaf of rye bread.

The pleasant encased feeling of the socks and boots on her feet made her think of something. This is the first time I have worn a shoe or a boot or anything but bedroom slippers in—how long? Three years, I think.

Many of the young people on the sidewalk wore T-shirts stamped with the names and crests of universities: Stanford, Ohio State, Tulane. Some of them seemed too young to be in college. Some too old. It was hard to tell. Were they fifteen or twenty-five? She felt like an old person to whom all young people look the same age.

As the jacket warmed in the sun, it gave off a pleasant smell of dry goods and gun oil. Perhaps it was the can of neat's-foot oil, which she had unscrewed and taken a sniff of. From the deep pockets of the jacket she removed several articles and lined them up on the bench beside her: the can of neat's-foot oil, five candles, the spiral notebook, her wallet, the calendar, her driver's license, and a map (Picturesque Walks around Linwood). She looked at the calendar and the date of the expiration of her driver's license. She made a calculation. Her driver's license had expired at least three years ago, no doubt longer.

She gazed at the photograph on the license. She read the name. Earlier in the Gulf rest room she had looked from the photograph to the mirror then back to the photograph. The hair was shorter and darker in the photograph, the face in the mirror was thinner, but it was the same person.

She uttered her name aloud. At first it sounded strange. Then she recognized it as her name. Then it sounded strange again but strange in a different way, the way an ordinary word repeated aloud sounds strange. Her voice sounded rusty and unused. She wasn't sure she could talk.

A youth wearing a Michigan State T-shirt sat down on the bench next to her display of articles. He looked good-natured and dumb. She decided to practice on him.

"Michigan State," she said. It came out not quite as a question and not quite as a statement. "You—?" This sounded more like a question.

"Oh no. Linwood High. I play for the Wolves."

"The Wolves. Oh yes." She noticed the banner. "Yes, but is that permitted?"

"Is what permitted?"

"The Michigan State T-shirt."

That was a slight blunder. For a moment she had imagined that there might be regulations preventing unauthorized persons from wearing university T-shirts, perhaps a semi-official regulatory agency. In the next instant she saw that this was nonsense.

But the youth did not see anything unusual. "You can get them for three and a half from Good's Variety."

"Are the Wolves—?" She paused. She was making two discoveries. One was that you didn't have to talk in complete sentences. People didn't seem to need more than a word or two to make their own sense of what you said. The other discovery was that she could talk as long as she asked questions. Making a statement was risky.

"If we win this one, we'll be state champs, single A," he said.

"That's—" she said and stopped. But he didn't notice. He must have been waiting for somebody, for suddenly he was up and on his way.

22

"Have a nice—" he said, but he turned his face away.

"What?" she asked in a very clear question. "Have a nice what?" But he was gone.

At first, after she had changed her clothes and sat on the bench, she had watched passersby to see if they noticed anything unusual about her. They didn't or at least gave no sign of it. She had felt like Rip Van Winkle coming down into town after a twenty-year nap. Surely dogs would bark at her and children would hoot and throw rocks. But nothing happened. She began to feel reassured. Only her hair felt like Rip's. It was heavy and long and still damp after the rain, weighing on her head and falling down inside her collar. It was too thick for her pocket comb. Her scalp itched.

Three women had gone into the barbershop and sat in the chair of the woman barber and got haircuts. One got a shampoo. When the third woman left, she felt confident enough to cross the street, open the door of the barbershop, go directly to the empty chair, and sit down.

"How you want it, honey?" asked the woman barber.

She had rehearsed what she was going to say. Or ask. "Could you cut it first, then wash it, then dry it?"

"Okay, honey. But how you want it?"

Brief panic. Then she saw something. "Like hers?" Though she had wanted to make a statement, her voice rose in a question.

"Like hers?"

She nodded toward the movie poster on the sidewalk. The poster showed an actress with blond hair pulled to one side. The movie was *Three Days of the Condor*. It must have been an old movie. The poster was faded and torn. Perhaps the theater was closed.

"You got nice thick hair. You'd be a honey blonde like her if you stayed out in the sun." The barber was a big mountain woman. She said *nahce* for nice and *hahr* for hair. The strong hands felt good on her scalp as they grabbed her heavy hair. She felt better every time a hunk of it was sheared off and hit the floor. The feel of the woman's fingers on her scalp made her eyes stare. A wall of glass bricks across the street glittered in the sunlight. A sign above the door written in script read *Le Club*.

When the woman barber finished, she swung her around to face the mirror and held a hand mirror behind her the way the man barber did for his customers. The steel base of the chair was ringed by windrows of dark blond hair.

Now she did look something like the actress except that her hair was cut higher in back, like a boy's, and showed more of her neck.

"Nice." She risked a statement. "Could you wash it now?" She noticed a basin.

"Come on over here, honey." The woman's eyes slid past her. "Don't I know you? Have you been working here summers?" The woman barber couldn't quite place her. Her unfashionable clothes made her look like a local. On the other hand, perhaps she talked like a tourist.

The woman barber's eyes reminded her of something she had forgotten. Strangers often thought they knew her. Was it her ordinary good looks or was it a way she had of listening to people and following them like a good dancer that made her seem familiar?

"You from around here?"

"No, I'm from—" She stopped. "Oh, by the way, what is today?"

"Wednesday."

"October—"

"Twenty-second."

She didn't dare ask the year.

After the shampoo she sat on the bench again. Her hair felt good, light and warm in the sun.

From the pocket of her jacket she took out the red spiral-bound notebook and opened it. At the top of the first page was written in blue ink and in her hand the following:

Date: October 15

Place: Room 212, Closed Wing, Valleyhead Sanatorium

Below, printed in capital letters and underlined, was the following:

INSTRUCTIONS FROM MYSELF TO MYSELF

What followed was written in her ordinary script:

As I write this to you, I don't remember everything but I remember more than you will remember when you read this. You remember nothing now, do you? I know this from experience. Electroshock knocks out memory for a while. I don't feel bad. To tell you the truth, I'm not even sure I'm sick. But they think I'm worse because I refuse to talk in group (because there is nothing to say) and won't eat with the others, preferring to sit under the table (because a circle of knees is more interesting than a circle of faces).

I, that is, you, but for the present as I write this, I—am scheduled to be buzzed early Wednesday morning. This is the beginning of the sixth (I think) course of electroconvulsive therapy, or ECT, known hereabouts as buzzing.

I am writing this in my room in the closed wing (you may not remember the room when you read this on October 22, but it will come back), from which there is no escape, else I'd be long gone.

After you get buzzed Wednesday, you'll be in recovery. The adjacent hall leads to the back door, which opens into the service yard, where the bread truck arrives about 11 a.m.

You may not remember this when you come to (about 9 a.m.). Your jaw will hurt and your teeth will be sore from the mouthpiece. You will be conscious but still paralyzed from the Anectine (curare), lying there bright-eyed and still, like a parrot shot by the poisoned arrow of a pygmy's blowgun (which you have been). You'll be drowsy from the Brevital and your mouth will be dry from the atropine. You'll be dressed in nothing but your hospital gown. But they like you to go back to your room under your own power, so you'll wait on the stretcher until you can make it to the cubicle. You'll have time—at least an hour. Nobody is going to bother you—they're too busy buzzing the others. In the cubicle you'll find your pj's, robe, and slippers. But there will be something new. You will find *this*, this notebook open to this page, on top of your clothes where you can't miss it. You will read it because there will be nothing else to do for a while and because you will not have entirely forgotten that you wrote it. There will also be the blue skirt and sweater (the only clothes thin enough to ball up and stuff into the pockets of the robe). Between the skirt and sweater you will find the wallet with four hundred dollars in fifties (a little anxiety here: somebody could swipe it while you're buzzed).

As you read this, it will not be entirely new to you—it will be like remembering a dream. But if you did not read it, you would not remember what you, I, had decided to do.

You are now sitting in the cubicle and reading these words. You have time. They don't expect you to walk back to your room for a while.

The cubicle, you will notice, has two doors, one opening into recovery, the other opening into the hall.

Ordinarily you leave by the hall door, turn right, and return to your room.

Do not do this.

Do this. Put on your pj tops and skirt and slippers. Pull on sweater. Pull out pj collar—it looks something like a blouse. Do you remember our trying this? These slippers have heels and look something like loafers.

Leave robe in cubicle.

Put wallet and notebook in skirt pocket.

When you feel strong enough, look out into hall. If it is clear, leave, turn left, not right, to back door, go out and straight across service yard to big laurel next to water tank.

Sit under it and far enough back to be out of sight.

Wait for the bread van.

The driver will deliver the bread and spend at least ten minutes inside with McGahey (I think you might remember this). He's got something going with McGahey. The sliding panel door will be on your side (the laurel's side).

Walk straight into it. Do not go to the rear, where the bread cartons are, but toward driver's seat. Next to partition is some kind of carton (not bread) which is there every trip—perhaps a carton of paper bags. Do you remember studying the truck through the binoculars? I think there is enough room between carton and far wall.

He will make several more deliveries, the last one in Linwood at the Red Barn (I got this from McGahey).

When you see him unload the last carton, you count to thirty and go out too.

I can remember Linwood but I cannot remember whether I could remember it the last time I was buzzed. It varies. One time I couldn't remember my name for a week. When you get out you may know exactly where you are and what to do. But you probably won't. So I'll tell you.

Go down the hill to K-Mart and Good's Variety. Buy clothes and articles (see list below).

Go back up hill to Gulf station. Change clothes in rest room.

Check into Mitchell's Triple-A motel one block east. Don't worry about not having car or suitcase. You will have knapsack and they're used to it. Pay in advance. Check your driver's license to be sure you remember your name. Sometimes I, you, forget after a buzz.

Take a hot bath. Eat and sleep for twenty-four hours. You'll be very hungry after the buzz (remember?) and tired and sore. You'll feel like a rape victim in every way but one.

I wonder how you're feeling now. It varies so much, remember?

There will also be something good about having gone through the bad experience, the buzzing, for the last time and having survived—the bad maybe even being the condition of the good, I don't know. Like that man who crawled out of the plane crash in West Virginia last summer, remember? Everybody else dead or dying and he with a cut lip and, realizing he didn't even have to crawl, not knowing what he was doing, not even remembering it later, simply walked away like a man getting off a streetcar, walked into the woods. They found him hours later two miles from the plane sitting on a highway culvert calm as you please, but saying nothing. In a state of shock, they said. Sitting there blinking and only mildly bemused. Yes, but also, in another way, in his right mind, as if he had crossed a time warp or gone through a mirror, no, not gone through, come back, yes, the only question being which way he went, from the sane side to the crazy side like Alice or back the other way. They took him to the hospital, sewed up his lip, and let him go. Do you remember thinking about him getting on the bus and going on into Huntington, and walking home, hands in his pockets (no suitcase)?

The only question is how the buzz job will go this time, how much of the feeling will be bad, the real done-in rape-victim feeling, and how much of the feeling of the good, the survivor.

STOP YOUR CUBICLE READING HERE. CONTINUE YOUR READING AFTER YOU'VE RESTED IN LINWOOD AND FEEL STRONG.

A bareheaded policeman stood on the corner. Feeling stiff, she rose, stretched, and walked down the block a short distance. Her knapsack was hanging from the back of the bench. From time to time she turned to keep it in sight. Leaving the bench was for her a foray. The bench was home base. She could venture halfway down the block, keeping the knapsack in sight, before turning back. The knapsack was for saving her place on the bench. Could one ''save a place'' on a public bench? She couldn't remember. Soon it was possible for her to observe people as well as clothes. Though she could still not be certain of their ages, she began to notice that there were two kinds of people. There were those who had plans, whose eyes and movements were aimed toward a future, and those who did not. Some youngish people, that is, between twenty and thirty-five, sat on the sidewalk in silence. Though they sat or lay in relaxed positions, time did not seem to pass easily for them. They looked as if they had gone to great lengths to deal with the problem of time and had not succeeded. They were waiting. What were they waiting for?

Another group of people, older and better dressed, stood at the window of a real estate office looking at photographs of homes for sale, mountain cabins, expensive condominiums. They talked, took notes, compared prices. Their eyes glistened. In their expressions she could see the pleasure of the prospect of moving, of the exhaustion of the possibilities of an old place and the opening of the possibilities of a new place. Perhaps they lived in places like Richmond or Atlanta or Washington. Undoubtedly they had plans to buy a mountain cabin for vacations or a condominium for retirement. They had plans and the plans took up their time.

It was as if she belonged to both groups. It was not clear which was better off or which she would join if she had the chance. It seemed that she had plans for the immediate future, but she didn't know what to do with the rest of her life.

The old tightness came back and clenched under her diaphragm. She turned back to the bench. For her, too, it was a question of time. What would she do with time? Was there something she was supposed to do?

Her body was sore. Her arms and legs hurt, one side of her jaw was swollen, her ribs felt as if she had taken a beating. But there was also the feeling that she was over the worst of it. Perhaps, she thought, it was like the pain one feels after being in a fight and winning. It was the kind of soreness the sun cures. The bench and her position on the bench had been arranged so that the morning sunlight hit the sore parts of her body. She felt like a snake stretched out on a rock in the sun, shedding its skin after a long hard winter.

Her hands were open on her knees. She turned them over. There were fingernail marks in both palms, not severe enough to break the skin but deep enough to cause bruising. They were the sort of marks one might make waiting a long time, fists clenched, for something frightening to happen.

At that moment something inside her relaxed. A muscle, which had been clenched so long she had forgotten it, suddenly unclenched. It let go and she closed her eyes and took a breath of air into a new part of her lungs.

It became possible, she noticed, to look at things rather than watch out for things. A line of ants crawled past her foot. She picked out one ant which carried a neatly cutout section of a green leaf, holding it vertically aloft like a sail, and followed it as it made its way over the coarse granules of the sidewalk. As the sun warmed her, she studied the clothes of the passersby. Many people, she noticed, seemed to dress as they pleased. Nobody paid much attention. Had this always been the case? Surely it had been different the last time she was in a street, one, two, three years ago.

What year was it? Nineteen seventy-nine? eighty? eighty what?

The sidewalk was crowded. When she made her forays, she was afraid of running into someone. Then she realized that she was not accustomed to seeing people going somewhere or doing something. It seemed more natural for people to be sitting silently or standing and gazing or being taken somewhere. What if she ran straight into someone? But oncoming people seemed to know without looking at her exactly when to veer slightly and miss her. The veering occurred when the other person was about five feet away, a turn of a degree or so to the right or left. It must be a trick, an exchange of signals which she must learn. Otherwise, she might find herself confronting a person, step to the right with him, to the left, and so on. What then? What she feared was a breakdown in the rules of ordinary living which other people observed automatically. What if the rules broke down? Suddenly she remembered that she had once been an A student. But what if she flunked ordinary living?

Just before she reached home base, the bench, a young woman approached and did not veer. They stopped, facing each other. Oh my, she thought, this is it. But the woman was smiling, for all the world as if she knew her. Oh my, she thought, perhaps she does and I am supposed to know her. Indeed, she seemed to belong to a past almost remembered. She was dressed in the old style, skirt, blouse, cardigan sweater, shoulder bag, penny loafers. Her long black hair was parted in the middle and framed her oval face like a madonna's. Seen close, she was not so young. Her face was chapped. Evidently the woman had something to say to her or expected her to say something, for she did not step aside. As she watched the woman's radiant smile and cast about in her mind for where she might have known her, she noticed that the woman held a sheaf of pamphlets in one hand and that her fingers were ink-stained. From the pressure of the strap of the shoulder bag on the wool of the sweater, she judged that the bag was heavy. Perhaps it was filled with more pamphlets. The woman, still smiling, was handing her a pamphlet. Anxious to make up for not being able to recognize the woman, she began to read the pamphlet then and there. The first three sentences were: *Are you lonely? Do you want to make a new start? Have you ever had a personal encounter with our Lord and Saviour?* While she was reading, the woman was saying something to her. Was she supposed to listen or read?

Later, from the bench, she observed that other people dealt with the woman differently. Some ignored her, veered around her. Others took the pamphlets politely and went their way. Still others stopped for a moment and listened (but did not read), heads down and nodding. But for her, questions asked were to be answered, printed words were to be read.

Facing the woman, she considered the first sentences of the pamphlet. "Yes," she said, "there is a sense in which I would like to make a new start. However—"

But the woman was saying something.

"What?"

"I said, are you alone? Do you feel lonely?"

She considered the questions. "I am alone but I do not feel lonely."

"Why don't you come to a little get-together we're having tonight? I have a feeling a person like yourself might get a lot out of it."

She considered that question. "I'm not sure what you mean by the expression 'a person like yourself.' Does that mean you know what I am like?"

But the woman's eyes were no longer looking directly at her, rather were straying just past her. The smile was still radiant but in it she felt a pressure like the slight but firm pressure of a hostess's hand steering one along a receiving line.

"Won't you come?" said the woman but steering her along with her eyes. "The address is stamped on the back. I promise you you won't regret it.'' Her voice was still cordial, but the question did not sound like a question and the promise did not sound like a promise.

Sitting down again, knapsack beside her, she reflected that people asked questions and answered them differently from her. She took words seriously to mean more or less what they said, but other people seemed to use words as signals in another code they had agreed upon. For example, the woman's questions and commands were evidently not to be considered as questions and commands, then answered accordingly with a yes, no, or maybe, but were rather to be considered like the many signboards in the street, such as Try Good Gulf for Better Mileage, then either ignored or acted upon, but even if acted upon, not as an immediate consequence of what the words commanded one to do.

Such a code, she reflected, may not be bad. Indeed, it seemed to cause people less trouble than words. At one time she must have known the code. It should not be hard to catch on to.

A man sat down on the bench beyond her knapsack. She couldn't tell if he was twenty-five or thirty-five. On the one hand, he was as slender as the first youth, but the curly hair which hugged his scalp was as dry and crinkled as a thirty-five-year-old's. A blue vein throbbed in his slightly hollow temple. He wore matching red sweatshirt and pants, with a white stripe running along the seam of the pants, and odd shoes which were like sneakers except that the sole ran up the back of the heel. He was breathing heavily. These details she had observed in one glance. Now from the corner of her eye she became aware that he was looking at her and wished to speak. It was also clear to her, though she could not have said how, that ordinarily he was shy but that some unusual circumstances had given him leave to speak to her.

''I just ran eighteen miles.'' He closed his eyes and took a deep breath.

''Why?''

''I've been into running for three months.''

''You've been what?'' What was the meaning of the expression ''into running''? Perhaps he was in trouble. He was on the run.

''It's changed my life.''

She didn't understand him but it was clear that he was speaking of something commonplace, something she might be expected to understand if she had not been away for a long time.

"How has it changed your life?"

"It got me out of my head."

"You mean—" She was not certain what he meant. Had he gone crazy?

"In another three weeks I expect to be up to twenty-six."

"Why twenty-six?"

"That's the marathon distance. But this is no ordinary marathon."

"It isn't?"

"No. I'm getting ready for the Richmond marathon, but I'm doing it by running on the Long Trail—that's what it was originally called and is still called in Vermont. I like that better than the Appalachian Trail, don't you? You can run it from here north because once you get up it's mostly flat, but very high. You're right on the crest of a ridge, with nothing but valleys and clouds on either side. By the way, I'm Richard Rountree." He held out his hand. She took it. It was very slender, dry, and fibrous. He seemed to be all gristle and bone.

"I'm—" She began and stopped. She wanted to look at her driver's license.

He didn't notice. "Would you like to go to Hattie's tonight?"

"Hattie's?"

"You know, down the hill. It's nothing but a barn but the food's not bad. The music is country and Western. Runners hang out there."

While he was talking, she was planning a declarative sentence. "I don't know what I'm going to do," she said, uttering one word after another. The sentence sounded flat but she finished it and her voice did not go up into a question. "I don't know where I'll be staying tonight."

Though her voice sounded flat to her, like a person recovering from a stroke, like Rip coming down from the mountain and speaking to a villager, he didn't seem to mind. In fact, he drew closer, crowding the knapsack, and crossed one thin leg over the other toward her. As his eyes dropped, showing the damp bluish skin of his eyelids, she seemed to remember something from her girlhood. It was the way her mother had of talking to her about "a boy" and "a girl," "when a boy does such-and-such" or "leading a boy on." Perhaps something she had said had led him on, because he yawned, laced his fingers together, and bent them backwards in a way that seemed familiar to her.

"Look," he said, stretching out his laced-together hands. "I know a shelter on an unused spur of the trail, the spur to Sour-wood Mountain. In fact, it's closed, the spur, that is. In fact, that's where I stayed last night. It's not used at all. It's clean and when the clouds break there's a lovely view through the pines. Would you like to crash there tonight? You'd be welcome.''

Though she had not heard the expression ''crash'' before, she could tell that he was using it in a way that was not natural to him. Suddenly she saw that he thought it was the sort of expression she would use. ''Lovely'' in ''lovely view'' sounded natural in him, though she couldn't remember a young man saying ''lovely.''

''Thank you,'' she said. ''It sounds good. But I have a great many things to do. For example, I have to locate and take possession of a house. I had planned to go to a motel but I don't think I will. I have here a set of instructions on how to locate the house, things to buy, and so forth.''

Her words sounded strange and formal to her, as if she were reciting them from memory. She found herself taking out notebook and wallet as if to prove something to him.

''Like a treasure hunt,'' he said, sounding disappointed.

''Treasure hunt,'' she repeated.

''Richard Rountree,'' he said again, unlacing his fingers and holding out his hand. She took it again. He gave her a strong grip. His hand was as fibrous as a monkey's. Had he forgotten he had shaken hands already, or did she only imagine he had shaken hands before? It occurred to her that he was more uneasy than she.

Maybe he had been running too much. They seemed to have something in common, having been alone in the mountains too long and feeling strange in the village. Then why wasn't she attracted to him?

At that moment she was looking down at her driver's license in her open wallet.

''I'm Allison,'' she read, then remembered something. ''Allie,'' she said suddenly and smiled, looking up at him.

''Allie,'' he said. He let her hand go. ''Will you be coming back here, Allie? I mean to the bench.''

''Very likely.''

''This time of day?''

''Probably.'' Something else her mother told about ''boys'' came back to her. Don't ever turn down a boy completely. Keep your options open. You never know. Her mother called this "keeping a boy on your string."

But he did not look much like a "boy" with his dry crinkled hair coming forward in the middle to make a W-shaped hairline, and his dry narrow fibrous hands.

"I'll see you, Allie."

As he walked quickly away, the broad white stripes on his running pants flashed like scissors. His back looked as if he knew she was watching him.

The sun was high. She felt warm and drowsy. Perhaps it was noon. For some time, perhaps five minutes, perhaps twenty minutes, she had been watching the column of ants. They traveled past the toe of her boot. Most but not all carried cutout pieces of green leaves. They followed the same path, climbing over the same granules of concrete, then descending into a crack at the same place, then climbing out of the crack at the same place.

The ants were headed toward the curb at the corner where the policeman stood. His thick yellow-gray hair was creased at the back from wearing a hat or cap. Did his not wearing a hat or cap mean he was off duty? He had a large high abdomen. From a wide black cartridge belt a heavy revolver in a holster was suspended. The belt crossed his abdomen just below its fullest part. The position of the belt and the weight of the pistol created in her a slight discomfort. She wished he would hitch up his pants. How old was he? Forty-five? Fifty-five? Sixty-five?

She opened the spiral notebook.

INSTRUCTIONS FROM MYSELF TO MYSELF (PART 2)

When you read this, you should feel better, rested at least and not so sore. Feel your jaw and your teeth. Are they sore?

She felt her jaw and her teeth. They were sore.

Your memory will not be good, but that varies. Test it. Do you remember your name?

Only after I read it.

Do you remember how old you are?

Yes. No. Eighteen? Twenty-one?

Do you remember how long you were in the sanatorium?

Three years, I think. Or perhaps two. Possibly four.

You will have forgotten most very recent events, but they should come back. You should now begin to remember events that happened long ago. What can you remember?

THE SECOND COMING

I can remember skating on summer evenings. This coarse-grained sidewalk reminds me of it. I could feel the vibration come through the steel wheels and up into the bones of my legs. The concrete of the sidewalk on Prince Avenue was coarse. I would skate until it was dark enough for the lightning bugs to come out. The cement of McWhorter's driveway was smooth and turning into it was like turning onto silk. The skate wheels were silent and my legs were still, yet I went faster and faster through the lightning bugs.

Don't worry. Your memory will improve. But even if it does not, it won't matter a great deal. There is not a great deal that is worth remembering. What information you need you will find here or in your wallet.

My own memory as I write this is far from perfect. There are, however, a few things of recent memory that you will need to know when you read this.

One thing in particular is important. You will have to know it to know what to do next. Do you remember Miss Sally Kemp? Aunt Sally?

No. Yes.

She died. I found out this morning, a week before you read this.

She left you her estate, which is much larger than anyone expected. In her will she said I was nice to her. This meant that I listened to her. Nobody else did. This is true. I, you, always listen closely to people.

It, the estate, is some money (I don't know how much), an island off the Georgia coast, and a piece of land with an old house on it, I think, near Linwood. Do you remember her joking about her island which was nothing but a sandspit and three pine trees and worthless unless the treasure Captain Kidd was supposed to have buried there was ever dug up and which nobody took seriously enough even to try, yet which you thought of often, not so much to get the treasure but to find it, to find a sign or a gold bug or a map?

Treasure. Yes.

Well, there's no Captain Kidd's treasure, but the Arabs want to buy it.

The place near Linwood should not be far from where you are presently reading this.

Find out where it is.

Walk there.

Move in.

Take possession. It is yours.

Live there.

Don't tell your parents or Dr. Duk where you are. They will find you soon enough.

Don't tell anybody where you are.

Find a lawyer you can trust. This is a problem. I've thought about this a lot. Aunt Sally died at home, so the will will be probated (?) there. There will be the question of your legal competence and whether or not Mother and Father should be your guardians. I've thought about this a lot. You could just walk into the first lawyer's office on the street. But it would be better to ask someone's advice. You could ask a doctor. Go see a doctor with a minor complaint (muscle soreness—tell him you fell off a mountain, in a way you did) and ask him what lawyer he trusts.

Don't be angry at Father and Mother. They love you as well as they understand that word, or as well as most people love. Come to think of it, who or what do you "love"? Do you "love" them? What is "love"? I am saying the word aloud. It sounds like something dark and furry which makes a lowing sound.

There is one thing you must not forget, or if you have forgotten, be reminded of it here and now. It is the discovery I made last week (you made? we made?). Do you remember?

It took me (you? us?) all my life to make the discovery. Why so long? And then I (you, we) had to go crazy to do it. Why was the discovery so difficult? Because it is the very nature of the thing to be discovered and the very nature of the seeking that it could not be found by asking somebody or by reading a book. Imagine being born with gold-tinted corneas and undertaking a lifelong search for gold. You'd never find it.

What was my (your, our) discovery? That I could *act*. I was *free* to act. Is this something everyone knows or thinks he knows or, if he knows, knows in the wrong way? With gold-tinted corneas everything looks like gold but it's fool's gold.

Here was the kind of gold-tinted corneas I had: Dr. Duk told me many times I should be free to act for myself. I believed him. Just as I believed him when he suggested I take up bird-watching. So, clever straight-A student that I was, I set forth to act for myself. Which, of course, is not doing so at all. I was following instructions. Then how does one ever make the discovery that one can actually be free to act for oneself? I don't know. I don't even know how many people, if any, do it.

In my case I had to go crazy to make the discovery. It's like that man in West Virginia who walked away from the airplane crash. He walked through the woods until he came to a highway. Do you know what I think? That he felt absolutely free to turn right or turn left or sit down on the culvert.

At any rate, I acted for myself and here you are, we are, doing it.

Good luck.

For some reason she felt a need to count her money. Her wallet contained $326. There was seventy-six cents in change in the pocket of her new jeans. She folded her wallet and put it and the notebook and the knife in the deep pocket of her camouflage jacket. After thinking a moment, she packed the candles and the can of neat's-foot oil in her knapsack, between the sleeping bag and the wedge of cheese. She hung the knapsack on the back of the bench. Now only the map remained on the bench.

Drumming her fingers on her knees, she watched the ants carrying their little green sails toward the policeman. Rising suddenly, she took half a dozen steps and tapped him on the shoulder and in the same moment (this was wrong) asked him a question. He did not give a start but turned, his head already inclined and nodding as if he were prepared for her question. Many people must ask him questions. His eyes were darting around the concrete of the sidewalk.

"What's that?" he said, putting his great hairy ear close to her mouth.

She had asked her question too soon and in too much of a rush. Yet before she could repeat it, it seemed to her that he was backtracking and listening to her first question again.

"Whose place?" he asked.

"Miss Sally Kemp." She wanted to ask him to come to the bench, sit down, and look at the map. Instead, she found that she was giving a tug at his sleeve. "Would you—"

It was surprising how quickly he understood. In an instant they were sitting on the bench with the map between them. He went on nodding and gazing down at the map instead of the sidewalk. It was not a good map. A few trails crisscrossed. In the blank spaces between the trails were drawings of chipmunks and whiskey stills and mountaineers carrying jugs of "mountain dew" and wearing overalls with one shoulder strap.

In his eagerness to be helpful and even before he knew where she wanted to go, his forefinger began tracing the trails on the map. His fingernail was as large and convex as a watch crystal and, surprisingly, polished. The nail made a slight sound on the paper as it passed up and down the trails. As their heads bent close over the map, she could not hear him breathe in but his exhalations came out whistling and strong as a bellows. The sight of his large polished nail on the map and the sound of his breathing so diverted her that she could not collect her thoughts.

"I know where old Judge Kemp's summer place used to be. He used to come up here when I was a boy. I even worked in his greenhouse."

"Greenhouse?" she said drowsily.

"His daddy got the idea a long time ago of growing orchids and selling them to the rich people at the old Grove Park Inn where they used to have dances every night."

"That's him," she said but not really remembering.

"This is where it used to be." The gleaming watch-glass fingernail strayed off a trail into a blank space.

"Used to be?"

"It burned down years ago."

"It all burned?"

"The main house. Must have been bums or hippies living out there. Ain't nobody been out there for years."

"Show me how to get there." After she said it, she realized she had said it. She had uttered not a question, not a statement, but a request. How long had it been since she had said to someone: Do this, do that? Perhaps the secret of talking was to have something to say.

"Take this trail." The watch-glass nail glided, hesitated, then stopped like a Ouija in a white space. "It's just the other side of the golf course."

"How far is it from here?"

"Three, four miles."

"Do you mind telling how old you are?" It would help if she knew whether he was forty-five or sixty-five. But he went on nodding and didn't reply. Her question, she saw, was inappropriate, but he let it go.

Instead he looked at her and said: "Are you going to stay out there?"

"Yes. It's my place."

"Be careful, young lady."

"Why?"

"Hippies and bums stay out there. Last summer a lady got—hurt. Just keep your eyes open."

"All right."

He rose.

"It's a nice walk. Have a nice day."

"What?" She was puzzled by the way he said it, in a perfunctory way like goodbye. But what a nice thing to say.

But he only repeated it—"Have a nice day"—and raised a finger to the place where the brim of his hat would have been. He returned to his street corner.

After marking the trail with her Scripto pencil and making an X in the blank space, she folded the map carefully with the marked trail on the outside and stuck it in the breast pocket of her shirt. Opposite the Gulf station she stopped and looked down at her boots. They felt stiff. She went into the rest room, tore three coarse tissues from the roll above the washbasin, put the toilet seat lid down, sat and took off her boots, removed the can of neat's-foot oil from her knapsack and oiled her boots, using the entire can. Carefully she disposed of the oil-soaked paper and empty can. She washed and dried her hands.

In the street her boots felt better, light and strong yet pliable as suede. There was a small pleasure too in getting rid of the can. She meant to live with very few things.

Passing a drugstore window, she noticed a display of Timex wristwatches. Perhaps she should own a watch. Else how would one know when it was time to get up, eat meals, go to bed? Had there ever been a time in her life when she did not eat a meal when mealtime came? What if one did not? Who said one had to get up or eat meals at a certain time?

After a moment she shrugged and shouldered her NATO knapsack, this time using both straps, and walked on. The distributed weight felt good on her shoulders. For the first time in her life, she felt that it, her life, was beginning.

But maybe that was because she could not remember much about her old life.

III

UNDOUBTEDLY SOMETHING WAS HAPPENING TO HIM.

It began again the next day when he sliced out-of-bounds and was stooping through the barbed-wire fence to find his ball. For the first time in his life he knew that something of immense importance was going to happen to him and that he would soon find out what it was. Ed Cupp was holding the top strand high so he could crawl through, higher than he needed to, to make up for his, Ed Cupp's, not following him into the woods to help him find the ball. To prove his good intentions, Ed Cupp pulled the wire so hard that it stretched as tight as a guitar string and creaked and popped against the fence posts.

As he stopped and in the instant of crossing the wire, head lowered, eyes slightly bulging and focused on the wet speckled leaves marinating and funky-smelling in the sunlight, he became aware that he was doing an odd thing with his three-iron. He was holding it in his left hand, fending against the undergrowth with his right and turning his body into the vines and briars which grew in the fence so that they snapped against his body. Then, even as he was climbing through, he had shifted his grip on the iron so that the club head was tucked high under his right arm, shaft resting on forearm, right hand holding the shaft steady—as one might carry a shotgun.

He did not at first know why he did this. Then he did know why.

Now he was standing perfectly still in a glade in a pine forest holding the three-iron, a good fifty feet out-of-bounds and not looking for the ball. It was only after standing so for perhaps

40

thirty seconds, perhaps two minutes, that he made the discovery. The discovery was that he did not care that he had sliced out-of-bounds.

A few minutes earlier he had cared. As his drive curved for the woods, the other players watched in silence. There was a mild perfunctory embarrassment, a clucking of tongues, a clearing of throats in a feigned but amiable sympathy.

Lewis Peckham, the pro, a grave and hopeful man, said: "It could have caught that limb and dropped fair."

Jimmy Rogers, a man from Atlanta, who had joined the foursome to make it an unwieldy fivesome, said: "For a six-handicapper and a Wall Street lawyer, Billy is either nervous about his daughter's wedding or else he's taking it easy on his future-in-laws."

He hit another ball and it too sliced out-of-bounds.

The other four golfers gazed at the dark woods in respectful silence and expectation as if they were waiting for some rule of propriety to prevail and to return the ball to the fairway.

As he leaned over to press the tee into the soft rain-soaked turf, he felt the blood rush to his face. Jimmy Rogers had gotten on his nerves. Was it because Jimmy Rogers had messed up the foursome or because Jimmy Rogers had called him Billy? How did Jimmy Rogers know his handicap?

After teeing up the third ball and as he measured the driver and felt his weight shift from one foot to the other, he was wondering absentmindedly: What if I slice out-of-bounds again, what then? Is a game so designed that there is always a chance that one can so badly transgress its limits and bounds, fall victim to its hazards, that disgrace is always possible, and that it is the public avoidance of disgrace that gives one a pleasant sense of license and justification?

He sliced again but not out-of-bounds, having allowed for the slice by aiming his stance toward the left rough.

He said: "I'm picking up. It's the eighteenth anyhow. I'll see you in the clubhouse."

The slice, which had become worrisome lately, had gotten worse. He had come to see it as an emblem of his life, a small failure at living, a minor deceit, perhaps even a sin. One cringes past the ball, hands mushing through ahead of the club in a show of form, rather than snapping the club head through in an act of faith. Unlike sin in life, retribution is instantaneous. The ball,

41

one's very self launched into its little life, gives offense from the very outset, is judged, condemned, and sent screaming away and, banished from the pleasant licit fairways and the sunny irenic greens, goes wrong and ever wronger, past the rough, past even the barbed-wire fence, and into the dark fens and thickets and briars of out-of-bounds. One is punished on the spot. When his third drive dropped fair, he was lying seven.

It had been bad enough to begin with that he couldn't play with his regular foursome. For more than a week, his daughter's future father-in-law, a seven-foot Californian, had taken the place of Slocum McKeon, a local attorney and excellent golfer, a taciturn unambitious intelligent man who knew how to be both distant and amiable. To make matters worse, who should show up today but his brother-in-law Bertie, a benumbed addled aging New Yorker with no feel for the game or its etiquette, the sort who will drive into other players and fuddle on his way like Mr. Magoo, noticing nothing. This meant he couldn't play with Dr. Vance Battle, the happiest man he knew, a young husky competent G.P. who liked to get his hands on you, happy as a vet with his fist up a cow, mend bones, take hold of your liver from the front and back, stick a finger up your anus paying no attention to your groans, talking N.C. basketball all the while, pausing only to frown and shake his head at the state of one's prostate: "It feels like an Idaho potato."

The last time his foursome played, he fell down. Vance grabbed him and squinted at him. "You better come in, Will. I want to take a look at you."

As if this weren't bad enough, Bertie shows up with Jimmy Rogers, an old con man from the campus, an unwelcome wraith from the past, a classmate who had got blackballed even by the Betas. Who, what brought this pair together?

Maybe Vance was right. Something was happening to him.

A few minutes earlier, on number-sixteen green, he had suffered another little spell and had fallen down in the deep trap behind number-sixteen green. But he had gotten up quickly and no one had noticed. His brother-in-law was lining up a putt, crouched over his putter with its gimmicky semicircular head, elbows sticking out, right foot drawn back daintily. Though the sun shone brightly, the green seemed suddenly to grow dark as if the daylight had drained down the hole. The other players, waiting in silence for the putt, grew taller. After the putt Jimmy Rogers took his arm and drew close and said *Hail Caesar* and he said *Hail Caesar?* and Jimmy Rogers said *You really did it, didn't you?* and he said *Did* what? And Jimmy said *You picked up all the marbles, that's all. You married one of them and beat them at their own game in their own ball park.* Them? Who's them? Yankees? What game? Practicing law? Making money?

But then Jimmy drew close and looked solemn.

"I'm so sorry, old buddy."

"Sorry about what?"

"Your wife's passing."

"Oh. Thank you."

"What a wonderful person she must have been."

"Yes, she was."

Jimmy Rogers began to tell him a joke about a Jew and a German and a black on an airplane with a single parachute. A high-pitched keening filled the sky. Am I going crazy? he wondered curiously. Earlier he had seen a bird, undoubtedly some kind of a hawk, fly across the fairway straight as an arrow and with astonishing swiftness, across a ridge covered by scarlet and gold trees, then fold its wings and drop like a stone into the woods. It reminded him of something but before he could think what it was, sparks flew forward at the corner of his eye. He decided with interest that something was happening to him, perhaps a breakdown, perhaps a stroke. When his turn came to putt and he stooped over the ball, he looked at the hole some twenty feet away and at Lewis Peckham, who was tending the pin and who was looking not at him or the hole but in a small exquisite courtesy allowing his eyes to go unfocused and gaze at a middle distance. The green broke to the right. He did not know whether he was going to hit the ball five feet or fifty feet. It was as if the game had fallen away from him and he was trying to play it from a great height. He felt like a clown on stilts. Lewis Peckham cleared his throat and now Lewis was looking at him and his eyes were veiled and ironic (as if he not only knew that something was happening to him but even knew what it was!) and he putted. The ball curved in a smooth flat parabola and sank with a plop.

It was a good putt. His muscles remembered. When the putt sank, the golfers nodded briefly, signifying approval and a kind of relief that he was back on his game. Or was it a relief that they could play a game at all, obey its rules, observe its etiquette and the small rites of settling in for a drive and lining up a putt? He was of two minds, playing golf and at the same time wondering with no more than a moderate curiosity what was happening to him. Were they of two minds also? Was there an unspoken understanding between all of them that what they were doing, knocking little balls around a mountain meadow while the fitful wind bustled about high above them, was after all preposterous but that they had all assented to it and were doing it nevertheless and because, after all, why not? One might as well do one thing as another.

But the hawk was not of two minds. Single-mindedly it darted through the mountain air and dove into the woods. Its change of direction from level flight to drop was fabled. That is, it made him think of times when people told him fabulous things and he believed them. Perhaps a Negro had told him once that this kind of hawk is the only bird in the world that can—can what? He remembered. He remembered everything today. The hawk, the Negro said, could fly full speed and straight into the hole of a hollow tree and brake to a stop inside. He, the Negro, had seen one do it. It was possible to believe that the hawk could do just such a fabled single-minded thing.

Lewis Peckham did not offer to help him find his ball. He knew why. Because Lewis had helped him on the last hole, seventeen, where he had also sliced out-of-bounds and to do so now would be unseemly. In a show of indifference Lewis permitted him the freedom to look or not to look for the ball, to drop or pick up. It was a nice calculation. Your ordinary pro would make a great sweaty show of helping out.

It was not his regular foursome. It was not an ordinary golf game.

The first time he had sliced out-of-bounds, Lewis had gone through the fence with him and shown him something odd. At the base of a low ridge, they were halfheartedly poking at weeds, hoping to turn the new Spalding Pro Flite, when Lewis stopped and stood still.

"You notice anything unusual about that tree?" asked Lewis, nodding toward a flaming sassafras, not a tree really but a large shrub. The red three-fingered leaves caught a ray of sunlight and turned fluorescent in the somber laurels.

"No."

"Put your face next to it."

He did, expecting to smell something, perhaps licorice. Smelling nothing, he plucked a leaf for sucking, tasted the licorice stem. Lewis held a branch aside as if it were a drape at a window.

"Now?"

"Now what?"

"You still don't notice anything?"

"No."

"Come closer."

There was nothing to come closer to except a shallow recess in the rock of the ridge.

"Now?"

Something stirred against his cheek, a breath of air from the rock itself, then as he leaned closer a steady current blew in his face and open mouth, not like the hot summer breeze of the fairway, but a cool wet exhalation smelling of rocks and roots. His mouth tasted minerals.

"Where does that come from, a cave? I don't see an opening."

"Yeah. My cave."

"Your cave?"

"Lost Cove."

"Lost Cove cave? But that's down below."

"I know, but it's the same cave."

"Sure I remember. I remember every detail, the room where you found the saber-tooth tiger, the Confederate powder works. Where does the air come from?"

"It's a phenomenon around here. Like Blowing Rock. Warm summer air blowing up the gorge into the big entrance below, percolating up through the mountain, and coming out cracks like this, cool in the summer, warm in the winter."

"It's strange, but I remember every detail. I could go straight to the tiger's lair."

"Let me show you something."

A thousand feet below the sunny golf links the tiger had crawled into the cave thirty-two thousand years ago, lain down in darkness, and died so long ago that slender stalagmites and stalactites had grown together over the opening and zoo-caged him, him a bone, a skull and curve of tooth fused with the floor as if he were shaped from rock. For a while Lewis Peckham had charged admission, shown the Confederate powder works and the tiger until the state claimed him, broke into the stone cage, and hauled him off to Raleigh.

As he watched, Lewis seemed to vanish into the rock—and reappear as magically.

"How did you do that?"

"Look. It's a slot behind this rock. One step sideways and you're in the cave."

"It looks like a trick."

Lewis said it was, that the Confederates had used it as an escape exit.

Now he stood alone in the glade after slicing out-of-bounds on eighteen. He was holding the three-iron, not like a golf club or a shotgun now, but like a walking stick. Its blade resting on a patch of wet moss sank slightly of its own weight and the weight of his hand. Tiny bubbles of air or marsh gas came up through the moss next to the metal of the iron.

Once he was in the pine forest the air changed. Silence pressed in like soft hands clapped over his ears. Not merely faint but gone, blotted out, were the shouts of the golfers, the clink of irons, the sociable hum of the electric carts. He listened. There was nothing but the sound of the silence, the seashell roar which could be the *ee*ing and *oh*ing of his own blood or the sound of cicadas at the end of summer which seems to come both from the pines and from inside one's head.

Then he heard a chain saw so faraway that he could not make out its direction yet close enough to register the drop in pitch as the saw bit into wood and the motor labored.

The golf carts were going away. They had crossed a rise in the fairway. Through the trees he could see their white canopies move, one behind the other, as silently as sails.

He turned his head. Beyond the glade the pine forest was as dark as twilight except for a single poplar which caught the sun. Its leaves had turned a pale gold. Though the air was still in the forest, one leaf shook violently. Beyond the aspen he made out a deadfall of chestnuts. A flash of light came from the chestnut fall. By moving his head he could make the light come and go. It was the reflection of sunlight from glass.

Above him the branches of the pines came off the trunks at intervals and as regularly as the spokes of a wheel.

Lifting the three-iron slowly and watching it all the while, once again he held it like a shotgun at rest, club head high between his chest and arm, shaft resting across his forearm. Now, carefully, as if he were reenacting an event not quite remembered, as if he had forgotten something which his muscles and arms and hands might remember, he swung the shaft of the iron slowly to and fro like the barrel of a shotgun. He stopped and again stood as still as a hunter. Now turning his head and stooping, he looked back at the fence.

But he had not forgotten anything. Today for some reason he remembered everything. Everything he saw became a sign of something else. This fence was a sign of another fence he had climbed through. The hawk was a sign of another hawk and of a time when he believed there were fabulous birds. The tiger? Whatever he was, he was gone. Even the wheeling blackbirds signified not themselves but a certain mocking sameness. They flew up, flustered and wheeling and blown about by the same fitful wind just as they had thirty, forty years ago. There is no mystery. The only mystery is that nothing changes. Nothing really happens. Marriages, births, deaths, terrible wars had occurred but had changed nothing. War is not a change but a poor attempt to make a change. War and peace are not events.

Only one event had ever happened to him in his life. Everything else that had happened afterwards was a non-event.

The guitar sound of the fence wire stretched above him and the singing and popping of the vines against his body were signs of another event. Stooping now, he was trying to make his body remember what had happened. Suddenly it crossed his mind that nothing else had ever happened to him.

The boy had gone through the fence first, holding the new Sterlingworth Fox double-barreled twenty-gauge ahead of him, while the man pulled up the top strand of barbed wire. He had gone through the fence, but before he could stand up, the man had grabbed his shoulder from the other side of the fence in a grip that surprised him not so much for the pain as for the suddenness and violence and with the other hand grabbed the gun up and away from him, swung him around and cursed him. *Goddamn you, haven't I told you how to go through a fence with a loaded shotgun? Don't you know what would happen if*—suddenly the man stopped.

Now on the golf links years later he recognized the smell. It was the funky tannin rot of the pin-oak swamp as sharp in his nostrils as wood smoke.

The boy, who had already gotten oven the pain but not the surprise, stood looking at the man across the fence holding the two shotguns, still too surprised to feel naked and disarmed without his gun. Nothing would ever surprise him again. Once the surprise was gone and his heart slowed, he began to feel the first hint of the coolness and curiosity and watchfulness of the rest of his life. Is it possible that his eyes narrowed slightly (he wasn't sure of this) as he put his empty hands in his pockets (he was sure of this) and said:

If what?

They had gone into the woods after singles. The dog had run over the covey instead of pointing it, and the covey had flushed too soon and too far away for a shot, the fat birds getting up with their sudden heart-stop thunder, then angling off tilt-winged and planing into the trees. The man, white-faced with anger, cursed the guide, shot the dog instead of the birds, to teach the dog never to do that again, he said, not to hurt the dog bad what with the distance and the number-eight bird shot. The dog and the guide disappeared.

When the man handed the shotgun back to him, his eyes glittered but not in the merry way they did when a hunt went well. He had given the boy the new shotgun for Christmas and he had just finished trying an important lawsuit in Thomasville close by and this was the very place, the very woods where he, the man, once had had a great hunt, perhaps even a fabled hunt, with his own father. But this hunt had gone badly. The Negro guide was no good. The dog had been trained badly. The lawsuit was not going well. They, the man and the boy, had spent a bad sleepless night in an old hotel (the same hotel where the man had spent the night before the great Thomasville hunt). The hotel was not at all as the man had remembered it.

Here, said the man, handing him the shotgun and stretching up the top strand of barbed wire. The wire creaked. *I trust you now.*

Thank you. The boy was watchful as he took the gun.

Do you trust me? asked the man.

Yes. No.

You have to trust me now.

Why?

I'm going to see to it that you're not going to have to go through what I am going through.

What's that?

You'll just have to trust me, okay?

Okay, said the boy, eyes wary and watchful. The man sounded almost absentminded and his glittering eye seemed to cast beyond him to the future, perhaps to the lawsuit Monday.

Come over here a minute.

What?

Here. Over here by me.

Oh.

Now, as the boy stood beside him, the man gave him a hug with the arm not holding the gun. He felt the man's hand giving him hard regular pats on the arm. He was saying something. The boy, no longer surprised, did not quite hear because he was reflecting on the strangeness of it, getting an awkward hug from his father, as they stood side by side in their bulky hunting clothes in the wet cold funk-smelling pin-oak swamp. He couldn't remember being hugged before except at funerals and weddings, and then the hugs were perfunctory and the kisses quick cheek kisses and that was all right with him, he didn't want to be hugged or kissed then or now.

And now, standing in the glade with the three-iron, he was wondering idly. *Why?* Why is it that I would not wish then or now or ever to kiss my father? Why is it that it was then and now a kind of violation, not the violation of the man grabbing him across the fence but a violation nevertheless, and a cheapening besides. Italians and Frenchmen and women hugged and kissed each other and what did it signify?

What? asked the boy.

The man pulled him close and turned his face down toward him and the boy smelled the heavy catarrh of his breath with the faint overlay of whiskey from the night before. His father was understood to suffer from "catarrh" and all night long, while the boy lay still, watchful and alert, the man had tossed and breathed out his heavy catarrh-and-whiskey breath.

Two singles went in here. I'll take one and you the other. But the man didn't let him go, held him still and gave him regular hard pats.

The man liked to go after singles after the covey was flushed, veering from the fields and open woodlands which the dogs had quartered and plunge backward into thickets and briars where not even the dogs would go, turning and using his body as entering wedge, the vines singing and popping against the heavy duck of his pants and jacket. When a single got up and he shot it and found it (no thanks to the dogs), and held the bird in his hand for a moment before stuffing it into the game pocket, his eyes would grow merry as if he had set himself an impossible quest and won, had plunged into the heart of the darkness and disorder of the wet cold winter woods and extracted from it of all things a warm bright-eyed perfect bird.

But now the man was standing still, eyes glittering, holding the gun oddly and gazing down at it, the stock resting on the ground, the barrel tilted just back from the vertical and resting lightly in the crotch of thumb and forefinger.

You and I are the same, said the man as if he were speaking to the gun.

How?

You are like me. We are two of a kind. I saw it last night.

Here come the pats again, hard, regular, slow, like a bell tolling.

Saw what?

I saw the way you lay in bed last night and slept or didn't sleep. You're one of us, I'm afraid. You already know too much. It's too bad in a way.

Us? Who's us?

You'd be better off if you were one of them.

Who's them?

The ignorant armies that clash by night.

The boy was silent.

We have to trust each other now, don't we?

Yes, said the boy, rearing slightly so he could see the man better.

We're buddies, aren't we?

Yes. No. You're wrong. We're not buddies. I don't want to be anybody's buddy.

Okay. Let's go. There are two of them. You take the one on the right.

Okay.

Oh shit, said the man. Last hard pat, sock, wham, on the shoulder. *I'm sorry.*

The boy looked up not surprised but curious. He had never heard the man say *shit* before.

Now standing with the three-iron in the glade, he was thinking: he said that one and only *shit* in exactly the same flat taped voice airline pilots use before the crash: *We're going in. Shit.*

Now the man was looking more like himself again, cheeks

ruddy, cap pushed back on his head as if it were a summer day and he needed the air, though it was very cold. It was his regular chipper look but when the boy, going forward, looked at him sideways he noticed that his eyes were too bright.

They kicked up two singles but the birds flew into the trees too soon and there was no shot. The birds angled apart and the man and the boy, following them, diverged. A lopsided scrub oak, dead leaves brown and heavy as leather, came between them. A ground fog filled the hollows like milk. As the boy moved ahead silently on the wet speckled leaves, his heart did not beat in his throat as it used to before quail are flushed. Then it came, on the man's side of the tree, the sudden tiny thunder of the quail and the shot hard upon it and then the silence. There was not even the sound of a footstep but only a click from the Greener. Now the boy was moving ahead again. He heard the man walking. They were clearing the tree and converging. Through the leathery leaves and against the milkiness he caught sight of a swatch of khaki. Didn't he hear it again, the so sudden uproar of stiff wings beating the little drum of bird body and the man swinging toward him in the terrific concentration of keeping gunsight locked on the fat tilt-winged quail and hard upon the little drumbeat the shocking blast rolling away like thunder through the silent woods? The boy saw the muzzle burst and flame spurting from the gun like a picture of a Civil War soldier shooting and even had time to wonder why he had never seen it before, before he heard the whistling and banging in his ear and found himself down in the leaves without knowing how he got there and even then could still hear the sound of the number-eight shot rattling away through the milky swamp and was already scrambling to get up from the embarrassment of it (for that was no place to be), but when he tried to stand, the keening in his ear spun him down again—all that before he even felt the hot wetness on the side of his face which was not pressed into the leaves and touched it and saw the blood. It was as if someone had taken hold of him and flung him down. He heard the *geclick* and *gecluck* of the Greener's breech opening and closing. Then he heard the shot. He waited until the banging and keening in his head stopped. He did not feel cold. His face did not hurt. Using the gun as a prop, he was able to get to his knees. He called out. It had been important to get up before calling. Nobody, not him, not anybody, is going to catch me down here on the ground. When there was no answer, he waited again, aware only of his own breathing and that he was blinking and gazing at nothing in particular. Then, without knowing how he knew, he knew that he was free to act in his own good time. (How did he know such a thing?) Taking a deep breath, he stood up and exhaled it through his mouth *sheeew* as a laborer might do, and wiping blood from his lip with two fingers he slung it off as a laborer might sling snot. Twelve years old, he grew up in ten minutes. It was possible for him to stretch out a hand to the tree and touch it, not hold it. He walked around the tree before it occurred to him that he had forgotten his shotgun. At first he didn't see the man, because both the jacket and the cap had a camouflage pattern which hid him in the leaves like a quail and because the bill of the cap hid his face. The man was part lying, part sitting against a tree, legs stretched out and cap pulled over his face like a countryman taking a nap and there was the feeling in the boy not that it was funny but that he was nevertheless called upon to smile and he might even have tried except that his face suddenly hurt. He did not see the man's gun, the big double-barreled twelve-gauge English Greener. For some reason which he could still not explain, he went back to look for his own gun. It was not hard to walk but when he bent to pick up the gun his face hurt again. When he came back he saw the dark brown stock of the Greener sticking out from the skirt of the man's jacket.

Now the boy was squatting (not sitting) beside the man. He pushed his own cap back as if it were a hot day. He pulled the man's cap off. He was not smiling and his eyes were closed but his face looked all right. His cheeks were still ruddy.

He put his hand under the man's jacket but the Greener got in the way. He pulled the shotgun out by the butt and put his hand under the jacket again and against the man's chest. The heart beat strongly. But his hand was wet and something was wrong. The fabric of shirt and underwear was matted into flesh like burlap trodden into mud.

Now squatting back on his heels beside the man he took his handkerchief from his pocket with his dry hand and carefully wiped the blood from the other hand. Then he pushed his cap back still farther because his forehead was sweating. He blew into both hands because they were cold and began to think.

What he was thinking about was what he was going to do next

but at the same time he noticed that he did not feel bad. Why is it, he wondered, that I feel that I have all the time in the world to figure out what to do and the freedom to do it and that what is more I will do it? It was as if he had contracted into the small core of curiosity and competence he had felt within himself after the man had grabbed him across the fence, spun him around, cursed him, and took his gun away. Now he was blowing into his hands and thinking: This is a problem and problems are for solving. All you need to do anything is time to do it, being let alone long enough to do it and a center to do it from. He had found his center.

The guide doesn't live far from here. We passed the cabin. The Negro boy ran home when the man cursed him and shot the dog.

Now he was standing up and looking carefully around. He even made out a speckled quail lying in the speckled leaves. As he waited for the dizziness to clear, he watched the man.

Don't worry, I'm going to get us both out of here. He knew with certainty that he could.

Later, after it was over, his stepmother had hugged them both. *Thank God thank God thank God* she said in her fond shouting style. *You could have both been killed!*

So it had come to pass that there were two accounts of what had happened, and if one was false the other must be true; one which his stepmother had put forward in the way that a woman will instantly and irresistibly construe the world as she will have it and in fact does have it so: that the man had had one of his dizzy spells—he knows with his blood pressure he shouldn't drink and hunt!—and fell; that in falling he discharged the double-barrel, which wounded the boy and nearly killed the man. The boy almost came to believe her, especially when she praised him. *We can thank our lucky stars that this child had the sense and bravery to know what to do. And you a twelve-year-old*—mussing up his hair in front in a way she thought of as being both manly and English—*We're so proud of you. My fine brave boy!*

But it was not bravery, he thought, eyes narrowing, almost smiling. It was the coldness, the hard secret core of himself that he had found.

The boy and his father knew better. With a final hug after he was up and around and the boy had recovered, except for a perforated and permanently deafened left middle ear and a pocked cheek like a one-sided acne, the man was able to speak to him by standing in the kitchen and enlisting D'Lo the cook in the conversation and affecting a broad hunter's lingo not at all like him: *I'm going to tell yall one damn thing*—Yall? He never said *yall*. Talking to D'Lo, who stood at the stove with her back to them? *I'm getting rid of that savage*. He nodded to the Greener on the pantry table. *I had no idea that savage had a pattern that wide! So wide it knicked you—did you know that, D'Lo?* Hugging the boy, he asked D'Lo. D'Lo must either have known all about it or, most likely, had not been listening closely, for she only voiced her routine but adequate *hnnnonnhHM! Now ain't that something else!*—which was what the man wanted her to say because this was the man's way of telling the boy, through D'Lo, what had happened and soliciting and getting her inattentive assent to the routineness and even inevitability of it. Such things happen! *And I'll tell you something else*, the man told D'Lo. *When a man comes to the point that all he can think about is tracking a bird and shuts everything out of his mind to the point of shooting somebody, it's time to quit!* D'Lo socked down grits spoon on boiler rim. *You right, Mister Barrett!* Was she even listening? And now the man finally looking down his cheek at him hugged alongside: *Right?*

Yes sir. He waited only to be released from the hug.

There was silence. They spoke no more of it. We know, don't we, the silence said, that the man was somehow wounded by the same shot and there is nothing to be said about it.

But how did he miss the bird? How did he wound himself?

While the sheriff was taking care of the man in the swamp, the guide brought the two shotguns, a dead quail, and three empty shells into the dark clean room smelling of coal oil and newspaper and flour paste where the Negro woman was washing his face. She dried it and patted something light and feathery—spiderwebs?—on his cheek. He didn't feel bad but his ear still roared. *"Here dey,"* said the black youth. *They yours and hisn.* He looked down at the kitchen table at the two shotguns, the three empty Super-X shells, and the dead quail. This black boy was no guide. What guide would pick up empty shotgun shells? *You didn't see the other bird?* he asked the guide. *Ain't no other bird*, said the black boy. The white boy said: *There were two singles and he shot twice and he never misses*. The black boy

54

said: *Well he done missed this time.* The white boy heard himself saying: *You just didn't find the bird*, and getting angry and wondering: Why am I worrying about the second bird? *Nawsuh*, said the woman, whose black arms were sifted with flour. *John sho find your bird if he was there. Look, he even found your bullets. Must have been the dogs got him.*

He looked at the Greener on the kitchen table in the shotgun cabin, sat down, broke the breech, and took out the one empty shell and set it next to the shells the guide had found. As he gazed he put one hand to his cheek, which had begun to bleed again, and covered his roaring ear.

Now in a green forest glade near a pretty pink-and-green golf links, he touched his deafened ear. Did it still roar a little or was it the seashell roar of the silence of forest? Holding the three-iron in both hands he tested the spring of its steel shaft.

It was as if the thirty years had passed and he had not ever left the Negro cabin but, strange to say, had only now got around to saying what he had not said for thirty years. Again he smelled the close clean smell of kerosene and warm newspaper.

Now in Carolina in a glade in the white pines he said aloud: *There was only one shell in the Greener*, for some reason smiling a little and examining the three-iron closely as if it had a breech which could be broken, revealing the missing shell. But he only saw the green Winchester Super-X with its slightly wrinkled cylinder smelling of cordite. *What happened to the other shell?* Nothing. There was no other shell. I broke the breech of the Greener and there was only one shell. Why? Because he reloaded after the first shot. He shot the first single. Then there was a pause. It was then that I heard the *geclick* of the Greener breech opening and the *gecluck* of its closing. But why reload with one good shell left? That was all he needed for the second single if I missed it. Because he always liked to be ready. He liked to shoot quick and on the rise. And why, after the second shot, did he reload with only one shell?

Because— He smiled at the three-iron which he held sprung like a bow in front of him.

Because when he reloaded the last time, he knew he only needed one shot.

But why reload at all? He had reloaded before the second shot. After the second shot, he still had a good shell in the second chamber.

Wait a minute. Again he saw the sun reflected from something beyond the chestnut deadfall.

What happened? Here's what happened.

He fired once at the first single. Geclick. Eject one shell and replace it. Gecluck.

He fired the second time at the second single and also hit me. Geclick. Reload. Gecluck.

Why reload if he knew he only needed one more shot? He still had a good shell in the second chamber.

In the Carolina pine forest he closed his eyes and saw green Super-X shells lined up on the clean quilt in the Negro cabin.

There were *four* shells.

Faraway the golfers were shouting, their voices blowing away like the killdeer on the high skyey fairways. It was close and still in the glade. He was watching the three-iron as, held in front of him like a divining rod, it sank toward the earth. *Ah, I've found it after all. The buried treasure*, he thought smiling.

Strange to say, there rose in his throat the same sweet terror he had felt long ago when his father's old bitch Maggie (not the sorry pointer dog his father shot at Thomasville) pointed, bent like a pin, tail quivering, and they went slowly past her to kick up the covey, knowing as certainly as you can know anything that any second it would happen again, the sudden irruption at one's very feet, the sudden heart-stop thunder from the very earth where one stood.

Ah then, so that was it. He was trying to tell me something before he did it. Yes, he had a secret and he was trying to tell me and I think I knew it even then and have known it ever since but now I know that I know and there's a difference.

He was trying to warn me. He was trying to tell me that one day it would happen to me too, that I would come to the same place he came to, and I have, I have just now, climbing through a barbed-wire fence. Was he trying to tell me because he thought that if I knew exactly what happened to him and what was going to happen to me, that by the mere telling it would not then have to happen to me? Knowing about what is going to happen is having a chance to escape it. If you don't know about it, it will certainly happen to you. But if you know, will it not happen anyway?

2

On the first nine, his slices had carried him along the backyards of the new condominiums and villas which bordered the golf links. The condominiums were like separate houses of different colors and heights which had been shoved together, some narrow with steep roofs, some broad and balconied like chalets.

Youngish couples, perhaps weekenders from Atlanta, sat drinking and barbecuing under the pines. They did not seem to notice him as he pursued his ball through their backyards. Two young men, both thick-waisted, both mustachioed like Mexican bandits, Atlantans yes, stood gazing down at smoking briquets in an orange tub-shaped grill as he retrieved his Spalding Pro Flite.

He sliced into a pond. He sliced over a creek. He sliced into a patio party of more Atlantans. He sliced clean off the golf course, across a new highway. There were a few small flat-topped houses scattered among vacant treeless lots. A man was washing a camper. It had a Pennslyvania license. An old couple stood at the roadside, binoculars in hand, as if they were waiting for a bird. In the distance above scrubby pines rose a dark pyramid-shaped building with a lopped-off peak like a Hawaiian temple.

Though he'd have preferred walking or riding with Lewis Peckham, Jimmy Rogers insisted on renting a third golf cart and driving him around in pursuit of his errant drives.

Jimmy Rogers told him several jokes. He noticed that Jimmy would discuss various matters such as financial deals, real estate developments, as they sat side by side bouncing along in the cart, but that he would only tell a joke after they dismounted to make their shots. Then it was possible for Jimmy to confront him and, standing not more than a foot away, take hold of his arm and engage him with his eyes. As he listened to a joke, Jimmy's gaze fixed intently on him, darting ever so slightly. Jimmy seemed to be requiring something of him.

When Jimmy told him the following joke, seizing his arm and pulling him close, the sensation of Jimmy's eyes darting over his face was not altogether unpleasant. It reminded him of the touch of a doctor's hands examining his body.

Three women died and went to heaven.

The first, a white woman about fifty, arrived at the pearly gates. St. Peter asked her what she died of. She replied cancer of the breast. What a shame, said St. Peter, to be cut off from life in your prime but don't worry, daughter, you have arrived in heaven where eternal happiness awaits you. And he welcomed her in.

Then came the second woman, also white, but younger, about thirty-five. Again St. Peter expressed sorrow and asked her the cause of her death. She said it was leukemia. Again he said what a shame it was that one should die so young but that her eternal reward awaited her and so forth and told her to come in and take her place.

The third woman was a young black girl about eighteen. This time St. Peter expressed not only sympathy but shock that one so young should have died. What did you die of, daughter? Gonorrhea, said the black girl. Come on now, girl, how could that be? People don't die of gonorrhea. And the girl said: They does when they gives it to Leroy.

During the joke he was aware of Jimmy's casting about for slightly different ways of saying the same thing: "what a shame" and "expressed sorrow" and "expressed sympathy," "welcomed her in" and "told her to come in." Sometimes Jimmy filled in the blanks by saying "and so forth." As the joke approached its end, Jimmy's grip on his arm tightened and Jimmy's gaze seemed to dart deep into his eye like the ray of a doctor's examining scope.

Back at the cart Jimmy began to describe a real estate venture, an island off the South Carolina coast in which he and Bert Peabody—your brother-in-law, Billy—had an interest. Two Atlanta banks had made strong commitments and a personal friend, Ibn Saroud, had already put up one mill five.

"We're going to close this mother out next week."

"Ibn Saroud?" he repeated absently. Arabs in North Carolina. What had happened to the Jews? When the Jews appeared in history, Marion said, it was a sign. But what if they disappeared?

As Jimmy stopped the cart at his ball, which lay tree-bound in the rough and a good hundred and eighty yards from the green, the famous sixth, a swatch of billiard-table baize jutting above a neck of gold trees along a creek, a battlement from which a tiny pennant flew, ravined in front, and moated clean around by sand. A wind was blowing in gusts off the scarred mountain and into his face. As he looked at his irons he was thinking that it was the same warm wind which blew up the gorge and into Lost Cove cave and through thirty or forty miles of cool wet rock.

"A really fascinating person and a close personal friend. He speaks ten languages. Do you know how he brought me the money?"

"No."

"In a satchel! Like a fucking Fuller-brush man. What I'm telling you is that this sapsucker walks in with this satchel, opens it up, and there's the one mill five in fifties. I don't bat an eye. All I say is, Hold it, Ibn, till I get my own satchel. He liked that."

As Jimmy watched him from the cart, he gazed from the ball to the tree to the ravine to the green to the moon-faced mountain. The tree made a perfect stymie. Again he decided that something was happening to him. It took an effort to follow Jimmy's jokes and his plans for the island with its marina, its houses and condominiums invisible from the beach, its Championship Wilderness Golf Course. What plans! Jimmy was all plans and schemes and deals. Even his jokes were plans. When Jimmy told him a joke, what he heard was not the joke but the plan and progress of the joke. There was this German and this Jew and this nigger on this airplane, said Jimmy, and he could only watch and wonder how Jimmy would fare with his joke, his Arab, and his island—each a little foray into the future. Why would anyone want to make such plans now? He could not. He could not bring himself to tell a joke or even to consider that he had another twelve holes of golf to play. As for planning the next shot, he had no idea whether he would hit the ball three feet or three hundred feet. Did it matter?

The tree was a maple, and though it stymied him, the trunk was slender and the branches came off high enough to shoot under them with a long iron. His lie wasn't bad. Though the ball lay in the rough, it lay lightly and with a good cushion under it. He took out his two-iron and made his only good shot of the day. Closing the face of the club a little and opening his right hand on the grip, he hooked around the tree, caught the ball with the sweet spot of the iron, so that there was the sensation in his hands not of having hit anything but of a clicking through the ball as if he had tripped a switch. The ball took off low, turned like a boomerang, and as it went high over the ravine of gold trees caught a gust and settled like a bird on the tiny green.

There is a kind of happiness in golf, he thought, still feeling the sweetness of the shot in his hands and arms. Look at Bertie. He lives for nothing but to break a hundred, works on his game the livelong day, yet when he hits the ball, he looks like a man having a seizure. Nevertheless, wasn't Bertie a lucky man?

"You're going to like that one," said Jimmy Rogers absently and not paying attention. "I only wish I could offer you a piece of the action on my island."

"What action? What island?" Jimmy had forgotten golf and he had forgotten the island.

"Bert wants in and I've promised him though it was all I could do to talk that mother Ibn into letting him have a little piece of it. But there is something you might want to do."

"There is?"

"Not for me. Not even for Bert. But for an old friend of yours."

"Who's that?"

"Katherine."

"Katherine?"

"Katherine Vaught Huger."

"Oh, Kitty."

Jimmy's arm, which had been stretched along the back of the seat, turned and his thumbnail touched him between the shoulder blades. It was a meaningful thrust signifying something about Kitty. They were rolling down the sunny fairway, the electric cart humming sociably. Jimmy gazed fondly ahead, eyes crinkled, as if they were old friends.

"Yes, it's Katherine's island and she has a little problem that only you as an old friend can help her with. Those are her words. She'll be waiting for us. Your daughter Leslie was gracious enough to ask me over for a drink. Actually she said I was to get you home by five, and I'm not about to get in trouble with those two gals."

They were not exactly old friends, though Jimmy seemed to know more about him than he knew himself. He, Jimmy, knew about his old girlfriend, his wife's death, his money, his wife's money, his brother-in-law's money, his honorary degree, his man-of-the-year award.

When he first spied Jimmy headed for the foursome, ambling along in his perky way, hands moving around in his pockets, elbows sticking out, head cocked, pale narrow face keen as a knife, one eye had gleamed at him past the rim of his hollow temple.

That eye had gleamed at him for years, not frequently and in unlikely places. Somewhere, sometime, that eye would gleam at him again. No matter when and where it happened, however unlikely the place, it never came as a surprise. Each time it was as if he had caught a glimpse of himself, a narrow keener cannier self, in a mirror.

Did he imagine it or hadn't that eye gleamed at him once in Long Island City years ago when he had had a wreck driving into Manhattan from the North Shore? And found himself sitting on a curb outside a Queens Boulevard bar & grill, shaken up and therefore vulnerable to the stares of passersby and also open to chance happenings. At such times, he had noticed, coincidences occur. They not only occur, they are called for. If one gets wounded in a war and is lying shot up in a ditch and J. B. Ellis, whom one had known years ago in Birmingham, shows up, who would be surprised?

Lives are lines of force which ordinarily run parallel and do not connect. But that day Robert Kennedy had been shot and he had had a wreck. Lifelines were bent. He sat embarrassed and bloody on a Queens Boulevard curbstone while bar-&-grill types came and went, looming hungrily above him, consuming him, eating him with their gazes, then back to the bar to gaze at Kennedy lying in a hotel pantry—a feast of gazing! What was more natural than that in the crowd of onlookers he should catch a familiar gleam of eye like himself looking at himself—Jimmy Rogers! What was more natural than that Jimmy Rogers should be living in Long Island City and doing PR for Long Island University? Jimmy rescued him from the feasting crowd, took him in, and was kind to him, sent him on his way. Kennedy was killed. Lines of force were bent. It was natural on such a day to have a wreck and see Jimmy Rogers.

Perhaps, he thought, even God will manifest himself when you are bent far enough out of your everyday lifeline.

Now here was Jimmy Rogers again. Had something happened? Was something about to happen? As assassination was imminent.

There was something both mysterious and unadmirable in his dealings with Jimmy Rogers. They had come from the same town but had not known each other well. Jimmy's father was a butcher. They attended the same university, where he but not Jimmy had joined a good fraternity, a small band of graceful Virginians and Northerners who wore their pants high, did not talk loud, or vomit when they drank. Over the years he had had not much to do with Jimmy. They spoke when they met on campus paths. He knew now that he had been snobbish toward Jimmy and that it could not be helped. Jimmy joined the Rho Omega Kappas, the Rocks, who wore sweaters under their double-breasted suits and showed too much gum when they smiled.

He had not been admirable in his dealings with Jimmy Rogers.

On the other hand, Jimmy always had stuff between his teeth and came too close, breathed on you, and touched you when he talked. No wonder he got along with Arabs.

Then Jimmy had been kind to him in Long Island City, ministering to him among strangers.

Now here is Jimmy again, coming too close and telling jokes and making deals with Arabs.

Did this mean that lifelines were back to normal, that is, nonconverging and parallel to infinity? Or had something happened and their lifelines had bent together?

They were waiting for Bertie to hit a fairway wood. Jimmy stopped the cart a little too close to him. Why would Jimmy not know that ten feet is too close and fifteen is not?

Bertie shot. His body remained still and erect as a post while his arms swung and his legs jerked. The ball shanked, rustled like a rat through the thick grass. Bertie actually said *pshaw*.

A club flashed above the deep far bunker, sand sprayed, and a ball arced high over the green and back down into the ravine. Lewis Peckham clucked and cocked his head a sympathetic quarter inch. "He sculled it." Ed Cupp was at least six feet eleven inches tall but only his shining blond head showed above the bunker lip. He climbed out cheerfully and went striding off, swinging his sand-iron like a baseball bat. He played golf like a good athlete who had just taken it up, with a feel for the game and a toleration for his mistakes. Though he was in his late forties, he looked like a UCLA forward—which he had been—swinging across campus. Do native Californians stay blond and boyish into old age? Yet when he spoke—and he spoke often, mostly about a warranty problem with his Mercedes which had broken down in Oklahoma—it was with the deliberation of an old man, a ninety-year-old sourdough telling you the same long story about the time somebody jumped his claim.

Lewis Peckham looked at his, Will Barrett's, two-iron shot which lay hole-high and three feet from the pin. He nodded twice. "That was a good golf shot."

In the cart Jimmy leaned close and again put a thumb in his back, signifying Kitty.

"Do you remember when Kitty was queen and you presented her at the Fall Germans?" he whispered.

"Ah—"

"She was—still is—the best-looking white girl I ever saw—she's certainly been lovely to me and I really appreciate it. Don't you remember? I got Stan Kenton."

Strangely, he had forgotten about Kitty being queen but not about Stan Kenton. In college Jimmy quickly learned the ropes. He had gotten to be manager of this and that, manager of stadium concessions, of the yearbook, of the cap-and-gown business, manager in charge of decorating the dance hall and hiring an orchestra. Jimmy was making money long before the Arabs.

"What I am saying is this," said Jimmy and the thumbnail turned like a screw, not unpleasantly, into his spine. "Kitty is going to rely on you for something. She has enormous respect for you, you know. We all do." The eye gleamed and the thumbscrew went in a little too hard. "You old rascal, you did it, didn't you?"

"Did what?" He smiled. He frowned. He was almost surprised. The thumbnail going in so hard and the "rascal" was not like Jimmy.

"Nothing. You just sat back like you always did and picked up all the marbles. That's what I call class."

"Class?"

"You made it in the big apple, you married a nice Yankee lady who owns half of Washau County, you retired young, you came down here and you helped folks, poor folks, old folks, even built them a home, helped the church, built a new church, did good. Now your lovely daughter is getting married. Joy and sorrow, that's life. But yours seems mostly joy. You know what you did."

"No, what?"

"You won. That's what you did, you old—" The eye glittered and the thumbnail screwed into his back. "You won it all, you son of a bitch, and I love you for it."

The thumbnail signified love and hatred.

Through the not unpleasant pain of the thumbnail he wondered where Jimmy had picked up these expressions, "big apple," "class," "I love you for it." He sounded like an old Broadway comic. Playing Long Island City.

Jimmy Rogers loved him and hated him. This kind of love-hate, pleasure-pain, had not happened to him for a long time. After you grow up, you stop having fistfights, cursing, getting drunk, and talking about women. You begin to banter. He had bantered for thirty years.

But now, with Jimmy coming at him with thumbnail screwing into his back, coming close as a lover, eye glittering with love-hatred, it was difficult to pay attention. He could not bring himself to be aware of more than a mild stirring of curiosity, like the prickling that Jimmy's thumbnail sent up his neck. A little something or other was happening, but no more than that. It was as if he had been living in a prison cell for so long that he had come to believe that nothing was really happening anywhere—when one day he heard a footstep. Someone was coming.

It was at this moment that he saw the bird. A small cloud passed over the sun, the darkness settling so quickly it left the greens glowing. A hawk flew over, a dagger-winged falcon, its flight swift and single-minded and straight over the easy ambling golfers. When it reached the woods it folded its wings as abruptly as if it had been shot and fell like a stone.

3

He stood in the glade, both hands resting on top of the three-iron. The blade of the iron pressed hard enough into the wet moss to make bubbles come up. There was no sound except the distant power saw. He must have stood so and perfectly still for a long time because a tiny bird, no larger than his thumb, lighted on a twig not three feet away, stared at him with a single white-goggled eye, then turned its head clean around to look with its other eye. Deeper in the pine forest, beyond the chestnut fall, the poplar made an irregular cone of sunlight and leaves. He had been gazing at a figure behind the poplar. Was someone standing there or, more likely, was it a trick of light, a pattern in the dappled leaves? It did not matter. Not caring who it was or even if anyone was there, he gazed vacantly and, unaware that he did so, changed the grip on the club. Idly, like a golfer practicing, he took hold of the grip with both hands interlocked, right little finger overlapping left forefinger, and began a backswing. Then, turning the club head up and fitting it against his shoulder, he sighted along the shaft as if it were a gun barrel and swung it a few degrees laterally to and fro.

The figure moved behind the poplar, or perhaps a breath of air stirred the leaves. He went on gazing but could not bring his eyes to focus. Something distracted him. Though his gaze was fixed, it was unseeing. He seemed to be listening, head slightly cocked.

Something was close. He knew it as surely as if he had been carrying a Geiger counter and it had begun to click. There is a moment of discovery when the discoverer is so certain of his find that his only thought is to keep still for a moment, wait and watch, before taking it. When Maggie the pointer pointed a covey dead ahead, his father would stop too, raise a hand toward him: *Just hold it*, his lips said silently.

Until today he had not thought of his father for years.

Now he remembered everything his father said and did, even remembered the smell of him, the catarrh-and-whiskey breath and the hot, quail reek of his hands.

And, strange to say, at the very moment of his remembering the distant past, the meaning of his present life became clear to him, instantly and without the least surprise as if he had known it all along but had not until now taken the trouble to know that he knew.

Of course, he said, holding the three-iron across his arm like a shotgun and smiling at the figure dappled by sunlight beyond the poplar, of course. Ever since your death, all I ever wanted from you was out, out from you and from the Mississippi twilight, and from the shotguns thundering in musty attics and racketing through funk-smelling Georgia swamps, out from the ancient hatred and allegiances, allegiances unto death and love of war and rumors of war and under it all death and your secret love of death, yes that was your secret.

So I went away, as far as I could get from you, knowing only that if I could turn 180 degrees away from you and your death-dealing there would be something different out there, different from death, maybe even a kind of life. And there was.

I went as far as I could go, married a rich hardheaded plain

decent crippled pious upstate Utica, New York, woman, practiced Trusts and Estates law in a paneled office on Wall Street,
kept a sailboat on the North Shore, played squash, lived at 76th
and Fifth, walked my poodle in the park, went up an elevator
to get home, tipped three doormen and four elevator men at
Christmas, thought happily about making money like everyone
else (money is a kind of happiness), made more money than
some, married a great deal more money than most, learned how
to whistle down a cab two blocks away and get in and out of
"21" in time for the theater, began to enjoy (thanks to you)
Brahms and Mozart (no thanks to you). Music and making
money is to New Yorkers what music and war was to the Germans. And I was never so glad of anything as I was to get away
from your doom and your death-dealing and your great honor
and great hunts and great hates (Jesus, you could not even walk
down the street on Monday morning without either wanting to
kill somebody or swear a blood oath of allegiance with somebody else), yes, your great allegiance swearing and your old
stories of great deeds which not even you had done but had just
heard about, and under it all the death-dealing which nearly
killed me and did you. God, just to get away from all that and
live an ordinary mild mercantile money-making life, do mild
sailing, mild poodle-walking, mild music-loving among mild
good-natured folks. I even tried to believe in the Christian God
because you didn't, and if you didn't maybe that was what was
wrong with you so why not do the exact opposite? (Imagine,
having to leave the South to find God!) Yes, I did all that and
succeeded in everything except believing in the Christian God—
maybe you were right about one thing after all—what's more
even beat you, made more money, wrote a law book, won an
honorary degree, listened to better music.

Now Marion is dead and I can't believe I spent all those years
in New York in Trusts and Estates and taking dogs down ele-
vators and out to the park to take a crap.

In two seconds he saw that his little Yankee life had not
worked after all, the nearly twenty years of making a life with
a decent upstate woman and with decent Northern folk and
working in an honorable Wall Street firm and making a success of it too. The whole twenty years could just as easily
have been a long night's dream, and here he was in old Carolina, thinking of Ethel Rosenblum and having fits and falling

down on the golf course—what in God's name was I doing there, and am I doing here?

He gazed at the figure which seemed to come and go in the trembling dappled light of the poplar.

You were trying to tell me something, weren't you?

Yes.

That day in the swamp you were trying to tell me that this was what it was going to come to, not only for you but in the end for me, weren't you?

Yes.

You did it because you hoped that by having me with you when you did it you would show me what I was up against and that if I knew about it that early, I might be able to win over it instead of it winning over me, didn't you?

Yes.

Then it's not your fault. It's not your fault that after all this time here I am back where we started and you ended, that there is after all no escaping it for us. At least I know that, thanks to you, you tried, and now for the first time since that day you cursed me by the fence and grabbed my gun, I don't hate you. We're together after all.

Silence.

Very well. At least I know why I feel better holding a shotgun than a three-iron.

He walked through the chestnut fall to the poplar. The figure changed in shape, disappeared, returned as a solid of darkness bounded by gold leaves, then vanished altogether. Glass winked in the sunlight. The leaf shook violently as he went under it.

Once he cleared the screen of leaves the sun behind him suddenly went down and came up in front, blazing into his eyes. Holding one hand against the light, he sidestepped into the shade of the pines until he could see. The sun behind him was reflected from a bank of windows. It was a house of glass. He went on circling until he reached the darkness of a great pine and the house came into such an angle with his eye that no part of it reflected the sun.

It was a greenhouse, such as he had never seen before, freestanding but sheltered at one end by the ridge, with a wall of lichened concrete and a tall gambrel roof. It looked as big as an ark. The sun, sunk behind the pines, had come straight off the lower, more vertical of the glass slopes. A steep copper hood, verdigrised green-brown, shaded the front door like a cathedral porch. Iron spikes and fleurs-de-lis sprouted from the roof peak. Virginia creeper and saplings thrust through broken windows. The glazing on the lower tier was intact. The dusty glass was gilded by the sun and he could not see inside. The greenhouse, he judged, was a good fifty feet long and twenty-five feet wide. As he watched it, his head moved slightly as if he were appraising the width of a green or the length of an iron shot. A single huge pine near the porch towered over the whole forest.

"Are these yours?"

One heart-jump not from surprise but from anger at being taken by surprise, for in his circling he had, without thinking about it, backed into the fork of cloven pine, a vantage point from which he could see without being seen. He turned, frowning.

The youth held out two golf balls. He took them, still frowning and inattentive as if it were no more than he expected, a caddy retrieving lost balls, and thanked the youth—no, not a youth he noticed now, another miscalculation: he had at first thought long-haired youth with unchanged voice but no, it must be short-haired girl with woman's voice—and still frowning, examined the balls.

"Yes. Spalding Pro Flite and Hogan four. Yes, that's them all right. Thanks." He held out a dollar. Nice going, youth-girl caddy. But the slender hands which had given him the golf balls didn't move.

Frowning still—he was still off-balance—he shrugged and turned to leave.

"This one woke me up."

"What?"

"Hogan woke me up."

"Hogan woke you up?"

"It broke my window." She nodded toward the greenhouse.

"Which one?"

"Not those. At the end of my house, where I was sleeping. The surprise of it was instigating to me."

"Okay okay. Will five dollars do it?" He fumbled in his pocket.

No answer. Eyes steady, hands still.

"Did you say your house?"

"Yes. It is my house. I live there."

There was a window broken in the lower tier. His slice could hardly have carried so far. On the other hand, he had hit the first drive very hard, too hard (Was that it, his anger, that was causing the slice? Never hit a golf ball or a child in anger, said Lewis Peckham), and it went high, curving very foul, and did not hit wood. A real banana ball, said Lewis the first time.

"Okay. How much do I owe you?"

"It was peculiar. I was lying in my house in the sun reading this book." She had taken a book from the deep pocket of the jacket and handed it to him, as if to prove—prove what?—and as he examined it, a rained-on dried-out 1922 *Captain Blood*, he was thinking not about Captain Blood but about the oddness of the girl. There was something odd about her speech and, now that he looked at her, about her. For one thing, she spoke slowly and carefully as if she were reading the words on his face. The sentence "I was lying in my house" was strange. "The surprise of it was instigating." Though she was dressed, like most of the kids here, in oversize men's clothes, man's shirt, man's jacket, there was something wrong—yes, her jeans were oversize too, not tight, and dark blue like a farm boy's. Yet her hair was cut short and brushed carefully, as old-fashioned as the book she was reading. It made him think of the expression "boyish bob."

"I was lying in my house in the sun reading that book. Then *plink*, *tinkle*, the glass breaks and this little ball rolls up and touches me. I felt concealed and revealed." Her voice was flat and measured. She sounded like a wolf child who had learned to speak from old Victrola records. Her lips trembled slightly, not quite smiling, her eyes not quite meeting his yet attentive, sweeping his face like a blind person's.

Oh well. She was one of the thousands who blow in and out every summer like the blackbirds, nest where they can, in flocks or alone. Sleep in the woods. At least she had found a greenhouse.

As he turned away, gripping the three-iron with a two-handed golfer's grip and with a frowning self-consciousness which almost surprised him, she said: "Are you—?"

"What?" He cocked the club for a short chip shot and hung fire.

"Are you still climbing on your anger?"

"What?"

When he swung around, she was closer, her eyes full on him, large gray eyes set far apart in her pale (Yes, that was part of the oddness, not the thinness of her face but its pallor. Her skin was as white as a camellia petal yet not unhealthy) face. Her gaze was steady and unfocused. Either she was not seeing him (Was she blind? No, or she'd have never found the Hogan let alone the palding Pro Flite) or else she was seeing all of him because all at once he became aware of himself as she saw him, of his golf clothes, beltless slacks, blue nylon shirt with the club crest, gold cap with club crest, two-tone golf shoes with the fringed forward-falling tongues, and suddenly it was he not she who was odd in this silent forest, he with his little iron club and nifty fingerless glove.

Where had he seen her before? For one odd moment she was as familiar to him as he himself. He who remembered everything remembered those fond hazed eyes from Alabama twenty years ago. But maybe she wasn't born then.

Oh well. She was on something and couldn't focus her eyes.

He gave her the book. My God, what a nutty world, she zonked out on something, reading Rafael Sabatini and holed up alone in a ruined greenhouse, while grown middle-aged men socked little balls around a mountain meadow and hummed along in electric carts telling jokes about Jews and Germans and niggers. Atlanta and Carolina invaded by Arabs. No wonder my father wanted out.

"Angry? No, I'm not angry. What did you mean by still angry?"

"I mean over there." She pointed to the chestnut fall. "Where you were standing."

She had been watching him.

"Why did you think I was angry?"

"You were holding your golf stick in the thicket. I wanted to give you back your little golf balls but I was instigated by fear. I thought you were going to hit someone. Or shoot."

"You were watching me."

"Yes."

He looked down at his hands gripping the club. He became aware that he was nodding.

"You look angry again."

"I didn't know anyone was watching me."

"Why did that make you angry? I wasn't spying or denying. I was afraid."

Again the slow scanning speech. He looked at her. Yes, she was on something.

Maybe they're better off, after all. At least they are unburdened by the past. They don't remember anything because there is nothing to remember. They crawl under the nearest bush when they're tired, they eat seeds when they're hungry, they pop a pill when they feel bad. Maybe it does come down to chemistry after all. But if it does, then *he* was right. He wouldn't have it, the way they are, and though I wouldn't have him, I won't have it either.

Already walking out of the woods, he had forgotten her but only after remembering that there was something familiar about the way her upper lip had a little down and was shortened, pulled up in a gentle arc just clear of the lower in a pert familiar way out of keeping with her soft dazed eyes. Passing through the glade he swung the three-iron at the skunk cabbages, clipping the fat little purple pods as neatly as he had hit the Pro Flite with the two-iron.

Strange: he was slicing his drives from a proper tee with a proper fairway before him and hitting his irons like Hogan, from the rough, in the woods, behind trees. He shot better in a fen than in a fairway.

As he climbed through the fence and walked toward the clubhouse, it occurred to him that for the first time in years, perhaps in his life, he knew exactly what was what and what he intended to do. He remembered everything. He fell down again but not seriously, springing up immediately and hardly missing a step. Had the girl seen him fall?

It did not end quite as I expected, he thought, with a smile, as the poker dice rattled in the leather cup. His good friends greeted him in the fragrant and cheerful little locker-room bar. Towering above them in a great photomural, Jack Nicklaus blasted out of a sand trap, his good Ohio face as grim as a crusader, each airborne grain of sand sparkling like a jewel in the sunlight.

It did not end quite as I expected but it did end and I did find out how it would end, he thought as a yellow eye gleamed at him. Jimmy Rogers took him by the flank and drew him close as a lover. Jimmy wanted to tell him a joke. I know what I must do.

He listened calmly and even attentively. He remembered everything, even the joke which Jimmy had told him twenty years before. He even remembered the future. His entire life lay before him, beginning, middle and end, as plain as the mural of Jack Nicklaus blasting out of the sand trap.

He remembered everything.

IV

SHE REMEMBERED NOTHING. IT DOES NOT MATTER THAT I DO
not remember the past, she thought. What matters is finding
shelter, a safe warm place in these great cool dripping rhododendrons. Water tinkled down the rocks of the ridge and made
a little stream.

The safest place, she decided, was the little room at the end
of the greenhouse. The greenhouse backed up against the ridge.
Why did they build it like that? A stranger would hardly know
the room was there, grown up as it was with weeds and laurel
from the ridge; the laurel hiding the small door and holding it
shut. If you tried to open it from the inside it was like pushing
against a child who was trying to keep you in. But you could get
out.

It was possible to enter the room by way of the greenhouse,
pick one's way through the jungle to an intervening door which
could be bolted. Though many of the windows were broken, as
soon as one entered, there it was in the nostrils, a trace of the
closeted hot leaf-damp of greenhouses.

The small room must have been a potting shed. There
were flanged tables and shards everywhere. Yet the roof was
glazed. Why? Had they used it like a cold frame to grow
seedlings?

One bench she cleared for her possessions. Another she
pushed into the corner. The greenhouse was built under the
ridge on an east-west axis, leaving one corner of the potting
room, the southeast, sunny. After spreading her sleeping bag on

the table, she stuffed the empty knapsack with black moss (peat? sphagnum? Spanish?) and made a pillow.

Try it. The bed wasn't bad. If it got too hard, she could make a moss mattress. The corner was a good place for sitting propped up in the sun. A lookout was necessary but the glass was so dirty it looked frosted and she could see nothing but bright dusty sunlight. By calculating angles and declinations and wetting her handkerchief in the rivulet and rubbing glass inside and out, she cleared two saucer-size spots through which she could see in two directions, one with no trouble at all, beyond the little waterfall and up the path which she had taken from the hiking trail; the other by turning her head and looking over her shoulder, a little vista through a clearing made by huge dead mostly fallen chestnut trees. A few yards farther, she calculated from her map, the golf course must begin. Though she could see neither trail nor golf course, now and then she could hear the shouts of the golfers. The path ascended the ridge so steeply to the trail that when hikers passed, only the upper half of their bodies was visible. If anyone approached from the direction of the trail or the golf course, she would see them. If anyone came into the greenhouse, she would hear them.

How dangerous was it to live in this world?

The sun was still high and warm. Too warm. Something was wrong. Two windows in the upper tier directly above her bunk were broken out. Only splinters of glass remained in the steel frames. The sun shone directly through. It felt good on her face. Her new clothes grew warm and gave off a pleasant dry-goods smell. But what if it rained? What if it got cold? What manner of creature might fall in her lap in the dark? Dark? When would it get dark? She remembered the candles she bought in town.

She went exploring in the ruins of the house. There were three great blackened chimneys far apart (could this have been a single building?) with mounds of brick and rubble, grown over by creeper, between. What was she looking for? Anything flat enough, light enough, and wide enough to cover the hole: tar paper, tin, glass, boards. But there was nothing but brickbats, vines, and chipmunks, until she found the cellar—by falling into it. After giving up the search and heading for the greenhouse, she dropped suddenly, two feet, three feet, grabbed vines and didn't fall. There were steps. She went back for a candle and

Scout knife. The vines needed clearing, the cellar was dark. There could be snakes as well as treasures.

Down stone steps and into root-smelling dark: perhaps the cellar had been sealed off from vandals, like King Tut's tomb. Yes, some few treasures had fallen down the steps and been covered by creeper: an iron stove, two books, and a grimy transom-size window. The books were *Captain Blood* by Rafael Sabatini and *The Trail of the Lonesome Pine* by John Fox, Jr., both books rain-soaked, sun-dried, and swollen to fat loaves. She opened *Captain Blood*, sat on the steps, and read:

> Picking his way daintily through that shambles in the waist came a tall man with a deeply tanned face that was shaded by a Spanish headpiece. He was armed in back-and-breast of black steel beautifully damascened with golden arabesques. Over this, like a stole, he wore a sling of scarlet silk, from each end of which hung a silver-mounted pistol. Up the broad companion to the quarterdeck, moving with easy assurance, until he stood before the Spanish Admiral.

The words were still clear on the thick yellow page but the paper crumbled like bread and a bakery smell rose in her nostrils. Words surely have meanings, she thought, and there is my trouble. Something happens to words coming to me from other people. Something happens to my words. They do not seem worth uttering.

People don't mean what they say. Words often mean their opposites.

If a person says to you: *I hate to tell you this, but*—she doesn't hate to tell you. She likes to tell you. This is a good place to make a new start with words. A man wrote these words over fifty years ago and here they've been ever since, lying in a dark cellar. She read the phrase aloud: *a tall man with a deeply tanned face*. It sounded strange in the dead silence and the warm Carolina sunlight.

A large brindled dog came down from the trail, straight across the ruins, sat down and looked at her, not panting and not wagging his tail. He did not have a collar. His head was as wide and flat as an anvil. No doubt he belonged to a hiker but he did not leave. His clear hazel eyes looked from her to the book and back to her. An orange tuft above his eye moved like a man cocking an eyebrow. When she met his gaze, he cocked the other eyebrow and looked at a chipmunk. Can a dog be embarrassed?

She opened *The Trail of the Lonesome Pine*—it smelled more of school library than bakery—and read:

> Knowing nothing of the ethics of courtship in the mountains—how, when two men meet at the same girl's house, "they makes the gal say which one she likes best and t'other gits"—Hale little dreamed that the first time Dave stalked out of the room, he threw his hat in the grass behind the big chimney and executed a war dance on it, cursing the blankety-blank "furriner" within from Dan to Beersheba.

Yes, that's it, she thought, forgetting about the dog. Ordinarily people have ways of doing things—like the people who lived in this house long ago and read this book. It was up to the "furriner" to catch on. As for her: either she had not caught on to the way people do things, or people did not know what they were doing and there was no use trying to catch on. In either case, this seemed as good a place as any to make a start.

Make a start at what? For one thing, she could read these books for more clues, go to town, visit the public library, obtain a library card, take out more books, speak to the librarian, sit on the bench, observe people, speak to them, and either catch on to their ways or, if they didn't have any ways, make up one's own.

She examined the window. It must have been a glass transom for a double door, for it had a big brass latch and it was almost too heavy to wrestle up the steps and through the vines. Panting, she propped it against a chimney and knelt for a look. It was not broken. Cellar rootlets stuck to the glass. No, not rootlets, they were lead cames. When she leaned over to see if the lead went through, the sun made dull colors through the dust. The panes were stained glass.

Dragging the transom to the foot of the path, she leaned it under the dripping rock and went to get soap, rag, and moss. The dog followed, his serious hazel eyes attentive but unable to meet her gaze.

It gave pleasure to make a soft soaped Brillo pad of moss and scrub every inch of glass, frame, lead, and brass, doing one camed section at a time and rinsing it under the trickle. The water was not cold and had a mineral reek.

Downhill and easy going to the greenhouse, but her arms trembled as she pushed the transom up the wall until it rested on the concrete ledge. Now the trick was to stand on the ledge and slide the transom up the first slope of glass without falling off. It couldn't be done. There was no getting a purchase on it. But it was possible to stand on the ground and push it up with a forked stick of dogwood until the transom was balanced on the gambrel. Then, half propping, half holding stick on ledge, she climbed up beside it. Now the angle was right. She could lean forward against the lower slope, ah safe! both hands free to push transom past the gambrel angle and let it down carefully on the upper slope—but there was no sliding it laterally now, it must be lined up carefully.

Hope rose in her, then a confidence, that the random fit of transom to hole would somehow work out better than if she had measured hole and designed window to fit. It did. It was better than a fit. The frame of the transom overlapped the steel sash of the greenhouse, the scuffed wood engaging rusty metal all around, and weighted down in a friction bond so strong she couldn't even budge the transom toward her down the slope.

A fit by chance is romance, she said to herself.

Climbing down, she was already thinking how to fasten it more securely. A strong wind could blow it off. Perhaps a few nails in the frame, the nails above wired to the iron fleurs-de-lis and below to the mechanism of the window vents.

Tired now, she stretched out on her bunk. The afternoon sun shone directly on the upper slope of stained glass. The light broke into colors which filled the little room. Perhaps she had stirred up a suspension from the potsherds and the moss. The gold was like dust in the air and the violet made a vapor.

She gazed up at the transom. A cornucopia dumped out its fruit and flowers, purple grapes, yellow corn, scarlet strawberries, golden pumpkins, boxy pink rhododendron, the harvest tumbling down a blue sky to a green earth where fascicles of pine needles spelled out Autumn. Rhododendron! Then the stained glass had been designed for this place, my place. What had happened to her Winter, Spring, and Summer? Carted off by Tut tomb robbers. But perhaps they and many other treasures are hidden in the cellar. Kegs of nails, books, such as the Swiss family of Robinson found on their wrecked ship.

Something bumped the potting table. She leaned out. The dog was turning round and round in the moss to make a bed.

She took a nap.

When she woke, violet vapor swarmed in her eyelashes. She took out her Scripto pencil and notebook and wrote:

I am here.

I need from town: milk, matches, dog food, saw. There is plenty of stove wood, dead chestnut I think. When did all the chestnuts die? What about bathing? How to get the stove up from the basement? What kind of stove is it? How does a stove work? Does it burn wood or coal? Does it heat water?

I need to make a living. I do not have a house but I have a greenhouse. I can live here and either get a job in town or make a living from the greenhouse. How do you make a living in a greenhouse? With greens.

I need to remember what I knew when I wrote to myself in this notebook, for example, that this is my place. Because now I can only remember things after I see them (somewhere I must have worked with stained glass, knew about cames).

In order to make a living I must remember what I can do.

Remember. Start at the beginning. My name is Allison. I was born in nineteen-fifty-something, sixty-something?

Try.

The first thing I remember is my embarrassment with strangers. No, embarrassment *for* strangers. They seemed so vulnerable. What if one should hurt their feelings? Once as a child when I was walking home from school I stopped to talk to a colored maid hanging out wash. She seemed very nice. But I began to worry how to break off the conversation and leave. I could not think of a way that might not hurt her feelings. So I had to wait until she finished hanging out the wash and went inside.

Very well, start at the other end. Yesterday. Last week.

After you make a living, then what do you do? How do you live?

When she leaned back on the knapsack pillow wedged into a corner of glass, a ruby swatch of light fell across her face. The down on her cheek turned fiery.

Yes, now I remember something. It was because she had sat so in the closed ward in the same lookout position, head wedged in an angle of the wingback chair. From here too she could see the two places people come from, the highway which ran past the main gate and the door to the hall.

Using the binoculars her father had given her for birdwatching, she was watching out not for the birds but for the bread truck. A car came over the hill, its top appearing first as a swelling in the hot asphalt. In the binoculars it seemed not to approach but to swell and rise until it was a few inches clear of the highway and riding on thick shimmering air. The car, a yellow Continental, was foreshortened and set off at an angle so that the four women passengers, two in front and two in back, appeared to be seated in a row. They were dressed as if they were going to a party, hair done neatly, but at this hour they could only be visiting antique shops or views of valleys and mountains of red leaves. Yes, they were leafers. The car had a Florida license.

Dr. Duk came in. He knocked on the door after opening it and coming in.

Knock knock, he said, hiding in the little foyer.

Who's there, she said.

Ivan.

Ivan who?

Ivan to be alone.

This was a bad sign. When Dr. Duk felt obliged to be funny, she was in for it. By enlisting her in his joke, he was trying, one, to be funny, and, two, to give her a "language structure" so that she, who had stopped talking because there was nothing to say, would have a couple of easy lines, straight man to his comic.

When he said *Knock knock*, it was not hard to say *Who's there?* Or *Ivan who?* Perhaps he was right. She could never lead off with a *Knock knock*. So she had lost most of her speech except for short questions such as *Who's there?* and *Ivan who?*

Where did he get these knock-knock jokes? Not even her father had told a knock-knock joke for years. Dr. Duk was English. Had knock-knocks just got to England? But Dr. Duk was not quite English. He sounded English and his first name was Alistair, but a faint sootiness underlay his white skin. It reminded her of her mother stirring carbon black into her Williamsburg white paint. Kelso said his real name was Dr.

Dukhipoor. Had he got his knock-knock jokes from old Milton Berle reruns in Pakistan? The patients called him Dr. Duck.

Her eyes were asking him something and he knew what it was, but he felt obliged to talk first about his hobbies, birdwatching and gardening. Maybe he was English. There is an advantage to being a small insular people, he said. We make a virtue of our limitations—ah, but you Americans and the Russians with your great continental soul-searching—heavy, man!—all very well indeed I'm sure but it's not a bad thing to do a bit of gardening and take a good look at a pine warbler. D'you know the first thing I do when I go to a convention to read a scientific paper? Register in the motel, then take a turn around the block with my glasses. Have a look-see. Nobody walks in your suburbs. Children look at me with absolute astonishment. Parents suspect me of being a molester. Dogs try to bite me. Last year in Phoenix I took a turn with my glasses, stopped at a vacant lot filled with the usual rubbish and weeds, spotted a bit of a commotion, put my glasses on it, and what d'you suppose it was? A canyon wren! Can you imagine? A canyon wren in a vacant city lot!

Maybe he's right, she was thinking at the edge of her mind but really watching his face for a sign, a pudding face framed by black hair combed low across his forehead and straight down the sides like Robert Newton. Maybe the Englishman can keep sane in a mad world by watching wrens and puttering about his garden—ah, she thought in her greenhouse, I can have my garden now, yes, more "grandiose" than his, he would say, because it's a crystal palace and I'm going to live in it and make a living from it. With greens. A greenhouse is for growing greens. But maybe he's right, and it's one way to keep from going nutty, but maybe there's something nutty too about an Englishman puttering about his mums while the sceptered isle slowly sinks into the sea.

No, he wasn't quite kosher with his too black hair and his puddingish Robert Newton face, and his sooty white skin. Anyhow, the English don't go around talking about "the English" and "your suburbs" and saying "heavy, man."

Her eyes kept asking him the question, so he answered her, coming smoothly off the knock-knocks and the bird-watching and swinging round to her but offhandedly as if the birds were the important thing and her illness a detail to be polished off on his way out. Yet it was his very offhandedness which caused the familiar sweet doomstroke in her throat. What is this sweetness at the horrid core of bad news?

No—ah—I just thought praps you might do with a light massage of your neurones. Not even a major ECT series. A small refresher course. To get you ready for the big world out there.

You're going to buzz me again. (Her unfamiliar voice sounded loud and crackly like the intercom.)

Only a refresher course. I would imagine it to be your last.

Why?

Why what?

The asking in this case is like the answering, she said. I mean—she stopped.

Yes?

She had trouble talking. It was like walking out on a stage. She could answer questions, play straight man to his knock-knock routine, even ask questions. But to make a statement on your own, surely you had to know what you were talking about.

No buzzin cousin, she said. (A lame statement and she saw what she was doing, trying to slip in a statement in his joking style, by cockney rhyming Southern-style.)

You'll feel much better.

I feel bad? Which I? It was the lilt at the end of a question that let her say it, freed her up. She did not want to go down just yet the way a statement goes down flat and hard, ends. Isn't there a difference between the outside-I, the me you see, the meow-I and the inside deep-I-defy? Back to the old meow-I.

I'm talking to the deep-I or the I-defy—only I thought we had agreed it became the I-define. Your I as you want to define it.

Okay, she said, what what what.

Okay, you want my reasons for suggesting a little refresher course.

Yes. Yes, that is, sir.

Don't be afraid. No, it's just that you don't eat. You won't talk to the others, staff or patient. You've stopped participating in group. You have stopped functioning.

I don't eat?

Only the morsels you smuggle back to your room in a napkin, like a chipmunk.

Morsel. She liked the word. It was folded on itself and had a taste. It was dark and nourishing, better than a snack. She also liked his *rubbish*. It was cleaner and firmer than our *trash*.

How about group?

Group? she said, meaning: I still go to group.

He understood.

Yes, you go to group, but you sit under the table.

Knees are easy. Faces are defacing.

Ha. I like that. I quite know what you mean. I'd prefer to look at knees rather than some of the defaced faces in staff conference and seminars. All the same, we're stuck with these faces and we have to make the best of it.

I'll take the knees.

There you go.

Now he was trying to sound like Dennis Weaver and didn't. She was embarrassed for him. How could he stand to speak himself? You'd have to be crazy to make such a fool of yourself. How could he stand to be so out-of-focus? a bogus Englishman doing knock-knocks. I'd rather be crazy. Or maybe the question was, why did she have to know everything before she could say anything?

I—she began and stopped.

Yes?

(Here came her statement because this was the one thing she knew.)

I have to go down first. You're trying to keep me up.

Down?

I have to go down down down before I go up. Down down in me to it. You shouldn't try to keep me up by buzzing me up.

Down and down I go, round and round I go. He twirled around, keeping hands in pockets. God, she thought, if I were him I'd be crazier than me.

Tacky-tacky, she said. I need to go down to my white dwarf.

White dwarf?

You know stars? He did know stars, often spoke of the constellations. To stay sane, learn about wrens, mums, Orion.

What about stars?

A red giant collapses into a white dwarf. Hard and bright as a diamond. That's what I was trying to do when my mother found me in the closet going down to my white dwarf.

Ah. Quite a speech, although I suspect you meant going down to become my white dwarf, I think.

I have to get down to it, to me. And you won't let me. You want me up before going down.

Ah, but what if the star collapses all the way into a black hole? (This pleased him.) How will we find you in a black hole? (The more he thought about it, the more pleased he was.) I'm not up to a time warp.

No buzzin cousin.

Your parents are coming this afternoon.

A bang by the gang.

There you go.

When's the buzzing?

Oh, tomorrow. Ninish.

Now she wanted him to leave. One advantage to being crazy is that one is given leave to be rude. Had she gone crazy so people's feelings wouldn't be hurt? She turned her face into the wing of the chair until he left.

When she heard the door close, she put the binoculars in her lap and watched the highway where it came over the hill beyond the cedars. She was waiting for the bread truck.

When the bread truck came, she looked at her watch, opened her notebook, and began to write.

2

When she woke in the morning it was cool enough in the greenhouse to make her think about keeping warm when winter came.

The stove was her best hope. The only alternative was to buy a kerosene heater in town, if such a thing was available. That cost money and meant buying and lugging fuel and stinking up the greenhouse, which still had its faint reek of root rot and tropic orchid damp.

But how to move the stove from the cellar of the ruin to the potting shed? It was too heavy to move more than an inch or so along the cellar floor, let alone haul up the steps.

But she thought it would do. Big and black and iron, it was a Ben Franklin maybe or a potbellied. No, it didn't have a belly but an oven and firebox as big as a dollhouse and capped by iron lids the size of dinner plates and a balcony of warming compartments (she guessed). It even had a water tank. And its name was not Ben Franklin but Grand Crown. Mica windows, crazed and brown and glittering with crystals, let into the dark room of the oven. There were pipes of light fluted blued metal, one an elbow—fluted flues? It was a cook stove! But didn't cook stoves warm rooms? Was it also a water heater?

Then why hadn't she asked the man with the golf stick to help her? He was strong enough. They could have got it out with ramps and ropes like the Egyptians building the pyramids. Had she been put off because he was angry and out of it, sunk into himself, beheading skunk cabbages and aiming the golf stick like a gun? No, for that very reason he'd have done it—for the reason that he was, she saw at once, out of it, out of his life, he'd have been glad to do anything at all except whatever it was he was doing or not doing. So that she had only to say to him in the glade do this, do that, and he'd have done it, not for her, not even seeing her, but for the pleasure, the faint ironic pleasure of the irrelevance of it, of helping a stranger move a stove in the woods.

Though she could not have said so, she could tell that he had reached such a degree of irony in his life that he would as soon do one thing as another. He'd have been glad to help her move the stove just for the oddness of it. "Where have you been?" his golfer friends would ask him. "I sliced out-of-bounds on eighteen and met a girl who asked me to help her move a stove into her house." "Right," they would say. "What else?"

No, she hadn't asked him because she didn't want to ask anybody. Asking is losing, she might have said. Or getting helped is behelt. It is not that a debt is incurred to a person for a thing as that the thing itself loses value. It was her stove and her life and she would move the stove and live her life. Sitting on the step beside the dog, she felt the porcelain shield and the blue enameled trademark Grand Crown and tapped the mica window. It was as solid as quartz. The stove was heavy. She could barely pick up one corner.

There was time to get it out. The October sun was warm. Get it out how? With ramps? pulleys? slaves? She didn't know. All she knew for sure was that she could do it and do it alone. Anything is possible if you have time and take thought over it. She had found a treasure. You don't ask a stranger to help you move a treasure. You don't ask friends either. And you certainly don't ask family.

She had at least a month. If she had to she could take it apart piece by piece and move it like the Statue of Liberty.

Wasn't there a picture in a dictionary showing a child picking up a horse, using a system of pulleys and ropes? She could go to the hardware store but she needed a word. What was the word for such a thing? If she didn't have the word, they wouldn't give it to her. Never mind. She'd look until she found it, then point. I hate to go into hardware stores and not know the name of a thing.

Go to library, get book on greenhouses, look up pulley in dictionary. There might be a picture of different kinds of pulleys with names.

Move stove, she wrote. She wrote:

Consider water problem, i.e., taking a bath. It appears stove has small pipes for heating water. Water supply?

Two more problems:

One: How to live. How do you live? My life expectancy is approximately another fifty or sixty years. What to do? One good sign: I can already feel myself coming down to myself. From giant red star Betelgeuse, Dr. Duk's favorite, trying to expand and fan out and take in and please the whole universe (that was me!), a great gaseous fake of a star, collapsing down to white dwarf Sirius, my favorite, diamond bright and diamond hard, indestructible by comets, meteors, people. Sirius is more serious than beetle gauze.

Two: Memory. It's coming back. I can say sentences if I write them because I am writing to myself. Speak memory. Why? Only because I have to know enough of where I've been to know which way I'm going.

I remember my father: passing me in the downstairs hall on his way out to play golf Saturday morning. He's forgotten I'm home to stay. Now he remembers I didn't finish school, I didn't get a job, I didn't get married, I didn't get engaged, I don't even go steady. I didn't move on like I was supposed to. I made straight A's and flunked ordinary living. My father's expression: surprise and a quick frown: *Hi.* (What are you doing here?) He sees my failure and feels sorry for me but wants no part of it or me and just forgets.

My mother: finding me sitting in closet of my apartment on Front Street (where I was first trying to go down to it, my white dwarf), bends over me, the little push of air carrying her Shalimar perfume, cashmere sleeves pushed up 1960 coed style, showing her tan too tan even a little branny arms, shimmer of gold, gold jewelry, gold-streaked hair, heavy clunk of bracelets (the real thing, like the *chunk* of a Cadillac door closing, not a

Chevy). Now now, now now, this won't do, what are you doing sitting in there? *Go-ing, go-on, Gawain, go-way, gong, God, dog*, I said, not knowing what I meant—do I have to mean something?—maybe just go way, maybe dog-star = Sirius = serious = God—but she as usual insisting on making her own strong sense of everything even my nonsense *(leave me my nonsense, that's the way, the only way I'm going to get out and through—okay, Ducky, Dr. Duk, maybe you're right, maybe I will collapse into a black hole, but if that's the case then I have to and I will)*. My mother: thinking I was saying *going going gone*, so she said: going going gone my foot (I like her old Alabama slang coming out), you're not going anywhere but out of there, and the only thing that's going to be gone around here is all this dust, get a rag.

Stop trying to make sense of my nonsense.

My mother refused to let me fail. So I insisted.

Sarge: spending week with him at Nassau doing what I pleased or what I thought of as doing as I pleased. Sarge, a thin mustachioed blond Balfour salesman (fraternity and sorority jewelry) from Durham, who knew his catalogue of pins and drop letters and crests so well he had won a salesman-of-the-month trip to Nassau. Tickets for two. I, not a sorority sister, Sarge not a fraternity man, but he "pinned" me with four different pins, Chi O, Phi Mu, KD, Tri Delt, and we thought that was funny. Sarge always going by the book, Sarge and I in bed looking at a picture book and he doing the things in the book with me he thought he wanted to do and I doing the things I thought he wanted me to do and being pleased afterwards then suddenly knowing that the main pleasure I took was the same as doing well for my father: look at my report card, Daddy, straight A's, A Plus in music.

But what do you do after you get your straight A's for Daddy and Sarge?

Drugs: not bad. In my bed in Front Street apartment or in closet, getting out of it with yellowjackets and going down down down toward *it*, Sirius or the black hole, but not really, only seeming to, because when you come out of it you're nowhere, not an inch closer to Sirius, not out the other side of the black hole but just back where you were, only worse, like dreaming that the plane has taken off and it never does. But drugs not bad if you don't have to come off drug and come back. Because:

drugs = illusion of going down down down to *it*, and if there is no *it*, the illusion is better than nothing.

One thing is sure. Never again will they lock me up and buzz me.

The sun shone straight down the cellar steps, warming her back. While she ate a sandwich of rye bread and cheese and sliced luncheon meat, her gaze wondered from the stove to the finials on the greenhouse to the dog. How could she keep meat cold? She gave the dog the luncheon meat. While he chewed it, he was able to meet her eye, giving himself leave to watch her, cocking first one eyebrow then the other at her. As long as he chewed, he could look at her. When he finished, he licked his chops and settled his complex mouth but his lip stuck high and dry on a tooth. It embarrassed him. But the dog's embarrassment did not embarrass her. Wasn't this a good sign?

All next morning from sunrise to the noon she worked in the greenhouse. What to do and where to start? Clean out the jungle. Start in the corner near the door, which as soon as the sun hit it began to smell of florist damp and root reek and rain forest. Could those be orchids gone to seed in big wire baskets hanging from the roof or some kind of air-feeding lianas trailing down like snakes?

At first she thought the laurel and rhododendron had fallen through the rotten benches and rooted in the earthen floor, but the floor under an inch of mulch was concrete. Take hold of a small tree and up it came easily with its flat fan of roots. The trouble was getting the junk out. Bush, tree, bench she dragged out and pushed into the fen. Using a piece of copper flashing from the ruins, she shoveled out root rot and potsherds, and by the time she got hungry, she had cleared a quadrant of concrete ten or twelve feet on edge. Sitting in the sun with the dog, she ate again and brushed the floor lightly with her freehand: good solid old trowel-smoothed uncracked cured concrete, iron-colored and silky as McWhorter's driveway. Two more items for her shopping list: broom, shovel.

Tired, she curled up in her bunk and fell immediately to sleep with only time to think: God, I am going to sleep without a pill!—and woke as suddenly. What woke her? The violet vapor from the glass grapes falling straight in her eye? No, the dog had barked. Or rumbled a deep throat rumble. He was sitting up, ears erect, hackles bristling along his spine like a razorback hog.

Someone was coming down the trail.

It was a troop of Girl Scouts, all but one hefty, most fat. They had shoulder patches which she could not make out. The fattest girl and the thinnest girl carried between them a banner which rippled but she could make out: Troop 12, Laf—? In—? Lafayette, Indiana? Surely Girl Scouts couldn't be older than fourteen or fifteen, yet they looked at least twenty and bigger than life. Their legs were like trees.

The fattest girl had straight blond hair that came straight down over her ears like eaves, like Kelso's.

Kelso grabbed her in the dayroom.

I know where you're going.

She did. Kelso knew everything.

You got visitors. Your folks come to see you. What they doing here? They only been here twice. Maybe they come to take you out of here. How come they keep you here? Don't they know what a dump this is? Don't they know they don't buzz you any more at good hospitals? You want to know what this place is for? This is for people who are too proud to go to state and too poor or stingy to go to a good private hospital. You want to know what it costs them here to keep us? Less than half what it does at state. They making money on us, honey.

Kelso had been at Valleyhead for fifteen years. When she was not too sick, she was canny and told the truth, but one look at her and you knew she could not make it for long in the world. There was no place for her to go. She was smart and had been a bookkeeper with Sears, but that wasn't enough. Sometimes she went to Atlanta, to her parents' house. Though she sounded countrified and looked like a fat lady running a service station in south Georgia, her father had a big house in Druid Hills. But she always came back fatter than ever, stiff as a board and obedient, hair coming straight down all around her head like a funnel. So stiff and obedient that once McGahey told her to sit down and she sat for hours until McGahey noticed there was no chair under her.

Isn't your father a doctor, Allie?

She shook her head.

A dentist, right. He could afford it. Maybe they taking you out.

She shrugged.

You could make it, babe. You're a smart cookie and you know how to get along if you wanted to. How come you don't try?

She shook her head.

I saw them coming in, all dressed up. They must be passing through.

She shrugged.

Talk to me, babe.

Okay, Kelso. (She jumped. Her voice sounded strange.)

Kelso laughed. I know why you don't talk. You so scared, you can't talk. I'm so scared I eat all the time. Now that's something. I'm so scared I get stiff so they'll buzz me. You're so scared you play dumb so they'll buzz you. Maybe we're crazy ha ha. But you're crazy like a fox. Come here, babe, I'll give you a hug.

Kelso gave her a hug.

You think I'm pretty, Allie?

She nodded and smiled.

You're pretty too, honey. You're going to make it.

She smiled and gave Kelso a hug.

Kelso, you are right about my parents. They were going somewhere. To a party evidently. Her mother was aglow in the drab little parlor next to Dr. Duk's office, tan skin glowing (and unbranny) against creamy linen, real old-fashioned linen with irregular weave, gold streak in her hair swept straight across her forehead, giving as always the effect of dash and motion even when she was still, gold aglow at her ears and wrists. Even sitting still she shimmered. Gold glinted. Her father in his candy-striped seersucker smiled and nodded, crouched in his chair, feet drawn under the chair and springing slightly. The two of them blew in like tropical birds. Dr. Duk in his tacky double knits and me in my T-shirt and jeans look like inmates and, she fancied, smell slightly sour.

They were going to a party but they came mainly to see her, they said. They had plans for her. They argued about the plans. There was this pleasant sense of plans being made for her, like her mother putting her on a plane for summer camp: now here's your money and here's your schedule and here's what you do during the three-hour layover in Atlanta . . .

Then there was this disagreeable feeling when they changed the subject from her to the party. They talked about Will Barrett. *Talk about me. Make plans.*

One thing I must do: get past the point where I need other people to make plans for me.

I'll tell you whose party it is, Alistair, said her mother.

Somehow her mother had managed in three visits to get on a first-name basis with Dr. Duk. They were buddies. She too was a bird-watcher and had enlisted him in her Christmas bird count. Dr. Duk: nodding and smiling, straining every nerve, blood rushing forward to his face, to keep up with this dashing exotic person—his buddy?

It's a very dear and old friend, said her mother.

An old boyfriend, said her father absently, grinning his eye-tooth grin, feet springing under him.

It's Will Barrett, said her mother. You know the Barretts of Linwood-Asheville?

She could tell by the way her mother hung fire ever so slightly, eyes flicking, that she was waiting for Dr. Duk's reaction.

You mean—! said Dr. Duk, straining forward another inch.

Yes, Will married a Peabody. They own the joint. She died. Now he owns the joint.

The joint? said Dr. Duk. All the grass, eh?

(Jesus, don't try to make jokes, Docky Duck. You're much better in your listening-doctor position, legs crossed, thigh hiked up as a kind of barricade, gazing down at your unlit Marlboro as if it were a Dead Sea scroll.)

Yeah, all the grass, Alistair. They own the whole joint, half the country, the mills, the hotel. And that rascal Will! Not only did he marry a Peabody, he also made it on his own, from editor of the *Law Review*, straight into the top Wall Street firm, one of the Ten Most Promising Young Attorneys, early retirement, man-of-the-year here—I mean, he did it all! I should have known better—but he was always out of it when I knew him—little did I realize what was going on behind that absentminded expression. Just wait till I get my hands on that rascal! So who do I end up with? Old blue-eyes here. But he's cute. Aintcha, hon?

Her mother leaned over and poked her father under the ribs.

There was Dr. Duk straining every English-Pakistani nerve to catch on to the peculiar American—or were they Southern?—ways of this dashing woman, her odd abusive banter about her old boyfriend (!) in the presence of her husband (!); who sat there grinning and not paying attention, getting her hands on that rascal (!). It's a long way from Dukhipoor, Doc. But he laughed and kept up as best he could, looking only slightly beleaguered.

Knock knock, Doc.

The party is for Will's daughter, who is getting married to a wonderful boy, said her mother, an architect from Stanford, who happens to be the best man in the entire country at restoration. And guess where they're going to live, honey?—in the old Hunnicutt house next to us! And guess—

She stopped listening until they began talking about her.

They began to argue about something. She heard her name and pricked up her ears.

They were arguing about the plans for her future.

Kelso, why are they suddenly interested in my future?

Her mother had plans for her.

Her father had different plans for her. ·

They argued about the plans. She was amazed and pleased. There were plans for her!

The pleasant feeling came back. They argued angrily, but the anger was between them and not toward her. Dr. Duk once again in the familiar territory of ill will, relaxed, hiked up a thigh, took out a Marlboro.

Her mother's plan (her mother: sitting bolt upright now, leaning forward, hand open to Dr. Duk, eyes fine): I want Allison to come home with us, Alistair. Not to your old room, honey. I know you don't want that, but listen to this. Jason Cupp is restoring downtown Williamsport. We have a chance to buy the old Hunnicutt place for a song. Jason and Leslie will live there and restore it. And guess what's out back? Remember? The old carriage house. It's so lovely, the old bricks weathered and worn into scoops outside and down to cobblestones inside. You can move in in three weeks. Wait, dear! You haven't heard the best part. We're also converting the old Atlantic Coast Line railroad station into, guess what, a community art center! Painting, music, plays, you name it. And guess who we want for our music director? It wasn't my idea. The board wants her.

The Board or *Aurora bora*? she said.

Boring or beautiful? said Dr. Duk, looking at her with a smile (they were after all two of a kind, she and Docky, compared with these exotic outsiders). I think beautiful.

She skipped three grades, said her mother. She was the youngest girl ever to enter Mary Baldwin. She won the music prize her sophomore year and gave a concert her junior year, the only time it's ever been done.

Yeah, I was smart. I opened my mouth and nothing came out. I forgot the words. Forgot the Schubert, blew the Wolfe. I stood still and looked at them. Time passed. People looked away. They were embarrassed. Not only embarrassed but frightened and hateful. Who are you, you bitch, to do this to us when we didn't want to come here in the first place? What to do? Leave. Check out. Went off the stage, straight out the fire-escape door, into the street, and right on out of town.

Clink clunk. As I see it, said her mother, all the ingredients are there: she'll be at home among family and friends, she'll have her own lovely little place. But what's most important she'll be working at something she's good at and something we need— she's wonderful with children. And just to be on the safe side, we could all fly up here every weekend to check in with you. What do you think, dear?

Nnnnaaaaahrgh.

Yes. Well, I agree, honey, it must come as quite a shock. But think about it. What do you think, dear?

If I think about it, all I can think of is those scooped-out bricks and those cool dead colonial blues and grays and me lying in a closet with the shakes.

But what she said aloud was: Things though loose can be jammed nevertheless. Blue is for you but the instigation of color is climbing on the Sirius me.

What? said her father. What did she say? he asked her mother. I know, dear, said her mother, aglint and fond.

Her father's plan (her father, hitching forward and putting one forefinger on the other forefinger): No, Doc, no way. Allie is not ready to leave your care. (Why were they all of a sudden making these plans?) But I don't see why she should be cooped up here. What do you say to this: a house, her own house, here in the neighborhood, under your wing, so to speak, close enough so she can take part in groups and crafts and so forth. The nicest place money can buy. What's money if you can't make your kid happy? As a matter of fact, we saw one of these chalet-duplex-condos this morning which would be perfect.

For you to come up and play golf, said her mother. But if we restored the Hunnicutt house—

So you could be national secretary of the Dames, said her

father, smiling back to his eyeteeth, feet springing under the chair.

Now Walter, said her mother.

She could see that Dr. Duk was just beginning to see that her father smiled all the time and that all his expressions, even frowns, occurred within the smile. For example, now he was grinning angrily, not smiling.

She used to work for her father, as assistant to the dental hygienist, after she flunked life and had come home but before she curled up in a closet. He had passionate and insane views on every subject. She was certain that one reason he had taken up dentistry was so he could assault helpless people with his mad monologues. In he'd come, smiling and handsome, hands scrubbed pink, breath sweet with Clorets, and while she kept the patient's mouth dry with a suction tube, he'd stuff the same mouth with hot wax and crowns and fillings and fingers and then he'd come out with it: "What's wrong with Mao?" or "What's wrong with Franco?" or "Do you know what I'd do with them"—striking coal miners, hippies, queers, niggers, Arab sheiks, Walter Cronkite, George Wallace (yes! a hick, a peckerwood), media Jews, Miami Jews (but not Israelis!), Ronald Reagan (yes! a two-bit actor), Roosevelt (!), Carter, Martin Luther Coon, Kennedy, Nixon (yes! a crook), the Mafia, Goldwater (yes! he runs Arizona with Mafia help), J. Edgar Hoover (yes! a homosexual fascist punk). He liked General Patton. He had seen *Patton* eight times. "You know what I'd do with all of them? Line them up against that wall and go down the line with my BAR"—he grinning and boyish all the while, she embarrassed for him (was that her real sickness, that she was embarrassed for everybody? and for a fact everybody did so badly!), the patient's eyes rolling. "You want to know my philosophy? Shape up or ship out. If the cat keeps crapping on the rug, the cat goes—that's all! If the cook sasses me, the cook goes. What's wrong with that?"

What do you think, Allie? her father asked her. You take the top of the chalet. There's a room in the back with a balcony and the damnedest view you ever saw. Well?

Wif you? Wiv view? she heard herself say.

Why did she sound so crazy around her parents? Because no matter what she said or did, her mother would make her own sense of it and her father wouldn't like it. So it didn't matter what she said. It was like being alone in a great echoing cave. There was a temptation to holler.

A view! said her father. You wouldn't believe the view!

Interesting, said Dr. Duk, safe behind his thigh and therefore more able to conceal himself. You thought she said *with view*, meaning room with view. But thought I heard *with you*, meaning praps she might have some reservations about living with you. With you both. With yall.

Dr. Duk smiled, pleased with himself. He could talk Southern. They all looked at her.

She shrugged. She didn't know which she meant or whether she meant anything.

Dr. Duk's plan: I think yall are overlooking one little thing. Both plans are excellent. But the fact remains that Allison is not quite herself yet—though she is clearly making progress, progress toward a decision to have something to do with us. My own feeling about Allison is that she knows a great deal more than she lets on. Right, Allison?

Wraing.

You see, said Dr. Duk. What she said was halfway between *right* and *wrong*. She's afraid to commit herself. My own wish is that she have a final little refresher course of treatment.

I don't think she needs any more shock treatments, said her mother. There's nothing wrong with Allison except that she's an extremely sensitive person who is more subject to tension than most people. So am I! Tension! That's the enemy. She gets wound up just like me. You know what I do? Stretch out and tell my toes to relax, then my knees—they do it!

You want to know what I think it all comes down to, said her father to the world around, looking at no one in particular. It all comes down to accepting your responsibility. Once you do that, you got it made.

Shape up or ship out, she thought. Right. I'm shipping out.

This little refresher course is my own contribution, said Dr. Duk. I'm reading a little paper on it in San Francisco. My finding is that a refresher course of six treatments in selected cases is even more effective than the usual thirty.

No buzzin cousin. It was her voice but it sounded like a radio with a bad volume control.

They all looked at her.

She herself will tell you, said Dr. Duk, that after receiving my own modified ECT, she feels better, relates better to people and her environment, speaks freely, eats better, sleeps better.

Fried is crucified, said the radio.

They all looked at Dr. Duk, she too.

Dr. Duk smiled down at his little Dead-Sea-scroll Marlboro. Allison is giving us her own theory of why ECT works—which is as good as any, to tell you the truth. Namely that going through the ordeal of ECT is a kind of expiation for guilt. Having expiated, one naturally feels better.

Guilt? said her mother, arching her back so suddenly that gold shivered and glinted. Guilt for what?

That is something we might well get into, said Dr. Duk. Now. How does this grab you? I wonder if you two would be interested in coming up, participating in some family sessions. Some studies have been done on the subject and are quite promising. Come to think of it, I might just mention that our Founder's Cottage here is available and you might consider that in lieu of the chalet—

Look, Doc, said her father. He was on his feet and for the first time unsmiling. It made him look queer. White showed in the smoothed-out crow's-feet. Taking off his new pink crinkly jacket, he draped it carefully over the back of the wooden chair. Now he faced them unsmiling but nodding, hands resting lightly on his hips (seeing himself, she knew, as General Patton surveying the mess at Kasserine Pass). Let's get this show on the road, Doc.

Show? said Dr. Duk, turning to *her* for translation.

She translated: *you and them but not me.*

That's right, Doc. We got some business to talk over that Allison is not interested in. Could we talk in your office?

Oh, said Dr. Duk. He rose in some confusion. Okeydoke.

You know what we do at home, Doc, when we have a little problem, said her father. I call a conference, around the dining-room table, after Dinah the cook leaves. I believe in getting it all out on the table. Then we take a vote.

Then the chairman decides, said her mother.

Chairman? Again Dr. Duk asked *her.*

Of the boring board.

In the confusion of ushering them into his office, Dr. Duk got crossed up between wanting to please her father, wanting to get the show on the road, wanting to rent (or sell?) the vacant Founder's Cottage, and forgot about her. Dr. Duk smelled the money, Kelso said. Your folks must have struck oil, babe. He forgot to call McGahey to come get her, forgot even to send her back to her room. They all forgot her.

Alone in the parlor, she felt good. She had been given leave, sanction, through omission, She felt like a child left at the movies and forgotten. She could see the best part again.

No sooner had the office door closed than she knew what she would do. Her father wanted to get down to business with Dr. Duk—bidness he called it—and the business had to do with her. Therefore it was her business.

It, the moment of the closing of the office door, was the beginning of her freedom. As she sat alone, it crossed her mind for the first time in her life: What if *I* make the plans for me? What then? Is there an I in me that can start something? An initiating I, an I-I. What if I had left the black maid hanging out clothes, broke off the conversation and left, would it have killed her? Would my embarrassment kill me? Perhaps not.

Why of all places, in this sour little parlor, should it have come to her, not only that she could make a plan but the plan itself? She knew what to do and how to do it. All her life she had watched people do things. She knew that Dr. Duk would be sitting behind his desk in the casemented bay. A Nikon camera fixed to a tripod stood next to him. One window, the one with the feeding station, was always cranked open in good weather. If an evening grosbeak or a goldfinch showed up, Dr. Duk could snap the camera by moving his hand only an inch or so to a remote-control device. Sometimes he kept the shutter switch in his hand. If she was talking to him and he heard a bird alight behind him, his eyes did not move from her face yet he seemed to be looking through the back of his head. A thick tree-sized pittosporum smelling of bitter bark covered window and feeding station.

Under the station was a space, a little leafy room where one could sit in comfort on a limb of pittosporum.

3

Tuesday the man came again. Again it was she who saw him before he saw her. She was in the shadow of the rock filling a Clorox jug from the tiny waterfall. The dog rumbled and his spine hairs went stiff as boar bristles.

The man was walking toward the greenhouse from the glade. His hands were in his pockets. Something in brown paper was tucked under his arm. The sunlight made a glint on a facet of his forehead and his brown hair, which had streaks on it. Was it turning gray or was it burnished and bleached by the sun? Was he gray-haired or a platinum blond? He was not good-looking. His eye sockets were too deep, his eyes too light, his mouth too grim, his skin burned too dark by the sun. Her father always smiled; he never smiled. A shadow like a German saber scar crossed one cheek. Today he was dressed differently. Instead of golf clothes, he wore an ordinary white shirt and ordinary pants. No, not ordinary. The shirt was tailored and had a soft rolled buttoned-down collar and the pants were narrow in the cuff and at least two inches above the dirty tennis shoes. Was he dressed carelessly as her father would dress if he put on shirt and pants on Saturday morning? No, he thought about how he would dress. The way he walked reminded her of the yachtsmen who stopped in Williamsport and strolled about town: not exactly ambling and not striking out, foot coming down heel first, but toed in, left shoulder coming forward with left leg. It was either a Northern walk or a yachting walk.

Yes, that's what he was, she thought watching him through the waterfall, a Northern millionaire with his platinum-streaked hair growing carelessly-carefully under and over the soft collar, who would spend a hundred dollars for corduroy pants so they would look uncreased and too small but too small in the right way not the wrong way like her father's khakis, which made his stomach look too big, or Dr. Duk's double knits, which were too tight in the crotch.

Just as before, his head was turned slightly—was he listening for her in the greenhouse?—so that he faced her but did not see her though she was less than twenty feet away. Under the jut of his brow, his eyes were cast into deep shadow but as she watched they seemed to open and close, now shut and dark, now open and pale, like a trick picture of Jesus. Yes, it was a trick of light or of her own retina. She shut her eyes. The image of him went dark then bright with eye sockets like a skull.

There at her door he stood in the same odd and absolute stillness, the same way she had seen him standing in the glade. Ha, what to do at a greenhouse door clearly full of nothing but plants? ring a doorbell? knock on glass? Yes, because he was lifting a hand to the door.

Perhaps she had opened her mouth to say something or perhaps she had moved, but before she could do anything else and just as the man's hand touched the house, the dog charged. The man had time to turn, it seemed to her slowly, the sunlight striking a different plane of his forehead, and held out his hand palm down to the dog. Too slowly it seemed to her: was this too part of his studied Northern nonchalance? No, because even now his eyes could not or would not focus on the dog. He didn't care whether the dog bit him or not!

It was not courage, not even inattention but rather, she saw, a kind of indifference yet a curiosity with it. Would the dog attack? Would tooth enter flesh? If it did, would it matter?

The hand was held out like a piece of meat proffered by the man. It was easy to imagine him examining the wound as if it belonged to someone else.

She hollering something, the bristle-backed dog charging flat out, past all snarling, and even as he took the hand in his mouth in the same instant fetched up stiff-legged, shoulders jutting up one then the other like a reined-in horse, sliding to a sit, pushed the hand out of his mouth with his tongue and cocked a yellow tufted eyebrow around but not quite to her. Embarrassed again.

They watched as the dog settled his mouth and looked away. The man came over to the rock.

"Did he stop because of my saying or because of your not saying?" asked the girl.

"I'm not sure. Probably because of your saying. Would you give me a drink of water. I've had a long walk."

It was sweat, she saw, that made his hair and forehead shine.

He followed her into the greenhouse. Without raising his head, he looked around, his lightish eyes moving in deep sockets. "It still smells like a greenhouse. Once I was in Cincinnati. I liked the smell of a greenhouse there so much I worked in it for six months."

"Doing which and how and was it for consideration? How much?" she asked, eyes widening with interest. "Would you—" She stopped. Would he what?

"Work for you?" he said. "How much do you pay?"

"Never mind." She gave him the Clorox bottle. He drank a long time.

"Thank you. Is this where you have to get your water?"

"Yes. How thirsty. It's been a long time."

"Since what? Since seeing anybody thirsty?"

"Something—something is up front but not all the way."

"You mean you're having difficulty remembering things and that you almost remembered something?"

"Yes, that's—"

"I had that once. In my case it was a question of not wanting to remember. In fact, I remembered something here in this spot that I hadn't thought of for years."

"Was it for a gladness or the same old Sunday coming down?"

"No, it wasn't the same old Sunday coming down. I can't say it was a happy memory but I was glad I remembered. I feel much better. You will too. Thank you for the water."

"You are— Are you?"

"I brought you something."

"What?" She noticed the brown bag. "Oh, I don't need. I am fine though I was in the hospital for—it is the time I can't remember."

"I know."

"I was somewhat suspended above me but I am getting down to me."

"Good."

She was about to say something but she saw in his eyes that he had drifted away.

They stood in silence. It was not for her like a silence with another person, a silence in which something horrid takes root and grows. What if nobody says anything, what then? Sometimes she thought she had gone crazy rather than have to talk to people. Which was worse, their talk or their silences? Perhaps there was no unease with him because he managed to be both there and not there as one required. Is it possible to stand next to a stranger at a bus stop and know that he is a friend? Was he someone she had known well and forgotten?

"Are you—?"

"Am I what?"

"Are you my—?"

"Am I your what?"

For a moment she wondered if she had considered saying something crazy like "Are you my lover?" Or "Are you my father?"

She sighed. "You said the bag."

"What? Oh yes. I brought this for you." He gave her the bag.

She opened it. "Avocados? I think. And—what? A little square can of—" She read: "—Plagniol."

He watched her.

"What a consideration! But more than a consideration. The communication is climbing to the exchange level and above. And the Plagna is not bologna."

Gazing at her, he almost smiled. In her odd words he seemed to hear echoes of other voices in other years. One hundred years ago Judge Kemp might have said on this very spot: "How considerate of you!" with the same exclamatory lilt. But there was another voice, something new and not quite formed. Did she mean that his consideration (being considerate) was more than just a consideration (a small amount), more than exchange (market value of the Plagniol), which was after all baloney?

"I think you will like that olive oil. It is very good. Some friends brought the avocados from California. They're the best kind, not hard and green, but a little soft and brown. They're very good for you. You're too thin. Fill a half with olive oil."

The avocados were as big as coconuts. "I'll plant the pits in the greenhouse," she said. "No tricks with toothpicks."

"Right. Plant them in soil."

Later she tried to decide why she felt so free to talk or not talk with him. Was it because of her, that in her new life she could have gotten along with anybody? Was she just lonely? Or was it a certain tentativeness in him that waited on her, like the dog, even now and then cocking an eye in her direction? Or could it be a Northern awkwardness in him that brought out her Southern social graces because she was ha ha her mother's daughter after all?

Her fingers felt the rough pebbled texture of the avocados. "Why are they here?"

"Why did I bring them? I thought you might like them. For another thing—"

"Yes?"

"They are the most nourishing of all vegetables."

"What is entailed with you?"

"Nothing. Why?"

"You seem somewhat pale and in travail. Is the abomination at home or in the hemispheres?"

"I don't know. Maybe both. You mean my brain. I don't feel very well, to tell the truth."

Later he irritated her and she got rid of him. He was standing by while she told him what she meant to do with the stove. There it was hanging from a rope suspended between two chimneys. It looked like a small iron house ripped from its foundations, pipes and connections dangling. She explained.

"I bought the thing which is called a block-and-tackle. I tied the ropes on the chimneys which have shoulders like steps." Listen to me talking good, she thought. Perhaps in order to talk all you need to do is do something, then explain what you have done. "Tomorrow the stove will go from here to there."

He stood, hands in pockets, looking up at the stove from under his eyebrows as if it had descended from another world.

"How?" he asked.

She did not reply.

"What—?" he began and stopped.

He is in some kind of distress, she thought.

After a moment he said: "You got that thing up there all by yourself?"

"Yes."

"How are you going to get it over there?"

"It's downhill."

"I know, but—" He stopped.

"Yes?"

"Ah, why do you want it over there?" He sounded as if he had a hundred questions and picked this one at random.

"To keep warm."

"You're going to put it in the greenhouse?"

"Yes. What type of stove do you call it?"

"It is a cook stove."

"Does it burn wood?"

"Yes."

"Will it both keep me warm and cook?"

"Yes. It also has a water tank."

"Then it will have hot water?"

"If it gets cold water and then you feed it wood."

She clapped her hands without smiling. "The climb is underway."

"Yes, right. The climb may be underway, but"—he turned toward her, shoulder turning with his head, but did not quite meet her eye—"you see, it has pipes which you connect with a plumbing system. And I don't believe—"

"I can bring water down from the rock."

"Well, yes, you could if—"

"Do you have my dossier?"

"Your what? Oh, you mean how do I know about you?'

"You look like you know about me."

"I know something about you."

Her eyes fell. Forehead muscles pushed her eyebrows down into a shelf. Then he had come from her parents.

"Then the word came from the bloard."

"Bloard?" He didn't know what she meant. From the board? the broad? blood? blood kin? bloody broad? All these?

What she meant was board and bored, meeting of her father's board which was boring because it bored into you.

"Look. I'll be back in half an hour."

"No no. Naw."

"I didn't mean to upset you. I'm going to get a golf cart from the club and a trailer and a couple of men and we'll put the stove where you want it."

"Oh no."

"No? Why not?"

"Because there I will be with people having put the stove where I want it. And that's the old home fix-up which is being in a fix. Then what? The helping is not helping me."

"I see." After a while he said: "You mean you would rather do it yourself."

"The arrangement is the derangement. When the arrangement is arranged, then you know what the ensuement is."

"No, what is the ensuement?"

"The ensuement is: then I am with the arrangement."

"Yes, I see that. But does that also mean that you can't accept anything from anybody?"

She tightened her arms around the brown bag. "The contents are intense and also tense."

"Why is that?"

"Because of the thanks. After thanks come blanks."

"Not necessarily. The avocados are yours. You don't owe me any thanks. But if you did thank me, it wouldn't take anything away from the avocados. They wouldn't become blank. They're solid."

"That is not the climbing question."

"What is the climbing question?"

"When are you going to leave?"

"Oh."

"You see."

"What?"

"The feelings are more than revealing."

"Yes, I see what you mean. Yes, you may have hurt my feelings a little, but maybe not as badly as you think. At any rate, it is not an awful thing. I'll leave so you can enjoy the avocados."

"It's not you."

"You mean it's not that you dislike me but you don't know how to get rid of me and that makes you nervous. What if I don't leave? Yes, it's a problem sometimes. I developed an art of moving people out of my office. It was a matter of placement of chairs and of getting up and moving in such a way that the other person moves in front of you and finds himself at the door without knowing how he got there."

"Le cool is coming soon," she said, gazing around.

"Le cool? Yes, fall is upon us."

"Le dad is no better than le doc and what are you in le plan?"

"Well, I don't know. But I wasn't trying to be your father or your doctor."

"Understanding can also be a demand. De man. Le mans."

"Yes. I guess you are fed up with people trying to understand you. And I guess I was sounding like—who? De man. What man is that, I wonder. I'm making you nervous. I'll be going."

"Yes, I have to go also." She hugged the bag. "They're mine when you leave."

"They're yours now."

"But I cannot inspect them with your inspection."

"I understand. Very well, I'll leave so you can inspect them."

"Okay then."

She waited. Why didn't he leave? It is difficult to talk to people, to stand around wondering what to say and what to do with your eyes. Maybe it is easier to be crazy than to put up with people's pauses. Suppose he didn't leave.

He left. Whew. She began to think of topics of conversation in case he should come again.

Later the dog walked toward the chestnut fall, sat, and cocked his head.

The man was getting up from a log where he had been sitting (watching her?). He began to walk and fell down. She hurried to help him but he was up quickly, brushing himself off.

"What happened?" She took his arm and was thinking not so much about him but about herself, the sudden weakness at the pit of her stomach when he fell, her heart still racing. What happened to me? she meant.

"I fell down."

"I know that. But why?"

"I don't know. Lately I tend to fall down."

"That's all right I tend to pick things up. I'm a hoister."

"We'd make a twosome."

"Don't joke."

"All right."

Was that the world's secret then, that you have to joke all the time? Is that how you live?

The man was sitting on a polished chestnut log, one arm stretched over his knee, hand open. He seemed to be looking at the barbed-wire fence. Now he stood and putting his hands in his pockets bent over them as if he were cold.

"What?" she asked.

"Nothing. I—" He looked at his watch. His brown smooth hand still had tooth marks from the dog. She could not take her eyes from his hand.

"I love—" she began.

"You love what?"

She loved his hand.

"Is it time and if it is, time for what?" she asked.

"Time? Yes." He was gazing at the fence in an absent staring way. He broke away, blinked. "Yes. I have to be somewhere at five-thirty."

"I don't."

"I know. This is your home."

"Where is your home?"

"Over there." He nodded toward the one-eyed mountain.

"You own a home on the mountain?"

"I own the mountain."

"Okay. Then go home."

"Right." They were both startled by her command. He left. She watched as he stepped through the fence, paused, then went quickly through. Now, standing and facing her from the golf links, he seemed to feel freer, as if the fence allowed a neighborliness.

"Perhaps you would not mind a suggestion," he said.

"No, I wouldn't."

"Do you know what a creeper is?"

"Virginia creeper?"

"No no." If he could have smiled, she thought, he would have smiled. "No, it's a little platform on wheels which mechanics lie on when they work under cars."

"I know it but not the word."

"You have some planks, but you're going to need a creeper to get the stove down the hill."

"Thanks for the word."

He noticed that she treated the gift of the word exactly like the avocados. She'd have to think about it after he left.

As she listened she noticed he was white around the eyes. Did he usually wear sunglasses? His eyes, his face reminded her of something, what? yes, of the face and white eyes of combat soldiers she had seen a long time ago in *Life* magazine. The eyes of the soldiers could not or would not bring themselves to focus.

Why could she remember perfectly an old *Life* magazine but could not quite remember why she had decided to come here?

"Go to Washau Motors in town," the man said. "They sell Fords. I own it. But you won't have to mention my name. So I am not doing you a favor. Ask for Jerry, the parts man. Through an error, probably Jerry's, we have on hand one hundred creepers. Jerry is why I'm not making money. He would be glad to lend or give you an old one."

"What will I say?"

"Say 'Jerry, I'd like to borrow one of your old creepers.' "

"The word is creeper."

"Yes. And there are two other things you're going to need."

"What?"

"You are probably going to have to take the stove apart to move it and to get it through the door of the greenhouse. You're going to need two ten-inch crescent wrenches and a can of WD-40 to loosen the rusty bolts."

"Give me the words." She took out pad and pencil. He wrote: *Creeper. Ten-inch crescent wrench. WD-40.*

"Good."

"I found the word 'block' in the dictionary in the library under the word 'pulley.' So I knew what to ask for in the hardware store."

"I see."

"Thank you."

"You're welcome."

"I'd be glad to lend you—"

"No thank you."

After the man left, she sat in the sun under the poplar. Though the air was still, one gold leaf shook violently. The bark had a bitter smell.

4

In the dim light and damp bitter-bark smell of the pittosporum there was the sound just above her head of a bird on the feeding tray. It was scratching seed with its feet like a chicken. The only way she could get comfortable sitting on the not quite horizontal branch was to slump against the trunk.

Through the open casement of Dr. Duk's office came her father's voice, faint then louder, going away then coming back. He was pacing up and down, shirt-sleeved, hands on hips, getting the show on the road. Dr. Duk would be sitting four feet from her, safer now behind his desk and swiveled around in his chair, keeping one eye on the feeding station and one hand near the tripoded Nikon in case a painted bunting should show up. Did buntings kick seed around like chickens?

Her mother? She must be sitting in the patient's chair across the desk, bolt upright, one little finger in her mouth, eyes lidded and ironic as she watched her husband.

—might disagree on the particulars, Doc, said her father, coming close now. But one thing we can sure as hell agree on and that's Allison's well-being. It's her happiness and health which comes first, now and always, right?

Right on, said Dr. Duk.

(No, dumb Docky Duck. Not right on. Like Kelso says, when you try to sound like something, you don't sound like nothing.)

Get to the point, Tiger, said her mother dryly. A muted clunk, heavy gold striking gold, and she knew without seeing that her mother pursed one corner of her mouth and stuck her fist into her waist, jangling her bracelets.

Not point, said her father. Points. Okay.

Point one: We have the obligation to act in Allison's best interests, right? You, Dr. Duk, in her medical interests, we,

Katherine and I, in all her other interests, home, family, finances, future, and so forth.

Yes? said Dr. Duk, perking up. He did after all have an ear for such things and knew when something was up. At this moment he was looking at her father and thinking, as Kelso would say: What's this dude up to, dropping by on his way to a party with all these plans for Allison when he hasn't showed up twice in the past year? And what are these two all steamed up about with their competing plans, and what's coming up now, the real plan? What's this about finances? Have they suddenly gotten rich?

Point number two: As Allison's parents we are also her guardians, right? I mean especially since Allison is hardly competent to manage her own affairs.

Well—

Would you believe, Doc, that in this state under a new law there is a difference between a person being mentally incompetent and legally incompetent? That even a person committed to a mental institution can inherit property?

Would I believe, you ask. Yes, I think I—

Would you believe this, Doc?—and this is the bottom line, folks—that even in such a case the parents do not automatically qualify as guardians?

Well yes, as a matter of fact—

I mean, what the hell is happening to the American family? Her father's voice swept around the room like a searchlight. You know what I would do with people like Earl Warren?

You don't have to. Earl Warren's dead, said her mother wearily. Why don't you get to the point, Tiger?

Would you believe, Doc, that in order for us to be Allison's legal guardians, we have to petition the court and that it is up to the judge, any damn local redneck judge, to decide?

Well—

(What's up, Doc? Your ears are standing straight up, aren't they?)

That's where you come in, Alistair, said her mother crisply, clinking and gathering herself. I'm quite sure you know the new laws better than we do. Namely, that a legal procedure is involved and that your testimony as to Allison's legal competence will be crucial. I mean, my stars (now her eyes would be going up to the ceiling), you could testify in good conscience to *my* legal competence.

Of course. Quite. Dr. Duk's voice was going down. No doubt he was rolling his unlit Marlboro cigarette. The little Dead Sea scroll was still undecipherable, but there was something here!

The only thing I don't quite see, can't find the handle of, said Dr. Duk carefully, is why all of a sudden the issue becomes important at this point in time.

(This point in time. Oh, Docky, now we're Nixon. The question is, who are you, Docky, and what are you doing here at this point in time?)

She stopped listening and let her weight slump her hard against the trunk. She closed her eyes and ears to the words. The voices rose and fell, mounted against each other, glanced off, went away, came back, joined. It was like being a child and listening from the top of the stairs. Voices can be understood without words. Her father's voice now had the same ragging importunate tone she heard from the landing when he was winning at poker. Dr. Duk's was tentative, premonitory—like a prospector whose Geiger counter begins to click: hold on, what's this? what have we here? Her mother's voice was foot-wagging, eyes going around, exclamatory, impatient: oh, for heaven's sake, let's get this over with!

She started listening again when after a silence her father's voice changed, fell into a quiet storytelling cadence. Such-and-such happened. So-and-so did it. Everyone listens when someone tells the news of a happening. Something had happened, and he was telling it as much to himself as to them, as if only in the telling, the saying out loud, could he believe it.

She pricked up her ears. They were talking about her.

—and would you believe, Doc, that the old lady, Aunt Sally, was not even her aunt? She was her real aunt's friend, Aunt Grace. The two of them had lived together for thirty years, fought like cats and dogs most of the time. They used to come over every Sunday for dinner, so Allie naturally called Miss Sally Aunt Sally. Sure, we knew Miss Sally was fond of Allie ever since Allie was a little girl—for one thing Allie was the only one who would listen to her because the old lady could talk the ears off a jackass and frankly I couldn't stand it more than a few minutes—

(That was because I thought I was supposed to and did not know how not to listen or what would happen to a person if one got up and went away.)

—and it was a good two weeks after she died that Ludean,

the old nigger maid the two of them had had for twenty years, brought it over to me, this old metal Crailo candy box with a piece of ruled paper inside and about three lines in Miss Sally's handwriting—the paper wrinkled from having been balled up once just before being thrown away, because Ludean was cleaning up Miss Sally's room and you know how niggers like those old candy boxes to keep things in—

(Now how in the world would Docky know anything about niggers and Crailo candy boxes?)

—I still don't know how Ludean had sense enough to save it but there it was, carefully uncrumpled and smoothed out, saying: Being of sound mind I hereby leave all my worldly goods to my dear little friend, Allison Hunnicutt Huger. What had happened of course was that she and Grace had had a fight and she had changed her will, so Grace should have gotten it but we'll take care of Grace—so there it is, a perfectly good holographic will dated last month and I'm mainly thinking that it's funny because it will screw up her lawyer who is sitting there with probably six previous wills in his safe—you know what I would do with lawyers, don't you?

Yes, we know, Tiger, said her mother. We have to leave in ten minutes.

So I'm thinking mainly it's funny and certainly no big deal since her worldly goods consist of only two items she was always joking about: her grandfather's poor little old dirt farm on the side of a mountain which she used to say was so steep the mule had to grow longer legs on one side to plow it, and the other, a sandspit of an island off Georgia which had two pine trees and whose only value was the treasure Captain Kidd was supposed to have buried and nobody had ever found.

(Yes, and that's one reason I'd listen to her—I'd see myself on the island with a map, climbing up one tree and sighting through the other. It wasn't even the treasure I liked but the island and the idea of something being hidden there and finding it through a geometry of pine trees.)

So all this time she had been paying her taxes and talking about her dirt farm and her island and nobody had been listening but Allie. How about that?

Get to the point, Walter. I'm leaving, said her mother.

Okay. The point is, to make a long story short, that her poor little old dirt farm is eight hundred acres next to the Linwood golf course and her sandspit of an island is over two thousand acres, more of a wilderness than Cumberland which you've heard of, and that the Arabs have already offered two mill one for it. That's getting to the point, isn't it.

Two mill one? said Dr. Duk.

Two million one hundred thousand dollars, Doctor.

(How about that, Doc?)

Silence. Sounds only of fingers drumming on wood—Dr. Duk's on his desk?—and bird scratching feed—painted bunting? Docky, you've plumb forgot the birds, haven't you?

You said get to the point, didn't you, Mrs. Huger? said Dr. Duk in a new voice, a deeper richer crisper voice. Well, Allison is the point, isn't she? Clearly you have much to think about but equally clearly we can agree on one thing, can't we? That no matter which of your plans seems more feasible when Allison is well enough to leave here—assuming she is well enough but as I don't have to tell you, Dr. Huger, there is no such thing as a guarantee in either dentistry or psychiatry, is there? But we can agree that no matter what comes to pass, we will bear any burden, pay any price, to do what is best for Allison. Right?

(Jesus, Docky, first Nixon, now Kennedy?)

You got it, Doc. That is certainly true of us. I gather you have the same concern for Allison.

You better believe it.

(Not bad, Doc. You almost got it right.)

Okay, said her father. Now have we got our ducks in a row?

Ducks? said Dr. Duk suspiciously. He knew people called him Dr. Duck.

One, you do what is right for Allie medically. Go ahead with your treatment. Two, meanwhile we'll all three do what is right for Allison legally. Three, Katherine and I will come up with a long-term plan, maybe a place for Allie in Linwood, maybe a place at home, maybe we'll take over your Founder's Cottage for family sessions or whatever—is the place for sale, by the way? Anyhow, we'll see—

Again the meaning of the words went away and there was only the feint and parry of the voices, and then the goodbye sound of words swerving together before going away. Chairs scraped. They were on their feet.

There was not much time, not more than two or three minutes. That was enough, because she knew what she wanted to do.

No, there was plenty of time, as it turned out. They were still talking in the office when she reached the parlor, the tone of their voices rising but not quite reaching the penultimate break-point of goodbye. She figured she had another thirty seconds. And she did, time enough to reach her father's pink-crinkly jacket still carefully draped over the back of her wooden chair, from it take out the blue-leather passport-size wallet she knew he used when he wore a jacket and from it four of the one-hundred-dollar bills she knew he took on a trip (You know what I would do with American Express?), and was out and down the hall and halfway up the stairs so quickly and yet so silently that she could hear their voices as the inner door of the office opened.

In her bathroom she folded the bills lengthwise once and put them under the loose leather lining in one of her slippers. Then she lay on her bed and waited for her parents to come tell her goodbye.

After they left she sat at her window, head wedged in the corner of her wingback chair, took out her notebook, and began to write.

V

NOW THAT HE WAS MAKING HIS WEEKLY VISIT TO THE NURSing home his wife's money had built, he realized that he was doing exactly the same things he did when she was alive, taking the same route through the gleaming halls, even visiting the same patients. The only difference was that instead of pushing Marion ahead of him in her wheelchair, he had Jack Curl the chaplain in tow.

But something was different. Ordinarily Jack Curl would have distracted him. All his life he had waited on people, tuned in on them, attended them. Now for some reason it didn't matter.

As Jack Curl talked, Will Barrett stood in the hall moving his head a little to make the bright sunlight race like quicksilver around the beveled glass of the front door. He seemed to remember halls, the hall of the hospital where his father stayed in Georgia, the hall of the hospital where Jamie died in Santa Fe. How odd, he thought smiling to himself, that then I didn't know what to do with myself and now I do. The only time I knew what to do was when something bad happened to somebody. Disaster gave me leave to act. Between times I didn't know what to do. Now I know.

Now he remembered that after he had gone to find the Negro guide and sent him for the sheriff, he had returned to his father lying in the pin-oak swamp. He sat down beside him to wait. The man's eyes opened. His father did not speak but in his eyes there were both sorrow and certitude. *Now you know,* the eyes said. *I'm sorry. I was trying to tell you something and I didn't. Now you'll have to find out for yourself. I'm sorry.*

Very well, he thought. I found out. Now I know what to do.
"What?" he said. Jack Curl had asked him something.

"I said what I remember about Marion was the way she not only knew about all the patients but the help too. You were wonderful with her. I'm so glad you've continued her wonderful idea of inviting patients to your home. She'd have liked that. This week it's Mr. Arnold's turn, isn't it? Do you remember how she always asked about the janitor's grandchildren—by name? Now I'm the janitor. She'd have liked that too. Do you remember?"

"Yes." No. What he remembered was the weight of her, the angle and set of his own body when he levered her out of the Rolls and in one motion around and into the wheelchair.

A tuft of bronze hair curled through the zipper of the chaplain's jump suit. Jack Curl's muscular jaw swelled like a pear under the temples just as his lower body swelled like a pear in the jump suit. Yet he was as light on his feet as a good dancer. He danced around in front of him like a child to catch his attention. Today for some reason it was possible to observe the smallest detail about Jack Curl, for example, the way he was letting his sideburns grow longer by shaving a little below them. The short new hair did not match the long hair of the sideburns. But more than that: he suddenly saw the purpose of the jump suit and Jack Curl's shambling way of walking and his not quite clean hands and the pliers in his hip pocket and the way he moved his shoulders in the jump suit. Jack Curl was saying: I am more than a clergyman going about doing clerical things. I am also a handyman, a super, something of a tough really. Somebody has to fix the plumbing and wiring. To do God's work, it is necessary to come off manual work. Like Paul fixing tents.

He took a good look at Jack Curl.

How did it happen that now for the first time in his life he could see everything so clearly? Something had given him leave to live in the present. Not once in his entire life had he allowed himself to come to rest in the quiet center of himself but had forever cast himself forward from some dark past he could not remember to a future which did not exist. Not once had he been present for his life. So his life had passed like a dream.

Is it possible for people to miss their lives in the same way one misses a plane? And how is it that death, the nearness of death, can restore a missed life? Marion knew this. She loved to go to funerals. They went to funerals in Manhattan, Long Island, Utica, and all over the South; funerals of her uncles and aunts and cousins, his uncles and aunts and cousins, kinfolk he'd never seen. Funerals made her solemn and vivacious. The old folk here died off like flies. She attended every funeral and volunteered him as pallbearer. Suddenly he had become pallbearer to friend, kin, and stranger. It became clear why Presidents like to go to funerals. The worse things got for Lyndon Johnson, the more funerals he went to, there he stood grave and silent, dispensed. Like a President, Marion stood in her braces at a hundred gravesides, solemn and exultant.

Why is it that without death one misses his life? When Marion was dying, he was standing at the window of the hospital room, hands in pockets, gazing down at the bluish-white street light above the empty corner. It was four o'clock in the morning. She spoke to him in a different voice. In the dark her jaundice—she was yellow as a gourd—did not show, but her voice was quavery with fever. "Yes?" he said and came to the bed. She looked at him calmly. Had they looked at each other in years? "I want you to do something," she said. "All right," he said. "Keep the house for Leslie." "All right," he said. "She is going to need a place," she said. "She is going to California but she will want to come back here, won't she?" "Yes," he said. "Very well. I will."

She spoke with the quietness of people after a storm which had drowned out their voices. What struck him was not sadness or remorse or pity but the wonder of it. How can it be? How can it happen that one day you are young, you marry, and then another day you come to yourself and your life has passed like a dream? They looked at each other curiously and wondered how they could have missed each other, lived in the same house all those years and passed in the halls like ghosts.

"Let me say this, Will," said Jack Curl, dancing around and stopping him in a kind of mock confrontation.

"O.K."

"Marion, your dear wife, my friend, the only benefactor these old people had, is gone. Right?"

"Right."

"Do you know the last thing she told me before she died?"

"No."

"She wanted to go ahead with the one project closest to her heart."

"What was that?"

"You know. Her idea of a retirement village. A total love-and-faith community."

"Ah."

"What do you think of this for a name? The Marion Peabody Barrett Memorial Community."

"Sounds fine."

"Does it sound too much like a commune?"

"No, it sounds fine."

"All I ask of you is what you yourself want: to carry out her wishes."

All you ask from me is three million dollars. Well, why not?

How could he not have noticed this about Jack Curl before? that even as he was moving his shoulders around under his jump suit, playing the sweaty clergyman doing good, that Jack too was trying to catch hold of his own life? that in the very moment of this joking godly confrontation—sure, I'm trying to con you out of three million, Will, but it's a good cause and I'm God's own con man, okay? and so forth—here was Jack Curl trying to catch hold. And wasn't he doing it? Wasn't he doing everything right? Yet when you took a good look at him, this sweaty Episcopal handyman, this godly greasy super, you saw in an instant that he was not quite there. Looking at him was like trying to focus on a blurred photograph.

But you, old mole, you knew otherwise, didn't you? You knew the secret. I could see it in your eyes, open and clear and brown, when you were run to ground in a Georgia swamp and looking up at me. You shot yourself, and then we could talk. You knew the secret. But how can that be? How can it be that only with death and dying does the sharp quick sense of life return? For that was your secret, wasn't it? That it was death you loved most of all and loved so surely that you wanted to share the secret with me because you loved me too.

One night after the war and during the Eisenhower years the father was taking a turn under the oaks. The son watched him from the porch.

"The trouble is," the man said, "there is no word for this."

"For what?"

"This." He held both arms out to the town, to the wide world. "It's not war and it's not peace. It's not death and it's not life. What is it? What do you call it?"

"I don't know."

"There is life and there is death. Life is better than death but there are worse things than death."

"What?"

"There is no word for it. Maybe it never happened before and so there is not yet a word for it. What is the word for a state which is not life and not death, a death in life?"

"I don't know."

"I wonder if it ever happened in history before?"

"I don't know." Where is the word, the girl in the greenhouse would say, and look around.

Hands in pockets, he looked at the chaplain and past him to the sunlight, which had turned yellow and now shone straight through the front door. I wonder what you would have thought of rich Christian Carolina, old mole.

"What?"

"I said what a great lady Marion was to give so unendingly of herself. There was so much to give."

"Do you mean because she was so rich or because she was so fat?"

"Ha ha. That's a winner. Touché. Marion would have loved that. Yes, Marion was far too heavy. God knows I tried to tell her. She said look who's talking." He put his hands on his side, a jolly fat lightfooted friar in a jump suit. "Marion and I had much in common. We loved all the good things God gives us. In a word we like to eat. But no, that's not what I meant by her heart's desire. You know what I meant."

"What?"

A clock struck. The sun was setting.

"I am talking about Marion's dream of a community of people living out their lives married, together, not burdening anybody, a true love-and-faith community lived according to the rhythm of God's own liturgical year."

God, love, faith, marriage. The old words clanged softly in the golden air around them like the Westminister chimes of St. John's steeple clock.

"Actually, Will, it was your other lady I wanted to talk to you about."

"What other lady is that?"

"Ha ha. I'm talking about my favorite girlfriend, the apple of your eye, your lovely daughter Leslie, a real sweetheart."

Leslie a sweetheart? lovely? the apple of his eye? Leslie, his daughter, was a tall sallow handsome dissatisfied nearsighted girl whose good looks were spoiled by a frown which had made a heavy inverted U in her brow as long as he could remember.

"What about Leslie? Is she giving you trouble?"

"You better believe it."

"What does she want now?"

"She wants to write her own wedding ceremony."

"Could it be any worse than your new liturgy?"

"Ha ha. That's a winner. But what are we going to do?"

"We?"

"You don't have a bishop looking down your throat."

"I sure don't."

Jack pulled him close. They were standing outside the open door of a room. Jack almost whispered.

"I want you to meet our newest couple. Tod and Tannie Levitt. Actually they're our oldest couple. We've stretched a point and allowed them to share the same room. They're eighty-five and eighty-seven. In the same room! Big deal, right? Bear with me. I have my devious reasons. They're cute as they can be. You'll love them. But, more important, I think you'll see the possibilities of a real couples' community even in this bareass hospital room. I want you to imagine Tod and Tannie in a rustic setting, a simple but homey apartment with a balcony opening onto the entire Smoky Mountains. Did you know that the hundred twenty-first psalm was Marion's favorite? I will lift up mine eyes unto the hills, from whence cometh my help. And you better believe that's where hers came from."

Tod and Tannie were sitting slumped in their wheelchairs between two beds. The television was mounted on a steel elbow high above them, too high to see. The *Crosswits* was on without sound. Tod was nodding and both hands in his lap were rolling invisible pills. Tannie was no bigger than a child. Her back was bowed into a semicircle so that she faced her knees. Her eyes were closed. But her bed jacket was a cheerful pink, all silk and ribbons and lace, and her soft white hair was as perfectly combed and curled as a Barbie doll's.

"Will," said Jack Curl loudly. "I want you to meet Tod and Tannie, our first resident couple."

Tod went on nodding. Tannie did not open her eyes. A sound like a soft whistle came from her.

"They're this week's winners on the dating game," said the chaplain, winking at him. "So they're shacking up with us. Right, Tod?"

Tod nodded, had not stopped nodding.

He gazed down at Tannie's little stick arms. The skin was white and paper dry but a vein, thick and powerful as a snake, coiled on her wrist.

"Now watch this," said Jack in a lower voice but not minding if Tod and Tannie overheard him. "This is what I mean by an ongoing couple relationship. Tod!"

Tod went on nodding and rolling pills.

"Tannie!" cried the chaplain.

Tannie went on snoring, chin on her chest.

"Tod and Tannie! Give us a little song!"

Tod did not stop nodding but one hand seemed to rise of itself and give Tannie a poke in the ribs. "Sing, Mama!" said Tod in a hoarse whisper.

As if he had pressed a button, Tannie's head flew up, her eyes opened, showing milky-blue, and she began to sing in a high-pitched girlish voice. Tod's hand conducted and his head lilted from side to side instead of nodding. He came in on every third word or so.

> Daisy, Daisy, give me your answer true.
> I'm half crazy, all for the love of you.
> It won't be a stylish marriage,
> I can't afford a carriage,
> But you'll look sweet upon the seat
> Of a bicycle built for two!

"For two," said Tod.

The instant the song was finished, Tannie's head sank to her chest and she began to snore. Tod stopped conducting and went back to nodding and pill rolling.

"Well?" asked Jack Curl in the hall.

"Beats television," he said vacantly, moving his head to make the yellow light race around the beveled glass of the front door.

"You better believe it. Now, Will."

"Yes?"

"Now. What I want you to imagine is the two of them, Tod and Tannie, and two hundred couples like them, from sixty-five on up, each with their own little rustic villa, coming back after evensong and lifting up their eyes to the hills. What do you think?"

"Okay," he said, unable to move his eyes from the sunlit door.

"Okay?" Jack Curl rounded, came closer, in excitement. "You mean—"

"I mean I will do as you say. I will imagine them."

"Oh. Good. I think."

When an old person died at St. Mark's, often there was no one to claim the body Marion would go to great lengths to trace the family and arrange the funeral. Yamaiuchi would chauffeur them in the Rolls, leading the way for the hearse to distant Carolina towns, Tryon or Goldsboro, where after the funeral in an empty weedy cemetery they would head for the nearest Holiday Inn in time for the businessman's lunch. Marion, animated by a kind of holy vivacity, would eat the $2.95 buffet, heaping up mountains of mashed potatoes and pork chops, and go back for seconds, pleased by both the cheapness and the quantity of food. Like many rich women, she loved a bargain. All the while he gazed in bemusement at the ragged Southern cemetery, empty except for the Rolls, the hearse, Yamaiuchi, and three Asheville morticians (he was usually the fourth pallbearer for the casket light with its wispy burden), and then gazed around the bustling new Holiday Inn and the local businessmen come to eat. Live men and dead men.

The shotgun lay beside the man on the wet speckled leaves. In his father's eyes he saw a certitude. He had come into focus. How does it happen that a man can go through his life standing up, not himself and dreaming, eating business lunches and passing his wife in the hall, that it is only when he lies bleeding in a swamp that he becomes as solid and simple as the shotgun beside him?

"What?" He gave a start. The chaplain was saying something.

"I said when I come over tomorrow, perhaps you and I and Leslie can have a little powwow. About this ah do-it-yourself wedding."

"Sure."

"I want to get your old friend Mrs. Huger in on it too. I have a feeling she can handle Leslie. She's quite a lady."

He was looking down at his hand. A shaft of light struck it. The yellow light, refracted by the prism, shaded into blue and red on his skin like a bruise. It was still possible to feel the buck of the Luger in the bones of his wrist.

"You're so lucky Mrs. Huger turned up when she did, Will. You've no idea how helpful she's been. Isn't she an old flame of yours? She's a doll. Did you know she's my main contact with Leslie and the groom's family? Why is it women know so much more than we do?"

"Who?"

"Mrs. Huger. Your old—"

Oh, Kitty. Kitty Vaught Huger. My old flame. What in hell was Kitty doing up here? She and her grinning dentist-husband. They were everywhere, all over the golf course and in his house. Kitty had a woman's managerial way with her. For a fact she had been helpful. Even Yamaiuchi liked her. Last Saturday when the Cupps flew in from California she and Yamaiuchi had fixed the hors d'oeuvre. What did she want? What did her husband want? Like many people who want something, he had a way of coming at you from the side and grinning back to his eyeteeth. Both came closer than people usually do. When they greeted you, they fell forward and laid hands on you. When Kitty touched him, he felt showers of gooseflesh but not exactly excitement. It was the sort of gooseflesh you feel when a child, not knowing about such things, puts his hands on you.

Kitty had changed. When he thought of her, he thought of sitting next to her in the Alabama twilight in her father's Lincoln, her knees together, eyes cast down, silent; crossing lonesome red-clay railroad cuts filled with ironweed and violet light. But now she came shouldering up to him. She was bolder, lustier, better-looking but almost brawny, a lady golfer, brown and freckle-shouldered. Her voice was deeper, a musical whiskey-mellowed country-club voice with a laugh he didn't remember. When he sat, she straddled good-naturedly, opening her knees. When she leaned toward him, her heavy gold jewelry clunked.

He was sitting in the Mercedes looking at the Luger. It was getting dark. A few old people were in the Kennedy rockers on the front porch, but most were inside watching giant-screen TV. Mr. Arnold, one of Marion's patients who had come to the house, spied him and tried to say something, but one side of his face was pulled down and his lips blew out like a curtain. One hand was fisted and held close, cradled like a baby by the other arm.

The Luger felt good. Its weight and ugliness and beauty made him smile. He shook his head fondly. Why did he feel good? Was it because for the first time in his life he could suddenly see what had happened to his father, exactly where he was right and where he was wrong? Right: you said I will not put up with a life which is not life or death. I don't have to and I won't. Right, old mole, and if you were here in rich reborn Christian Carolina with its condos and 450 SELs and old folks rolling pills and cackling at *Hee Haw*, you wouldn't put up with that either.

Ah, but what if there is another way? Maybe that was your mistake, that you didn't even look. That's the difference between us. I'm going to find out once and for all. You never even looked.

Is there another way? People either believe everything or they believe nothing. People like the Christians or Californians believe anything, everything. People like you and Lewis Peckham and the professors and scientists believe nothing. Is there another way?

He hefted the Luger. His father took it off an SS colonel, it and the colonel's black cap with its Totenkopf insignia and some photographs—his father: a captain in the 10th Armored Division, which joined Patton at Saarburg, where he, his father, had his picture taken standing up in the hatch of an M4 Sherman tank, which did not look at all like the snapshot of the SS colonel standing in the hatch of the Tiger tank taken in the Ardennes (even though I somehow know it was exactly what he, my father, had in mind when he had his picture taken: the Tiger in all its menacing beauty). Strange that he, my father, often spoke of the Ardennes and the Rhine and Weimar but never mentioned Buchenwald, which was only four miles from Weimar and which Patton took three weeks later, never mentioned that the horrified Patton paraded fifteen hundred of Weimar's best humanistic Germans right down the middle of Buchenwald to see the sights, Patton of all people, no Goethe he who said to the fifteen hundred not look you sons of Goethe but look you sons of bitches (is not this in fact, Father, where your humanism ends in the end?). Yet he, my father, never mentioned that, even though I read about it in his own book, a history of the Third Army, that the 10th Armored Division was there too. Why did he keep the photographs of the SS colonel standing in the hatch of the Tiger tank which I found in the attic in Mississippi and not one word about Buchenwald? Why did he talk about the SS colonel so much if the Nazis were so bad and why did he think Patton not the SS colonel ridiculous with his chrome helmet and pearl-handled revolvers?

He talked about the SS colonel as much as he talked about Marcus Flavinius, the Roman centurion. He knew by heart the letter which Marcus had written his cousin Tertullus in Rome, where he, Marcus, had heard things were going badly what with moneygrubbings, plots, treasons, sellouts. He, Marcus, wrote:

When we left our native soil, Tertullus, we were told we were going to defend the sacred rights of the empire and of the people to whom we bring our protection and civilization. For this we have not hesitated to shed our blood, to sacrifice our youth and our hopes. We regret nothing. Please tell me the rumors I hear of treachery at home are not true and that our fellow citizens understand us, support us, protect our families as we ourselves protect the might of the Empire.

Should it be otherwise, Tertullus, should we leave our weary bones to bleach on the tracts of the desert in vain, then beware of the anger of the Legions.

> Marcus Flavinius
> Centurion of the Second
> Cohort of the Augusta Legion
> SPQR

Anger. That was it! His anger! You were possessed by anger, anger which in the end you turned on yourself. You loved only death because for you what passed for life was really a death-in-life, which has no name and so is worse than death. Is that what you envied the SS colonel, his death's-head?

Very well, perhaps you were right, but what if you were not? Did you look?

What if there is a sign? What about the Jews? Are the Jews a sign? And if so, a sign of what? Did you overlook something? There were the Romans, the Augusta Legion, yes. There was the Army of Northern Virginia, yes. There was the Afrika Korps, yes. But what about the Jews? Did you and the centurion overlook the Jews? What did you make of what happened to them?

What to make, Father, of the Jews?

He smiled again.

What to make, reader, of a rich middle-aged American sitting in a German car, holding a German pistol with which he will in all probability blow out his brains, smiling to himself and looking around old Carolina for the Jews whom he imagined had all disappeared?

Somehow he had got it in his head that all the Jews had either been killed in the Holocaust or had returned to Israel.

The missing Jews were the sign his father had missed!

What would have happened if a bona fide North Carolina Jew had walked up to the car and introduced himself?

Now he was talking aloud to himself: Father, the difference between you and me is that you were so angry you wanted no part of the way this life is and yourself in it and me in it too. You aimed only to make an end and you did. Very well, perhaps you were right. But I aim to find out. There's the difference. I aim to find out once and for all. I won't have it otherwise, you settled for too little.

He had waited too long. The chaplain, leaving St. Mark's, spied him and caught him before he could start the Mercedes.

For a moment he was afraid the chaplain was going to get in the car but he leaned in the window. In the second his head was above the Mercedes there was time to put the Luger under his thigh.

"Will! I'm glad I caught you. I forgot the main thing I wanted to ask you." He tapped his temple. "The mind is going."

"Yes?"

"I'm giving a retreat at Montreat next week. It crossed my mind you might come along."

"A what?"

"A religious retreat. It's our regular yearly number. And our regular gang. Actually a wonderful bunch of guys. A weekend with God in a wonderful setting. It's an ecumenical retreat. I'm double-teamed with a Roman Catholic priest from Brooklyn, a real character—he looks so much like Humphrey Bogart everybody calls him Bogey. What a card. They call me Hungry Jack. Hungry Jack and Bogey. Actually we're not bad together. Incidentally, the food's first-class. But the important thing's it's a weekend with God. That's the bottom line."

"Leslie tells me I should do something else."

"What's that?"

"Have a personal encounter. Leslie believes she has had a personal encounter with Jesus Christ and has been born again."

"There you go."

"There I go what?"

"There are many mansions and so forth. It's not my gig but if it's hers, more power to her."

"What does that mean?"

"Why don't you come to the retreat and find out. We've got all kinds in our gang—Protestants, Catholics, Anglicans, unbelievers, Jews—all wonderful guys, the kind of guys you'd like to spend a weekend with or fishing or just shooting the breeze. We call ourselves the Montreat Mafia. They're darn good guys and I promise you'd like—"

"Did you say Jews?"

"Yes. Last year we had two Jews. One a judge, the other—"

"What kind of Jews?"

"What do you mean, what kind?"

"I mean were they ethnic Jews or believing Jews?"

"God, I don't know. I didn't inquire."

"Where are they from?"

"Where are they from? One's from Florida, the other from New York, I think."

"Yes, it must be."

"What must be?"

"Nothing."

"Will you join us?"

"Will you tell me something, Jack?"

"You better believe it."

"Do you think the Jews are a sign?"

"The Jews?" Again the quick second look. He did say Jews. And he is smiling. Are we kidding?

"Marion thought the Jews, the strange history of the Jews, was a sign of God's existence. What do you think?"

"Oh wow. With all due respect to Marion, God rest her soul, hopefully we've gotten past the idea that God keeps the Jews around suffering to avenge Christ's death."

"I didn't mean that. I meant the return of the Jews to the Holy Land. The exodus from North Carolina."

Then it's a joke, said the chaplain's smile. But what's the joke? Better take out insurance against it not being a joke.

"Well, to tell you the truth, I'm less interested in signs of the apocalypse than in opening a serious dialogue with our Catholic and Jewish friends, and I can tell you we've gotten right down to some real boilerplate at Montreat—will you think about it?"

"I just thought about it."

"We're leaving here next Thursday, by early afternoon hopefully."

"I would hope that you would go in hope."

"Eh?" said the chaplain cocking an ear. "Right. Well, anyway—"

"Do you believe in God?" Will Barrett asked with the same smile.

"How's that?" asked Jack quickly.

"You know, God."

In the fading light the chaplain looked at him closely, smiling all the while and narrowing his eyes in an especially understanding way. But Jack Curl wished that Will Barrett would not smile. The chaplain's main fear was not of being attacked or even martyred—he thought he could handle it—but of being made a fool of. It was one thing to be hauled up before the Grand Inquisitor, scorned, ridiculed, tortured. He could handle that, but suppose one is made the butt of a joke and doesn't get the joke? He wished Will Barrett, who seldom smiled, would stop smiling.

In the fading yellow light he could see the chaplain eyeing him uneasily to see if he was joking.

"I'm trying to ask a serious question. That is difficult to do these days."

"You can say that again. Fire away."

The Luger was hard under his thigh. Jack Curl's face loomed pale in the darkness.

"Do you believe in God, Jack?"

In the fading light he could see the chaplain look at him swiftly as if there were a joke to be caught. Then the crow's-feet suddenly ironed out, making him look white-eyed and serious.

"Well, if I didn't, I'd say I needed some vocational counseling, wouldn't you?" The chaplain's head loomed in the Mercedes, his face large and solemn. "Seriously—and you can check me out on this—I seem to be picking up on some vibes from you lately—that you might be thinking of entering the church— am I out in left field? I was lying a while ago when I said the one thing Marion wanted most was her new community project. No, what she wanted more than anything else was your coming into the church."

"Ah."

"Do you know where I've found God, Will?" The chaplain's round face rose to the Mercedes roof like a balloon.

"No, where?"

"In other people."

"I see."

"Don't you think you belong here in the church? With your own people. This is where you're coming from. Am I reading you right?"

"My people?"

"Weren't they all Episcopalians?"

"Yes."

My people? Yes, they were Episcopalians but at heart they were members of the Augusta Legion and in the end at home not at St. John o' the Woods but with the bleached bones of Centurion Marcus Flavinius on the desert of the old Empire. They were the Romans, the English, Angles, Saxons, Jutes—citizens of Rome in the old Empire.

"Don't you think you belong with us?"

"Ah." The Luger thrust into his thigh like a thumb. He smiled. Not yet, old Totenkopf. "You didn't answer my question."

"What was the question?"

"Do you believe God exists?"

"Yes," said the chaplain gravely. The chaplain's face, he imagined, went keen and fine-eyed in the failing light. Could it be? the lively expression asked. A God-seeker? A man wrestling with Doubt? (He, the chaplain, had never made a convert.)

"Why?"

"Perhaps he is trying to tell you something at this moment," said the chaplain solemnly. (God, don't let me blow this, I've got a live one hooked.)

"What?"

"Grace is a mysterious thing," said the chaplain.

"What does that mean?"

"Perhaps the answer lies under our noses, so to speak, in fact within ourselves. If only we would take the trouble to ask the question."

"I shall put the question—as a matter of form—and I shall require an answer. But the answer will not come from you or me," he said softly.

"What's that?" asked the chaplain quickly, leaning in. "I didn't quite catch—"

"I said only that the question can be put in such a way that an answer is required. It will be stipulated, moreover, that a non-answer, silence, shall be construed to mean no."

"There you go," said the chaplain uneasily. It made him uneasy to talk about religion. Marion Peabody Barrett had terrified him with her raging sarcastic attacks on the new liturgy and his own "social gospel." There is a time to talk religion with women, to be God's plumber, to have solemn yet joyous bull sessions with men during a weekend with God, to horse around at a party. He was at home doing any of these but not when they were mixed up. The trouble with Barrett's queer question and peculiar smile was that you couldn't say which he was doing. The truth was Barrett was a queer duck. Rich, powerful, of one's class, but queer. Sly. What to do, then? Listen. Listen with all your might. Determine whether he's kidding or not. The chaplain narrowed his eyes and leaned several degrees toward Barrett.

"I think I know how to ask such a question," said Will Barrett.

That was your trouble, old mole, you didn't even bother to ask and you should have, if only from Episcopal rectitude and an Episcopal sense of form—as one asks routinely of an empty house before closing the door and leaving: Is anybody home?

The question should be put as a matter of form even though you know the house is empty.

Then no one can complain of your leaving.

To his relief the chaplain pushed himself away, gave the Mercedes top a slap with both hands. "Why don't you put your question on the retreat?"

"I'll give it some thought."

"Give it some prayerful thought."

"Very well. I'll see you tomorrow. You deliver Mr. Arnold because Marion would want that and I'll try to deliver Leslie because that's what you want."

"You got yourself a deal."

When he moved his thigh and picked up the Luger between his legs, the metal felt hotter than his own body.

The glass doors of St. Mark's closed behind the chaplain. Closing the door for the last time. That was it. That's why everything looked so clear. He knew he would not come here again. When you leave a house for the last time and take one last look around before closing the door, it is as if you were seeing the house again for the first time. What happened to the five thousand times between?

2

He had not known who the girl in the greenhouse was until Kitty told him twice, once before the girl ran away from the sanatorium and again afterwards. But even when he found out and at the same time saw that Kitty did not know where her daughter was, he could not bring himself to pay close attention. Something else engaged him even as Kitty and her grinning dentist husband and grinning Jimmy Rogers pressed in upon him. They wanted something from him. It was clear but not from what they said. They were telling jokes and saying something about property, Arabs, money, state laws about guardianship and inheritance, developing an island. An island? Though he was not listening closely, there was the unmistakable feeling in the back of the neck when someone wants something and is casting about for a way to ask. Not finding a way, they move closer, heads weaving like a boxer's, looking for an opening.

What did they want? Money? Free legal advice? Both? It seemed to be Kitty who wanted it most. At least she came closest, touched, hugged, kissed, poked, jostled, swayed against, jangled, shimmered.

What did she want?

Though he faced the husband, now not three feet away, it was hard to take in more than the grin, white teeth, styled hair, pink clothes.

Instead he gazed past them, past the white wicker and stuffed linen furniture, the lacquered ivory-colored tables, blue porcelain lamps—it was Marion's Chinese Export blue-and-white room, what in the South used to be called a sun parlor—to Leslie and the Cupps and Jack Curl, past Lewis Peckham the golf pro listening politely to Bertie, Bertie making grips on an invisible golf club; past the others, guests and waiters, past the huge Louis XV secretary with its doors open to show the decoupage panels, to the bank of windows broad as a ship's bridge opening onto a short steep yard dropping off to the gorge and the valley beyond.

A gazebo perched on the lip of the gorge.

A twist of cloud, thick as cotton, rose from the gorge behind the gazebo and a small scarlet oak he had never noticed before. It was stunted and lopsided and black. The few leaves that hadn't fallen hung straight down as if they had been tied on by a child. The white gazebo was almost whited out by the cloud.

From beyond the post oak in the silent swamp came the *ge-click* of the Greener breech being broken and presently the *ge-cluck* of its closing.

That was when you reloaded.

But you had only shot once, at the first single. You had another shell. Why not wait until the second shot at the second single to reload?

Because you knew you only needed three shots, two for the quail and one for you.

Wait a minute. There were *four* empty Winchester Super-X shells afterwards, three on the quilt beside him in the Negro cabin where he was lying after the woman wiped the blood from his face, and a fourth in the Greener the guide had brought back with the shells. The cabin smelled of kerosene and flour paste. Newspapers were freshly pasted on the walls.

But there were only three shots.

Wait a minute. Is it possible to fire both barrels of the Greener at once? There were two triggers.

"Wait a minute," he said aloud. Then he smiled and shrugged. What difference did it make?

The three Arabs were pressing in upon him. That's what they looked like, Arabs: the dentist, Jimmy Rogers, and Bertie: brown-skinned, coming too close, smiling, nodding—Jimmy Rogers was even rubbing his hands together.

"Excuse me," he said. "I have to go upstairs and tend to some business."

"What business?" asked Kitty, frowning.

Her closeness and nosiness gave him a shower of goose-bumps, a peculiar but not unpleasant sensation.

"I'm looking for an old shotgun." He noticed absently that it had become possible to tell the truth, that it was no longer necessary to make an excuse, go fix a drink.

"What are you going to do, shoot us?" asked Kitty with a mock falling away. She told the others: "He was always like that, ready to have a shoot-out if somebody crossed him, right here and now."

No, I wasn't always like that.

"That was the way it was where we came from, wasn't it, Will?"

"I was going to look for an old shotgun that belonged to my father and grandfather."

"You didn't mess with them either," Kitty told the others.

"Where we came from, if you fell out with somebody, you didn't smile at them and go around behind their backs. You called them out and had it out with them."

That's right. We call ourselves out and have it out with ourselves. Famous one-man shoot-outs.

"I keep a shotgun loaded with double-ought buckshot under my bed," said the grinning dentist-husband. "I fixed a rack just inside the rail. All I got to do is reach down with one hand. Just let some sapsucker come in the door or window. Just let him come. I know a man, a substantial man no redneck, who just the other day bought a shotgun and a .357 Magnum and two cases of shells, and he's a college graduate, not one of your nuts."

The grin, he noticed, went back to the eyeteeth. What's this guy so angry about? His wife? Being a dentist? His daughter? No wonder his daughter's nuts. Who does he want to shoot? Probably niggers.

"Speaking of the Wild West, guns, and shoot-outs," said Jimmy Rogers, coming even closer, close as a lover, and, putting his head down in their midst, told them one of his jokes.

Though he tried to listen to the joke, his mind wandered. Jimmy pulled him close and then gave him a final little tug. The joke must be over. "I have to go," he said.

"Hold on, son," said Kitty, but it was she who held on, laughing and grabbing his arm with both hands, wrists all aglint and ajangle with gold. There was about her a rushing way he didn't remember of coming close and pushing ahead of her the smell of her hair and a perfume—Shalimar? How did he remember after all these years? It smelled like Shalimar sounded—and a friendly kind of jostling, jostling him with arm, shoulder, elbow, hip, hair swinging past the hollow of his throat. What he did remember, not he but his body, was the warmth in the places where she touched him. It was curious. Spots she touched grew warm as if he had had a positive skin test. His antibodies remembered her body. "Hold it, son. I need to have a word with you." Curious! Something was both strange and familiar. Suddenly he realized he had not thought about women for a long time, not since Marion's death, not since long before Marion's death—except for the time he thought about Ethel Rosenblum and fell down in a bunker. For three years he had lived in a dream of golf and good works.

"What?" he said, turning an ear down to her upraised face.

She wanted to whisper something. The Arabs fell back, stopped smiling, bent forward in a huddle, made plans.

"Look, Will. The summerhouse is lost in the cloud."

"Yes, it is."

"Do you realize what happened to us?"

"No, what?"

"We passed each other like ships in a fog. I was a fool. I should have grabbed you when I could."

"As it has turned out, I don't think—"

"Let's go get lost in the fog," she whispered. She couldn't quite whisper but like a child trying to whisper sputtered in his ear. His hair raised. He nodded.

"Could you meet me in the summerhouse?" she asked. "I have a bug to put in your ear."

Welts sprang out on his neck.

"There's something I have to do."

"What?"

"I have to find the shotgun."

"I don't mean now. I mean after dinner. After the others leave. Is there a side door?"

"Yes."

"I'll go out the front door to get a breath of air. You go a different way. You're always dropping out anyway. You know what Marion said about you?"

"No, what?"

"You were just not *there* half the time. But what she didn't understand, and what you and I do, is that now and then you and I just have to drop out, don't you?"

"I suppose."

"Very well. Can you keep me from the foggy foggy dew?"

"Sure," he said absently.

This time when she jostled, she managed to sidle and give him a friendly kidding hip-bump such as you used to do in high school corridors or playing basketball.

His body seemed to remember something and, turning toward her, confronted hers like a man moving in his sleep.

The cloud had come over the cliff. As it came up the short steep yard it seemed to thin and turn into fog. Wisps of fog curled around the tree, which looked more and more like a common Mississippi scrub oak than a stylish Carolina scarlet oak.

Before they came to the tree his father said: There are two singles. You take one and I'll take the other.

Then they went ahead until the tree came between them.

One single got up, the one on the man's side of the tree. He had hardly heard the furious wingbeat against the tiny drum of body before the first shot came blotting out everything in the shockroar which went racketing through the swamp. His father always shot on the rise.

Before he could reach the door, his daughter stopped him. Her face was cross, the frowning U cut deep in her forehead.

"You've got to get that shaman off my back."

"Who?"

"Father what's-his-name."

"Oh, Jack."

"Yep. He's getting on my nerves. Tell Jack he's not marrying me and Jason. We're marrying each other."

"Okay. Anything else?"

"The only reason we're doing this here is that I promised Mother."

"Okay. I have to go."

"Go? Where?" Her glasses flashed. "You're not pulling another fade-out."

"Fade-out?" He tried to focus on her.

"That little number you do, now you see me now you don't—though I'll give you this much, sweet Poppy"—and she gave him an absentminded hug, still frowning—"you always turned up when I needed you."

"Not this time."

"What?"

"Nothing."

I'll be damned, he thought. Nothing changes. Am I doing to her exactly what he did to me, leaving her? But there's a difference. She doesn't need me.

And for a fact she had already turned away, her frowning crossed-up face thrust toward Jack Curl and the Cupps.

"Wait," he said.

"What?" she said, stopping but not turning toward him.

"Ah—well."

Ah well. Yes. That's it. Maybe there had been a time when there was something to say and maybe the time would come again, but it was not now.

"What?" said Leslie.

"Goodbye," he said.

"What?" she asked vacantly and nodded. "Okay." She nodded again, eyes fixed in a stare. "Okay."

"Give me—" He held out his hand.

"Oh, Poppy," said Leslie, turning back and giving him a cheek hug but still frowning past him. She hadn't heard him.

Just before he turned away, he took a last look at her. Is it possible to see someone here and now? Her hair was perfectly straight, a long shining fan spread across her shoulders, as bright and clean as a happy child's. She was a child, hardly more. But when she turned, her face was cross and thrusting, moving in a kind of tic against her hair. When he looked at her, the flashing granny glasses, the inverted U on her forehead, the chewed lip, she slid away from him back in time and he seemed to see her as a child when he passed her in the foyer on 76th Street on her way to Central Park with the nurse, she giving him the same quick fretful cheek hug, and then slid away again but forward in her own time, casting ahead of herself to the park, worrying about . . . Are women beside themselves from the beginning?

3

In the upstairs study, built with a widow's walk above it like a Nantucket house, he found the Greener in a broom closet behind the Electrolux and the waxer. The straps and buckles of the old stiff scuffed case were hard to undo. He gazed at the gun. It was one of four things he had saved from Mississippi. The other three were the Luger, his grandfather's *Ivanhoe*, and his father's *Lord Jim*. It figured. Both his grandfather and his father had enemies. One, like Ivanhoe, had enemies he hated. The other had the guilts like Jim and an enemy he hated, himself. And one had the shotgun, the other the Luger. What do you do when you are born with a love of death and death-dealing and have no enemies?

He had not looked at the shotgun or *Lord Jim* or *Ivanhoe* for twenty years.

Fitting barrel into stock, he clicked it out straight and snapped on the forestock. The gun was shorter and heavier than he remembered, short as a carbine, both barrels cylinder-bore. God, no wonder they were good shots. How could you miss anything with a cannon full of birdshot? The metal was not rusty but the bluing had long since worn away to greasy steel. Only a faint design, fine as scrollwork on money, remained. He broke the breech and sighted at the windows through the barrels. White light from the cloud came spinning down the mirrored bore. There was a faint reek of gun oil and powder from the last shot. Who had cleaned the gun? the sheriff? I? I. On the rib between the barrels he read: *W. W. Greener, 68 Haymarket, London. Best in all trials 1875–1888*. The grip was worn smooth as a police pistol. The wood of the forestock had shrunk around the bone ornament like an old man's muscle.

He closed the breech, hefted the gun, sighted it again, pulled the two triggers, first one then the other, then both together. Again, he broke and closed the breech to cock the firing pins. Again he pulled both triggers.

I'll be damned. You can fire both barrels at once.

Wait a minute. You shot the single. There were two singles. That left one shell for the other single.

But you reloaded.

Why? Why didn't you wait for the second single and the second shot before reloading?

But you reloaded, then swung around to track the second single, swung so far around and so intent on the tracking that you forgot I was there, didn't see me through the post oak, and got me too.

Then you reloaded again with one shell. Because one shell was all you needed.

Wait a minute.

There were four empty shells, three the guide had picked up and put on the quilt beside me in the Negro cabin, and one in the breech of the Greener. "Here yo bullets," the guide said, not even knowing that spent shells are worthless.

Wait a minute.

Then you had to have fired both barrels at the second single. Why?

You don't unload two Super-X's on one small quail.

Wait a minute.

There was no second single. If there had been, I'd remember, because I remember everything now. I'd have heard him get up before you shot, heard the sudden tiny thunder. I knew that all along. Why didn't I know that I knew it?

Then both barrels were for me, weren't they?

Well, I'll be damned. No wonder the Greener spit fire and smoke like a cannon.

So that was it.

Will could not take his eyes from the shotgun. An electric shock seemed to pass into his body from the greasy metal clamped in both hands like an electrode. A violent prickling went up his back and into his hairline.

His diaphragm contracted. He found that he had laughed.

Well, I'll be damned. Is it possible that I knew it all along and until this moment did not know that I knew it? Or did you miss me? Or am I killed and until this moment did not know it? Can you be only technically alive?

Well, as you used to say, it's a different ball game now, isn't it?

Hm. Why do I feel relieved, even dispensed, as if somehow I were now free to do what I am going to do?

Smiling, he turned the carbine-length shotgun, swinging the muzzle toward him. Easily done: you can even put both thumbs on both triggers.

Let me get it straight now.

You shot the first single.

Then you broke the breech, removed the one spent shell, and reloaded.

Then you fired both barrels.

Then you broke the breech, ejected the two, and reloaded, but with one shell.

One shell for the single, two for me, one for you.

Then how did you nearly miss me?

You couldn't miss a quail on the wing with one barrel at fifty feet. Yet you nearly missed me with both barrels at fifteen feet.

What happened at the very last split second that you pulled up?

Was it love or failure of love?

And how did you miss yourself?

Well, whatever the reason, you corrected it the next time, didn't you? In the attic, in Mississippi. But why didn't you take me with you then, if you knew something and were that sure you knew it?

The sorrow in your eyes when I came over and sat beside you in Georgia—were you sorry you did it or sorry you didn't?

He was smiling down at the shotgun and shaking his head.

Sorry you didn't do it. Because the next time you took no

chances and did it right, used both barrels, both thumbs and your mouth.

I remember now. I cleaned the gun when I got it back from the sheriff in Mississippi. Both barrels. Wouldn't one have been enough? Yes, given an ordinary need for death. But not if it's a love of death. In the case of love, more is better than less, two twice as good as one, and most is best of all. And if the aim is the ecstasy of love, two is closer to infinity than one, especially when the two are twelve-gauge Super-X number-eight shot. And what samurai self-love of death, let alone the little death of everyday fuck-you love, can match the double Winchester come of taking oneself into oneself, the cold-steel extension of oneself into mouth, yes, for you, for me, for us, the logical and ultimate act of fuck-you love fuck-off world, the penetration and union of perfect cold gunmetal into warm quailing mortal flesh, the coming to end all coming, brain cells which together faltered and fell short, now flowered and flew apart, flung like stars around the whole dark world.

4

"Going hunting?"

"No." It was Lewis Peckham standing in the doorway behind him. He wondered if anything could surprise him.

"I got an old cornfield the hogs have been into. It's full of doves. You could come down this afternoon."

"No thanks." He unlatched the forestock of the gun, broke the breech, replaced the parts carefully in the plush cavities of the heavy fitted case.

"What's the matter?"

"What?"

"I said what's the matter?"

"What do you mean what's the matter?"

"Something's been the matter with you."

"It's okay now." He laughed.

"You do seem better. What was it?"

He looked at Lewis. It was unusual for him to ask questions.

"It was something I didn't know that was bothering me. Now I know."

"I could tell you how to correct your slice, but that's not it, is it?"

"No."

Lewis Peckham's face, narrow and dark as a piece of slab bark, was as usual slightly averted.

"But the slice is part of it, isn't it? I'll tell you a funny thing. I can watch a man swing a golf club and tell you more about him than a psychiatrist after a hundred hours on the couch."

It was probably true. Lewis had a shrewd grave watchful intelligence which, however, was almost spoiled by a restlessness under the quietness. He was not what he appeared. It had at first appeared that Lewis was a natural man, one of the few left, a grave watchful silent courteous man, a Leatherstocking. But he was not. He was a discontent golf pro. He looked like a Cherokee scout but his family was old-line Tidewater and he had played golf at the University of Virginia. He was an unhappy golf pro. Maybe books had ruined him. What a shock to learn from this grave silent man that he wrote poetry in secret! Imagine Leatherstocking a poet. Lewis knew a great many things, could read signs like an Indian but unlike an Indian he did not know what he could not do. He thought he was a good poet but he was not. He thought books could tell him how to live but they couldn't. He was a serious but dazed reader. He read Dante and Shakespeare and Nietzsche and Freud. He read modern poetry and books on psychiatry. He had taken a degree in English, taught English, fought in a war, returned to teach English, couldn't, decided to farm, bought a goat farm, managed a Confederate museum in a cave on his property, wrote poetry, went broke, became a golf pro. Lewis showed him some of his poetry once. It was not good. There was one poem called "New Moon over Khe Sanh," which was typed in the shape of a new moon:

> The
>   rounds
>   incoming
>   bright sliver
>   of moon reflected
>   in foul funkhole
>   bright sliver of
>   metal destined for
>   my brain is no
>   Carolina
>   moon
>   No

How could Lewis who could locate others so well, so misplace himself? How could he read signs and people so well, yet want to be a third-rate Rupert Brooke with his rendezvous with death at Khe Sanh? Why would he even want to be a first-rate Rupert Brooke? On the other hand, what was Lewis supposed to do? be an Indian scout? goatherd? English teacher? golf pro? run a Confederate cave? Lewis didn't seem to know. But what was good about him was that he remained himself despite himself. Books had not spoiled him. He knew a great deal he hadn't learned from books. The trouble was he didn't set store by it.

Will Barrett smiled. All at once he knew what Lewis was supposed to do and what would make him happy. After all the local Angles and Jutes and Saxons have driven each other crazy over niggers and gone to war for lack of anything better to do, Lewis is the fellow who keeps his head and goes around picking up people with his pickup and saving a remnant in his cave.

"You're sure you're okay, Will?"

"Sure."

"You want to know what I think?"

"Yes."

"I think you're in a clinical depression. I believe you might do with some counseling. Have you heard of logotherapy?"

Logotherapy. Jesus Christ. What's he been reading now? English teacher, goatherd, spelunker, poet, golf pro, now a psychiatrist.

Lewis inclined his head gravely. "The trouble is you and I share something that sets us apart."

"What's that?"

"We're the once-born in a world of the twice-born. We have to make our way without Amazing Grace. It's a lonely road but there are some advantages along the way. The company, when you find it, is better. And the view, though bleak, is bracing. You see things the way they are. In fact, don't you feel sometimes like the one-eyed in the land of the blind?"

He frowned. Why was Lewis's unbelief so unpleasant? It was no better than the Baptists' belief.

If belief is shitty and unbelief is shitty, what does that leave?

No, Lewis was even more demented than the believers. Unbelieving Lewis read Dante for the structure. At least, believers were consistent. They might think Dante is a restaurant in Asheville but they don't read Marx for structure.

"Have you considered analysis, Will?"

"Analysis of what?"

"Of you. Psychoanalysis."

"I did that. Three years of it."

"Analysis? No kidding." Lewis brightened. Lewis thought better of him! Lewis envied him! Lewis wanted to be analyzed! "Then you of all people should know that depression is eminently treatable, right?"

Lewis waited, not quite watching him, as grave and courteous as if he were waiting for a putt.

"Maybe you're right."

"Of course I'm right. What is more, you know as well as I do that such a reaction is quite common following the death of a spouse."

A spouse. Marion was a spouse. But did Marion's death depress him or mystify him?

"Also, if you want to know the truth, Will, I think you retired too soon."

"May be," he said absently.

"Early retirement is one of the major causes of depression."

"Is that right?"

He took a good look at Lewis, at the dark slab-sided face and straight black hair which was too long for a golf pro and too short for a poet. There was a space in him where a space shouldn't be, where parts were not glued together. What it was was that there is nothing wrong with being a goatherd-poet-golf-pro but there was something wrong with the way Lewis did it. What?

"After all, Will, you got it all. You got everything a man needs. And you're a good athlete. You could play scratch golf if you put your mind to it."

"What would you do if you had it all, Lewis?"

"I'd raise beef cattle, listen to Beethoven and Wagner, read and write," said Lewis without hesitation.

Two fingers strayed along the greasy steel of the Greener barrel.

"You don't enjoy such things, Will?"

"Sure."

Lewis touched his arm, a rare thing. Leatherstocking didn't touch anybody. "Tell you what, Will. They don't need the father of the bride around here. Let's me and you cut out, go down to my spread, crack a bottle, and put on the Ninth Symphony."

"No thanks, Lewis." Dear Jesus. Sitting with Lewis in his farmhouse, listening to the Ninth Symphony.

"Name one thing better than the Ninth Symphony."

Kitty's ass. "I'm not in the mood." He looked at his watch. What did Kitty have in mind?

"You and I know that golf is not enough."

"Right."

"You couldn't do without them any more than I can, Will."

"Do without what?"

"The finer things in life."

"Right."

"Man does not live by bread alone and we make plenty bread at golf."

"Right." Why was it that the thought of the finer things in life, such as the Ninth Symphony, made his heart sink like a stone? For a fact, the Ninth Symphony was one of the finer things. On the other hand, Lewis's proposal was so demented he had to laugh: he and this solemn poet-golf-pro music lover listening to the *Ode to Joy* of an afternoon in old Carolina.

"You want to know what I've decided over the years, Will?"

"What?"

"I've decided the worst thing that can happen to a man is to lose his heritage."

What heritage? Tidewater unbeliever who had read Dante six times for the structure, could draw the circles of hell, the platforms of purgatory, and the rose of heaven? When you came down to it, Lewis took Erich Fromm more seriously than God, Dante, or Virginia. Was this not madness pure and simple, to come from Tidewater Virginia, read about Dante and God, read the *terza rima* aloud with such admiration that tears came to his eyes—and top it off with Erich Fromm?

"I got to get back to the party." And then to Kitty's ass. "I promised Marion to get Leslie married up proper."

"Yes. What a lovely girl. That reminds me. This may make you laugh but it's something I promised Marion."

"What's that?"

"Before she died Marion asked me to tell you something."

"What's that?"

"Funny she wouldn't tell you. You and Marion didn't communicate much, did you?"

"No, we didn't communicate much. We had what you call a communication breakdown."

Lewis laughed, himself again despite himself. "Marriage is hell, ain't it? Cindy is a wonderful wife but she hasn't grown."

"That's too bad." Grown to what? "What was it you were supposed to tell me?"

"Oh, Marion said: just make sure he gets to the wedding and all, that if he wants to pull one of his little fade-outs, she's not going to be there to cover for you." Lewis laughed. "She knew you pretty well, Will."

"Yes."

"I told her, shit, Will will be there, don't worry about it."

"You didn't say shit to Marion."

"No, I didn't."

"Right."

"You won't come down later to crack a bottle and listen to some music? I just got the whole Ring."

"No." Jesus, no.

"Or shoot doves. Or sit in the cave. Or whatever."

"The cave? Shoot doves?" A strange thought flew into his head. He looked at Lewis. "Okay. I will."

After Lewis left, he stood for a moment looking down at the Greener. For the second time in a week, he remembered a movie actor he had only heard of once. No, he didn't even remember the actor. He remembered his father remember the actor as they were driving in Hollywood in 1950. After the Georgia hunt they had gone West. At the end of the continent they found themselves driving down Sunset Boulevard in his father's big black 4-hole Dynaflow Buick. His father, who had not spoken for a thousand miles, said: "You see that corner?" "Yes sir." "Once I was here before." "Is that right?" "I was here for the Olympics of 1932. On that corner I saw an actor by the name of Ross Alexander. It was before his death." "Is that so?" "One night he was giving a party at his house. In the middle of the party he got up and said I think I'll go outside and shoot a duck. No one thought anything of this announcement. He went outside to the garage and shot himself. No one thought much of that either. Similar events were occurring in Rome in 450 before its sack by the Vandals." "Is that right?"

Will Barrett snapped the leather case of the Greener and put it away in the closet behind the Electrolux.

5

"What a wonderful person your wife was," said Kitty.

"Yes, she was."

They were watching his daughter Leslie as she talked with Mr. Arnold from the nursing home. Despite his stroke he could get around with a walker. One fierce eye gazed around the room under a small bald head white as an onion. One side of his face was shut down. Eyelid, cheek, lip fell like a curtain.

"Marion was a saint in this world," said Kitty.

"Yes."

"And you were so wonderful with her. I've seen you pushing her in the A & P, helping her in and out of the car."

"Yes."

"If she hadn't been so heavy, she would have been a lovely woman."

"Yes."

No. Marion was not lovely, even before she got "heavy," never had been lovely except for her good gray eyes and heavy wide winged eyebrows.

Why had he married her? It was not, was it? because she was Bertie's sister and Bertie owned the firm and Marion owned forty million dollars?

No, he married her, hadn't he? because she was touching, with her not too bad polio limp, and even pretty in a gawky Yankeefied way—even now when he thought of her at Northport, he saw her in a blue middy blouse—middy blouse? was such a thing possible, was it in a photograph, or did he imagine it?—and her direct gray-eyed gaze a whole world removed from a Sweetbriar girl or a Carolina coed who had six different ways of looking at you and with all six had seen you coming before you saw her.

No, he married her because he pleased her so much. It is not a small thing to be able to make someone happy so easily.

No, he married her for the very outlandishness of it, marrying her in Northport being as far as he could get from where he had come from.

No, he married her because she was such a good cheerful forthright Northern Episcopal Christian and wanted him to be one too and he tried and even imagined he believed it—again for the very outlandishness of it, taking for his own a New York Episcopal view of an Anglican view of a Roman view of a Jewish

Happening. Might it not be true for this very reason? Could anybody but God have gotten away with such outlandishness, contriving to have rich Long Island Episcopalians who if they had no use for anything had no use for Jews, worship a Jew?

No, he married her for none of these reasons and for all of them. Marry her for money and the firm? Yes and no. Marry her because he could make her happy? Yes and no. Marry her because she was as far away as he could get from Mississippi? Yes and no. And from you, old mole? Yes. And get Jesus Christ in the bargain? Why not?

Yes, it was all of these but most of all it was the offhandedness and smiling secret coolness with which he did it, getting it all and even going the Gospels one better because the Gospels spoke of the children of this world and the children of light and set one against the other and he was both and had both and why not? Why not marry her?

Wasn't it possible to believe in God like Pascal's cold-blooded bettor, because there was everything to gain if you were right and nothing to lose if you were wrong?

For a while it seemed that it was possible.

Then it seemed not to matter.

In all honesty it was easier to believe it in cool Long Island for its very outrageousness where nobody believed anything very seriously than in hot Carolina where everybody was a Christian and found unbelief unbelievable.

After he married Marion, she seemed happier than ever, gave herself to church work, doing so with pleasure, took pleasure in him—and suddenly took pleasure in eating. She married, gave herself to good works, heaved a great sigh of relief, and began to eat. She ate and ate and ate. She grew too heavy for her hip joint already made frail and porous by polio. The ball of her femur drove into the socket of her pelvis, melted, and fused. She took to a wheelchair, ate more than ever, did more good works. She spent herself for the poor and old and wretched of North Carolina. She was one of the good triumphant Yankees who helped out the poor old South. In and out of meetings flew her wheelchair, her arms burly as a laborer's. Fueled by holy energy, money, and brisk good cheer, she spun past slack-jawed Southerners, fed the hungry, clothed the naked, paid the workers in her mills a living wage, the very lintheads her piratical Yankee father had despoiled and gotten rich on: a mystery. Another mystery: her sanctity and gluttony. She truly gave herself

143

to others, served God and her fellow man with a good and cheerful heart—and ate and ate and ate, her eyes as round and glittering as a lover's.

It had been a pleasure for him to please and serve her. Only he, she said, had the strength and deftness to lean into the Rolls, take her by the waist while she took him by the neck, and in one quick powerful motion swing her out and around and into the wheelchair. Yamaiuchi was strong enough to do it but she wouldn't let him. That's why Yamaiuchi hates me, he thought. Had she promised him something in her will and hadn't come through? To the A & P, then push her by one hand and the cart by the other while she snatched cans off the shelves, Celeste pizzas, Sara Lee cream pies, bottles of Plagniol, brownies, cream butter, eggs, gallons of custard ice cream. For her the pleasure came from the outing with him and from her "economizing" by doing her own shopping.

Twice a week he took her also to St. Mark's Home, where he wheeled her down the halls and she knew every resident by name and visited, wheelchair to wheelchair. Looking down, he could see her welted forehead and cheeks foreshortened and her burly forearms, resting now, while he pushed.

She ate more. She grew bigger, fatter, but also stronger. She ate more and more: Smithfield hams, Yamaiuchi's wife's shirred eggs, Long Island ducks. Cholesterol sparkled like a golden rain in her blood, settled as a sludge winking with diamonds. A tiny stone lodged in her common bile duct. A bacillus sprouted in the stagnant dammed bile. She turned yellow as butter and hot as fire. There was no finding the diamond through the cliffs of ocherous fat. She died.

Both Marion and Leslie his daughter were religious in ways which were both admirable and daunting. He could not disagree with them nor allow himself the slightest distance of irony. How could he disagree with them? Both seemed to be right or at least triumphantly well-intentioned. It was odd only that though he had no quarrel with them, they quarreled with each other.

Marion had been an old-style Episcopalian who believed that one's duty lay with God, church, the *Book of Common Prayer*, family, country, and doing good works.

Leslie, his daughter, was a new-style Christian who believed in giving her life to the Lord through a personal encounter with Him and who accordingly had no use for church, priests, or ritual. She believed this and Jason believed a California version of this. They got along well together, did good works, and seemed to be happy. How could one find fault with Leslie?

Leslie was leaning forward, speaking slowly to Mr. Arnold. She was helping him with his speech. She was a speech therapist. When he tried to say something, his lips on the slack side blew out like a drape. Leslie grimaced impatiently.

Now Leslie was arguing with Jack Curl, the minister. The three Cupps stood by silent and agreeable, tall as trees. The argument was not disagreeable, there were smiles and laughter, but it was an argument nevertheless. He could tell by the arch of Leslie's back and by Jack Curl's terror. Serious arguments, especially theological arguments, terrified Jack. They were probably arguing about the wedding. Marion had wanted a traditional ceremony. Leslie and Jason wanted to write their own ceremony.

Marion had been a conservative Episcopalian and had no use for the changes in the church.

Leslie and Jason were born-again Christians and had no use for anything, liturgy or sacrament, which got in the way of a personal encounter with Jesus Christ.

Ed and Marge Cupp were Californians.

Jack Curl, the minister, had no strong feelings about woman priests or the interim prayer book. He had been terrified that Marion, who had found him through her search committee and who considered the interim prayer book an abomination, would fire him. He attended ecumenical councils in the Middle East and Latin America. He had even visited a Russian bishop in Odessa and had started a collection of ikons. He wore jump suits.

Kitty believed in astrology.

Yamaiuchi was a Jehovah's Witness. He believed he was one of the 144,000 who would survive Armageddon and actually live in their bodies on this earth for a thousand years—and reign.

Yamaiuchi's wife, the cook, was a theosophist, who believed in reincarnation. She believed she had once been a priestess on Atlantis before it sank.

Is this an age of belief, he reflected, a great renaissance of faith after a period of crass materialism, atheism, agnosticism, liberalism, scientism? Or is it an age of madness in which everyone believes everything? Which?

The only unbelievers he knew in Linwood were Lewis Peckham and Ewell McBee, and they were even more demented than the believers.

Leslie, who was sitting bolt upright on the couch, legs folded under her, took off her glasses to clean them, a habit she'd always had, leaving her eyes naked and hazed. Looking at her, his daughter, he found himself thinking not about her or the wedding or the argument but, strangely enough, about how the girl in the woods might see her. In her nutty way with words, she would have seen Leslie in her name *Leslie* and now he too could see her, had always seen her as a *Leslie*, the two syllables of the name linked and hinged and folding just as her legs folded under her and the stems folded against her glasses, the whispering of her panty hose and the slight clash of the glasses connoted by the *s* in *Les* and the *Leslie* itself with its *s* and neuterness signifying both prissiness and masculinity, a secretarial primness which indeed Leslie had and which was all the more remarkable what with her being born-again. It was impossible to envision her personal encounter with Christ as other than a crisp business transaction.

Yet once he saw her at the end of a prayer meeting when everyone smiled and cried and hugged each other. She had removed her thick glasses. It made her look naked and vulnerable. She smiled and hugged and cried too. It struck a strange pang to his very heart to see her like that. For some reason, tears sprang to his eyes too. What to make of all this melting belief? Did he like her better cool and distant behind her glasses? What was wrong, he asked himself, with opening up and loving everybody? What was wrong with their loving Jesus? I don't know. Something.

Marge Cupp cupped her hands and made swimming motions. An ex-Olympic swimmer, she was telling Jack Curl how she taught children to swim before they walked. Like many Californians, she knew how to expand the particular into the general, turn a hobby into a religion, and what's more make it credible. It was easy to believe her and see her in the surf, a blond not-so-young Juno, waves foaming at her knees, her swimcoach tank suit well worn and dry, the hem slightly frayed over her strong dark marbled legs, launch happy babes into the Pacific, the Aquarians of a new age. Who knows? Maybe she was right: going back where we came from, back to the primal sea. That was her California principle, leaving the sad failed land life behind and leaving it soon enough and young enough before it screwed you up for good, and going back to the original environment, the ocean (which had the same salt content as blood and the amniotic fluid where we were happy), and, age ten months to ten years to a hundred, frolic like porpoises in the warm Cretaceous sea.

Jack Curl was trying to listen but he was terrified. Jump suit or no jump suit, he was terrified. Wouldn't he have been better off rid of his genteel Virginia Episcopal tight-assed terror if Marge had got hold of him age six months and pitched him into the ocean?

Ed Cupp bunched the fingers of his left hand (which was big enough to hold a basketball from the top) and drove them up into his right. He was describing to Lewis Peckham the proper insertion of a Mercedes oil filter. There was a warranty problem with his car, whose engine had burnt up in Oklahoma City, where the Mercedes dealer had refused to honor the warranty, claiming that the oil filter had been inserted improperly. It was impossible to insert the filter improperly, said Ed Cupp, German engineering had seen to that. It was all he could think about. He too was credible. Listening to him, one shared his outrage and wished him well in his lawsuit against the Oklahoma dealer.

Leslie, leaning forward, smiling yet intense, was giving Mr. Arnold speech lessons, making a *p* by compressing her lips and puffing out the *p* against her hand, then holding her hand to Mr. Arnold's mouth, but when he tried to say *p*, his slack lips blew out on the left side. Mr. Arnold looked around angrily and made motions toward his mouth. He was hungry. Leslie was angry with him.

The tree was disappearing. There was a ripple in a glass windowpane. He knew that particular ripple. Sitting in a certain chair, not reading, not talking, not listening to music, he had discovered that the ripple lined up with the far rim of the gorge so that when he moved his head a wave seemed to run along the rocky ledge.

Something was happening. Suddenly, with a little surge of satisfaction under his belt, he knew what it was. Everything had the look about it of coming to an end. There was nothing more he wished to say to the Cupps. There was nothing more for them to say to him. Things do come to an end. There was an end to this room. It was impossible for him to imagine entering this whited-out room tomorrow and lining up the ripple in the glass with the rim of the gorge. The tree was vanishing for good into the cloud.

For at least a hundred times in past years he had lined up ripple of glass with rim of gorge. A novel thought occurred to him. Sooner or later there comes along a lining up which is the last—number 101 or 102. Ordinarily one does not keep track and does not imagine that there will be a last lining up. But why not decide which lining up will be the last? Very well. This one. He lined up ripple with the beginning of the gorge rim like the two points of a gunsight and moved his eye. The ripple ran along the rim until it came to the scarlet oak which hid the target like the tree in front of the Texas Book Depository. Anyhow, the tree had almost vanished in the fog.

Suddenly he knew why he remembered the triangular patch of woods near the railroad tracks where he wanted to make love to Ethel Rosenblum. It was the very sort of place, a nondescript weedy triangular public pubic sort of place, to make a sort of love or to die a sort of death.

The silence of the cloud seemed to press in upon the house like cotton.

Did you not then believe, old mole, that these two things alone are real, loving and dying, and since one is so much like the other and there is so little of the one, in the end there remained only the other?

Silence.

Very well, old mole, you win.

6

Kitty touched him, jostled him with her hip, shoulder, elbow. She looked at him. "You look as though you just made up your mind to do something, decided what you wanted, and know just how to get it."

"Ah."

"What is it, Will?" She moved closer.

"Ah."

Her eyes widened. "Is it me?"

"Ah—"

Kitty laughed, put her arm around his waist, and said she had a favor to ask of him. He smiled and nodded, noting with curiosity that everywhere she touched him a welt rose to meet her.

His body swelled. It occurred to him that it would be pleasant to take her hand and hold it against him. He turned his back on the others. But before he could take her hand, she laid both hands on him and tugged him playfully roughly into the corner beyond Marion's Louis XV secretary. As they went past, Kitty's hand went out to touch one of the brilliant enamel-like decoupage panels. Hand and eye made one swift appraisal. "My God, would you look at that," she said absently to no one and in a different voice.

"Now, old dear friend Will, my first and only love. Oh, it's so good to see you. Do you remember Central Park?"

"Yes."

"What a dummy I was. I should have taken you up. But you were always so vague. I never knew when you were going to wander off in one of your funks."

"Taken me up on what?" he said absently, watching the tree. The room was closed up in a cloud, a white room whited out by a white cloud, but no one seemed to notice.

"Ha ha, haa haa. Don't give me that, son," said Kitty, coming even closer.

"All right."

Maybe he had "proposed" to her. In any case, he saw that Kitty had made over her past life in her head so that it became as clear and simple as a movie. He had proposed to her and she had turned him down. If she had taken him up, it was possible for her to think she would have been happy. But she hadn't and so her life had been screwed up. If only— But even an "if only" is not so bad if it is simple. Regret can be enjoyed if it makes sense. The difference between them was that the older she got the more sense her life made. Yet she was not altogether serious in her swaying and swooping against him and her "if onlys." The seriousness showed in her quick sure appraisal of the Louis XV secretary, the split-second touch-and-look. She knew what she wanted. What did she want from him?

The tree grew dimmer. Some of the leaves came off and blew straight up. There must be an updraft from the gorge.

"What a good-looking couple we made, Will!"

"We did?"

"Do you remember what my housemother told me at school?"

"No."

"That you and I were not only the best-looking couple she had ever seen but the most distinguished."

Distinguished. What could Kitty mean? Undoubtedly Kitty was making up her own bad but clear fiction and the always unclear fact. What could the housemother have meant? What was distinguished about a coed cheerleader and an addled ATO who didn't know whether he was coming or going? Ah, suddenly he saw what Kitty meant. She meant *now* they were a distinguished couple, he with his silvery temples, she with her lithe branny brown arms and gold swatch of hair.

Kitty drew closer. "Stop giving me that Scorp look. It takes one to know one you know."

"What?"

"You haven't forgotten that we are both Scorps?"

"Scorps?"

"Scorpios." She jostled him. "Don't hand me that." Perhaps he had not remembered everything. "Did you think I had forgotten your birthday? It's next month, the day after mine, remember? Not that I needed to know. I could take one look at you, the way you stare right through people, and know you were a Scorp. And I got news for you, son."

"What?"

"Pluto, who governs both the positive and negative aspects of sex, is at this moment entering his own sign, which happens to be our own sign."

"Is that good?"

"Not good or bad as you damn well know. It all depends on the Scorps themselves. And I'm here to tell you one thing about one Scorp."

"What?"

"I'm no longer the little gray lizard Scorp you once knew. You're looking at a fully evolved eagle Scorp, with the well-known Scorp sexuality and only us Scorps know what that means."

"I believe I am."

"And as for you—"

"Yes?"

"Clearly you are somewhere in between, in transit. That's fine—as long as you don't forget one thing."

"What?"

"What happens when two fully evolved Scorps get together."

"What happens?"

"They can save a country. Or destroy it. Or have an awesome love affair. Hepburn and Burt Lancaster are Scorps."

"That's not—"

Kitty's face came into his neck. "Actually, that's not why I grabbed you."

"Why did you grab me?"

"I wanted to tell you where I'm coming from."

"Where are you coming from?"

"I'm fixing to beat Marion's time. And it's perfectly all right with Marion. She gave me permission before she died. In fact, it was her idea."

"Beat Marion's time," he mused. "I haven't heard that for a long time." He couldn't seem to tear his eyes from the tree, which had all but vanished.

He was trying to listen. Kitty was talking about what a good person Marion was, he was, she Kitty was. She was. He was. It was true. They were. Ah, what had happened to them all, all these good persons, all those good things Marion stood for, God, church, home, family, country? Why had he always felt glum when Marion spoke of these good things? What had happened to marriage? Why was not goodness enough for marriage? Why did good married couples look so glum? Old couples, young couples, thirty-five-year-old Atlanta couples in condos, sixty-five-year-old Ohio couples in villas, each as glum as if one had got stuck with the other at a cocktail party for two hours. Two hours? Ten years! Thirty years!

"What?" he said and gave a start. Kitty seemed to be talking about her daughter.

"Schizophrenics often are."

"Are what?"

"Shrewd. Walter wanted to call the cops when she escaped but Alistair said that Allison is very shrewd in her own way— it's true!—and that she'll probably come back to Valleyhead."

"Then you don't know where she is," he said absently. Now he knew why the girl in the woods looked familiar. She had the same short upper lip, the little double tendon below her nose pulling the lip into a bow and just clear of the lower. The first time he had seen Kitty on a park bench, lips parted so, he had wanted her mouth.

"Actually, I think I do. She has some hippie friends in Virginia Beach. Yes, I'm sure that's where she is. Actually I think it might do her good. She's no dumbbell. She planned the whole thing, swiped four hundred dollars from her father, and disappeared into thin air. I'm going to give her a few days and then go find her. That's what I wanted to talk to you about. Do you mind having your old flame in your hair for a few days?"

"Ah no."

There were three shells on the quilt of the Negro cabin where he was lying. The Negro boy had brought them, and even the one dead quail, and put them on the bed beside him. Some guide. What guide would retrieve empty shotgun shells? The Negro woman wiped the blood from his face with the clean damp rag. "You ain't hurt bad. You just lay there until the high sheriff comes." The room smelled of kerosene and flour paste. Fresh newspapers covered the walls. She leaned over him. The movement of the rag against his cheek and lip was quick and firm but did not hurt. "Your daddy be all right. Ain't nothing wrong the good Lord cain't fix," the woman said. He turned away impatiently. "Where's the shotgun?" The Greener lay on the other side of him. The guide had found it and brought it back. He broke the breech. There was a single shell in the right barrel.

Yet only now, thirty years later, did he do the arithmetic. One shell for the quail, two for me, and one for you.

Well well, he thought, shaking his head and feeling in his pockets for the Mercedes keys. He must have been smiling because Kitty gave him a jostle. "What's the matter with you, you nut?"

To his surprise—yes! now he could be surprised!—a strange gaiety took hold of him. Something rose in his throat. What? Laughter. He laughed out loud.

"What are you laughing at, idiot?"

"Everything. Nothing. I'm sorry. What were you saying about ah—"

"Allison."

"Allison?"

"My daughter, dummy. Allie."

Allie. Yes. That was her name. That was Allie sitting on the stoop of the greenhouse reading the fat pulpy *Captain Blood.* Allie.

"I want you to meet her, talk to her, listen to her. I want her to get to know you. She can't talk to people but somehow I know that she would talk to you. I can't tell you how many times the thought has come to me that if only you had been there all along Allison would have been all right. And here's the strangest thing of all. Sometimes I have the strongest feeling that you could be or ought to be her father—ha! fat chance, yet there is a slight chance, remember?"

"Remember what?" Had he forgotten something or had Kitty rewritten the entire book of her life? His eyes went unfocused on the white cloud.

"No, really, Will. There is something about her, about us, about Allison. We were together once in another life."

"What?" He gave a violent start.

"I said— What are you smiling about, you nut?"

"Was I smiling?"

"Like a chess cat."

"A what?"

"Like somebody had let you in on a big secret."

"A secret. Yes."

He looked at Kitty. In the corner of his eye he could see Leslie talking to the Cupps. She was nodding and frowning. They were arguing, he knew, about the after-rehearsal party. It was the custom for the groom's family to give the party. The Cupps proposed to rent the Buccaneer Tavern at the Holiday Inn. Leslie looked sullen.

Kitty's hand, he noticed, was on his arm. He gave a start. He had not been listening.

"Don't forget," whispered Kitty in his ear but not quite managing to whisper.

"What?"

"Three o'clock."

"Okay," he said absently.

"Isn't it a shame that we waste so much time figuring out what we want," said Kitty. "To think of the years—"

"Right." Marion had wanted to serve God, eat, and to do good. Jimmy Rogers and the dentist wanted money. Kitty wanted what? him? his money? out from the dentist? He wanted what? Kitty's ass? Death? Both?

Kitty's face had gone solemn. Her eyes were shining.

"You will help me with Allison?"

"Sure," he said absently.

"The child hasn't learned that she has to get in touch with her feelings before she can get well. When things don't go just right, she thinks she has to crawl into a hole. Or hit the road, change, move, go."

"Yes," he muttered. "Sometimes you have to go. Get out. I've done that."

"You? You've never copped out. You were a good husband. Marion told me."

"Actually I wasn't. Did she tell you what I did last year?"

"No."

"One Sunday after church Marion sent me to town for some booze. We were entertaining Bertie and some of his Palm Beach pals. It was not that I couldn't stand Bertie and his pals, though in fact I couldn't. In fact, I don't know exactly why I did it. Instead of going to the liquor store I went to the bus station and took the first Trailways. A week later I found myself in Santa Fe. You know who I was looking for? Your brother Sutter."

Kitty made a face. "What was he doing?"

"He was sitting in an imitation adobe house watching M*A*S*H. He would only talk to me during commercials. He was working in a V.A. hospital for paraplegics and had one more year to go before his pension. After a while I left. I don't think he noticed."

"Sutter is a mess," said Kitty absently and took hold of him, coat, shirt, flank, and gave him a hard pinch as a mother might. "Don't forget," she said. "Three o'clock. The summerhouse."

"What? Oh. No. I won't forget."

7

Leslie looked up at him briefly and went on with her argument with the Cupps. No, it was Leslie and Jack Curl who were arguing. Or rather Jack Curl who was listening, pale as a ghost, as Leslie said: "Okay, big deal. First you have the *Book of Common Prayer*, then the green prayer book, then the red book, then the zebra book, then the interim book—and that was all I ever heard you and Mother talk about. Big deal."

As he watched Jack Curl, who was smiling and frowning and had opened his mouth to say something, he heard himself say: "Am I not also a member of the wedding?"

No one paid attention. Leslie's face was heavy with dislike, her lower lip curled. The Cupps were still smiling but their teeth looked dry. Mr. Arnold pointed his finger at his open mouth.

He was hungry. Jason sat listlessly, big hands dangling between his legs. They were all angrier than he thought. Were they arguing about religion or the rehearsal party?

"Very well," said Will Barrett, clearing his throat. "It seems I am not a member of the wedding." When no one answered or looked at him, he cleared his throat again. "Okay. I have one suggestion before I leave"—when he said "leave," Leslie looked up briefly and nodded ironically—"to go on an errand. It is this. It is my understanding that according to custom and the book of etiquette we are not supposed to have the rehearsal party here in this house, though as Marge and Ed well know, it would please me to do so. If Ed and Marge wish to give the party at the Buccaneer Room of the Holiday Inn, it is quite all right with me. After all, one place is as good as another. If, however, there is some dissatisfaction on this point, may I suggest as a tertium quid, ha ha, that if Ed wishes me to, I can put him in touch with Arthur at the club and the two of them can work out what they want. It is done all the time and it will cost Ed so much it will take his mind off his Mercedes."

"There you go," said Ed, cheering up.

Leslie held up both hands. "Now hear this, folks," she said, taking off her glasses and folding the stems. Her hazed eyes went from one to another. She nodded grimly. Her thin lips curved in satisfaction. She looked like Barbara Stanwyck in that part of the movie where she tells everybody off. "Number one, there is not going to be a rehearsal party for the simple reason that there is not going to be a rehearsal. The reason there is not going to be a rehearsal is that there is not going to be any ceremony to be rehearsed. Since when do you need a ceremony for two people to come together in the Lord? Number two. As for this book I keep hearing about, the only book I go by is the Gospel of our Lord and Saviour Jesus Christ. Number three. The only reason Jason and I are here at all is because you want us to be. We love you all dearly and wish to please you but we cannot compromise our beliefs. Number four. As far as such quaint customs as 'giving the bride away' is concerned, forget it, folks. I don't mean to hurt your feelings, Daddy, but nobody can give me away because I've already given myself away, to the Lord and to Jason. Number five. As far as a priest is concerned, an intermediary between God and man, no hard feelings, Jack, but the Gospel commands us to call no man father."

Jack Curl opened his mouth to everyone. "Father? Nobody calls me father. Who here calls me father?"

But no one answered. Everyone seemed sunk in thought. Only Mr. Arnold tried to say something but his lip blew out. He pointed a finger straight into his mouth. Across the room Yamaiuchi was leaving fast with a tray of empty bloody-Mary glasses. Will Barrett called to him and made a motion. It was possible for Yamaiuchi, whose eye had not quite met his, to pretend he hadn't heard him. He called to him again. He knew that Yamaiuchi heard because his ears fluttered even closer to his glossy head, but he did not turn around. It was rare for anyone but Marion, who had hired him and sent him to forestry school in Asheville, to give him orders. For this reason it now became possible for Yamaiuchi to pretend not to hear him.

For some reason this made him angry with a quick hot anger. He lost his temper. He had not been angry or surprised for thirty years—no, once before, when Kitty's brother was dying and the stupid nurses wouldn't do anything—and in the very instant of feeling the anger rise in his throat, he remembered that it was with exactly the same sudden rage his father had turned on the black guide. His father, known as a nigger-lover, cursed the guide like a nigger-hater.

He, Will Barrett, meant to say: Get your ass or perhaps even get your yellow ass (his father said black ass) over here, but he felt the room go silent and felt himself shrug and laugh as Yamaiuchi wheeled with the tray. He beckoned to him. Yet even now the Japanese looked for the briefest instant in Leslie's direction, decided she wasn't boss, and came over, smiling angrily.

"Bring this man a plate of food," he said, pointing to Mr. Arnold, who was pointing a forefinger straight into his mouth.

"Y'sah," said Yamaiuchi. "The buffet is urready." Again his eye slewed toward Leslie. Was he saying, I'd rather take orders from her?

"Do it now," he said, smiling angrily. He was genuinely puzzled: I wonder why this Japanese is playing this game, calculating decimal points of insolence.

"Y'sah." Yamaiuchi bowed, two degrees too far, and left.

Someday I'm going to hit that little grinning bastard, he thought, drive him right into the ground with both fists.

An instant later he thought with amazement, where did that

rage come from? I could have killed him. My father could have too: he could as easily have shot the guide as he shot the dog.

You're one of us, his father said.

Yes, very well. I'm one of you. You win.

Where does such rage come from? from the discovery that in the end the world yields only to violence, that only the violent bear it away, that short of violence all is in the end impotence?

8

He gazed at himself in the bathroom mirror, turned his head, touched his cheek like a man testing whether to shave. Presently his face canceled itself. The bright-faceted forehead went dark, the deep-set eyes began to glow, the shadowed pocked cheek grew bright. The mirror, he noticed, did not reflect accurately. It missed the slight bulge of forehead, the hollowing of temple which showed in photographs. Even when he turned his head, his nose did not look snoutish as it did in a double mirror.

Something stirred in him. He looked at his watch. In three minutes Kitty would slip out into the cloud. When he thought of her standing in the summerhouse, hugging herself, wrapped in fog, he smiled. Then she would sit on the damp bench, straddling slightly, her thighs broadening and filling the creamy linen skirt. Yes, it was in her, not in a mirror, he would find himself. Entering her, he would be answered, responded to, delineated. His life would be proved by her. She would echo him, print him out, trace his shape like radar. He could read himself in her.

His heart gave a big pump. Did Kitty want what she appeared to want? Did she want him to fuck her in the summerhouse? Yes! And it was Kitty's ass he wanted. Yes! He blinked in astonishment. It was as if he had forgotten about women, about loving women, about having a woman's ass or loving a woman, one woman, one's own heart's love, love her heart, mind, soul, sweet lips, ass and all. A violent shiver took hold of him; hairs on his arm raised. What was he afraid of? of being caught? that he shouldn't? that he couldn't?

Heart beating in his neck, he hurried down the back stairs to the garage—and fell. Either fainted or fell, or slipped and fell, and knocked himself out, or perhaps had a fit, one of his "petty-mall" spells. Fit or fall, it seemed to him that he drifted down weightlessly, careening softly off the walls of the stairwell, and fetched up comfortably at the bottom of the steps. If he had been knocked out, he must have come to instantly, in decent time to collect himself, not get up but arrange himself in a sitting-lying position on the bottom step.

There was a sound. Someone had entered the garage.

The narrow stairwell was dark. The bright cloud seemed to fill the garage. He could see the three cars and most of the floor without being seen.

Methodically he felt his arms and legs and clenched his fists. Had he had a stroke? Would he have to carry one fisted hand in the other like a baby? No, his hands worked. Something wet and warm ran into the orbit of one eye. He touched his cheek. It was blood. Above, at his temple, rose a clotted swelling. Though it seemed to be growing larger, it didn't hurt.

The cat sat in its usual place under the Rolls. Tendrils of fog drifted across the clean floor. The light from the cloud struck the concrete at such an angle that he could make out the faint arcs of the mason's trowel. The fog crept under the Mercedes, where it vaporized and disappeared. Perhaps there was a faint warmth in the motor.

He noted with curiosity that there seemed to be no hurry, that there was all the time in the world, time to take account of small events in the garage. More important, it had become possible to take stock of himself, assess the extent of his injuries, and make his plans accordingly. Curious! Suddenly he had come into himself like the cat, got rid of the ghost which stood aside from himself, forever rushing ahead or hanging back. Here he was in the real world of cats and concrete! He smiled. Perhaps something had been knocked loose in his head. Or perhaps something loose had been knocked together.

Someone had come from behind the Rolls and was standing over him. Leaning on one elbow, he cocked his head to look up.

"Lawyer Barrett?"

"Yes?"

It was Ewell McBee.

"Lawyer Barrett, I needed to tell you something."

"You already told me. You apologized for the shot. Don't worry about it," he said dreamily. Ewell loomed against the white cloud. As he shaded his eyes with one hand to see him better, he noticed that Ewell's head silhouetted against the whiteness showed a slight hollowing at the temple oddly like his own. And when he turned his head, there was a familiar snout-ishness about the nose.

"I needed to ask you something."

Ewell did not seem to find it remarkable that he was lounging in the dark stairwell.

In his strange new mood he made the following observation: people notice very little indeed, ghost-ridden as they are by themselves. You have to be bleeding from the mouth or throwing a fit for them to take notice. Otherwise, anything you do is no more or less than another part of the world they have to deal with, poor souls.

You worry about what you are supposed to do. The funny thing is, no matter what you do, people believe it is no more or less than what you are supposed to do.

"I'm going to make you a proposition you can't turn down, haw haw," said Ewell. He hawked, spat, hiked a foot up on the Mercedes bumper, settled his crotch.

"Your video-cassette company? How much do you want me to invest?" He seemed to understand everything Ewell said before he said it. He tried to stand but something was wrong with his left leg; it gave way. It was possible to resume his lounging position in such a casual way that Ewell did not seem to notice.

"I want you to hear about it from my potner," said Ewell, placing one hand softly on the Mercedes hood. "We going to have us a little party tonight. At my villa. A private screening of her latest film. It's called *Foxy Frolics* and it's a winner, I guarantee. Just me and my potner and you and her leading lady. She's actually a wonderful girl named Cheryl Lee from Chapel Hill and she's as smart as she can be. What she really wants to do is play the violin for the Appalachian symphony. She's into erotic movies for the money. What she really is is a musician. What talent! The party is her idea. She wants to meet you. For some reason she thinks you're the smartest and sexiest man she ever saw. I told her you were as dumb as me, just richer, har har."

A rushing black tide seemed to be filling one end of the garage. When he closed one eye, then the other, it did not go away. But when he turned his head a little to confront it, the wall of darkness retreated.

Ewell hawked. "We can have us a party. First I make us some toddies like your daddy used to make, then Norma Jean will cook us a steak, then we'll show the film and I promise you

you'll have the finest time you ever had. Cheryl is a little armful of heaven, but she is also smart. You and me understand each other, don't we?''

He cocked his head, the better to see the looming figure of Ewell McBee, the slightly hollow temple, the snoutish nose. It seemed strange to hear Ewell, who once was a bully and jerk-off artist who wore bib overalls and had thick white country-white skin talking about ''films'' and ''screening'' and being ''into'' this and that.

But he was only half listening. He tested the strength of his hands, moved his legs. I believe I can walk after Ewell leaves. The rushing darkness had fallen back. Is it a tumor or stroke or what? he wondered. It did not seem to matter. The newfound core of calmness and freedom seemed safe from such things, even from the tide of darkness trembling at the corner of his eye.

Unhurriedly he began to listen to Ewell, who was talking about his, Will Barrett's, father.

''He was the smartest man I ever knew and he would bet on anything. He would bet you five dollars a mockingbird would sit still while he hit a niblick out of the sand.''

Yeah, that's real smart.

''He would always give me ten dollars after a round—that was a lot then. Once I was caddying for him and Judge Pettigrew and Senator Talley and an insurance man and I heard him buy a one-million-dollar life-insurance policy, just like that.''

That was real smart too. Buy a million-dollar life-insurance policy, then scatter your brain cells over the state of Mississippi.

''I never will forget one thing he told a preacher. One time they had a preacher in the foursome. A big famous preacher from Montreat. I could tell he was getting on your daddy's nerves. He couldn't cuss. The preacher kept talking about his church, how much money he took in, and saving souls, ten thousand souls in this one church in Charlotte. Oh the soul this and the soul that, praise the Lord and so forth. Your daddy didn't say a word. But he was getting hot under the collar. Then he said something to the preacher I will never forget. You know what he said?'' Ewell hawked and hiked himself.

''No.''

''He said to him right in the middle of number-six fairway. He said let me tell you something about all those souls you're bragging about. In the first place, you want to know what a soul is? I'll tell you. A soul is a man like you and me and Ewell here. You want to know what a man is? I'll tell you. A man is born between an asshole and a peehole. He eats, sleeps, shits, fucks, works, gets old, and dies. And that's all he does. That's what a man is. That's what he said. I'm telling you, your daddy was a pistol-ball.''

"Yes." That's what he was, a pistol-ball.

"Well, we going to have our little party?"

"Party?" he said absently.

"If you don't, Lawyer Barrett, you'll be making the mistake of your life. Here is this beautiful talented girl who has the hots for you, and you may not have another chance because I guarantee you she's on her way up. Just you remember her name, Cheryl Lee. That's her stage name. Her real name is Sarah Goodman from Wilmington and she's going to be famous."

"Will she be famous for *Foxy Frolics* or for her violin playing?" He pricked up his ears. "Did you say Sarah Goodman?"

"Yes."

"Is she Jewish?"

"Jewish? Why yes."

"Are you sure?"

"Sure I'm sure. Her old man is Sol Goodman in dry-goods."

"Did you say she was from Wilmington?"

"Yes, but—"

"Wilmington, North Carolina?"

"Why yes. Do you know her?"

"And you say she's leaving? She's going back to Israel, right?"

"Israel? Why no. If she passes her audition, she's moving to Asheville. If not, she'll come back to Highlands and make movies with Norma Jean. I think she ought to do that anyhow. She's a real fine little actress."

"I see." He brightened. "Are you sure she's Jewish? I mean, after all you can't go by a name. Rosenberg was a Nazi."

"Is the Pope Catholic? I'm telling you, I know her old man, Sol Goodman."

"I see."

"Cheryl could make it either way. She's got it all. Do you know who she looks exactly like? Remember Linda Darnell? Imagine a Linda Darnell who can play the violin like Evelyn and Phil Spitalny. In fact, now that she's finished this film, she's getting ready for her first recital."

He must have had a lapse of inattention or perhaps even another spell. Did he blank out? How much time passed? In any case, he must have seemed rude because the next thing he knew, Ewell McBee was standing directly over him, feet apart, hands on his hips, speaking loudly. He seemed to be in a rage.

"You want to know what your trouble is, Lawyer Barrett?"

"Why, yes," he said with genuine curiosity, cocking his head to look up.

"The trouble with you is you always thought you were too good for anybody or anything. Nothing is ever good enough for you."

"Really?" he said, peering up at Ewell with interest. "How is that?"

"You always thought you were so damn smart. You and your daddy. But I'm here to tell you something. The only difference between you and me is money. Outside of that, you and I are exactly alike. You and your daddy are smart all right but there is such a thing as outsmarting yourself. You even think you're smarter than your daddy, don't you?"

"Is that right?" Well, yes.

He gazed up at Ewell with curiosity. Enemies, he knew, often tell the truth. And these days enemies, honest enemies are few and far between. Nobody says anything unpleasant. Enemies will often tell you unsuspected truths about yourself, just as a photograph or a double mirror will show your snoutish nose.

"You know I'm right, Lawyer Barrett."

"About what?"

"About us being exactly alike."

"How is that?"

"You know as well as I do we could have us a fine time having a party with Cheryl and Norma Jean, looking at the film and having some drinks and later having a real party. I mean a *fine* time. A little pussy never hurt anybody. You like pussy as much as I do, don't you?"

"I hadn't thought about it lately," he said, but thinking now of Kitty's ass. Well, yes. How could it have slipped my mind? What time is it?

"But you don't talk about it because you think you're too good to have a party with me."

"A party with Sarah Goodman is not out of the question."

But Ewell's anger carried him beyond listening. In a way, he's taking another shot at me, he saw.

162

"Me and you are alike as two peas in a pod," said Ewell, moving his shoulders. "The only difference between us is that me and my daddy had to work like niggers and you and your daddy had your own niggers and enough money to learn lawyering and how to talk. Otherwise, we just the same."

"How are we the same?" he asked curiously, straining up to see and hear.

"Your daddy said it. What's more, we both love money, only you were smarter about getting it and so you don't have to talk about it. You marry the richest lady in the state, so you don't have to worry about it. Then you can go around giving it away, so you can be man-of-the-year. Like money don't matter to you. You're right. It don't matter if you got it. But if you didn't have it, it would matter. You act like you was so sorry your wife passed. Maybe you was. She was a real fine lady. But maybe it didn't exactly kill your soul that you inherited all that money. But you would never say. The only difference between us is that I would say. I married the meanest damn white woman in Henderson County and I was glad she passed and I don't mind saying so. But you're smart. And you're ever bit as cold-blooded as I am, only you don't have to talk about it because you got money. Money may not be everything but it sho lets you act nice. My daddy used to tell me: make the money then act as nice as you please. You're even smarter than your daddy. Look what happened to him. But not you. You setting there right this minute eyeing me and listening and figuring something out, ain't you?"

"What do you think I'm figuring out, Ewell?"

"I don't know because you don't say. You never did. But you're figuring hard as you can. And you setting there acting polite and you ain't about to come to my house for a party."

"As a matter of fact, I would like to meet Sarah Goodman, that is, Cheryl Lee." Kitty told him he had been Jewish in another life. Perhaps he had. Could it be that a native North Carolina Jewish girl was still here? that she had not only not returned to Israel but was hanging around Highlands making erotic movies and having parties in villas with Gentiles, Jutes like Ewell? If so, what did that signify? And why did he want to see her? to have her ass or to find out if she was going to Israel?

Ewell, he saw, had reached that degree of anger where everything is received as a provocation. On he came, shouldering. The only thing that prevented a fistfight was that he, Will Barrett, was lounging at his ease on the steps, sitting-lying, propped on one elbow, head cocked, eyeing him.

A strange thought occurred to him. Perhaps Ewell was the last hater. Has a time come when not only has love left the world but hatred also and nothing is left but niceness?

Ewell went on talking but with a slackening of anger, with even a hint of affection, perhaps the sort of affection which follows barroom brawls, but he didn't listen closely.

Ewell was making plans for the party. "Don't worry about a thing. You and me going to have us a fine time."

The white cloud which filled the wide doorway had grown as dense and solid as a pearl. No doubt the sun shone directly upon it, for it was shot through with delicate colors.

Again the ripple of darkness came forward at the corner of his eye but it went away when he tried to look at it. Instead, he looked at the three cars. The three, one English, one German, one Japanese, seemed as beautiful as birds poised for flight at any moment from the immaculate concrete.

Perhaps I am having some sort of an attack, he thought with interest, a stroke, hemorrhage, tumor, epilepsy. But if something is wrong with me, how is it that I can see so clearly and calmly, that I do not cast forward or backward from myself, am here in the here-and-now, and know what I am going to do?

But for a fact he may well have had one of his spells, for when he looked up, Ewell McBee had vanished without a trace. Swallowed up by the thick opalescent cloud.

9

So here he was, the engineer, as Will Barrett used to think of himself in the early days when he wandered around in a funk in New York trying to "engineer" his own life, now years later, after a fairly normal life, a fairly happy marriage, a successful career, and a triumphant early retirement to enjoy the good things of life. Here he was, more funked out and nuttier than ever, having experienced another of his "spells" as they used to be called in his childhood, which were undoubtedly a form of epilepsy to say the least and perhaps a disorder a good deal more serious. Here he was, pacing up and down his room, sunk in thought, smiling from time to time, and once snapping his fingers softly like a man who has suddenly hit upon the solution to a difficult problem. And indeed he had, or thought he had. So intent was he in planning his new "experiment" that he had forgotten about lunch, about his daughter's impending wedding, about his guests downstairs and, for the moment at least, about his tryst with Kitty in the summerhouse. (Yet why did he look at his watch?)

The plan of action he had hatched would surely have seemed lunatic and laughable to the good folk of Linwood, or to any sensible person for that matter, if it were not fraught with dangerous, even fatal consequences. Though he had given up his peculiar preoccupation with the Jews—the Jews, it seemed, had not left North Carolina—he had conceived an even more outlandish scheme and now was making plans for putting it into action. It is one thing to labor under the delusion that all Jews had left North Carolina. It is something else to embark upon an adventure which would surely endanger his life.

What a shame he could not have relaxed and enjoyed life like his friends and neighbors in this, one of the pleasantest of all places. Good people they were by and large, business and professional men like himself who had worked hard, made money, raised families, been good citizens, and now were able to enjoy summer places or retire into condos and villas and savor the fruits of their labors. They walked in the woods ablaze with fall colors, played golf on a famous and sportive old links, went shopping for quilts or jellies or antiques, or simply sat about their patios having a sociable drink or two against a backdrop of Sourwood Mountain, gorges, and the faint blue hulk of the Great Smokies.

What a shame, considering his wealth and talents and general likableness, that he could not have enjoyed his life rather than raging at it, that he could not have gone on with his many charitable works as he had when his wife was alive.

Or, if he had no use for the company of ordinary retirees, there were more cultivated people available, classical-music-lovers, book readers, folk-music-lovers, serious bird-watchers, and the like. What indeed is wrong with listening to the Ninth Symphony, or discussing Erich Fromm with Lewis Peckham, and why did the prospect of spending time doing so make him groan aloud? No doubt Lewis Peckham and the doctors were right. Such negative feelings could only be symptomatic of a physical or nervous disorder.

No, instead of savoring the ordinary pleasures of leisure or gleaning the rewards of philanthropy or enjoying intellectual companionship, he must concoct one of the strangest schemes ever hit upon by the mind of man. He was right about one thing: it is doubtful if anyone had ever thought of it before.

And yet his "experiment" seemed to him the very model of logic, elegance, and simplicity. Such was his state of mind.

Ewell McBee, though an ornery unlettered covite despite his Jaymar Sansabelt slacks, a mountain man meaner than most, was right about one thing, he said to himself, pacing back and forth, setting fist softly into hand. He, Will Barrett, had learned over the years that if you listen carefully you can hear the truth from the unlikeliest sources, especially from the unlikeliest sources, from an enemy, from a stranger, from children, from nuts, from overheard conversations, from stupid preachers (certainly not from eloquent preachers!). When he used to go to church with Marion, he discovered that if you listen carefully to a dumb preacher, he will almost invariably and despite himself say something of value.

"As anyone can plainly see," said one dullard called in from Asheville by Jack Curl to pinch-hit, "all the signs of Armageddon are present." And in a droning voice he listed them, including the return of the Jews to Israel. On a beautiful Sunday morning in the mountains of North Carolina no one in the congregation paid the slightest attention—except Will Barrett, who, head slightly cocked to favor his good ear, had listened to every word—just as he had listened to Ewell McBee.

Are not great discoveries also made at the unlikeliest moments, such as listening to a droning preacher? His discovery had been made as Ewell McBee, towering over him in the garage, was going on and on about their childhood, about my daddy and your daddy, how much alike we are, and so forth. Ewell had given him the clue when he said how "smart" he, Will Barrett, was, smarter even than his daddy. "You don't say nothing, Will, you just lay back like you doing now, listening and thinking, like you going to make some great discovery."

What was the Great Discovery? We may as well say it right out. It dawned on him that his father's suicide was *wasted*. It availed nothing, proved nothing, solved nothing, posed no questions let alone answered questions, did nobody good. It was no more than an exit, a getting up and a going out, a closing of a door.

Most of all, it offended Will Barrett's sense of economy and proportion, of thrift, that so much, a life no less, could be spent with so little return. If one is going to do a dire thing, one may as well put it to dire practical use. In his Trusts and Estates law practice, he had learned that one often does well to attach huge conditions to huge bequests.

I will not waste mine, he thought, smiling.

Redneck Ewell was right, wasn't he? It was his, Will Barrett's, own sly way of "being smart," that is, of standing aside and keeping quiet, looking on, observing commonplace disaster which everyone else accepts as a matter of course, then figuring something out which converts a necessary evil to an ingenious good.

"You remind me of the fellow in charge of a garbage dump who discovered he could run his car on garbage," Ewell told him. "That way you do two things, get rid of the garbage and beat the Ayrabs—you like killing two birds with one stone, don't you?"

Yes. Again snapping his fingers softly, he sat down at his desk, a fine colonial pine piece his wife had given him and where he had never sat before. He smiled again. It was a pleasure to sit at a proper desk, take out stationery and pen, hatch out a plan, and write the necessary documents to bring it to pass.

The "documents" were two letters, one to Lewis Peckham, the other to Dr. Sutter Vaught.

Dear Lewis:

This letter is a simple precaution. When you receive it, you can destroy it without reading further, for I intend in fact to see you today before you receive this letter tomorrow.

I take the precaution upon your own advice. In our spelunking days you told me never to enter a cave alone without telling someone where I was going.

In a word I am accepting your invitation to visit you this afternoon and I shall walk down to your farmhouse via Lost Cove cave, entering by the upper Confederate "escape hole" you showed me when I sliced out-of-bounds and exiting at the main entrance near your house in the valley below. Though I am not familiar with the upper reaches of the cave, there is only one way to go, down, and I remember the lower part, the "commercial" cave, very well.

For one thing, I have a sudden hankering to visit the haunt of the saber-tooth tyger you discovered.

Mentioning the "tyger" lair is an essential part of the plan, he thought with a smile. First, it would tickle Lewis's literary fancy. Tyger Tyger and Lewis would have them off in a Blakean exploration of mythic depths. Second, and more important, it would establish a destination, a place in the vast, still not wholly explored, cavern.

The prospect of bourbon and Beethoven is irresistible.

This was the only lie in the letter. The prospect of having a tad of bourbon and branch water, as Lewis would say, and listening to Beethoven's Ninth Symphony was not only not irresistible, it was horrendous. The mere thought of it was enough to make him grimace and shiver like a bird dog with the squats.

If I haven't turned up by the time you receive this, send out the St. Bernard with a cask of Wild Turkey.

Take care,
Will

He addressed the envelope, licked the flap, sealed it, stamped it, felt and admired the heavy creamy embossed stationery, which Marion had given him and which he had never used. Why was it no longer possible to sit at a desk and write a proper letter like a character in an old-fashioned novel who as a matter of course might write any number of such letters to friends, members of family? If his daughter should receive such a letter from him, or he from her, each would faint.

It is only possible to write a letter now, he reflected, if it is part of a larger plan which could settle things once and for all, for himself, his daughter—and everyone else, for that matter.

The second letter was addressed, on a larger envelope, to Dr. Sutter Vaught, 2203 Los Flores Boulevard, Albuquerque, New Mexico.

Dear Sutter:

I have a favor to ask of you. One reason I ask you is that there is no one else I would trust to do it. Another reason is that the nature of the favor is such that, though somewhat burdensome, I am confident you will grant it.

Knowing you perhaps better than you think, I have reason to believe that aside from the urgency of my appeal it is the very strangeness of my request which will insure its being carried out.

You told me once that nowadays no one knew anything with sufficient certitude that he could tell anyone anything, and that if a man ever came along who really knew and could speak with authority—do this, do that—millions would follow him.

I tell you, not millions, to do this one thing for me. I do not ask you, I tell you: do this.

I am enclosing a stamped sealed envelope addressed to one Lewis Peckham of Linwood, North Carolina. Do this. After you receive this letter, wait three weeks. If by this time you have not heard to the contrary from me, proceed as follows: Come to Linwood, North Carolina. Go to the post office, fold and soil the letter to Lewis Peckham, and drop it in the mail slot marked "local." It will be assumed by the addressee that the letter was mislaid by a postal employee, dropped behind a radiator, kicked under a table, belatedly discovered, sneaked into the "local" bin by the guilty clerk, and so belatedly postmarked. It will be assumed by the postal authorities, should it come to this, that the letter was dropped inadvertently outside the post office, discovered, and mailed by some helpful soul.

After you do this, leave town immediately and say nothing of this to anyone.

Be assured that you are not being asked to become a party to a fraud or worse crime.

This is a good deal of trouble, I realize, to get from Albuquerque to Linwood, North Carolina, without a car, since you did not replace your Edsel, but I am confident that you will do it. Please believe me when I tell you that it is absolutely necessary that you do this, that you destroy this letter and that you never speak of this matter again.

Of course it may come to pass that you will hear from me before the deadline, in which case your mission is to be abandoned. In this event, I shall explain further.

Perhaps I owe you some explanation of this unusual request. I shall give you a partial one, at the risk of offending and alarming you. But at least you will see that no harm can come to anyone but me, and possibly not even to me, but that there is nothing you can do to prevent it in any case—and that a great good may come to many people.

If you do not hear from me in three weeks I shall be dead

by the time Lewis Peckham receives the letter you will mail in Linwood. There is nothing you can do to prevent this. In fact, the only chance of preventing it will depend upon your carrying out these instructions to the letter. If you will recall, I once performed a similar service for you.

The purpose of the delayed mailing is to make sure that my body will be found and found under such circumstances as to preclude suicide and the nonpayment of my life insurance.

Fraud is not involved—though a case for it would undoubtedly be made by the insurance company, since a payment of one million is involved. Under the law, life insurance must be paid in the event of death by natural causes, accidents, or acts of God. My death, if it occurs, shall occur not by my own hand but by the hand of God. Or rather the handlessness or inaction of God.

If I die, it will not be by my own hand but through the dereliction of another. It is not my intention to die but to live. Therefore, should I die, it will not be suicide.

This is what you might call the ultimate scientific experiment in contrast to dreary age-old philosophical and religious disputations which have no resolution. I say "ultimate" because God is the subject under investigation.

I aim to settle the question of God once and for all.

The Prudential Life Insurance Company quite properly did not pay me, the beneficiary of my father's policy, since he died by his own hand. I freely acknowledge this, even though I was sole beneficiary and could have used the money. Nevertheless I feel euchred out of that million. He paid for it and I could have used it. Without it, his death made no sense.

But in my case, if I die, it will be God or the absence of God which is responsible. Neither God nor the absence of God are listed as causes of death in my Prudential policy. Nor are they listed as the causes of suicide. Therefore the policy must be paid to my beneficiary, and my claim is not fraudulent.

The Rock will pay because the law requires it. The purpose of my request to you is to insure that the law not be circumvented.

It is not in your interest to know what I plan to do. Suffice it to say that for once in my life I know what is what, what I know, what I don't know, what needs to be done, and what I shall do. If you remember, it was your constant complaint that I was forever looking to you for "all the answers." However much you find yourself inconvenienced by this request, it should at least please you to know that I have at last understood you. One must arrive at one's own answers.

I may not know the answer, but I know the question. And I know how to put the question so that it must be answered. So certain am I of my own course of action that I do not require your approval. What I require from you is that you do what I say, and I charge you to do so on the pain of having my death on your conscience.

I will say only that the action I propose to take comes as a consequence of my belated recognition of my lifelong dependency on this or that person, like my father or yourself (who I supposed knew more than I did) or on this or that book or theory like Dr. Freud's (which I thought might hold the Great Secret of Life, as if there were such a thing). My equally belated discovery is the total failure, fecklessness, and assholedness of people in general and in particular just those people I had looked to. This includes you. Maybe you most of all—for it was you, it seemed to me—if you recall, I had good detection devices, excellent radar for knowing who knew what—it was you of all the pleasant prosperous gregarious denizens of our dear old Southland (to say nothing of the even more fucked-up remainder of the U.S.A.) who seemed to be on to something.

My father seemed to know what was what and ended up distributing his brain cells over the attic—after trying to take me with him.

Perhaps he was right. I aim to find out. I have found out how to find out.

You seemed to know what was what and you end up how? Marking time with the V.A. and watching M*A*S*H. Toward what end? So you can retire on your pension and watch the soaps all day?

Quite properly, you refused to give me any answers. Perhaps you didn't have any. It doesn't matter now. But I have a question and a way of asking it which requires an answer. A non-answer is not possible. But this does not concern you.

So much for you. My quarrel with the others can be summed up as a growing disgust with two classes of people. These two classes between them exhaust the class of people in general. That is to say, there are only two classes of people, the believers and the unbelievers. The only difficulty is deciding which is the more feckless.

My belated discovery of the bankruptcy of both classes has made it possible for me to take action. Better late than never.

Take Christians. I am surrounded by Christians. They are generally speaking a pleasant and agreeable lot, not noticeably different from other people—even though they, the Christians of the South, the U.S.A., the Western world have killed off more people in recent centuries than all other people put together. Yet I cannot be sure they don't have the truth. But if they have the truth, why is it the case that they are repellent precisely to the degree that they embrace and advertise that truth? One might even become a Christian if there were few if any Christians around. Have you ever lived in the midst of fifteen million Southern Baptists? (Of course you have. You're from Alabama.) No doubt the same might be said of Irish Catholics and Miami Jews. The main virtue of Episcopalians is their gift for reticence. Seldom can an Episcopalian (or an Anglican) be taken for a Christian. Perhaps that is what I like about them. A mystery: If the good news is true, why is not one pleased to hear it? And if the good news is true, why are its public proclaimers such assholes and the proclamation itself such a weary used-up thing?

If the good news is true, the God of the good news must be a very devious fellow indeed, fond of playing tricks.

But perhaps two can play at that game.

As unacceptable as believers are, unbelievers are even worse, not because of the unacceptability of unbelief but because of the nature of the unbelievers themselves who in the profession and practice of their unbelief are even greater assholes than the Christians.

The present-day unbeliever is a greater asshole than the present-day Christian because of the fatuity, blandness, incoherence, fakery, and fatheadedness of his unbelief. He is in fact an insane person. If God does in fact exist, the present-day unbeliever will no doubt be forgiven because of his manifest madness.

The present-day Christian is either half-assed, nominal, lukewarm, hypocritical, sinful, or, if fervent, generally offensive and fanatical. But he is not crazy.

The present-day unbeliever is crazy as well as being an asshole—which is why I say he is a bigger asshole than the

Christian because a crazy asshole is worse than a sane asshole.

The present-day unbeliever is crazy because he finds himself born into a world of endless wonders, having no notion how he got here, a world in which he eats, sleeps, shits, fucks, works, grows old, gets sick, and dies, and is quite content to have it so. Not once in his entire life does it cross his mind to say to himself that his situation is preposterous, that an explanation is due him and to demand such an explanation and to refuse to play out another act of the farce until an explanation is forthcoming. No, he takes his comfort and ease, plays along with the game, watches TV, drinks his drink, laughs, curses politicians, and now and again to relieve the boredom and the farce (of which he is dimly aware) goes off to war to shoot other people—for all the world as if his prostate were not growing cancerous, his arteries turning to chalk, his brain cells dying off by the millions, as if the worms were not going to have him in no time at all.

On the contrary. The more intelligent he is, the crazier he is and the bigger an asshole he is. He becomes a professor and forms an interdisciplinary group. He reads Dante for its mythic structure. He joins the A.C.L.U. and concerns himself with the freedom of the individual and does not once exercise his own freedom to inquire into how in God's name he should find himself in such a ludicrous situation as being born in Brooklyn, living in Manhattan, and being buried in Queens. He is as insane as a French intellectual.

It has taken me all these years to make the simplest discovery: that I am surrounded by two classes of maniacs. The first are the believers, who think they know the reason why we find ourselves in this ludicrous predicament yet act for all the world as if they don't. The second are the unbelievers, who don't know the reason and don't care if they don't.

The rest of my life, which will be short, shall be devoted to a search for the third alternative, a tertium quid—if there is one. If not, we are stuck with the two alternatives: (1) believers, who are intolerable, and (2) unbelievers who are insane.

I may be a member of the second class, the unbelievers, and no doubt an even greater asshole than they since they generally perform good works, help niggers, pore whites, etc., but at least I'm not crazy.

Unlike them I demand an explanation and at last have contrived a way of determining either what it is or that there is none.

For some time I had believed that the Jews were a sign, a clue to the mystery, a telltale bent twig, a blazed sapling in an otherwise riotous senseless jungle.

But now it appears the Jews may have not left North Carolina after all, and in fact are making porno flicks and building condos and villas in Highlands, enjoying the leaves, and in general behaving like everyone else. There goes the last sign.

Granted then that the situation is unacceptable, that both parties, the believers and unbelievers, are not only equally repulsive but also equally unpersuasive, what is one to do?

To the best of my knowledge, only one man in history ever made a practical proposal, that is, a proposal of which the rare sane unbeliever could at least make a modicum of sense. That was the famous wager of Pascal, who was the last French intellectual who was not insane. Though it has never been taken seriously, it does after all make sense. One makes the bet that God exists, though one doesn't know for sure. One could just as well bet that he does not exist. But it is better to bet that he does because if he does, the bettor wins and picks up all the marbles. If God does not exist, the bettor has lost nothing. He has everything to win and nothing to lose. If he bets against God, he has everything to lose and nothing to win.

But it is after all ludicrous to reduce the question to a crap-shoot at Vegas.

My father knew all about this, about believers and unbelievers and Pascal's bettor. What he said was I'm having no part of any of you. Excuse me but I won't have it. Good day, gentlemen.

That's one way. The trouble with Pascal's wager is its frivolity.

The trouble with my father's exit is that it yields no answers. It doesn't even ask a question.

I've discovered a better way, a more scientific method, in fact an experiment. If I'm going to spatter my brains around the Great Smokies, it will happen because my question was not answered, not because it wasn't asked. And I will not pull the trigger. And my beneficiary will be assured of receiving his million from Prudential.

There is an extra pleasure in killing two birds with one stone: solving the so-called mystery of life and beating the Rock at the same time.

My project is the first scientific experiment in history to settle once and for all the question of God's existence. As things presently stand, there may be signs of his existence but they point both ways and are therefore ambiguous and so prove nothing. For example, the wonders of the universe do not convince those most conversant with the wonders, the scientists themselves. Whether or not this testifies to the stupidity of scientists or to God's success at concealing himself doesn't matter.

The peculiar history of the Jews may be a sign but no one sees it as such except possibly the Jews themselves. But if the Jews have stayed in North Carolina (I must verify this) and not returned to Israel, their staying is no more a sign than the blacks leaving for the North or the blacks returning to the South.

But what if one should devise a situation in which one's death would occur if and only if God did not manifest himself, did not give a sign clearly and unambiguously, once and for all?

Would not the outcome of such an experiment be a clear yes or a clear no, with no maybes?

Unless I am mistaken, I've hit on the perfect, the definitive experiment—as definitive as the famous Michelson-Morley experiment which asked a question about the nature of space which could only be answered by a yes or a no, no maybes allowed.

We have had five thousand years of maybes and that is enough.

Can you discover a single flaw in this logic?

I've got him!

No more tricks!

No more *deus absconditus*!

Come out, come out, wherever you are, the game's over.

No, I do not mean to joke. What I am doing is asking God with the utmost respect to break his silence.

No, not asking. Requiring.

Didn't Jacob, a Jew, require an answer of God by hanging

on to him, rassling him until God got fed up with this Jew (what have I done to have picked out such a nagging stiff-necked people?) and gave him what he wanted. How odd of God to choose the Jews.

God no longer makes appearances as a rassler, but I have my own way of getting at him.

I shall do this by waiting him out.

My experiment is simply this: I shall go to a desert place and wait for God to give a sign. If no sign is forthcoming I shall die. But people will know why I died: because there is no sign. The cause of my death will be either his nonexistence or his refusal to manifest himself, which comes to the same thing as far as we are concerned. Only you know the nature of the experiment. I give you permission to publish the results in a scientific journal of your choice.

Will it not be a relief to all of mankind to have this dreary question settled once and for all, proved or disproved? Imagine! We shall no longer have to listen to preachers haranguing unbelievers about God's existence, and professors haranguing people about God's nonexistence and mythic structures?

For obvious reasons I cannot tell you where I am going to conduct this experiment. For if I did and the result was negative, you might spill the beans, mount a search, which would of course jeopardize the beneficiary's claim to the insurance.

Who is the beneficiary?

You are the beneficiary.

Does that surprise you?

Then it shall happen so: either you shall hear from me within three weeks or you shall not. If you do not hear, then I ask that you carry out the mission, make the trip to North Carolina, mail the soiled envelope at the Linwood post office.

If you do hear from me, I will at that time tell you the nature of the affirmative result of my experiment, that is, the nature of the sign I have received.

The reason I make you beneficiary is twofold. One, as you may have surmised, is to increase the incentive for your visit to North Carolina, whether you think I am crazy or not. For if the enclosed letter does not reach Lewis Peckham, my body will never be found and your insurance payment will be delayed seven years.

The other reason is that even if the answer to my little experiment is no, I wish you to continue the experiment and confirm it. Though I cannot enforce my request, I nevertheless make it and hope that you will continue the investigation, particularly since you will have the financial means of doing so and I expect you will also be interested.

To be specific: I wish you to monitor the demographic movement of Jews not only from North Carolina but from other states and other countries as well, to take note of any extraordinary changes which go contrary to established demographic patterns—such as the emigration of blacks from the South (and their present return). If, for example, there has occurred or should occur a massive exodus of Jews from the U.S. to Israel, I request that you establish an observation post in the village of Megiddo in the narrow waist of Israel (the site, as you may know, of ancient Armageddon), where a foe from the east would logically attempt to cut Israel in two. From this point you can monitor any unusual events in the Arab countries to the east, particularly the emergence of a leader of extraordinary abilities—another putative sign of the last days.

I can't see any reason why you can't just as easily live in the Israeli desert as the New Mexican.

Instead of watching TV docudramas, why not a ringside seat for the real thing?

I shall leave it to your best judgment how to evaluate such events and what action, if any, to take, e.g., whether to inform the media what is afoot. Though I am no great lover of mankind, I believe that people have the right to whatever information may help them to reach the right decision. If you had proof that Southern California would slide into the ocean next Tuesday, would you not at least put a notice in the L.A. *Times*?

Finally, I trust that none of these unusual requests will be necessary, not the delivery of the letter to North Carolina, not your removal to Megiddo, that instead you will receive a telephone call from me. A few days will tell the story.

Again: please destroy this letter after reading and digesting it.

Sincerely yours,
Will B. Barrett

Having finished this outlandish document, Will Barrett rose from his desk and paced up and down, hands deep in pockets, frowning, lips pursed, for all the world as if he were back in his

Wall Street office rehearsing an argument before a probate judge. But what a difference! What would Dr. Sutter Vaught make of this letter? Imagine Sutter in Albuquerque, picking up his mail, turning on Cronkite, flopping down in his recliner after a day's work with paraplegics in the V.A. hospital, opening his beer, then opening a letter which proposed first a trip by plane and bus to North Carolina (he had not owned a car since his Edsel gave out), then a permanent removal to a fleabitten village in Israel—to say nothing of the references to God's existence or nonexistence, Armageddon, and the appearance of the Antichrist during the Last Days!

Leaving aside what any psychiatrist—or any sensible person—would think of Barrett's preoccupation with God, Jews, Armageddon, and suchlike, one might nevertheless wonder how in fact Sutter would respond to this strange request: to journey to North Carolina and mail a soiled letter in the Linwood post office. The fact is that Will Barrett, crazy or not, might well have made a shrewd choice of a confidant. Even if Dr. Sutter Vaught thought he was as mad as a hatter, he would nevertheless very likely carry out the assignment, whether as a matter of curiosity and the simple oddness of it, or from a kind of quirky sense of obligation, or as an investment in the interesting role of beneficiary of a million-dollar life-insurance policy. Can a madman change his beneficiary? Who can say?

At any rate, Will Barrett suddenly bethought himself and, seating himself again at the desk, took up pen and added a postscript.

P.S. I wish there was a way to tell my daughter Leslie goodbye but there is not. Perhaps you will do it for me if it is necessary. If the result of the experiment is positive, then she and I will have found common ground. I will acknowledge her Lord. If not, and you do not hear from me, I ask you to choose a time at your convenience and convey this message to her: that even though she never seemed to need me, I am sorry I was such a rotten father. No doubt the fact that she never needed me sprang from her perception of my unavailability, coldness, shutoffness. These awful distances within a family—was it always so? But I've always been suspicious of the word "love," what with its gross abuse and overuse. There is no cheaper word. I can't say tell her I "love" her, because I don't really know what "love" means except as it applies to

178

one's feeling for children—and then it may only mean one's sense of responsibility for their terrible vulnerability, which they never asked for. One loves children, especially one's own, because there they are, through no doing of their own, born into the same low farce you and I are living but not knowing it yet, being in fact as happy as doodlebugs and you and I would do anything to keep them so. Wouldn't we? Is that love? Perhaps my experiment will shed some light that will be helpful to them later. But there is nothing I can say to her now. She is a Christian and the angriest person I know. When she was five years old and we were living in New York, she got hit by a car in Central Park. I thought she was going to die. She was in great pain. When she lay in her hospital bed she looked up at me and asked me, "Why?" "Why what?" I said, but I knew what she meant. I opened my mouth to say something, but there was nothing to say except that I didn't know why and that I would gladly have given my life to stop her from hurting, but she didn't want to hear that. I gnawed my arm at the prospect of her suffering. Is that love? Now when she finishes a Pentecostal service, she loves everybody with a swooning melting tearful smiling love which scares hell out of me. Is that love? Count me out.

Leslie will inherit a great deal of money. She hasn't needed me since she went to the Brearley School in New York. (Or is it that I imagined that I didn't need her?) But if my little experiment works out, I hope to find common ground with her, perhaps enough to share with her in her "love-and-faith community"—Jesus, why does this expression give me the creeps?

If not, tell her in your own words, that I love—tell her.

Moving quickly now, he folded the pages and inserted them with the letter to Lewis Peckham into the larger envelope, which he carefully sealed.

Opening a wall safe, he removed an insurance policy, read it, took down his old Harvard hornbook on Wills & Testaments, and wrote a letter to the Prudential Insurance Company requesting a change in beneficiary. He directed them to send the new policy to Dr. Sutter Vaught of Albuquerque, New Mexico.

So it was that Will Barrett went mad. His peculiar delusion and the strange pass it brought him to would be comical if it were not so perilous. This unfortunate man, long subject to "spells," "petty-mall" trances, and such minor disorders, had now gone properly crazy. This is how crazy he was. He had become convinced that the Last Days were at hand, that the world had fallen into the hands of the only species which knew how to destroy itself along with all other living creatures on earth, that whenever in history this species had invented a weapon, it had forthwith used it; that it was characteristic of this species that, through a perversity or an upsidedownness peculiar to it, while professing a love of peace and freedom and life, secretly it loved war and thralldom and death and loved them to a degree that it, the species, in these last days behaved like creatures possessed by demons; that the end would come by fire, a fire such as had not been seen in all of history until this century of demons, a fire which would consume the earth. The very persons who spoke most about "people's democracy" or "the freedom and sacredness of the individual" were most likely, he was convinced, to be possessed by demons.

Madness! Madness! Madness! Yet such was the nature of Will Barrett's peculiar delusion when he left his comfortable home atop a pleasant Carolina mountain and set forth on the strangest adventure of his life, descended into Lost Cove cave looking for proof of the existence of God and a sign of the apocalypse like some crackpot preacher in California.

VI

ALLISON SQUATTED IN THE SUNLIGHT ON THE CREEPER, A coil of rope slung over each shoulder, a double metal block in one hand, single in the other, which she hefted absently as she gazed up at the stove.

It was getting cold. A cirrus feather of ice crystals stood in six miles high from Canada. During the day she and the dog followed the sun to keep warm. At night she curled up in the NATO sleeping bag. How to heat the greenhouse? It was either move the stove or buy a new Peerless kerosene heater. But it offended her sense of thrift and propriety to waste the stove. And she didn't want to stink up the greenhouse. There was plenty of wood. Pine cones and dead chestnut from the forest and all manner of charred timber from the ruin. So the stove was the thing. Anyhow, she was a hoister, a mistress of mechanical advantage. And here was something to hoist. If she could hoist this monster of a Grand Crown stove, she could do anything in life.

But first count your money. Make your list, assemble your words, then visit the hardware store for blocks and tackle, wrenches, WD-40, plastic pipe and sleeves. Next, Washau Motors for creepers (she would need four, she figured, one for each foot of the Grand Crown).

It was only after she left the hardware store, coils of rope slung over each shoulder, plastic pipe tied in a surprisingly light bundle, backpack heavy with blocks, pulleys, hooks, and wrenches—she had all the words and got the things without pointing—and walked in the service entrance of Washau Motors, that she realized she had forgotten the most important word of all—no, not forgotten his name, had never had his name, never even thought of him as having a name. She had two names though, creeper and Jerry the parts man.

A mechanic was moving on a creeper under a car. It was only when he winked at her that she realized she had been watching him or rather watching the action of the creeper with its queer swiveling wheels.

She frowned and turned away, fell back to reconnoiter. How to get four creepers without the name of the creeper owner? It took a plan. She had one. She had a name, but she needed another. Next to a field of used cars she spied a husky young black man washing a Ford Galaxy on a rack. He wore a *Go Wolves* sweatshirt. She knew about the Wolves. She came up alongside him. He seemed pleasant and even deferred to her with a small courtesy, turning ever so slightly toward her as if he meant to share with her his hosing down the Galaxy.

"Do you play with the Wolves?"

"Yeah," he said, frowning. She perceived that he had second thoughts about his courtesy and decided to make up for it.

"Offense?"

He looked at the sky. "Cornerback."

"Are you going to win State?"

"You better believe it."

"I had better?"

"What?" he said heavily.

"Are you acting like somebody else?" she asked, eyeing him.

"What?" he asked quickly.

"Nothing. I hope you win."

"Why, thank you."

"What's the man's name here? I'm supposed to see him but I can't remember his name."

"The man?" He almost looked at her and almost smiled, trying, she saw, to figure out whether she was talking as she might imagine he talked. "You mean the boss or the owner?"

"The owner."

"Oh. Mister Barrett." Did she imagine it or was there a certain affection in his voice? Or was it a smiling indulgence?

"Right. John Barrett."

"No no. Will. Mister Will Barrett."

"Will Barrett."

Will Barrett. She repeated it to herself. How did the name go with him? How to take the name? She tried to locate him in the name. Was he a kind of Will Scarlet of the woods?

"What do you think of him?" This question, even she knew, was not suitable, but what did she have to lose? She needed to hear others speak of him.

"Of who? Mister Barrett? He nice as can be. He going to send me to Princeton"—he began but suddenly, taking thought, changed his mind and became chesty and huffy—"why you axing me?" His lip stuck out like Ludean's. "Like I told him, I already got six scholarship offers from the ACL prior to his."

Prior. She gazed at him curiously. Why did he flip-flop so fast, from courtesy to huffiness? "Why—" she began and fell silent. On the other hand, if you are curious, why not ask? Is there a law against asking? "Why are you pouting?"

"What's that?" He ducked his head toward her.

"Is it because your hands are cold and this is a poor job compared with a job inside as a mechanic or a salesman?"

"What? What you talking about, pouting?" He stared at her, open-mouthed. "Lady, what you talking about?"

"I was just wondering—"

"Lady, if you got any questions, ax inside."

"Very well. Thank you and good luck in the game."

"Sho," he said, nodding. "Have a nice day."

"I will. Goodbye." For some reason people had stopped saying goodbye. Very well.

Suddenly she noticed something. She could say goodbye! She wasn't afraid to state her business, say goodbye, and leave! She wasn't afraid of hurting feelings. No, her desire to please everybody had given way to an immense curiosity. What in the world made people so jumpy?

Jerry the parts man was sitting behind a counter reading a magazine named *Hustler*. She rapped. He looked up, frowning.

"Are you Jerry?"

"Yeah'm."

"I came by to pick up my creepers," she declared. She had no trouble making a flat declaration.

"What creepers?"

"Didn't Mr. Barrett call?"

"Oh yeah. You a friend of Mr. Barrett's?" His face had a new hooded expression. She frowned.

"Yes."

"Uh huh."

She was astounded. Was he leering at her? "I'll take four creepers," she said. *Don't give me that hustler look, you pimplehead, or I'll hustle you upside the head.* Why did she assemble these words, taking them not from the young black at the washrack but from Ludean the cook?

"He didn't mention four."

"I mentioned four. Call him. Tell him that will leave only ninety-six from the hundred you ordered by mistake."

"Yes ma'am."

While he stacked the creepers for her, she used the two nylon cords she'd already cut, one to lash the creepers together and lash the half-dozen lengths of ten-foot plastic pipe atop the creepers (the pipe as strong and light as weightless moon pipe), the other to tie to the bottom creeper as a pull cord.

Off she went down Church Street, backpack heavy with blocks, creepers rattling behind her, but feeling strong. Pavement lasted to the country club. Then: would the creepers creep on a dry golf links?

They did. But now as she surveyed stove and terrain, she had her doubts. There must be a better way than shoeing each foot of the Grand Crown with a creeper and dragging it over the littered ruin. She was a hoister, not a dragger.

The great stove had come out of the dark earth with a crack and a suck, roots popping. It reminded her of her father extracting a molar. The only trouble, requiring three false starts, came from knotting the sling properly and gauging the angle of pull in such a way as to clear the cellar stairwell with no more than a bump or two. A problem this and therefore a pleasure in the solving. But a pain also: the price of the rope. Figuring the weight of the stove at around eight hundred pounds—she could barely lift one corner as she reckoned she could barely lift a two-hundred-pound man—she calculated she needed an eight-to-one mechanical advantage. How to get it? with a tackle of one double block and one triple block! But there was another calculation: lifting the stove twenty-five feet would require not twenty-five but 5 times 25 equals 125 feet of rope! She settled on a half-inch W.P.S. nylon (mfg. in Madison, Georgia) at 35¢ @ foot, break strength 5,500 lbs. $42.75!!! The blocks were even worse; 2 simple pulleys @ $4.87 (for making a single block and tackle for smaller loads), 2 Wichita Falls steel double blocks @ $29.52, 1 triple block @ $43.71! Her cash reserve was devastated. She counted her money: $171.77—and she still had to buy plastic pipe and sleeves, stove polish, Brasso, and her meager groceries. But what blocks! Smooth satiny metal good for years of hoisting. And what a rope! Even as the blocks closed above her and the great ungainly molar of a stove popped out of its socket, the tackle running so smoothly through the blocks that she could pull with one hand, the tail of the rope lay loosely in her other hand as limber, supple, and heavy as a snake. There was always use for such a rope! In fact: why not rig a line from one chimney to the lonesome pine by the greenhouse, hang the stove on a pulley, and let it down the gentle slope like a trolley? Okay, except that, with her feel for angles and hefts, she gauged the distance from near chimney to greenhouse: yes, she could stretch the rope with the block and tackle as tight as you please, tighter than barbed wire, the break strength of the rope would stand it, but not the chimney. Her eye told her this. To clear the rubble and laurel and to allow for the down drag of the stove, she'd have to rig the rope high on the blackened chimney. The mortar mightn't hold. She couldn't take the chance.

Double half-hitching the tail around a stump of laurel, she covered the cellar hole with shards of stout two-by-six lumber and let the stove down.

Now that it was landed and only now did she give herself leave to take a good look at it.

What a stove! It was a castle of a stove, a rambling palace of a stove, a cathedral of a stove, with spires and turrets and battlements. A good six feet high and eight feet wide, it was made of heavily nickeled iron castings bolted together. Timidly she rubbed the metal with one finger. It was dirty but not rusty. Panels of porcelain enamel, turquoise blue for the oven doors and the four warming closets, little balconies jutting out head-high, snowy white for the splashback, were fused to heavy cast iron between frames of nickel. Bolted on one side was a nickel-iron box lined with heavy copper and fitted with a spigot. A water reservoir! On the other side, the firebox with a bay window of a door glazed with panes of mica, some crazed, some crystallized, but all intact. She opened the fire door. Inside was a grate, barely used to judge from the blacking, evidently a coal graté with four sides curling up like heavy petals, but observe: the end grates were attached by a single bolt and easily removable to accommodate logs, three-foot logs! Behind the firebox and attached by a short drawbridge loomed a squat Romanesque tower, yet another heater, it seemed, crowned by a nickeled dome, a great urn top fitted in turn with an ornamental temperature indicator (unbroken!). What was this? a newfangled 1899 water heater? (No, there was the copper reservoir which heated from the firebox.) A separate coal heater for sticking through kitchen wall into dining room? With a flue arrangement served by the main firebox so that, except in very cold weather, the two rooms could be heated from the firebox? She would see.

An hour she allowed herself and the dog to inspect her treasure in the sunlight, enough time to make sure it was in one piece and not only not rusted but, under the soot and grease and ashes, new. It must have been purchased shortly before the house burned, the super-stove of the nineteenth century, installed in the huge kitchen where during the fire it had the good fortune to settle early through the burning joists and into the cooled damped-down cellar where fire wouldn't burn. A great eighty-five-year-old brand-new stove! Tut can keep his gold mummy case.

Carefully, as the sunlight came full in her face, bejeweling her eyelashes, she sprayed the bolt on the coal grate with WD-40 and attached the two crescent wrenches (10″ Fullers, $7.95 each!). The nut held tight, but WD-40 seeped between metal. She wedged the inside wrench and took the outside in her strong boy's hands: no way for you to go, friend, but around. It went.

A decision must be made. If the Grand Crown could not be dragged or hoisted, how to get it to the greenhouse? Piece by piece, and why not, since she had to dismantle it anyway to get it into the potting room? Then I will, disassemble it piece by piece, clean and oil each bolt, polish the nickel, black the iron, wipe porcelain with a clean cloth. Then rebuild it in the potting room against the partition of double-hung sashes, open one to admit the drawbridge and connect the urn of a tower in the greenhouse proper—enough to keep the frost off her greens?

Screwed to the front, extending the length of the reservoir, oven and firebox, was what she could only think to be a towel rack, a heavy nickeled bar begrimed by grease and ash. No, not a rack for towels but for a wet wash on a rainy day! Unscrewing a can of Brasso ($2.05), which had an efficacious stink of ammonia and sulfur cream, she dabbed a clean rag (from a 1910 shirtwaist?) and scrubbed a length of bar. Under her hand the nickel winked in the sunlight like the sterling Ludean polished in the pantry on Saturday mornings.

She wrote in her notebook. For tomorrow: find rest of flue pipe in cellar. End of week: fit plastic pipe with sleeves and two elbows (one elbow under waterfall, other elbow over reservoir), string through laurels from waterfall to potting room (figure how to get pipe in without breaking a window: use hole in peak?). Slope is enough to permit a gravity flow yet gentle enough to rig a wire lift to stop flow: up equals stop, down equals flow.

The sun sank behind the pines. It must be four o'clock. Her back was cold. The dog stuck his muzzle under her knee. Let's start moving inside, she said to dog and stove. Working fast now with her wrenches, she unbolted the reservoir. The copper-and-iron box weighed as much as she but she didn't need hoist or creeper. She walked it, handling it downhill from corner to corner like the porter moving a steamer trunk from this very house. At the greenhouse porch she got it up (a hoist was too much trouble) and onto the creeper and zip, along silky cement to potting room. She eyed the sashes of the partition. Would the stove fit? Assuredly. The sashes worked. Better move stove from bottom up. Start with great nickel claw-and-ball feet, clean, reassemble, bolt to base, and build castle thereon stone by stone.

But, first, lay the Grand Crown over on its back, gently, using the block and tackle to pull it over and braking its fall with the half-inch nylon rappeled around the lonesome pine.

She looked at the sky. She figured she had a week.

VII

THE NEXT TWO HOURS PASSED AS SWIFTLY AS IF HIS SECRETARY, Miss Nabors, had walked into his Wall Street office and given him his appointment calendar.

After dressing in jeans, T-shirt, windbreaker, and tennis shoes, he went into the bathroom and emptied a bottle of Placidyl capsules into his hand, two handsful, one for each pants pocket—it was Vance Battle's prescription for his insomnia but he discovered he preferred lying awake—wrapped the empty bottle in toilet paper, crushed it with the Greener stock, flushed shards and paper. The plastic top wouldn't flush, so he opened a window and shied it into the gorge.

I could use about forty-eight hours' sleep, he thought. Then I'll be ready to wait and watch and listen. Then I'll take another little nap. And so on, until—

Sticking the flashlight in his hip pocket under the windbreaker, he scooped up envelopes, went out into the hall and down the back stairs to the garage, got into his Mercedes, and drove to town.

He bought four fresh alkaline batteries for his flashlight, a roll of aluminum foil, a manila envelope, visited the post office, where he bought stamps from Mrs. Guthrie and had a conversation about the fog. You look like you're going fishing, said Mrs. Guthrie.

He was surprised. Fishing? Yes, something like that, he said. A fishing trip. She would report the conversation later, it and his cheerfulness.

Another thirty minutes and the envelope had been stamped

188

and dropped in the slot, the Mercedes parked behind the bus station, and he was walking down the middle of number-fifteen fairway of the back eighteen.

The fog surrounded him. A hole in the cloud traveled with him. As he walked, the hole seemed to be still while the earth turned under him. Though he could not see the rough on either side, there was never a moment when he did not know exactly where he was. By dead reckoning he came onto number-seventeen tee, which loomed suddenly in the cloud like an Indian mound. The golf links was like his own soul's terrain. Every inch of it was a place where he had been before. He knew it like a lover knows his beloved's body. It was possible without looking to know that one particular spot on the tee, a patch of grass near the right blue marker, would be harder used than the rest, have more scuff marks, broken tees, tee holes, because the fairway doglegged to the left, so drivers teed up as far to the right as they could. He stopped and leaned over. It was even possible, he noted without surprise, to identify the exact spot, a tuft of grass with a bare spot behind it shaped like Arkansas, where he had teed up three days ago.

He walked straight to a pine tree near the edge of the rough. The trunk was bent into a flattened S. There had been a tournament over the weekend. Golf balls had bombarded the tree. Chips of bark littered the grass at the base.

The shell of a cicada hard as a gold bug had been clamped to the tree for three years. His fingers felt the slit in the shell where the creature had escaped.

It seemed to grow colder. Something else was different. Perhaps it was the silence that pressed into his ears. He looked at his watch. It was five o'clock.

It was only at this moment that he remembered his tryst in the summerhouse with Kitty. It was enough to bring him up short, but after shaking his head and smiling at it—perceiving, let us admit it, a mild pang of regret in the groin—he was on his way again. Who knows, he thought smiling, in one week, two weeks, I may be sitting with Kitty in the summerhouse enjoying the fall sunshine. Kitty's ass will keep for two weeks or for eternity.

Without further ado he walked quickly to the out-of-bounds fence, straddled it (no more ducking through), then moving more slowly, sidling through briars and laurel, came straight to the sassafras no larger than a shrub growing at the base of the ridge.

It had fewer leaves now and they were more speckled. He picked a small one shaped not like a three-fingered hand but like a mitt with a thumb. As he sucked the stem, air stirred against his cheek. It was not cooler or warmer than the cloud but different. The cloud smelled of complex leaf rots, bark tannin, and funky anise from the gorge. The cave air was simpler. It had a wet metal culvert smell. He opened his mouth. Clean ferrous ions blew onto his tongue.

Pushing aside a branch of sassafras, he stepped into an inconsequential niche of rock which would have appeared as no more than a lichened recess even without the sassafras, then squeezed sideways through a crack (the Confederates were thinner, even, than he), in the same movement turning past a lip of rock as easily as stepping into the jogged entrance of a fun house, and was in the cave. It pleased him that the great cave should have such a banal entrance. Far below in the valley at the proper entrance to Lost Cove cave an underground river flowed into the sunlight through a cathedral arch of stone.

You disappeared, one second standing in a lichened niche, then a little jog and into the cave. Lewis Peckham said the entrance was too neat and therefore probably man-made or at least man-shaped, by the Confederates as an escape hole in case they got hemmed up below.

Down, down he crawled, letting himself feet first down a rockslide, first prone then supine because he needed the flashlight. There was no way, he figured, to go wrong going down. He wished for a miner's head lamp and, thinking of it, seemed to catch a whiff of acetylene. The slide leveled gradually and entered a crawl. Dry rock gave way to wet clay. The crawl was longer than he remembered, a good hundred yards. There were places where the ceiling came so close to the floor that he had to turn his head sideways like a baby getting through a pelvis. Progress could only be made by a slow scissors kick and rowing with his elbows. Once he got stuck. The mountain pressed on his back.

When the crawl opened suddenly into a chamber the size of a small theater, he stood and walked across as quickly as a man going to work, crossed the lobby of his office building, mounted a shelf of rock which fell away into another slide, longer but not as steep as the first. It was possible to go down standing, using the light and choosing his footing carefully. There was pleasure in planning each step, calculating distance and angle of rock and using his weight either to fetch up or to carry him onto the next step. It was not hard work but when he reached the stream at the bottom he was sweating. There was a curving beach of gravel. As he played the light into the clear shallow water, it was easy to imagine that it was a tidal rivulet. There were minnows. Perhaps they were blind. But when he shone the light up, it showed a glittering lopsided vault, one side sloping steeply to join a cliff across the stream. The glitter, he saw, came from needles of stone, each holding a drop of water.

Beyond a promontory crouched the three nuns, humpy becowled stalagmites. When the cave was open to tourists, there was a blue floodlight behind the nuns. Lewis said that what people liked was not nature but likenesses in nature. Rather than see stalagmites, they would rather see stalagmites that looked a little like nuns. There were also formations called the Old Man of the Mountain, and Honest Abe, and Marse Robert.

It took another hour to find the chimney. It began, he remembered, as a sort of flue above a tilted slab of a boulder. But there were many such slabs. Twice he passed the entrance to the lair where Lewis had found the tiger, but did not bother to enter. It was the chimney he was looking for. When he found it, the opening was higher than he remembered. Before he went up, he made sure to leave footprints of heavy wet clay in plain view on the rock. It took both hands to jump straight up into the dark and catch hold and double over onto a shelf of rock. The chimney was directly above, a rough skewed cylinder a yard or so wide. With each step up he had to wedge himself like a chimney sweep to free one hand and use the light to plan the next step. Could this have been another Confederate beaver hole to escape the blue tide? No, because at its top it opened not up and to the outside but to one side and into a small curiously shaped chamber elongated in one dimension but rounded top and bottom like a pod. Tiger bones had been found here too. A knob of rock the size of a hassock rose from the stone floor at the smaller blind end of the pod. It looked a little like the great flattened head of a tiger. One could even imagine the lip of bone on each side where the massive jaw muscle attached. Could the tiger's skull have fused into rock over the years, dripped on by jeweled drops and turned calcareous and huge? But no, it was a rock shaped vaguely like a tiger's skull, enough to allow the cave operator to call it the Sleeping Tiger. Lewis said the tiger had died here thirty-two thousand years ago.

Water dripped on one side of the chamber and filled a saucer of stone. Good! It would be uncomfortable and unnecessary to die of thirst. It was quite comfortable sitting against the curving wall. Head high, he found a dry alcove for the flashlight. Next to it he stood the four fresh batteries. Emptying his pockets of Placidyl capsules, he carefully lined them up on the floor and counted them. Ninety-six. The roll of aluminum foil fitted on the shelf. He could piss down the chimney but feces must be deposited on a square of foil, packaged, and put away, else he'd foul his own den. What had the tiger done?

He smiled. Here I am, he thought, folding his arms and nodding and smiling. Now. Now we'll see.

Who else but a madman could sit in a pod of rock under a thousand feet of mountain and feel better than he had felt in years, feel so good that he smiled again and snapped his fingers as if he had made a discovery? I've got you both, he said aloud, God-seekers and suicides, I've got you all, God, Jews, Christians, unbelievers, Romans, Jutes, Angles, Saxons, Yankees, rebs, blacks, tigers. At last at last at last. It took me a lifetime, but I've got you by the short hairs now. One of you has to cough it up. There is no way I cannot find out.

Even if worst comes to worst, he thought with a smile, to suicide, it will turn out well. My suicide will represent progress in the history of suicide. Unlike my father's, it will be done in good faith, logically, neatly, and unobtrusively, unobtrusive even to the Prudential Insurance Company. Moreover, I shall arrange to be found.

What is more, it will advance knowledge.

His plan was simple: wait. The elegance of it pleased him. As cheerfully as a puttering scientist who hits on a simple, elegant experiment which will, must, yield a clear yes or no, he set about his calculations. The trick was to devise a single wait which would force one of two answers, not more, not less. If a yes, then to be able to leave and act on the yes. If a no, then to act on the no and at the same time euchre the Prudential Insurance Company out of the money he felt coming to him, to leave Sutter one million richer, and so to be found with the Placidyl gone from the floor of the cave but gone also from his blood. Lewis would find him eventually—

—Ah, to make doubly sure, drop a note down the chimney. He did: *Help!* he wrote. *With tiger, fifty feet above.* He frowned. That's confusing. They might not know which tiger. He wrote another note. *I'm fifty feet above this place and can't move. I think I've had a small stroke or an arterial spasm.*

Vance Battle had told him about arterial spasms. They could mimic a stroke yet an autopsy would show nothing.

The second note he folded and dropped down the shaft.

Ninety-six capsules. Three a day could give him tranquillity for thirty-two days. Then he'd be too weak to move anyhow and yet live long enough to get rid of the drug.

This way everybody wins. God, if he exists, is not affronted. If he doesn't, Sutter gets the one million.

There will be plenty of time for asking God—that is called prayer!—between knockout drops. I am no hero! to sit here for a month and starve without a drug is too much of a bore to consider.

Speak, God, or be silent. And if you're silent, I'll understand that.

O ye mystics who go out in the desert and see visions, o ye old men who dream dreams, who believes you?

O ye suicides who go not so gently into that good nothing, you can't tell me either. But I've beat you both. In either case I'll know.

Speak, God, and let me know if the Jews are a sing and the Last Days are at hand.

If the Last Days are at hand, one shall know what to do. I shall go to Megiddo with Sutter and wait for the Stranger from the East.

If you do not speak and the Jews are not a sign, then that too is an answer of sorts. It means that what is at hand are not the Last Days but only the last days, my last days, a minor event, to be sure, but an event of importance to me.

2

Unfortunately for the poor man awaiting the Last Days and raving away at God and man in the bowels of Sourwood Mountain directly below thousands of normal folk playing golf and antiquing and barbecuing and simply enjoying the fall colors—for on the following day at the height of his lunacy the cloud blew away and the beautiful days of Indian summer began, the mountains glowed like rubies and amethysts, and leafers were out in force—unfortunately things can go wrong with an experiment most carefully designed by a sane scientist. A clear yes or no answer may not be forthcoming, after all. The answer may be a muddy maybe. In the case of Will Barrett, what went wrong could hardly be traced to God or man, Jews or whomever, but rather to a cause at once humiliating and comical: a toothache. So in the end not only did he not get a clear answer to his peculiar question, not a yes or a no or even a maybe—he could not even ask the question. How does one ask a question, either a profound question or a lunatic question, with such a pain in an upper canine that every heartbeat feels like a hot ice pick shoved straight up into the brain? The toothache was so bad it made him sick. He vomited.

There is one sure cure for cosmic explorations, grandiose ideas about God, man, death, suicide, and such—and that is nausea. I defy a man afflicted with nausea to give a single thought to these vast subjects. A nauseated man is a sober man. A nauseated man is a disinterested man.

What does a nauseated person care about the Last Days?

Whether it was God's doing or ordinary mortal frailty, one cannot be sure. What happened in any event, happened after seven or eight days.

It began well enough.

He swallowed three capsules. A complex comfort took root in his stomach and flowed along his spine and into his throat. A simple chemical taste, both bitter and reassuring, rose at the back of his tongue. He fancied it was the taste of the cave. He lay down happily in a hollow of rock and closed his eyes.

Now came a different taste and smell. The smell of a warm Negro cabin in the winter, the walls papered by layers of the rotogravure section of the *Atlanta Constitution* thick as quilt and everywhere the close clean smell of coal oil and cornbread and Octagon soap. When he had knocked, the woman had come to the screen door and looked at the blood on his face. She opened the door without a word. The boy John Washington whom his father had cursed was standing behind her, his eyes so big that white showed all around his irises.

Will Barrett, feeling the same dead calm and certainty he had felt when he knelt beside the man:

"I need some help. My father has been hurt in an accident. I would appreciate it, Mrs. Washington, if you would send your son John to get the sheriff."

The woman's steady eyes flicked only once as he spoke. Not taking her eyes from him when he finished, she told the boy: "John, you go get High Sheriff Thompson," and to him after John took off: "You come on over here, boy, and I'll wash your face." He, following her and thinking of nothing in particular except the smell of newspaper and coal oil. "You gon be all right." On his cheek he felt the wet rag in gentle but firm wipes like his mother washing his face.

Thirty-two thousand years ago the tiger had come here to die. Why? Had he grown old and lain down in darkness? Had she come here wounded or to whelp and died instead?

Thirty-one thousand nine hundred years later, some country boys dressed in butternut found a good place to make gunpowder, in Lost Cove and in the very cave where the saltpeter was mined.

"They gon find us in here sure'n hell."

"No, they ain't," said the sergeant.

"I heard they was coming up the valley."

"Let them come. We got the magazine mined. They can come right on and get their asses blown back to New York."

"Then how we gon get out?"

"I know another way out," said the sergeant, who didn't seem to care much one way or the other beyond a flicker of pleasure in having it both ways, escaping from the intruders and blowing up the same intruders.

He became his father. He was walking down Sunset Boulevard. Here came Chester Morris in a blue Packard convertible. He was wearing a straw katy.

After that, Ross Alexander killed himself.

After that, he was standing smiling and nodding in Lower Pyne at Princeton, his hands thrust in his pockets in a certain way.

Lindbergh shook hands with his grandfather and Eddie Stinson at the airport.

Bobby Jones and Richard Halliburton and Johnny Mercer and Johnny Mack Brown came to dinner. D'Lo served Bobby Jones from the wrong side but Jones, a gentleman, didn't let on that anything was wrong.

What are you doing down here in the cold cold ground, massa?

I don't know, D'Lo. He turned to his father. What am I doing down here under the earth with you, old mole?

Because there is no other place for you.

The hell there isn't.

Name one.

Atlanta?

No.

San Francisco?

No.

New Orleans?

No.

Santa Fe?

No.

Back home?

No.

Linwood in the beautiful fall?

No.

Israel?

No.

Portofino?

No.

La Jolla?

No.

Aix?

No.

Nantucket?

No.

Georgia?

No.

What's wrong with these places?

They're all closed down.

There must be a place.

After the Spring Regatta picnic at the Northport Beach Club and during the award ceremony when he received his cup, walking up to get it, feet toed in, pants high and dry, right shoulder moving forward with right foot as if he had lived in Long Island all his life, he had caught the eye of Martha Stookey, only daughter and only offspring of Bryan A. Stookey, who owned Stookey Tidewater, which leased a fair portion of the continental shelf and whose business the firm had been after for years. The Lester Lanin orchestra was playing in the pavilion, but nobody was dancing. Martha, who was not good-looking to begin with, had made a mistake. She had come dressed for a tea dance or maybe a garden party. She wore a big round off-the-face hat. Everyone else wore sports clothes or swimsuits.

Even in the shadow of the hat, he could see that her face was blotched with unhappiness.

Why did God make ugly girls? It is hard to say. That was God's affair. But one thing he, Will Barrett, could do was make ugly girls happy. Then was that why God made ugly girls? So that selfish people like Will Barrett could make them happy and feel less selfish, do two things at once? No, three things. Make money too.

He asked her to dance. Her hand, when he took it, was cold and trembling. She was a good dancer. Other people began to dance. He enjoyed dancing with her. She smiled. She was not ugly.

Old man Peabody was looking at him. The look said: That's my boy.

Later, when the firm got the Tidewater business, Mr. Peabody said to him: "I'm putting you in charge of Trusts and Testaments. That includes widows and green goods."

The man found him sitting at a table on a little peninsula in a lake in the lobby of the Peachtree Plaza hotel. The lobby was a hundred feet high. Vines as big as snakes grew up and grew down like lianas. A waterfall fell a hundred feet. He was waiting for the first session of an ecumenical council on race relations. When he moved to Carolina, he thought for a while it would be a good idea to help out the South "in the area of race relations."

The man, who looked something like him except that he had a mustache and wore a white linen suit with vest, shook his hand and made a grimace. He was an Atlanta lawyer.

"Well, the jury found you guilty as charged."

"Guilty of what?" Jesus, they found me out. Guilty!

"Oh, you know. Pandering and whorishness in the practice of law. But don't feel bad."

"Why not?"

"It's only for a year and at a minimal security place in Arizona. A very pleasant place, they tell me. Here's your bus ticket."

As he entered the gate of the correctional facility, which was nestled in the desert foothills under the Ghost Range, he met John Ehrlichman coming out.

"What was it like, John?"

"Not bad, though there is no substitute for freedom. I had a clean cell, good food. My job was to read the dials in the boiler room from midnight to six. I wrote a book."

"It sounds like a good place. You're looking fine, John."

"You don't, Will. What have you been doing?"

"I was sitting in the lobby of the Peachtree Plaza hotel when—"

"That's amazing. It just so happens that I am on my way to the Peachtree Plaza, where I am going to push my book at a meeting of American Booksellers."

"Good luck, John."

"That's the way it goes. But this is not a bad place."

Ehrlichman was right. It was not a bad place.

Roosevelt was elected shortly after he was born. Roosevelt grinned. Roosevelt was elected again. Roosevelt grinned. Roosevelt was elected again. Will Barrett had never known another President. He was sick of Roosevelt's grin.

Years passed. He woke many times. The cave was companionable. The living rock was warm and dry. There were times when the ceiling of the cave seemed to open to the sky. As he gazed up, the darkness turned bright. Yet he always knew this couldn't be so. He smiled at himself.

The war came. His father was happy. Most people seemed happy. Fifty million people were killed. People dreamed of peace. Peace came. His father became unhappy. Most people seemed unhappy.

The boy lay prone in the Georgia swamp, watchful and silent, unwounded cheek pressed against the ground, the Sterlingworth shotgun cradled in his arms. Ground fog lay straight as milk, filling the hollows between the pin oaks.

So this is how it is, the boy thought, grim and exultant. This is one of the secrets nobody tells you. There are two secrets to life nobody tells you: screwing and dying. What they tell you about is love and the hereafter. Maybe they are right. But it is screwing and dying you have to deal with. What they don't tell you is how good screwing is and how bad it is to grow old, get sick, and die. Very well.

He and his daughter Leslie were going home after Marion's funeral. Yamaiuchi drove the Rolls. The back of his head was as sleek as a seal. He looked like Sammy Lee, the small muscular Olympic diver. Will Barrett was watching the bare winter woods. Why do woods have a certain look after funerals? He and Marion had gazed at dozens of woods after dozens of funerals in North Carolina. He remembered going home after his father's funeral. When the limousine stopped at the railroad crossing on Theobald Street, a nondescript place he had passed a hundred times walking home from school, he noticed that this place had a different look, an air of suspension, of pause and hiatus, like the policeman at the cemetery who stood still in front of the stopped traffic. This was the same place where he had thought about Ethel Rosenblum and fallen down.

Leslie's granny glasses clashed as she folded the stems. Clearing her throat, she turned toward him. She crossed her legs. The panty hose whispered. Her face with its hazed eyes and thin handsome lips had the expression of Barbara Stanwyck in that part of the movie where she tells everybody off.

"Let me tell you something, Poppy."

"Okay." It is evident that she is not only going to tell me something but also tell me off in that sense in which some people conceive it to be an act of courage to ignore convention and usage and get it all up front as the saying goes (God, I hope she doesn't say, let's let it all hang out).

"Poppy, let me say this."

"Okay."

"You and Mom—God knows I love you both, but you blew it. You both blew it."

"We did?"

"You better believe it. You both blew it."

"How's that?"

"Neither of you was ever honest with the other—or with yourself."

"How's that?"

"Not once in your entire married life were you and Mom ever honest with each other. Yet I am grateful to you because I have learned from it."

"How's that?"

"You should at least have admitted to each other what your marriage was based on. Then who knows, something might have come out of it, something creative. I've discovered that the hard way: lying to yourself makes it impossible to be creative in a relationship."

"How were we dishonest?"

"You never once admitted to each other or to yourselves why you married."

"Why did we marry?"

"You married Mom to get the Peabody fortune. Mom married you—I would like to say you were a catch and I guess you were—mainly to get married. Now that's not a bad basis for a relationship—the French have been doing it for years—as long as you admit it. Mom could not conceive the future without marriage. Fortunately times have changed."

"I see."

"Jason and I level. We believe that only if people level is there a chance of a relationship."

"I see."

What he saw was Marion holding his hand, laughing and running, half dragged, up the slope from the rocky beach, her gray eyes under the wide unplucked brows full on him, never leaving him, and he: he with the sweet pang at his heart—pang for what? for the pleasure she took in him? for the pleasure he took in giving her pleasure? for the vulnerability of her which he vowed to protect? her: gawky, ungood-looking (Waal now, Will, she ain't exactly a queen, is she? his fraternity brothers might say) yet handsome and direct through the eyes and mouth. Or was it the bittersweetness of the sudden bargain he struck with himself during this very run up the slope, that he would marry her not because she was rich and decent and he could make her happy, but because his life had come to such a pass that he could at least do this, take an action just for the mystery of it, an action which couldn't be bad and might even be a great good. Why not marry her? Mightn't one as well marry as not marry?

"Poppy, with all due respect to you and Mom, I've got to have something better. I've got to have something better in the way of relationships and I've got to have something better in the way of a genuine faith community. Mom lived by ritual. You live by—what do you live by, Poppy?"

"Ah, I'm not sure."

"Well, I know what I live by and I want to thank you and Mom for giving me what you did and for making it possible for me to learn, to learn to level with myself and others."

"Ah, you're welcome."

Once he saw the tiger traveling the highways and byways. But perhaps it was only one of the little explosions of light and color which now and then lit up the fragments of road map, bits of highway, crossroad, dots of towns which drifted across his retina. In the gray watery world, anyhow, no one seemed to notice the tiger. Very well, he thought, neither shall I.

In New York, below Columbus Circle, on the platform of the downtown Eighth Avenue Express, hundreds of people stood waiting. Each wore a kind of hood not like a hangman's hood but lopped over at the peak.

He woke. The tiger was there, standing in the opening. There was nothing bright or fearful or symmetrical about him. His eyes were lackluster and did not burn. His coat was not thrifty. His muzzle looked more like a snout. Otherwise, there was nothing notable about him. He was as commonplace as the tiger in the picture book the child recognizes and points to. "Tiger," says the child. The tiger's head turned this way and that. He swayed as he stood. He was too tired even to unlock his legs and let himself lie down. It was clear he had come to die.

Without fear or even curiosity he watched as the beast lay down heavily, its bones knocking against rock.

Later when he happened to touch the tiger beside him, which was either dead or dying, he noticed without surprise that the fur and skin had grown as hard as rhinoceros hide.

That's unusual, he thought. Moreover, there had been an unusual expression through the eyes of the tiger before he lay down. The eyes were careworn and self-conscious. He felt toward the tiger as he often felt toward the patients at St. Mark's. Haven't you troubled yourself and fretted needlessly over the years? Did you ever really know your times and seasons? What a mystery that you should have come here without knowing! Were you ever really a splendid tiger burning in the forests of the night?

A dry rustle came from the dead tiger like wasps in a gourd. Something was stirring in the carapace of this beast. Perhaps it is a female tiger lying down to whelp. No, this was an old male tiger, a friendly senile child's-picture-book tiger. It was a death rattle.

As he absently explored the beast, hide now hardened and chitinous as a locust, his hand felt along the spine as if it were looking for the slit where the creature escaped. There was no slit, but the skin had loosened in preparation for the molt.

Molt? Tigers don't molt. Be logical. It can be figured out. Very well. Whatever is alive here is more than a dying tiger. Yet it is not a tiger giving birth or a tiger molting and being transformed like a cicada. It is the same tiger but different.

He watched curiously until he saw the joke. Then he grew sleepy and lay down beside the beast.

The joke was that for the first time in the history of the universe it was the man who knew who he was, who was as snug as a bug in his rock cocoon, and the beast who did not, who was fretful, unsure of himself and the future, unsure what he was doing here. The tiger asked: Is this the place for me? Will I be happy here? Will the others like me? Will my death be a growth experience?

But how can you be dead and grow? Dead is dead.

The man laughed, took three more pills, scooped up water from one of the holes which was as perfectly cylindrical as if it had been drilled by a bit. Tiger or no tiger, he thought, it's all the same. The experiment continues. That was no sign.

He was vomiting. The pain from the tooth forked up into his head like lightning.

I'm really sick, he thought with interest. Sick as a dog. What could have made me so sick? the drug? the toothache? How long have I been down here?

He looked at the row of Placidyl capsules. Not quite half were gone. Six days? Ten days?

There was the sound of water dripping.

A tiger? John Ehrlichman? He shook his head. It made him vomit again. But he shook his head again and, gathering flashlight and batteries, started for the opening. Let me out of here. It is astonishing how such a simple and commonplace ailment as pain and nausea can knock everything else out of one's head, lofty thoughts, profound thoughts, crazy thoughts, even lust.

Ooooooh, he groaned aloud.

Let me out of here, he said with no thought of God, Jews, suicide, tigers, or the Last Days.

When he wiped his mouth he felt more than the beginnings of a beard.

The trouble was he was weaker and more drugged than he knew. Halfway down the chimney, his knee gave way and he fell the remaining twenty or thirty feet, fortunately bouncing off the walls, else he'd have surely killed himself, and landed in a heap, bruised and bleeding, at the bottom.

He lay quietly for a long time before he began to feel himself for broken bones and serious bleeding. Save for a few scrapes and many bruises on his hips and arms and head, he didn't seem to be badly hurt. The dark pressed in. It didn't matter whether his eyes were open or closed. Suddenly his heart gave a thump. The flashlight! Certainly it was in his hand when he started down the chimney. How stupid of him not to have brought a spare, a little pocket penlight! Now, even if he found the light, it was undoubtedly broken. Not even a match or a lighter. The toothache and nausea, he noticed, were gone. Gooseflesh rippled like wheat along his flanks. His scrotum drew up tight as a slipknot. Does fear supplant nausea as nausea supplanted God? Taking care not to move his body, he felt every square inch around him. No flashlight. Getting up on hands and knees, he almost fainted. Then putting his head down like an anteater, he began to spiral slowly, sweeping the rock with the outer hand. What if the light had landed on a ledge above? But no. The flashlight was lodged face up in a crevice a good twenty feet from where he had fallen. When his hand closed over the plastic rim, one finger went inside. The glass was broken. But the bulb wasn't. He pushed the switch. Darkness pressed in. He pushed it again. Darkness pressed in closer. Ah then, this is how things are, things might be settled for me after all. If he hadn't been so weak, he would have laughed. What kind of answer is this to an elegant scientific question? This way Prudential is going to get euchred honestly, he thought, and tapped the butt of the metal case against the rock. The darkness sprang back like an animal.

Limping and aching in every joint, legs spraddled like a drunk's, he made his way slowly along the beach, not bothering to look for fish, past Honest Abe and the three nuns, and started up the slide. He crossed the theater, but when he came to the upper slide, it was necessary to stop and rest with every step. I'm weak. I must have been down there a week. His legs and arms trembled. Twice he fell, once badly. He was so weak that, when he felt himself fall, he cradled the flashlight in both arms and let go of his body like a sack of potatoes. It, his body, rolled down a flat rock and wedged under an outcrop. He turned off the light and lay in the dark for half an hour. The nausea and the toothache were better but he felt very weak and all at once very thirsty. Why was he weak? How long had he been in this cave haranguing with God, the Jews, tigers, and John Ehrlichman? Five hours? Fifty hours? A week? He felt his beard. At least a week.

This time when he checked his bones, he found that one was probably broken, the small bone below the knee. When he tried to stand, it seemed to want to come through the skin. But there was little pain. It was possible to go on all fours, knees spread. Perhaps the bone was only cracked.

It was only after an hour, when at least, by any calculation, he should have gained the top and the opening, that there came the awful sense of loss, like a traveler who even before he slaps his back pocket knows his wallet is missing. Something was missing. He had lost something. What? The crawl. He had misplaced the crawl.

No, he hadn't misplaced the crawl. The crawl opened into the theater. When he crossed the theater he should have entered the crawl. Instead, he had started up the slide. It was the wrong slide, however. He was lost. A cave is like a river. It is hard to get lost going down. Going up is something else.

Turning off the light, he made himself comfortable and took stock. All he knew for certain was that he could not go back to the theater, let alone negotiate the crawl and another slide. Well then—he thought, yawned, and either fainted or went to sleep.

When he woke, he found himself wondering where he was, what strange bedroom. The toothache was gone, he noticed. He spat out something. Probably pus. The abscess had drained. Then the bad memories opened in his head like doors. This was not a bedroom but a cave. He had lost the crawl. He was very thirsty. It took a long time to stand up. As he shone the light around, he realized he was looking for something, water.

One of the dark spots on the ceiling close above him drizzled. He reached up his free hand. It was not water. Furry bodies fell on him, around him, squeaking. Tiny fans of warm skin brushed against his face. Hooks went through his hair like a comb. The dark spot went away. The rock was dry. The spots were colonies of bats. It was the bats that drizzled. Then, whatever day it was, it was daytime. Bats roost during the day, don't they? How did the bats get out?

Did he imagine it or did another, stronger breath of air stir against his cheek. A great bat?

Down on hands and knees again and slowly up the slide. What to do when slide meets roof? For here in fact slide did meet roof and he crouched in the angle, cleaving against the roof like a bat. He turned off the light. It was only after a minute or so that he realized that it was not quite dark. Rather was it ordinary dark, not the blind black retinal dark of the cave. A breath of air stirred his hair.

Turning his head as slowly as a sick man greeting a visitor, he saw a shadow on the rock. It was only a shadow, he thought. But consider that my flashlight is turned off. It follows then that the shadow has been made by another source of light. As he crawled along the cave a light breeze sprang up, and by the time he reached the shadow, he could smell leaves and bitter bark and the smell of lichened rock warming in sunlight.

But when he turned, he saw, not sunlight but a lattice of vines which all but sealed a hole in the rock. The hole was square.

Well then, he said, and noticed that he was not excited about his deliverance from the cave.

Then there must be more than one opening in the ridge. But why the square hole? Perhaps this was the actual escape hatch for the Confederate moles. Even fat Confederates could use this hole.

Carefully inching his way to the light, he discovered that the opening was not more than a foot and a half square and head high, the head, that is, of a man on all fours. The square shape came not from the rock but from a wooden frame beyond the rock.

A rigor seized him and he shook like a leaf. His teeth chattered. Somewhere above the racket he was thinking that it would be a curious experience to emerge from the cave as a Confederate years later, like a Japanese holdout in the Philippines. Hey you in the Mercedes, who won the war?

Resting elbows on the sill, he meant to poke his head through for a look, but both vines and sill were rotten and he fell, thinking even as he fell that it couldn't be much of a fall, what with the vines and the ridge itself not being much higher than a man. But this was a fall through air not vines or bushes, through air and color, brilliant greens and violet and vermilion and a blue unlike any sky, a free-fall headfirst with time enough to wonder if he might not be dead after all, what with this tacky heaven and the great black beast of the apocalypse roaring down at him, eyes red, jaws open and ravening, when, wood splintering first then exploding into kindling, he hit the table, then concrete, but not too hard, with one shoulder mostly but with the back of his head some. He shut down, turned off like a light.

3

Something was trying to get into his mouth. He clenched his teeth.

"You were asking for water."

He opened his eyes. Something, someone, a person, a woman, a girl, bent over him with a paper cup.

"Okay."

He tried to raise his head to drink properly. It was impossible. Pains shot up his neck. Very well. He had broken his neck. He opened his mouth and she poured water into it. There are few joys greater than drinking cool water after a serious thirst.

The colors came from a stained-glass window set in a roof of clear glass. I'm in church.

"How did you find me and get me in here?"

"I didn't. You fell in."

"Fell in? From where?"

"There." She lifted her face.

In the peak of the gambrel roof, where the vent of an attic might be, a square window had been set in the wall against the ridge. He looked at it.

"How did I get up here on this table or bed or—"

"I got you up with my block-and-tackle."

"I see."

"How do you feel?"

"Bad."

"What hurts?"

"Everything, from my leg to my head. I think my leg is broken." If my leg hurts, he thought, I am probably not paralyzed.

"Take these three aspirin and go to sleep."

"Don't call anyone until I tell you."

"All right."

He took the three aspirin and went to sleep.

When he woke, she fed him a large bowl of oatmeal. Why had he never noticed how good oatmeal is?

"What were you doing? Where did you come from?" she asked after a while.

"The cave," he said absently. He had been looking at the framed hole in the roof peak a long time. "Do you feel anything?" he asked her.

"Yes, a breeze. I had not felt it before. Where does it come from?"

"From the cave."

"What's it for?" she asked.

"To keep the greenhouse warm in winter and cool in summer. How does it feel to you?"

"Cool. But did you notice my—"

"Yes, because it's still warm out."

"No, it's cold outside."

"I judge the cave air is about sixty degrees. It is said to come from air blowing up the gorge and into the cave mouth and across some hot springs."

"Yes, but did you notice that it is warmer than that in here?"

"Yes," he said absently. "Can you imagine that vent being there all along and you not noticing it?"

She nodded. "It is both revealing and appealing to me that you cleaned out the vines so my window could catch the breeze from the cave."

"What old Judge Kemp did," he said more to himself than to her yet watching her closely, "was to back this greenhouse against the vent in the ridge so he could keep it a steady sixty winter and summer."

"So the natural air-condition was for fruition."

"Yes," he said, closing his eyes. "He made a lot of money. It's warm in here, warmer than the cave. Hm."

"I know," she said. "Did you notice a novelty hereabouts?"

"A novelty?" He opened his eyes and followed her gaze.

There, fitted snugly under the raised sashes of the partition, squatted the huge old kitchen range, no not old but surely new, transformed, reborn. Its polished nickel glittered in the sunlight. Expanses of immaculate white and turquoise enamel glowed like snowy peaks against a blue sky. A fire burned behind amber mica bright as tigers' eyes.

"You moved it."

"I moved it."

"By yourself."

"By myself. Look, it also has a reservoir."

"I see."

"The water is hot."

"Good."

"I gave you a bath. To see you was not to believe you."

"Thank you."

"But for now, go to sleep. You're exhausted."

"Very well. Don't tell anybody I'm here."

"Who would I tell?"

PART TWO

I

IT WAS NO TROUBLE HANDLING HIM UNTIL HE CAME TO AND looked at her. She could do anything if nobody watched her. But the moment a pair of eyes focused on her, she was a beetle stuck on a pin, arms and legs beating the air. There was no purchase. It was an impalement and a derailment.

So it had been in school. Alone at her desk she could do anything, solve any problem, answer any question. But let the teacher look over her shoulder or, horror of horrors, stand her up before the class: she shriveled and curled up like paper under a burning glass.

The lieder of Franz Schubert she knew by heart, backwards and forwards, as well as Franz ever knew them. But when four hundred pairs of eyes focused on her, they bored a hole in her forehead and sucked out the words.

When he landed on the floor of her greenhouse, knocking himself out, he was a problem to be solved, like moving the stove. Problems are for solving. Alone. After the first shock of the crash, which caught her on hands and knees cleaning the floor, her only thought had been to make some sense of it, of him, a man lying on her floor smeared head to toe with a whitish grease like a channel swimmer. As her mind cast about for who or what he might be—new kind of runner? masquerader from country-club party? Halloween trick-or-treater?—she realized she did not yet know the new world well enough to know what to be scared of. Maybe the man falling into her house was one of the things that happened, albeit rarely, like a wood duck flying down the chimney.

But wait. Was he a stranger? Strange as he was, smeared with clay and bent double, there was something about the set of his shoulders, a vulnerability in their strength, that struck in her a sweet smiling pang. She recognized him. No, in a way she knew who he was before she saw him. The dog recognized him. It was the dog, a true creature of the world, who knew when to be affrighted and enraged, e.g., when a man falls on him, who therefore had attacked as before and as before had as quickly stopped and spat out the hand, the furious growl winding down to a little whine of apology. Again the dog was embarrassed.

Perhaps she ought to be an engineer or a nurse of comatose patients. For, from the moment of her gazing down at him, it was only a matter of figuring out how to do what needed to be done, of calculating weights and angles and points of leverage. Since he had crashed through one potting table, the problem was to get him up on the other one. But first make sure he wasn't dead or badly hurt. It seemed he was neither, though he was covered with bumps and scrapes and blood and clay. He smelled of a freshly dug ditch. A grave. Again her mind cast about. Had he been digging a well for her in secret, knowing her dislike of help? But how does one fall from a well? Perhaps he had found a water supply on the ridge above.

She tried to pick him up. Though she was strong and had grown stronger with her heavy work in the greenhouse and though he was thin, he was heavy. He was slippery. His long slack muscles were like straps on iron. When she lifted part of his body, the rest clove to the earth as if it had taken root. Now sitting propped against the wall, the dog's anvil head on her thigh, she considered. The block-and-tackle she figured gave her the strength of three men. Better than three men. Three men would have demoralized her. Her double and triple pulleys conferred mastery of energy gains and mechanical advantages. With pulleys and ropes and time to plan, one could move anything. Now that she thought of it, why couldn't anyone do anything he or she wished, given the tools and the time? It was hard to understand why scientists had not long ago solved the problems of the world. Were they, the scientists, serious? How could one not solve any problem, once you put your mind to it, had forty years, and people didn't bother you? Problems were for solving. Perhaps they the scientists were *not* serious. For if people solved the problems of cancer and war, what would they do then? Who could she ask about this? She made a note to look it up in the library.

She got him up by first rolling him onto a door from the ruin, then, using a single double-gain pulley, hoisted one end of the door enough to slide the creeper under it, then rolled him to her bunk, devised a rope sling for the door, a two-strand hammock, hoisted door by two double-blocks hooked to the metal frame of the gambrel angle in the roof where the vents opened. The trick was to pull the ropes to both systems, then when the pulleys had come together take both ropes in one hand and stack bricks under the door with the other and start over. When the door was a little higher than the cleared bunk, she eased him over door and all, hoisted one end of the door, the head end, high enough to put three bricks under it so water would run off when she gave him a bath.

The only real trouble was getting his clothes off. Pulleys were no use. Man is pitiful without a tool. It took all her sweating gasping strength to tug the slippery khaki over his hips and to roll him over far enough to yank one elbow clear of a sleeve. Why not cut his clothes off? Then dress him 'n what? She considered his underwear shorts. She wouldn't have minded him naked but perhaps, later, he would. She covered him with her sleeping bag while she drew two pots of water, one for him, one for his clothes, the clothes first so they would have time to dry in the sun. No, the sun would take too long. Instead, she hung the shirt and pants on the nickel towel rack of the great stove. Quel pleasure, putting her stove to such good use!

It took all afternoon. She didn't mind bathing a man. How nice people are, unconscious! They do not glance. Yes, she should be a nurse of comatose patients. Again it was a matter of calculating weights and angles and hefts. The peculiar recalcitrant slack weight of the human body required its own physics. Heaving him over to get at his back, a battleground of cuts and scrapes and caked blood and bruises, she wondered: what had he done, fallen off a mountain? His face! With its week's growth of beard, a heavy streaked yellow-and-white stubble, and the lump above his jawbone, he looked like a covite with a wad of chewing tobacco. But only when she finished did she stop to gaze down at him. No, not a redneck. Except for the golfer's tan of his face and arms, his skin was white, with a faint bluish cast. The abdomen dropping away hollow under his ribs, the thin arms and legs with their heavy slack straps of muscle, cold as clay, reminded her of some paintings of the body of Christ taken down from the crucifix, the white flesh gone blue with death. The closed eyes sunk in their sockets and bluish shadow. The cheekbones thrust out like knees. He had lost weight. While his beard grew he had not eaten.

Exhausted, she cooked a supper of oatmeal and made a salad of brook lettuce and small tart apples from the ruined orchard and hickory nuts. Her back felt looks. She turned around. The dog and the man were watching her, the dog with his anvil head between his paws, the man with his cheek resting on his elbow. The looks did not dart or pierce or impale. They did not control her. They were shyer than she and gave way before her, like the light touch of a child's hand in the dark. The man looked one way, the dog the other, as if she were not there. Was she there?

The man could not sit up to eat. She fed him. He ate heartily but his eyes, like the dog's, only met hers briefly and went away as he chewed. She put hot oatmeal in the dog's dry meal from the fifty-pound sack, which she had packed from town by tying it like a blanket roll in the lower flap of the Italian NATO knapsack. Her strength surprised her. She could hoist anything.

2

It wasn't bad taking care of him. To tell the truth, before he landed in the greenhouse, she had begun to slip a little. It surprised her. She liked her new life. Physically she was healthy and strong. The hard work of cleaning the greenhouse and moving the stove made her hungry and tired. She ate heartily and slept like a log. She gained weight. When she caught sight of herself in the shop windows of Linwood, she did not at first recognize the tan towheaded long-haired youth loping along.

But looks became more impaling. Some people, most Southern people, guard their looks as if they knew what she knew about looks: that they are not like other things. The world is full of two kinds of things, looks and everything else. Some people do not guard their looks. A woman met her eye in an aisle of the supermarket and looked too long. The look made a tunnel. The shelves of cans seemed to curve around the look like the walls of a tunnel. She knew she was not crazy because a can fell off.

Some people use their looks to impale. Once, as she walked

down the street, her thighs felt a look. She turned around. A dark stout man perhaps from Florida (most visitors were from Florida), perhaps a Cuban, perhaps South American, was not only looking at her buttocks but had bunched his fingers under his chin and was shaking them and making a sucking noise, not a whistle, through his pursed lips.

Time became separated into good times and bad times. The nights and mornings were good times.

Then along comes late afternoon—four o'clock? five o'clock? she didn't know because she had no clock and lived by forest time—but a time which she thought of as yellow spent time because if time is to be filled or spent by working, sleeping, eating, what do you do when you finish and there is time left over? The forest becomes still. The singing and clomping of the hikers, the cries of the golfers, the sweet little sock of the Spalding Pro Flites and Dunlop Maxflys, the sociable hum of the electric carts die away and before the cicadas tune up there is nothing but the fluting of the wood thrush as the yellow sunlight goes level between the spokes of the pines. By now the golfers, sweaty and hearty, are in the locker room tinkling ice in glasses of Tanqueray, and Diz Dean briquets are lighting up all over Linwood. Forest time turned back into clock time with time going out ahead of her in a straight line as a measure of her doing something, but she was not doing anything and therefore clock time became a waiting and a length which she thought of as a longens. Only in late afternoon did she miss people.

She said to the dog: This time of day is a longens.

The dog turned his anvil head first one way then the other. What?

In this longitude longens ensues in a longing if not an unbelonging.

What? said the dog.

One way to escape the longens of clock time marching out into the future ahead of her was to curl away from it, going round and down into her dog-star Sirius serious self so there she was curled up under, not on, the potting table. The dog did not like her there. He whined a little and gave her a poke with his muzzle. Okay okay. She got up. No, it wasn't so bad and not bad at all when it got dark and clock time was rounded off by night. She lit a candle and the soft yellow light made a room in the dark and time went singing along with cicada music and not even the screech owl was sad except that just at dusk there rose in her throat not quite panic but something rising nevertheless. She swallowed it, all but the aftertaste of wondering: tomorrow will it be worse, even a curse?

But in the dark: turn a flowerpot upside down and put the candle on it to read by, the dog now waiting for her signal, which is opening the book, hops up he not she spiraling round and down but always ending with his big anvil head aimed at her, eyes open, tiny flame upside down in each pupil, watching her until she starts reading her book: then down comes his head on her knee heavy as iron. She read from *The Trail of the Lonesome Pine*:

> Hand in hand, Hale and June followed the footsteps of spring from the time June met him at the school-house gate for their first walk in the woods. Hale pointed to some boys playing marbles.
> "That's the first sign," he said, and with quick understanding June smiled.

Sign of what? Spring?

3

One morning she woke and could not quite remember what she was doing in the greenhouse. But she remembered she had written a note to herself in her notebook for just such an occasion. The note read:

The reason you are living here is to take possession of your property and to make a life for yourself. How to live from one moment to the next: Clean the place up. Decide on a profession. Work at it. What about people? Men? Do you want (1) to live with another person? (2) a man? (3) a woman? (4) no one? (5) Do you want to make love with another person? (6) "Fall in love"? (7) What is "falling in love"? (8) Is it part of making love or different? (9) Do you wish to marry? (10) None of these? (11) Are people necessary? Without people there are no tunneling looks. Brooks don't look and dogs look away. But late afternoon needs another person.

What do I do if people are the problem? Can I live happily in a world without people? What if four o'clock comes and I need a person? What do you do if you can't stand people yet need a person?

For some reason when she read this note to herself, she thought of an expression she had not heard since grade school: "Doing it." Was "doing it" the secret of life? Is this a secret everyone knows but no one talks about?

She "did it" at Nassau with Sarge, the Balfour jewelry salesman, thinking that it might be the secret of life. But even though she and Sarge did everything in the picture book Sarge had, it did not seem to be the secret of life. Had she missed something?

On the days she walked to town she found herself sitting on the bench near The Happy Hiker. One day the marathon runner saw her and sat down on the bench beside her. Again he shook hands with his fibrous monkey hand. Again he asked her to crash with him in the shelter on Sourwood Mountain. Again she said no. Again he loped away, white stripes scissoring.

Another afternoon a hiker asked for a drink of water at the greenhouse. Unshouldering his scarlet backpack, he sat beside her on the floor of the little porch. Though he was young and fair as a mountain youth, his face was dusky and drawn with weariness. When he moved, his heavy clothes were as silent as his skin. He smelled, she imagined, like a soldier, of sweat and leather gear. They were sitting, knees propped up. His arm lay across his knee, the hand suspended above her knees. She looked at the hand. Tendons crossed the boxy wrist, making ridges and swales. A rope of vein ran along the placket of muscle in the web of the thumb. Copper-colored hair turning gold at the tip sprouted from the clear brown skin. The weight of the big slack hand flexed the wrist, causing the tendon to raise the forefinger like Adam's hand touching God's.

As she watched, the hand fell off his knee and fell between her knees. She looked at him quickly to see if he had dozed off but he had not. The hand was rubbing her thigh. She frowned: I don't like this but perhaps I should. Embarrassed for him, she cleared her throat and rose quickly, but the hand tightened on her thigh and pulled her down. Mainly she was embarrassed for him. Oh, this is too bad. Is something wrong with me? The dog growled, his eyes turning red as a bull's. The man thanked her and left. He too seemed embarrassed.

Was there something she did not know and needed to be told? Perhaps it was a matter of "falling in love." She knew a great deal about pulleys and hoists but nothing about love. She went to the library to look up love as she had looked up the mechanical advantages of pulleys. Surely great writers and great lovers of the past had written things worth reading. Here were some of the things great writers had written:

> Love begets love
> Love conquers all things
> Love ends with hope
> Love is a flame to burn out human ills
> Love is all truth
> Love is truth and truth is beauty
> Love is blind
> Love is the best
> Love is heaven and heaven is love
> Love is love's reward

"Oh my God," she said aloud in the library and smacked her head. "What does all that *mean*? These people are crazier than I am!"

Nowhere could she find a clear explanation of the connection between "being in love" and "doing it." Was this something everybody knew and so went without saying? or was it a well-kept secret? or was it something no one knew? Was she the only Southern girl who didn't know? She began to suspect a conspiracy. They, teachers, books, parents, poets, philosophers, psychologists, either did not know what they were talking about, which seemed unlikely, or they were keeping a secret from her.

Was something wrong with her? What did she want? Was she supposed to want to "do it"? If she was supposed to, who was doing the supposing? Was it a matter of "falling in love"? With whom? a man? a woman? She tried to imagine a woman hiker's hand falling between her knees.

Naargh, she said.

The dog cocked an eyebrow. What?

Is one supposed to do such-and-so with another person in order to be happy? Must one have a plan for the pursuit of happiness? If so, is there a place where one looks up what one is supposed to do or is there perhaps an agency which one consults?

Who says?

Who is doing the supposing?

Why not live alone if it is people who bother me? Why not live in a world of books and brooks but no looks?

* * *

Going home one evening, she passed Hattie's Red Barn. Young folk were dancing and drinking and joking. Couples came and went to vans. Someone beckoned to her from the doorway. She did not belong with them. Why not? They were her age. They were making merry, weren't they? and she would like to make merry, wouldn't she? They were good sorts, weren't they? Yes, but not good enough.

You have to have a home to make merry even if you are away from home. She had a home but it was not yet registered. A registrar was needed to come and register her home in the presence of a third party, a witness. Upon the departure of the registrar the third party would look at her and say: Well, this is your home and here we are. She would make sassafras tea. Then they could make merry.

Perhaps she had not sunk deep enough into her Sirius self. If one sinks deep enough there is surely company waiting. Otherwise, if one does not have a home and has not sunk into self, and seeks company, the company is lonesome. Silence takes root, sprouts. Looks dart.

On the other hand, look what happens to home if one is too long at home. Rather than go home to Williamsport, she'd rather live in a stump hole even though her parents' home was not only registered with the National Registry but restored and written up in *Southern Living*. Rather than marry and have a life like her mother, she'd rather join the navy and see the world. Why is a home the best place and also the worst? How can the best place become the worst place? What is a home? A home is a place, any place, any building, where one sinks into one's self and finds company waiting. Company? Who's company? oneself? somebody else? That's the problem. The problem is not the house. People are the problem. But it was their problem. She could wait.

4

The man watched her from the bunk but she didn't mind. His look was not controlling or impaling but soft and gray and going away. Her back felt his and the dog's eyes following her, but when she faced them, their eyes rolled up into their eyebrows.

The mornings grew cold. It was a pleasure to rise shivering

from her own potting-table bunk and kneel at the Grand Crown stove and start a fat-pine fire for its quick blazing warmth and busy crackle-and-pop which peopled the room. Outside, the great dark rhododendrons dripped and humped in close, still hiding croquet balls knocked "galley west" in 1890 tournaments. This dreary cold clime is not getting me down!

The first morning the man said: "You gave me a bath."

"Yes. And washed your clothes." She dropped the clothes on him. "You can put them on." She was stiff. She had slept with the dog on croker sacks. From the army surplus store she bought two scratchy Italian NATO blankets and made a bed of pine needles on a slatted flat, which she propped on four up-ended big pots.

They talked about the once cool-feeling now warm-feeling cave air blowing above them. He told her how Judge Kemp had saved the cost of kerosene for the greenhouse but think what you could save. Your overhead is zero. (It made her feel good that her *overhead* was not over head and pressing down on her but was nought, had gone away.) You could grow produce all winter and sell at one hundred percent profit. Grow what and sell where, she asked. I don't know, he said, but we can find out—is that what you want to do, make a living here? I don't know, she said.

One morning when she returned from her woods latrine, a comfortable fork in the chestnut fall, which she used and where she deposited his excretions from a Clorox bottle and a neatly folded packet of newspaper, she found him sitting in the doorway in the morning sun. His swellings had gone down except for the knee, the scrapes had dry scabs, and his eyes were all right, not the inturning Khe Sanh white eyes but gray and clear and focused on the dog. His scruffy yellow beard looked odd against his smooth platinum-and-brown hair. Was he nodding because he knew what he was going to do? He nodded toward the other doorjamb as if it were the chair across his desk. She took it, sat down.

"Now, you've done a great deal for me. I would thank you for it but won't, for fear of upsetting your balance sheet of debits and credits. I know you are particular about owing somebody something, but maybe you will learn that's not so bad. I don't mind being in your debt. You won't mind my saying that I would do the same for you, and take pleasure in it, and furthermore can easily see our positions reversed. What I wish to tell you is that I accept what you've done for me and that I have other things to ask of you. I don't mind asking you. There are things that need to be done and only you can do them. Will you?''

"I will," she said. I will, she thought, because now he knew exactly what had to be done just as she had known what to do when he lay knocked out on her floor. I'd do anything he asks me, she thought, hoist anything. Why is that?

"Do you have a calendar?" he asked.

She gave him her Gulf card.

He looked at it, looked up at her, smiled. (Smiled!) "Wrong year." She shrugged. She was afraid to ask what year it was.

"What is today?"

"The fifteenth."

"Hm. It seems I've been gone two weeks." His gray eyes met hers. She didn't mind. "How much money do you have?"

"One hundred and eleven dollars and thirty-one cents."

"What are you going to do when your money runs out?"

She shrugged. "Find employment."

"Doing what?"

"Hoisting maybe. Also gardening."

"Hoisting? Hoisting what?"

"Anything."

"I see. You wouldn't consider my paying you something, or lending, until you get paid for your ah hoisting."

"How much money do you have?" she asked.

"On me?"

"On you and off you."

"About fifty or sixty million."

"Gollee."

"That's enough to employ you."

"No, that would throw things off-balance and render my Sirius unserious."

"Why shouldn't I pay for my room and board?" he asked her.

"To give one reason if not others, you don't have a dime. I had to go through your pockets before washing your clothes."

He laughed then winced and put a hand to his side. "I can get some."

"When you do, there will be time for a consideration of remuneration. The only thing in your pockets was a slip of paper which said *Help! With tiger, fifty feet above.* I was wondering about the nature of the tiger you were over and above."

221

"It doesn't matter. Could you do the following things for me in town. Do you have pencil and paper?"

She opened her notebook.

"Go to Western Union, which is at the bus station, and send the following telegram to Dr. Sutter Vaught, 2203 Los Flores, Albuquerque, New Mexico. Send this message: Plans changed. Forget about letter. Read it if you like but tear it up. Don't act on it. Will write. Barrett. Send it straight message."

"Straight message," she repeated, hoping he would explain but he didn't. Probably he meant send it straight to Albuquerque and not roundabout by way of Chicago. "Is that all?"

"No. Go to Dr. Vance Battle's office. See him alone. Tell him I want to see him. Tell him where I am, tell him I want to see him today and ask him not to tell anybody or bring anybody with him."

"Anything else?"

"Go by the library and get a book on hydroponic gardening."

"Okay."

"Then go behind the bus station and see if my car is still there. A silver Mercedes 450 SEL. My keys are under the seat. Drive it to the country-club parking lot. Park at the far end, which is nearest to here."

"Okay." She swallowed. Very well. Drive a car? His car? Very well. If he asked her to drive the car, she could drive the car. "Okay. Why were you in the cave?"

"What? Oh." Now he was walking up and down the greenhouse not limping badly, shouldering, hands in pockets. Does he notice how clean and smooth the concrete is? She felt the floor with both hands; it was cool and iron-colored and silky as McWhorter's driveway. She wished he would notice her concrete, the best-cured concrete in North Carolina. "I go down in caves sometimes," she said. He told her about the tiger.

"But the tiger wasn't there."

"No."

"Then—?"

"Then what?"

"Then there was more than the tiger?"

"Yes."

"You were trying to find out something besides the tiger."

"Yes."

"What?"

"I was asking a question to which I resolved to find a yes-or-no answer."

"Did you find the answer?"

"Yes."

"Which was it?"

"I don't know."

"So you came back up and out."

"Yes, I came back up and out."

"Is that good?"

"Good?" He shrugged. "I don't know. At least I know what I have to do. Don't worry."

"About what?"

"About money. I'll pay you back."

"I don't worry about money. Money worry is not instigating."

"No, it's not. You'd better go."

She enjoyed her errands.

Straight to the bus station, where she found the silver Mercedes. Though she wanted to try the keys and practice starting the car, she decided not to. Someone might see her. She would do her errands, wait until dark, and drive to the country club.

Nobody saw her.

What pleasure, obeying instructions! Then is this what people in the world do? This is called "joining the work force." It is not a bad way to live. One gets a job. There is a task and a task teller (a person who tells you a task), a set of directions, instructions, perhaps a map, a carrying out of the task, a finishing of the task, a return to the task teller to report success, a thanking. A getting paid. An assignment of another task.

She clapped her hands for joy. What a discovery! To get a job, do it well, which is a pleasure, please the employer, which is also a pleasure, and get paid, which is yet another pleasure. What a happy life employees have! How happy it must make them to do their jobs well and please their employers! That was the secret! All this time she had made a mistake. She had thought (and her mother had expected) that she must do something extraordinary, be somebody extraordinary. Whereas the trick lay in leading the most ordinary life imaginable, get an ordinary job, in itself a joy in its very ordinariness, and *then* be as extraordinary or ordinary as one pleased. That was the secret.

On to Western Union, which was part of the Greyhound bus

station. As she wrote the message she tried not to make sense of it. The telegram cost $7.89. When the clerk read the message, she said to him casually but with authority: "Straight message, please!"

"Right," said the clerk, not raising his eyes.

Victory! She had made it in the world! Not only could she make herself understood. People even understood what she said when she didn't.

It was a pleasure spending her money for him. Why? she wondered. Ordinarily she hoarded her pennies, ate dandelion-and-dock salad.

She sat on her bench but in a new way. The buildings and the stores were the same but more accessible. She might have business in them. Le Club was still there, its glass bricks sparkling in the sun. A cardboard sign in the window announced a concert by Le Hug, a rock group. What a pleasure to have a job! Smiling, she hugged herself and rocked in the sun. Imagine getting paid for a task by the task teller! Money wherewith to live! And live a life so, years, decades! So that was the system. Quel system!

A real townie she felt like now, bustling past slack-jawed hippies, moony-eyed tourists, blue-haired lady leafers, antiquers, and quilt collectors.

When she went into a building, the dog stayed on the sidewalk paying no attention to anyone until she came out. He showed his pleasure not by wagging his tail but by burying his heavy anvil head in her stomach until his eyes were covered.

There was no way to see Dr. Battle except to sign a clipboard and wait her turn as a patient. She had to wait two hours. She liked him, though he was too busy and groggy from overwork and thought she was a patient despite her telling him otherwise, sizing her up in a fond dazed rush, not listening, eyes straying over her, coming close (was he smelling her?). His hand absently palpated her shoulder, queried the bones, tested the ball joint for its fit and play. Unlike Dr. Duk he didn't bother to listen, or rather he listened not to your words but your music. He was like a vet, who doesn't have to listen to his patients. There were other ways of getting at you. He saw so many patients that it was possible for him to have a hunch about you, a good country hunch, the moment you walked in the door. Better still, it was possible for her to subside and see herself through his eyes, so canny and unheeding, sleepy and quick, were they.

Well then, how did she look to him? Is my shoulder human? He cocked an ear for her music. The fond eyes cast about to place her, then placed her. She was classifiable then. She was a piece of the world after all, a member of a class and recognizable as such. I belong here!

He looked at her boots. "You just off the trail?"

"Well no, though I've been walking quite a bit."

"And you're feeling a little spacy."

"A little what?"

"Spaced out."

"What's that?"

"Are you on something or coming off something?"

"What?"

He didn't seem impatient with her dumbness. "Okay," he said, counting off the questions on his fingers. "Are you taking a drug? Are you taking the pill? Are you coming off the pill? Are you pregnant?"

"No to one and all." How would he treat her madness? ignore it, palpate her shoulder and tell her to lead her life? Would she?

"Okay, what's the trouble, little lady?"

"I'm fine. What I was trying to tell you was—"

"You look healthy as a hawg to me."

"—was to give you a message from—" She wanted to say "from him." What to call *him*? Mr. Barrett? Mr. Will? Will Barrett? Bill Barrett? Williston Bibb Barrett? None of the names fit. A name would give him form once and for all. He would flow into its syllables and junctures and there take shape forever. She didn't want him named.

Sluggishly, like a boat righting itself in a heavy sea, Dr. Battle was coming round to her. He began to listen.

"From who?"

"Your friend Barrett," she mumbled. The surname was neutral, the way an Englishman speaks of other Englishmen.

"Who? Will Barrett? Will Barrett's out of town," he said as if he were answering her questions.

"Yes."

This time his eyes snapped open, *click*. "What about Will Barrett?"

"You are to come see him this afternoon when you finish here."

"What's the matter with him? Is that rascal sick?"

225

Rascal. The word had peculiar radiations but mainly fondness.

"No. That is, I think he is all right now. He is scratched up and bruised and his leg is hurt but he can walk. This is in confidence. He doesn't want anyone to know about this message." It was a pleasure to talk to another person about him.

"In confidence?" For a second the eye went cold and flashed like a beacon.

"I have not kidnapped him," she said.

He laughed. "All right. Where is he?"

"He is at my—" My what? "—place."

"Oh. So." He cocked his head and regarded her. It was possible for her to go around behind his eyes and see her and Will at her place. "Well, I'll be dog. How about that? Okay. What's with Will? Has he got his tail in some kind of crack?"

She frowned and folded her arms. "He went down into Lost Cove cave, got lost, came back up, and fell into my place."

Though it was true, it sounded odd, even to her.

"Fell?" he said.

"That's what I said. Fell. Flat fell down into my place."

"He fell into your place from a cave," said the doctor.

"That's right."

The doctor nodded. "Okay." Then he shook his head. "He shouldn't be doing that."

"Doing what?"

"He doesn't take care of himself. With his brain lesion he won't—" His eyes opened. "All right. This is as good a chance as any to throw him down and look at him. Where is your place?"

"You know the old Kemp place?"

"Yes. Near there?"

"There. That's my place."

"There is nothing left there."

"A greenhouse is left."

"You live in the greenhouse?"

"Yes."

"Will is staying in your greenhouse?"

"Yes. He fell into the greenhouse from the cave."

"He fell into your greenhouse. From the cave. Okay."

It pleased her that Dr. Vance Battle did not seem to find it remarkable that the two of them, who? Will and who? Allie, Will and Allie, should be staying in the greenhouse. Only once

226

did he cock his head and look at her along his cheekbone. Will and Allie? Williston and Allison? Willie and Allie?

"It is a matter in confidence," she said. In confidence? Of confidence? To be held in confidence? Her rehearsed language had run out. She didn't know where to put *of*s and *in*s. It was time to leave.

"Right. Tell that rascal I'll be out this afternoon. We'll throw him down and have a look at him."

Right, she repeated to herself as she left. I will tell that rascal.

5

Why does the sun feel so good on my back, she thought as she sat on the bench counting her money.

Why am I spending all my money, she wondered at the A & P as she paid $44.89 for two rib-eye steaks, horse meat for the dog, two folding aluminum chairs with green plastic webbing, and a cold six-pack of beer. What am I celebrating? His leaving? He's leaving. Is he leaving?

What would she do when her money ran out? Shelter and heat were free, but what about food? She could hoard hickory nuts like a squirrel and perhaps even catch the squirrels and eat them. No, she needed money.

It was necessary to get a job.

"Excuse me," she said to the fat friendly pretty checkout girl after waiting for the right moment to insert the question, the moment between getting her change and being handed the bag. She had rehearsed the question. "What are job opportunities here or elsewhere?" She had watched the checker and noticed that she was the sort who would as soon answer one question as another.

"I don't know, hon. I'm losing my job here at Thanksgiving when the season's over and going back to Georgia and see if I can get my old job at Martin Marietta. Then you know what I'm going to do?"

"No."

"I'm going to grab my sweet little honey man of a preacher, praise the good Lord every Sunday, and not turn him loose till Christmas. He's no good but he's as sweet as he can be." The other checkers laughed. She noticed that her checker had raised her voice so the others could hear her. Her checker was a card.

Yet she saw too that her checker was good-natured. "Why don't you go back to school, hon?" the checker asked her. "You a school girl, ain't you?"

"Ah, no, I—" Then that is what people do, get a job, go to church, get a sweet honey man. All those years of dreaming in childhood, of going to school, singing Schubert, developing her talent as her mother used to say, she had not noticed this.

"What can you do hon?" the checker asked her.

"I can do two things," she said without hesitation. "Sing and hoist."

"Hoist?"

"With block-and-tackle, differential gears, endless-chain gears, double and triple blocks. I can hoist anything if I have a fixed point and time to figure."

"Honey, you come on down to Marietta with me. I'll get you a job. They always need hoisters."

She saw that the checker meant it. Then there was such a thing as a hoister. Then why not consider it: hoisting great B-52 bomber wings to just the right position to be bolted to the fuselage. (People were friendly!)

"You think it over, hon."

"I will. Thank you."

How good life must be once you got the hang of it, she thought, striding along, grocery bag in her arm, folded chairs hooked over her shoulder.

Consulting her list—I have a list!—she went to the library and, sure enough, found a book on hydroponic gardening. List completed!

Though it was not dark, she walked straight to the Mercedes, unlocked the door, pitched groceries and chairs inside, and drove off as easily as a lady leafer headed for the Holiday Inn.

The tape player came on, playing Schubert's Trout Quintet. Her eyes widened. The sound came from all around her. It was like sitting in the middle of the musicians. The music, the progress of the trout, matched her own happy progress. I'm going *along* now, I'm going *along* now, went the happy little chord. It was as if she had never left the world of music and the world of cars, hopping in your own car and tooling off like Schubert's trout. What a way to live, zipping through old Carolina in a perfect fragrant German car listening to Schubert on perfect Telefunken tape better than Schubert in the flesh. How lovely

was the old world she had left! Hm, there must have been something wrong with it, what? Why had she gone nuts?

Because he wasn't there? No, it wasn't so simple. She could
make it now, with him or without him. But think of life with
him there beside her in the Mercedes! Or in her greenhouse. He
would remember for her if she forgot. She would hoist him if
he fell. Now she knew what she did not want: not being with
him. I do not want him not being here.

But what if he left?

She parked the car at the country club and dove into the woods
before some official questioned her.

Why was she so happy now? Because like the checker she
hoped for a sweet honey man? No. Because she hoped to get
married? No. Married. The word made her think of the married
leafers up here, mooning around, fed up with the red leaves and
each other. What if they married? *Married.* The word was a
flattening out, a lightening, and a rolling up. Rolled up tight in
a light-colored rug. And a winding up and a polishing off. In
short, stuck like her mother and father. On the other hand, the
thought of marrying him made her grin and skip like a school-
girl. Ma-rry-ing. What an odd expression. Marry-ing. Is it
merry to marry or marred? What if we *marry*? What if we
*ma*rry?—she sang to the music of Schubert's Trout. She'd not
forget these words. Other marriages might get screwed up but
not theirs. Hm. Look at these old couples gazing at the lovely
scarlet Smokies with the same glum expression. She? She could
look at a doodlebug with him and be happy. With him, silence
didn't sprout and looks didn't dart. What happened after you
got married? Do you look at each other and say: Well, here we
are, me and you, what'll we do, tea for two? Then was she happy
because she was going to surprise him with a steak dinner? Not
exactly. Then was she happy because it is a pleasure to carry
out a task assigned by a task assigner? Yes, in a way. She looked
forward to reporting to him everything she had done. While the
doctor examined him, she could cook the steaks, put the beer
under the waterfall to keep cold, fix avocado salad with Plagniol
(goodbye dandelion-and-dock), unfold the chairs, upend two big
pots for tables, open the mica door of the firebox to see the
wood fire. What about wild shallots with the avocados? Should
she invite the doctor for supper? No.

She was planning her supper like any other housewife.

* * *

But he was gone. The potting room was empty. Leaning over, she felt for him in all parts of the sleeping bag as if he might have shrunk. Her stomach hurt where the rail of the bunk hit her. When she straightened up, she felt dizzy and nauseated. How could his not being there make her sick?

Yet even as she searched, uncovering pots, looking behind creeper, she could feel her eyes narrow, her lips begin to curl as her searching self turned round and went down into her Sirius self until she stood now, arms folded, in the corner next to the stove from where she could see all of the potting room and through the door into the greenhouse. She eyed the vent in the eave where the cave air entered and blew across the room and through the space above the partition. Not much warm air came down. The room was cold.

The room had the look of his not coming back.

She shrugged. Very well, then. She drummed her fingers on her thigh. Why did the room suddenly feel cold? The warm air blowing in from the cave needed to come down. There must have been a system of ducts here earlier, probably of wood which had rotted. It would be possible to make new ducts out of—there were piles of cardboard boxes behind the A & P, many of the same size perhaps for standard-size cans like Campbell's soup. One could cut out the ends and connect them. The only expense would be paper tape and wire to suspend them from the ceiling. It would be an interesting problem to make branches in the duct system, cut boxes at the proper angle to deflect air to the proper places. How to transport the boxes? Flatten them out, load them on the creeper, and drag them from town?

She was nodding and chewing her lip when she caught sight of the steaks on the stove, still wrapped in white butcher paper. Wet pink spots stained the paper. What to do with them? All at once her mouth spurted with juices. Eat them. She couldn't remember the last time she ate red meat.

Feeling sick about him is all right, but not all night.

After starting a fire of fat pine in the Grand Crown, she went with her Clorox bottle to the waterfall, drumming her fingers to the running chords of the Trout. It was almost dark—

—and there he was in the path as if he had just fallen down and was trying to get up, hand propped under him in the very act of pushing himself up, but he didn't. He couldn't get up.

When she knelt beside him (her stomach was hurting again), his one-eyed profile gazed not at her but at the wet cold earth inches away. The eye bulged in the terrific concentration of pushing the earth away. He didn't move. The eye didn't blink. Was he dead? Not knowing that she did so, she both lay on him and pulled him up, hands locked around his waist, then stopped still to see if he lived, because he was so cold, lying on him long enough to feel the onset of the rigor, which started like an earthquake tremor then shook him till his teeth rattled.

Then what will love be in the future, she wondered, lying on him cheek pressed against his, a dancing with him in the Carolina moonlight with the old world and time before you, or a cleaving to him at the world's end, and which is better?

"Don't worry. I'll get you back."

Straddling him and trying his pelvis for heft, she looked around, gauging trees and limbs for hoist points. But he could move, enough so that by rolling him and getting herself almost under him with his arm around her neck, he could help her push them up and, leaning heavily on her, walk. Staggering though she was, her eye for angles was good enough to bend at the right moment and lever him onto the bunk without hurting him. He shook like a leaf. There was nothing for her to do now but, spent, gasping, trembling, use her last strength and climb over him, cover them with the sleeping bag and hold him until she got stronger and he stopped shivering. Somehow she, they, got them undressed, his wet clothes her dry clothes off, her warm body curled around his lard-cold muscle straps and bones, spoon-nesting him, her knees coming up behind him until he was shivering less and, signaling a turn, he nested her, encircled her as if he were her cold dead planet and she his sun's warmth.

It was dark. There was no firelight from the stove. Flexed and enfolded she lay still, waiting for him to get warm, blinking in the dark but not thinking. Her arm went to sleep. She began to worry, about the doctor, that he might not come or that he might and find them so and that the stove fire of fat pine might go out.

Presently he stopped shivering and went slack around her. "Ah," he said quite himself. "You undressed me again."

"Are you all right?" she asked.

"Yes."

"I'm getting up to fix the fire. The doctor is coming."

"He came."

"What happened?"

"Nothing. He said my leg wasn't bad, didn't need a cast. He smelled me, looked in my eye, shook his head, and told me to come in tomorrow for a checkup."

"Is there something wrong with you?"

"No."

"Then what were you doing out there on the ground?"

"I went out to get some water and fell down."

"Why didn't you get up?"

He was silent.

"I mean either I am not understanding something or something is not understandable."

"I blacked out."

"Is there something serious wrong with you?"

"No. Except I tend to fall down."

"I am a good hoister."

"I know."

"When you fall down, I'll pick you up."

"I know."

"I have to fix the fire."

She got up naked but not shivering. The pine had gone out, but it was so fat, a new fire could be started with a match. Atop the blazing kindling she laid two short green maple logs and a heavy hunk of chestnut to press them down. She left the door to the firebox open. When she started to climb over him, she discovered that he had moved to make room. As she turned to nest again, he held her shoulder and she came down facing him. But he was bent a little away from her. She bent too. They seemed to be looking at each other through their eyebrows. The wind picked up and pressed against the greenhouse. The metal frame creaked. There was a fine sifting against the glass. At first she thought it was blown pine needles. The sound grew heavier. It was sleet.

Winter had come.

His hand was in the hollow of her back, pressing her against him. She came against him, willingly. It was a marvel to her this yielding and flowing against him, amazing that I was made so and is this *it* then (whatever *it* is) and what will happen to myself (do I altogether like the yielding despite myself and the smiling at it like smiling when your knee jerks when Dr. Duk hits it with his rubber hammer) and will I for the first time in my life get away from my everlasting self sick of itself to be with another self and is that what *it* is and if not then what? He

232

kissed her on the lips. Ah then *it* is that too after all, the dancing adream in the Carolina moonlight except that it was sleeting and it was firelight not moonlight on the glass.

"Oh my," she said. "Imagine."

"Imagine what?"

"Imagine having you around at four o'clock in the afternoon."

He laughed. "What's wrong with night? What's wrong with now?"

"Nothing. But—"

She was moving against him, enclosing him, wrapping her arms and legs around him, as if her body had at last found the center of itself outside itself. But he stopped her or rather took her face in his hands and looked she thought at her, the firelight making his eye sockets deeper and darker than they were.

"There is something I must tell you."

"Yes, but—" she said.

"Yes, but what?"

Yes, but not now. Yes, but why did you stop? *Keep on.*

"What?" he asked her.

"I said why did you stop. I mean I meant to say 'it.' Why did you stop? I think this is 'it.' "

"I have to leave," he said.

"When?"

"Now."

"Is the leaving—"

"I'll be back."

"When?"

"Soon. There are some things I must do."

"What about this? It? That is, us."

"What about us?"

"Is there anything entailed?"

"Is anything entailed between us?"

"Yes."

"What is the entailment?"

He lay back, his hand behind his head. The wind shifted to the south. The sleet turned to rain. Some of the drops on the glass beyond his head didn't run. In the big drops the open firebox was reflected in a bright curved stripe like a cat's eye. With his hand behind his head, his shoulders and chest bare, the firelight showing the line of his cheek and the notch of his eye, with my hair falling across my arm and touching his arm, we are like lovers in the movies. Men never wear pajamas in the movies. So Sarge didn't wear pajamas. My father always wore pajamas.

"There is something you need to know," he said.

Yeah, she thought, there is something I needed to know and I think I know. What I need to know and think I know is, is loving you the secret, the be-all not end-all but starting point of my very life, or is it just one of the things creatures do like eating and drinking and therefore nothing special and therefore nothing to dream about? Is loving a filling of the four o'clock gap or is it more? Either way would be okay but I need to know and think I know. It might be the secret because a minute ago when you held me and I came against you, there were signs of coming close, to *it*, for the first time, like the signs you recognize when you are getting near the ocean for the first time. Even though you've never seen the ocean before, you recognize it, the sense of an opening out ahead and a putting behind of the old rickrack bird-chirp town and countryside, something tasting new in the air, the dirt getting sandier, even the shacks and weeds looking different, and something else, a quality of sound, a penultimate hush marking the beginning of the end of land and the beginning of the old uproar and the going away of the endless sea.

Then why had he stopped and would she ever know the secret or if there was a secret?

"This is like running around at the Dunes Exxon a mile from the beach and going back to town," she said.

"What's that?" he asked quickly. He looked at her. "You mean the ocean, getting near the ocean."

"How did you know that?"

"Perhaps that is what I want," he said absently.

"The ocean?"

"Something like that. Now may I tell you something?"

"Okay."

He turned to face her. Her cheek was on his arm.

"How are you?" he asked her.

"I'm all right now."

"But not before?"

"I'm all right because you are doing the instigating and you seem to know what you are doing. I was a good dancer."

"So if I do the instigating you'll do the cooperating?" he asked.

"Ha ha. Very funny."

"Very well. I am going to tell you what has happened concerning you because you are entitled to know. I'm also going to tell you what I have learned because, for one reason, you may be the only person who would understand it."

"All right."

"First, your mother and I are old friends. That is, I used to know her a long time ago."

"You and my mother?"

"Yes."

"How about that?" she said in her mother's voice, using an expression her mother liked to use. "Did you and she—?"

"Hardly."

"Does hardly mean yes or no?"

"Why do you ask?"

"Could you be my father?"

"Hardly."

"Remind me to look up hardly."

"Okay."

"How do you know you're not my father?"

"If I were, I wouldn't be here."

"Then why is it I seem to have known you before I knew you. We are different but also the same."

"I know. I don't know."

"Then why does it seem I am not only I but also you?"

"I don't know."

"Could I have known you in another life? Kelso believes in that."

"I don't think so."

"Then why is it that I live this life as if it were a dream and as if any minute I might wake up and find myself in my real life?"

"I don't know."

"Doesn't that mean that I had a real life once and that I might have again?"

"I don't know. Could I tell you what I want to tell you?"

"All right." He thought: She says *all right* the same odd nonsignifying way as Jane Ace in *Easy Aces*.

"Because your mother and I are old friends, among other reasons, she has asked me if I will be your legal guardian—God, I hate this beard, I meant to ask you to buy me a razor."

"I bought one."

"You did? Why?"

"It pleases me to please you. It is also joyful."

"I see. Your mother does not know that you are here and she doesn't know that I know you."

"Legal guardian. What is there to guard?"

"Your real and personal property."

"My property. I own fifty-eight dollars and fifty-three cents."

"Your real estate. This property and the island you inherited. They are quite valuable. Your parents believe it is in your interest to be declared legally incompetent and for me to be appointed your guardian since the court will not appoint them."

"What do you believe?"

"In my opinion you are not incompetent in the legal sense or the medical sense. I think you are quite capable of taking care of your own affairs."

"Aren't you a lawyer?"

"Yes."

"What is your preference in this matter?"

"I'd as soon not be your guardian, though I'd be glad to help you any way I can. However, if your parents can get your doctor to go along they can probably succeed in having the court declare you legally incompetent. In that case, you might be better off having me as your guardian than, say, your aunt."

"Oh my stars yes," she said, using Aunt Grace's expression. "Tell me this please."

"All right."

"Are my parents out to screw me?"

"What an expression."

"That's Kelso's." I can talk like anybody but me, she thought. "Her parents never came to see her. Mine came twice—until Miss Sally died. Kelso said my parents are out to screw me."

"Well, I wouldn't put it that way."

"How would you put it?"

"That your parents are not out to screw you. Perhaps they are trying to help you. They have a right to be concerned. And they can be a big help to you. Anyhow, you think about it and tell me later."

"All right."

"There is something else I want to tell you. About me."

"All right."

"It's what I learned in the cave and what I am going to do."

But he fell silent and turned away to watch the raindrops.

"What did you learn?"

He turned back. Their foreheads touched. Their bodies made a diamond. "As you can see, I don't know much. You are always asking questions to which I have no answers. By the way, did you always ask so many questions?"

When he began to talk she found that she could not hear his words for listening to the way he said them. She cast about for his drift. Was he saying the words for the words themselves, for what they meant, or for what they could do to her? There was something about the way he talked that reminded her of her own rehearsed sentences. Was she a jury he was addressing? Though he hardly touched her, his words seemed to flow across all parts of her body. Were they meant to? A pleasure she had never known before bloomed deep in her body. Was this a way of making love?

He was using words like "my shameful secret of success as a lawyer," "phony," "radar," "our new language," "this gift of yours and mine," "ours" (this was her favorite), "being above things," "not being able to get back down to things" (!), "how to reenter the world" (?), "by God?" "by her?" (!!!!!), "your forgetting and my remembering," "Sutter," "Sutter was right," "Sutter was wrong," "Sutter Vaught."

"My Uncle Sutter? I remember him."

"You do?"

"What about him?"

"Nothing much."

"Did you know him?"

"Yes."

"Was he crazy and no good like they said?"

"No. What happened to your sister Val?"

"She became a nun."

"I know that. Is she still a nun?"

"Yes. The last I heard, which was two or five years ago."

"Two or five. I see. Where is she, still in South Alabama?"

"No, she's not there."

"Where is she?" He was watching her closely.

"She's teaching at a parochial school at Pass Christian on the Gulf Coast. The school is run by the Little Eucharistic Sisters of St. Dominic."

He was silent for a long time. He seemed to be watching the rain. He put his hand in the small of her back. Oh my, she thought. Lightning flickered. At last he smiled in the lightning.

"What?" she said.

"You remembered it," he said.

"What?"

"That outrageous name. The Little Sisters of what?"

"The Little Eucharistic Sisters of St. Dominic." She clapped her hands. "I did. I remember all about Val. She came to see me when I first got sick. In her old black nun clothes. She put her hands on my head and told me I was going to be fine."

"She was right."

"Maybe. No, not maybe. I'm fine. You feel so good. Me too. The good is all over me, starting with my back. Now I understand how the two work together."

"What two?"

"The it and the doing, the noun and the verb, sweet sweet love and a putting it to you, loving and hating, you and I."

He laughed. "You do, don't you? What happens to the two?"

"They become one but not in the sappy way of the saying?"

"What way, then?"

"One plus one equals one and oh boy almond joy."

He was laughing. "You're Sutter turned happy."

"I want you to be my guardian," she said. Even though he was not touching her, his words were a kind of touching. Did he intend them so? When he didn't answer, she went back over his words for the sense of them. "Will you be my guardian?"

"Yes."

"Why did you go down in the cave?" Now his hand was in the small of her back again, with a light firm pressure as if they were dancing.

"What?" he said, knitting his brows as if he were trying to remember something.

"I do that," she said, "I go round and down to get down to myself."

"I went down and around to get out of myself."

"Did you?"

"I don't know. I can't remember. Curious. Now that your memory is better, mine is . . . Anyhow, that's over and done with. The future is what concerns us."

"You seem different. Before, when you climbed through the fence and I saw you, you were standing still a long time as if you were listening. Now you seem to know what to do. Was it the cave?"

"The cave," he said. She could hardly hear him over the

rising din of the storm. Lightning forked directly overhead and a sharp crack came hard upon it. The dog, discomfited and frowning, got up and walked around stiff-legged. It was an electrical storm. Soon the lightning was almost continuous, ripping and cracking in the woods around them. Facets of glass flashed blue and white. It was like living inside a diamond. He seemed not to notice her or the storm. His eyes were open and unblinking. The hand behind his head was open, the middle finger touched her shoulder, which she bent close to him, still warming him, now a touch, now a jab, but he could have been poking his own knee. The finger moved as if it were conducting music she couldn't hear. Nor could she hear what he said in the racket. He was talking in a low voice. She strained against him. Was he talking to her?

"The fence . . . the cave . . ." His voice seemed to be inside her head.

The finger stopped touching and the hand opened wide, palm up, like a man shrugging. The lightning was getting louder and she was thinking, is it good or bad that the greenhouse has a metal frame? Perhaps good what with the finials sticking up like lightning rods when *crackOW* it hit. A ball of light rolled toward them down the center aisle of the greenhouse as lazily as a ball of yarn. The dog, lip hung on his tooth, eyed it in outrage and walked stiffly away. "Jesus Christ," she said. "Let's—" And hushed because he wasn't listening.

He held her close. Again as her body came against him, she felt her eyes smiling and going away. Ha, she said to herself, maybe he didn't find what he was looking for but I did. Ha. Maybe I'm nuts and he's not but I know now what I want. Ha. Kelso, guess what. I did it like you said. I broke out and found my place and "fell in love" and inherited a million dollars. Maybe sixty million, and I don't care if it's sixty cents. Guess what. I am in love. Ah ha, so this is what it is, this "being in love." This is what I want. This him. Him. The money is nice but love is above. Yes yes. Kelso honey, I'm coming back for you. You are going to help me raise hydroponic beans.

Lightning struck again. The glass house glittered like a diamond trapping light. Jesus, she thought, doesn't he know we could get killed? But he was humming a tune—the Trout?—and keeping time with his finger on her shoulder.

The lightning was going away. "What's going to happen now?" she asked him.

"Now? I'm going home now."

"What are you going to do, then?"

"What is expected of me. Take care of people who need taking care of. I have to see how my daughter is. I have an obligation to her. I have not been a good father. Then we'll see."

"Am I one of those people you're going to take care of?"

"Yes." He sat up. "I'm hungry."

"Me too." Juices spurted in her mouth. "I bought some steaks."

He didn't seem surprised. She put her marine jacket on. He lay quietly, watching her while she cooked. She didn't mind feeling his eyes on her back and her bare legs. She went outside, to get the beer. It didn't matter that it was cold and raining and she was barefoot.

The steaks were good. But he ate absently, as if they were in a restaurant and the steaks were no more or less than he expected. The rain stopped. It was still dark when he left. She didn't know what time it was.

She could not have said how long she stood in the doorway thinking of nothing, listening to the dripping rhododendrons, which were like large brooding presences stooping toward her—when he came back.

He was different. They stood, the candle between them. She didn't want to look at him.

"I forgot to tell you something. I will be your legal guardian if that is what you and your parents want. That will involve a fiduciary relationship which I will discharge faithfully, in your interest and to the best of my ability."

"Is that all?"

"Isn't that enough?"

"Is it enough for you?"

"Me?"

"Why do you sound so tired?"

"Me? It is not an interesting subject. At least not to me. The subject is closed, if not disclosed," he said, smiling.

"Ha."

"Thank you for taking care of me." He held out his hand. She did not take it. She hung her head like a mountain girl.

She did not seem to notice his leaving and stood thinking of nothing until it occurred to her that the dog hadn't been fed. It was pleasant to think of the dog's pleasure as she gathered up the steak scraps.

II

THE RAIN HAD STOPPED BUT IT WAS STILL DARK WHEN HE reached the Mercedes. He did not realize he was cold until he tried to unlock the door. His hand began to shake. Then, as if it had been given permission, his whole body began to shake. He opened the door. The courtesy lights came on. He looked at his watch. It was four o'clock. After he got under the wheel and closed the door, he waited for the lights to go out. The courtesy lights stayed on long enough to allow the driver to insert his key in the ignition. While the light was on, he was aware of a slight compulsion to do what the German light expected him to do, start the engine. The Mercedes was waiting for him.

But he did not start the engine. He sat shaking and smelling the car. It smelled of leather and wax and car newness. The shaking came in waves but he paid no attention. Three hundred yards away a naked yellow light bulb shone in the gable of a shed where electric carts were stored, each parked in its stall, plugged in and recharging. The shed hummed. A stray cart had been abandoned in the woods. Its roof supports were tilted at an angle but an empty Coke bottle hung vertically in its gimbel. The shaking stopped. Suddenly he became sleepy. It is possible, he thought, to drive home now, go straight up to the bedroom from the garage, sleep until eight, bathe, shave, dress, and appear for breakfast as usual in the sun parlor. In good weather the morning sun flashed on the polished silver and the soft white napery. Yamaiuchi's hand came twirling down with a melon, orange juice, shirred egg.

On the other hand, he was sleepy, as sleepy as he had ever

242

been in his life. Sleep came down around his ears like an iron hat.

Now sitting on the back seat, he felt for Marion's lap robe. It was thick, gray, heavy as a rug, smooth on one side and curly with lamb's wool on the other. It was the "cheap" lap robe, he remembered, which Marion had chosen rather than use the fur robe from the Rolls. Something winked in the feeble yellow light. It was the miniature bar fitted into the back of the front seat. She had given him the "little" Mercedes for their own outings. As she saw it, and as it pleased him to see her seeing it, in the Mercedes they were more or less like other Carolina couples in their Plymouths and Fords, which for a fact did look more and more like a Mercedes. No Rolls, no chauffeur, no fuss. Zip they went up the Blue Ridge Parkway, down to town for shopping, into Asheville to see her attorneys, over to Charlotte, Chapel Hill, and Durham for football and basketball games. What a pleasure for her and him, as much a pleasure for him to show her how the pleasure could be taken as to take it for himself, to set out on a fine football Saturday morning, meet the McKeons and Battles for a picnic at an interstate rest area, swing Marion into her wheelchair, tuck her legs in with the "cheap" lap robe, stand around drinks in hand, hampers open on tailgates, and with that festive fondness and the special dispensation conferred by the kickoff two hours away—and the extra pleasure too of the very publicness of the place, their own sector of clean public concrete staked out amidst the sleeping eighteen-wheelers and Florida-bound Airstreams, we taking pleasure from them, we on our way to the game, they coming and going in the old unheeding public world—tend the tiny bar, pour whiskey into gold-lined silver jiggers, and finally simply stand in the wine-colored Carolina sunlight sleepy and smiling and look at the colors of the leaves and of the bourbon whiskey against gold.

Now sitting in the back seat in the dark, he switched on the light and opened the bar and lifted the silver flask. It was full. He poured a drink and set it on the rectangle of polished walnut. His hand began to shake again.

There he sat in the same Mercedes, a 450 SEL 6.9-liter sedan, a badly flawed frazzled shaky American, as hollow-eyed as a Dachau survivor, still smelling of cave crud, in a perfect German machine redolent of leather, polished wood, and fine oil on steel.

The bar light was still on. By moving over to the right corner, he could see himself in the rearview mirror. How do I look in the face? Like General J. E. B. Stuart, whose last words were: How do I look in the face? Except for the beard, not different from the way I always looked, the same veiled eyes as dark and uncandid as Andrea del Sarto, the same curve of lip, the same sly uptilt of head showing nostril.

So he had looked thirteen years old when he had driven West with his father in a new Buick convertible. It took a week. It was the summer after the "hunting accident," as it became known. His father wanted them to be pals. But there was nothing to talk about. He didn't want to be anybody's pal. His father put the top down and drove faster and faster. The hot desert air roared in their ears. All day every day they drove in silence watching the center stripe on Texas highways and out old U.S. 66 for a thousand miles, two thousand miles, in silence while the boy watched girls in lonesome towns like Kingman and Barstow and squeezed his legs tight for the good feeling and speculated in amazement and hope that it would come to pass that there was a connection between girls and the good feeling. What wonders the future held in store! In silence they watched the bats fly out of Carlsbad Caverns at dusk and in silence rode the mules down into the Grand Canyon from Bright Angel Lodge. While the father drove ten, twelve hours a day, he slept on the back seat and between times sat up and gazed at the girls in Holbrook and Winslow and in the desert gazed at himself in the mirror. What a sly handsome lad you are. What the world must hold in store for you. What? Anything you want. Girls, money, God, fame, whatever you want. On they drove, faster and faster, roaring at ninety miles an hour through Needles, Arizona, where the heat lay puddled like mercury on the pavement. For a week he slept and gazed. His bowels did not move. In Los Angeles they did not see Chester Morris wearing a straw hat and driving down Hollywood Boulevard in a Packard convertible. Ross Alexander was dead. Groucho Marx was alive. Back East they roared in silence, the hot air singing in their ears, the man's gaze fixed on the highway, the boy's on girls or the face in the mirror then as now betrayed and victorious and sly. Even the man knew now they couldn't be pals.

Well then, does anything really change in a lifetime, he asked the sly sidelong-looking Andrea del Sarto in the Mercedes mirror? No, you are the same person with whom I struck the pact roaring out old U.S. 66 through the lonesome towns and the empty desert. You don't ever really learn anything you didn't know when you were thirteen.

And what was that?

All I knew for sure then and now was that after what happened to me nothing could ever defeat me, no matter what else happened in this bloody century. If you didn't defeat me, old mole, loving father and death-dealer, nothing can, not wars, not this century, not the Germans. We beat the Germans, nutty as we are, and now drive perfect German cars, we somewhat frazzled it is true, and shaky, but victorious nevertheless.

Ah, but what if the death is not in the century but in your own genes, that you of all men are a child of the century because you are as death-bound by your own hand as the century is and you of all men should be most at home now, as bred for death as surely as a pointer bitch to point, that death your own death is what you really love and won't be happy till you have, what then?

Then we'll know, won't we?

Grinning and shivering on the back seat thirty years later, teeth clacking, this raddled middle-aged American sat in his German car in the mountains of North Carolina hugging himself and making shoulder movements like a man giving body English to a pinball machine except that he was thinking about J. E. B. Stuart and Baron von Richthofen and World War II and fighting the Germans, which he had not done. Instead, he took two quick drinks from the gold-lined silver jigger and waited until the warmth bloomed under his ribs and the shaking stopped.

Something occurred to him. Excitedly he jumped out of the car and, paying no attention to the cold drizzle which had started up again, paced back and forth beside the silver Mercedes, smacking his arms around his body and now and then kicking the Michelin radials. If the girl in the greenhouse a few hundred yards away could have seen him, she would have shaken her head. Though it was she who had been the mental patient and he the solidest citizen of the community, early retiree, philanthropist, president of United Way, six-handicap golfer, surely it was he not she who was deranged now, who, after holing up in a cave for two weeks, now paced up and down the parking lot of the Linwood Country Club in the predawn darkness, kicking a German car, while sane folk snored in their beds. Now he snapped his fingers and nodded to himself, for all the world like a man who has hit upon the solution to a problem which had vexed him for years.

Ha, there is a secret after all, he said. But to know the secret answer, you must first know the secret question. The question is, who is the enemy?

Not to know the name of the enemy is already to have been killed by him.

Ha, he said, dancing, snapping his fingers and laughing and hooting *ha hoo hee*, jumping up and down and socking himself, *but I do know. I know. I know the name of the enemy.*

The name of the enemy is death, he said, grinning and shoving his hands in his pockets. Not the death of dying but the living death.

The name of this century is the Century of the Love of Death. Death in this century is not the death people die but the death people live. Men love death because real death is better than the living death. That's why men like wars, of course. Bad as wars are and maybe because they are so bad, thinking of peace during war is better than peace. War is what makes peace desirable. But peace without war is intolerable. Why do men settle so easily for lives which are living deaths? Men either kill each other in war, or in peace walk as docilely into living death as sheep into a slaughterhouse.

Why do men walk like sheep straight into the slaughterhouse? Why are people content to stand helpless while their lifeblood is drained away?

Men in this century are no different from the Jews at Buchenwald who did not give themselves leave to resist death.

I know your name at last, he said, laughing and hooting *hee hee hooooee* like a pig-caller and kicking the tires, and you are not going to prevail over me.

Old father of lies, that's what you are, the devil himself, for only the devil could have thought up all the deceits and guises under which death masquerades. But I know all your names.

Here are the names of death, which shall not prevail over me because I know the names.

Death in the guise of love shall not prevail over me. You, old father old mole, loved me but loved death better and in the name of love sought death for both of us. You only kissed me once and it was the kiss of death. True, death is a way out of a life-which-is-a-living-death. War and shooting is better than such a peace. But what if there is life?

Everybody has given up. Everybody thinks that there are only two things: war which is a kind of life in death, and peace which is a kind of death in life. But what if there should be a third thing, life?

Death in the guise of Christianity is not going to prevail over me. If Christ brought life, why do the churches smell of death?

Death in the guise of old Christendom in Carolina is not going to prevail over me. The old churches are houses of death.

Death in the form of the new Christendom in Carolina is not going to prevail over me. If the born-again are the twice born, I'm holding out for a third go-round.

Death in the guise of God and America and the happy life of home and family and friends is not going to prevail over me. America is in fact almost as dead as Europe. It might still be possible to live in America, said the nutty American dancing in place in old Carolina.

Death in the guise of belief is not going to prevail over me, for believers now believe anything and everything and do not love the truth, are in fact in despair of the truth, and that is death.

Death in the guise of unbelief is not going to prevail over me, for unbelievers believe nothing, not because truth does not exist but because they have already chosen not to believe, and would not believe, cannot believe, even if the living truth stood before them, and that is death.

Death in the guise of the new life in California is not going to prevail over me. Marin County and the Cupps are not going to prevail over me. But what if the Cupps and Marin County should prevail? Then the Germans and my father are right and war is better than peace, true death better than the living death. But it will not prevail over me because I know the names of death.

Death in the form of isms and asms shall not prevail over me, orgasm, enthusiasm, liberalism, conservatism, Communism, Buddhism, Americanism, for an ism is only another way of despairing of the truth.

Death in the guise of marriage and family and children is not going to prevail over me. What happened to marriage and family that it should have become a travail and a sadness, marriage till death do us part yes but long dead before the parting, home and fireside and kiddies such a travail and a deadliness as to make a man run out into the night with his hands over his head? Show me that Norman Rockwell picture of the American family at Thanksgiving dinner and I'll show you the first faint outline of the death's-head.

God may be good, family and marriage and children and home may be good, grandma and grandpa may act wise, the Thanksgiving table may be groaning with God's goodness and bounty, all the folks healthy and happy, but something is missing. What is this sadness here? Why do the folks put up with it? The truth seeker does not. Instead of joining hands with the folks and bowing his head in prayer, the truth seeker sits in an empty chair as invisible as Banquo's ghost, yelling at the top of his voice: *Where is it? What is missing? Where did it go? I won't have it! I won't have it! Why this sadness here? Don't stand for it! Get up! Leave! Let the boat people sit down! Go live in a cave until you've found the thief who is robbing you. But at least protest. Stop, thief! What is missing? God? Find him!*

Ross Alexander left his happy home in Beverly Hills, saying: I'm going outside and shoot a duck.

You gave in to death, old mole, but I will not have it so. It is a matter of knowing and choosing. To know the many names of death is also to know there is life. I choose life. *Hee hoo hee heee hooeee*. He was shivering and dancing in place, hands in pockets like an Irishman doing a jig. Is it possible that a man in the last half of his life can actually learn something he didn't know before? Yes! *Ha hee hooee.*

Death in the form of death genes shall not prevail over me, for death genes are one thing but it is something else to name the death genes and know them and stand over against them and dare them. I am different from my death genes and therefore not subject to them. My father had the same death genes but he feared them and did not name them and thought he could roar out old Route 66 and stay ahead of them or grab me and be pals or play Brahms and keep them, the death genes, happy, so he fell prey to them.

Death in none of its guises shall prevail over me, because I know all the names of death.

Having pronounced this peculiar litany, he hopped into the car, lay down on the back seat, covered himself with the lap robe, stuck his nose in a fragrant crease of leather, and went to sleep.

This is what is going to happen.

In the very moment of sinking into a deep sleep he had, not

a dream or a flight of fancy, but a swift sure unsurprised presentiment of what lay in store.

Thirty years earlier the child knew that something was going to happen, and that the something was all he ever wanted or needed to know, and that it only remained for him to wait for it to happen and to settle for nothing less until it did.

What was the something? Women? War? Or victory in life? Death?

Thirty years passed. He had women, war, and victory in life. But nothing changed. Thirty years later he knew no more than he knew in Dalhart, Texas, squeezing his legs together and looking at girls.

Yes, but you have just discovered again what you knew all along, that something is going to happen.

This is what is going to happen. All at once he knew what had happened and what was going to happen.

He found himself in a certain place. It was a desert place. Weeds grew in the sand. Vines sprouted in the rocks. The place was a real place. Its exact location could be determined within inches by map coordinates, ninety-one degrees so many minutes so many seconds longitude west, thirty-three degrees so many minutes so many seconds latitude north. He had been there forty years earlier. Then the place had not been deserted. It was a spot near a stream which ran through a meadow. The spot was in a springhouse on the stream where crocks of milk and sweet butter used to be stored. D'Lo still liked to keep her own buttermilk there because it was not far from her house, which had no refrigerator, and she could pick it up on the way home. She found him there in the cool darkness watching reflections of light play against the damp masonry. Boy, what you are doing down here? I been looking all over for you, it's your dinnertime. (He didn't answer.) Now you come on up and eat with D'Lo. (He didn't answer.) Don't you remember how you always used to sit with D'Lo in the kitchen while they ate in the dining room? And when you had your spells, you'd come running in the kitchen and jump up in my lap and put your head right here? Sometimes I'd hold you all day. (No, I don't remember.) You come on here, boy, and let D'Lo hug you. You po little old white boy. (She hugged him but he didn't feel anything except that he was being hugged by a big black woman. What's this about big black loving mammies?) You poor little old boy, you all alone in the world. Your mama dead, your daddy dead, and ain't nobody left in the house but you and me. (That's not bad. He thought of the novelty of walking home from school in the afternoons to the big house empty except for D'Lo shuffling around in her flattened-out mules. Strange! But not bad.) Sweet Jesus, what we gon do? (One thing we gon do, D'Lo, is you gon turn me loose.) He stiffened. She was angry. He knew she would be. He already knew enough about people to know what displeased them. He knew how to please people, even black people. He was everybody's nigger. He was even the niggers' nigger. (Her lower lip ran out. There came across her face the new peevish black-*vs.*-white expression—for a second he saw that she wasn't sure he hadn't stiffened because of the new-white-*vs.*-black business. She let go.) You poor little old boy, you don't know nothing. You don't even know what you need to know. You don't even know enough to know what you ain't got. (She wasn't angry now. He knew she wouldn't be.) But don't you worry, honey. You all alone in the world and you gon be alone a long time but the good Lawd got something special in mind for you. (He has?) Sho he has. (How do you know that?) Because he got the whole world in his hand, even a mean little old boy like you. (How do you know that?) Because, bless God, I know. You laughing at me, boy? (No, D'Lo.) You full of devilment but you messing with the wrong one this time. Now you get on up to the kitchen and we gon have us some pork chops and butter beans and then we gon set down on the back porch and listen to the radio. (Well, it beats sitting on the front porch and listening to Brahms.) What you say, boy? (Nothing.)

Then the spot became part of a country club, the exact patch of grass in the concavity of a kidney-shaped bunker on number-six fairway. For twenty years winter and summer thousands of golf balls, cart tires, spiked shoes crossed the spot.

After twenty years the country club became a subdivision. The spot was the corner of a lot where a ranch-style house was built for a dentist named Sam Gold. Weeds grew in the fence corner where not even the Yazoo Master mower could reach and covered an iron horseshoe for ten years. Though Sam Gold was a Jew, places meant nothing to him. One place, even Jerusalem, was like any other place. Why did he, Will Barrett, who was not a Jew, miss the Jerusalem he had never had and which meant nothing to Sam Gold, who was a Jew?

After twenty-five years the subdivision became a shopping center, with a paved parking lot of forty acres. The spot was now located in the mall between the Orange Julius stand and the entrances to H&R Block. The mall was crowded with shoppers for twenty years.

Now it was deserted. When he came to years from now, he was lying on the spot. The skylight of the mall was broken. The terrazzo was cracked. Grass sprouted. Somewhere close, water ran. Old tax forms blew out of H&R Block. A raccoon lived in the Orange Julius stand. No one was there. Yet something moved and someone spoke. Maybe it was D'Lo. No. Was it Allie? No, nobody. No, somebody was there all right. Someone spoke: Very well, since you've insisted on it, here it is, the green-stick Rosebud gold-bug matador, the great distinguished thing.

The ocean was not far away.

As he turned to see who said it and who it was, there was a flash of light then darkness then light again.

III

SUNLIGHT SHONE IN HIS EYES, THEN SOMEONE CAME BE-
tween, then sunlight shone in his eyes again.

"Could it be? It is. Is that you, Will?"

"Yes," he said, instantly awake, a thousand miles from
his dreams, as unsurprised as if he were back in his office
again. "Who—?" Holding a hand against the sun, he tried
to make out the dark eclipsed face inside its bright corona of
hair. What he recognized was the Alabama quirky-lilting
voice and the way the round bare shoulder hitched up a little.
"Kitty." He sat up.

"You stood me up, you dog. You no good scoun'l beast. Look
at you. You're a mess! Happy birthday yesterday."

"What? Oh."

"We had a date in your summerhouse. Don't you remember?"

He smiled. "What day was that?" What year was that? It
pleased him that she was no more than mildly outraged and
evidently found nothing remarkable in his absence or his appearance or finding him asleep in a car and looking like Ben
Gunn. "I was called away suddenly," he said. "I only just got
back."

"So I notice," said Kitty absently, gazing at him. How, in
what manner, was she gazing at him?

"Come around to the other side so I can see you."

Instead, Kitty got in the front seat and turned around to face
him. The sun shone on the tiny beads of sweat on the down of
her upper lip. She smelled of "prespiration," which is the name

we used to give lady sweat, which is a good name for it because it smells like prespiration, which smells more Presbyterian than perspiration. He smiled: I'm beginning to think like Allie.

"Who are you going to play golf with? Walter?"

"I already played eighteen holes, and not with Walter." Her strong brown arm hugged the leather seat. The hand swung free just above his belt buckle.

Then it was afternoon. The sun had not cleared the cart shed rising; it had cleared the Mercedes roof setting.

It was odd seeing Allie in her, not just the upper lip drawn short by its double tendon but the quick economical stooping movements, the bowing of neck which caused the vertebra to surface in the smooth flesh, the risible watchfulness of the eyes searching his face. Yet somehow the liveliness which in Allie was graceful and shy became in Kitty rowdy and jostling. The hand in its pendulum arc touched his belt. The same become opposites in mother and daughter yet still remain the same. Chromosomes cast inverted but recognizable shadows of themselves.

"How do you feel, Will?"

"Fine. I slept all day."

"Lewis is here. Do you want to see him?"

"Lewis Peckham?"

She nodded. He wondered if when the fingers touched him it would leave a welt like a pendulum. "He was in the foursome."

"With Walter and—?"

"Not with Walter. Walter is long gone."

"Gone?"

"I mean he's gone. Took off. All we have in common now is this business with Allie."

"I see. How did you find me?"

"That's my car. I parked next to you this morning."

"You mean you saw me this morning?"

"Yes."

He pondered the fact that Kitty had seen him, recognized him, and played eighteen holes of golf.

"Why didn't you wake me up?"

"You were sleeping very soundly and dreaming. Your lips and eyes were moving."

"I see."

"I did call your daughter Leslie, though. She's been terribly concerned about you."

"What did you tell her?"

"Only that you'd be coming home when you woke up. Will you?"

"Yes. You mean she's back from her honeymoon?"

"She doesn't believe in honeymoons. She and Jason stayed here. She's discovered backwoods churches where people speak in tongues. She and Jack Curl have gotten very close."

"Jack Curl?"

"Yes. It seems they have great plans for the Peabody Foundation." She looked at him.

"There is no Peabody Foundation—yet."

"Well, they are planning one."

"I see."

"Are you sure you feel well?"

"Yes."

"We missed you at the wedding."

"Wedding. Oh yes."

"Same old Will. Same old Huck Finn lighting out for the territory. You know we've always been two of a kind."

"We have? How?"

"Both of us can only stand the rat race for so long. Then bye-bye, folks."

"Was Leslie's wedding all right?"

"Sure. Leslie read from the Bible and Jason read from *The Prophet*. It was very casual. Nobody blamed you for ducking out. Leslie and Jason said they would do the same in your place. In fact, both of them think you're like them. Unstructured."

"I am?"

"Leslie understands you better than you think, Will."

"She does?"

"Please try to understand her."

"Okay."

"Poor Will." She clucked and shook her head.

"Why poor Will?"

"What are you going to do now, Will?"

"Go home. I want to see Leslie."

"She's not there."

"Where is she?"

"She and Jason have moved into a community down in the cove."

"A community?"

"A love-and-faith community. That's what she and Jack want to use the Peabody Foundation for, to found such communities around the world, communities for all ages. Maybe the kids know something we don't know, Will."

"Yes."

"Anyhow, she's closed the house, but she knows you are coming there."

"I see."

Kitty's hand came to rest on his thigh. His thigh swelled. "Now listen, Will. This is important."

"Okay."

"I think I know where Allie is."

"Allie."

"Oh, Will, I need your help, but just look at you. You're a mess!" Suddenly leaning over, she took hold of a handful of his flank and gave him a great friendly tweak. "Listen, Will, I need to talk to you." But even as she said this, her mind seemed to wander. Her eyes went away. "You see that car."

"What car?"

"My car. Right there. What does it remind you of?"

He looked at the car. It was a black Continental. "I don't know."

"Don't you remember Daddy's Lincoln?"

"Yes."

"Do you remember the last time?"

"The last time?"

"After you came back from Santa Fe. Before you took off for good?"

"Ah—"

"When we parked behind the golf course like this?"

"Ah—"

"Ho ho ho you remember all right. Now, Will, listen to me."

"All right."

"We need to talk. About Allie, for one thing. I need to see you. Go home. Get cleaned up. Shave. My God, where have you been, laying in some gutter? Tomcattin'?" She gave him a poke. "All this time you could have been at Dun Romin' with me taking care of you. After you get settled, come over to my villa. We need to talk about Allie. I'm right over there in number six, Dun Romin'—don't you like that?"

"Very well, but if it's about Allison, I'll need to talk to Walter too."

"Honey, I done told you. Friend Walter has split."

"Split."

"Checked out. Long gone. Headed for the islands, or rather the island. Come to Dun Romin' and I'll tell you all about it." She hooked three fingers inside his belt and gave him a tug.

"I see." He mused: Did Kitty's special boldness come from a special sadness? Or do women grow more lustful as they grow older? "You and Walter are separated?"

"I told you things have been popping around here!" Now swinging around merrily, she knelt as if she were in a pew, arms on the back of the seat. Was she merry or sad? "No, seriously. It's been in the cards for years. It's not that Walter has this thing for his little receptionists—the older he gets, the younger they get—I couldn't care less. What it is is there's nothing between us. Nothing. Maybe there never was. So we've split. And we've agreed. He gets the Georgia island. I get the mountain here."

"Don't they belong to Allie?" He was watching her eyes, which were rounded and merry but also going away.

"Did I tell you I think I found out where Allie is?"

"No."

"She's here!"

"Here?"

"Not a mile from this spot. Lewis told me without knowing he was telling me. He thinks the world of you, thinks you're the solidest citizen around. I didn't tell him otherwise, that you're the original flake and we're two of a kind, the original misfits. Oh, Will, you're the raunchiest loveliest mess I ever saw, let's get in the Lincoln—no, I'm kidding. Lewis just happened to mention that a girl's been living out at the old Kemp place, a shy blond little woods creature. She called it her place. Who else could it be? All he had to say was that she comes to town once a week, goes to the A & P, buys oatmeal, talks funny, says no more than three words, and I knew. It's Allie. I'm going to see her now. Lewis drew me a map. Want to come? No, you go home."

"What do you and Walter want to do with Allie?"

"Just me. Walter has copped out. He's agreeable to anything. All he can think about are what he calls his Ayrabs. He and his Ayrabs, as he calls them, are going to turn the island into a 144-

hole golf course with an airport big enough to take 727s from Kuwait.''

''Very well. What do you want to do with Allie?''

''Allie.'' For the first time the merry Polly Bergen wrinkles at the corners of her eyes ironed out, showing white. Her eyes went fond and far away. ''Allie Allie Allie. What to do with Allie?'' Her eyes came back. ''Let's face it, Will.''

''Okay.''

''Alistair's been telling me this for years but I couldn't or wouldn't believe him.''

''Alistair?''

''Dr. Duk.''

''What's he been telling you?''

''Will,'' said Kitty and in her voice he recognized the sweet timbre, the old authentic Alabama thrill of bad news. ''Will, Allie can't make it. Allie is not going to make it, Will. She can't live in this world. No way.''

''Me neither.''

''What?'' said Kitty dreamily.

''Nothing. How do you know she can't make it?'' On the contrary, he thought. She may be the only one who can make it.

''Because Alistair told me. And because I know her and I know what happens when she tries. Do I ever know.''

''What happens when she tries?''

''At first she's bright as can be. Too bright. Everything is Christmas morning. And that's the trouble. She can only live if every day is Christmas morning. But she doesn't know how to live from one Christmas to the next.''

''What happens when she tries?''

''She can't cope.''

''What does that mean?''

''I mean that she literally does not know how to live. She can't talk, she can't sleep, she can't work. So she crawls into a hole and pulls it in after her. Twice I've saved her from starvation. I can't take that responsibility any more.''

''What do you want to do with her?''

''What is best for her. The best-structured environment money can buy, and all the freedom she can handle.''

''You mean you want to commit her.''

''I've talked it over again with Alistair. She can have her own cottage. She can do anything that you or I can do. The only difference is that I intend to make sure she will not injure herself. She will be around people who understand her and with whom she can talk or not talk as she chooses. She will have everything you and I have—books, music, art, companionship, you name it. And you and I will be here if she needs us.''

He must have fallen silent for some time because the next thing he knew she was poking him in her old style.

"What?'' he said with a start.

"Wake up. I was talking about Allie.''

"I know.''

"Tell me something, Will.''

"Okay.''

"Does Allie's life make sense to you?''

"Well I don't—'' he began.

"It's like Ludean said. Ludean, Grace's wonderful old Nigra cook. You know what she told me? She said: That chile don't belong in this world, Miss Kitty.''

He was silent. He was thinking about firelight on Allie's face and arms and breasts as she knelt to feed logs into the iron stove.

"You know what she meant, don't you?''

"No.''

"In her own way she was expressing the wisdom of the ages. I'm sure Ludean never heard of reincarnation, but what she was saying in her own way was that Allie had come from another life but had not quite made it all the way. That does happen, you know. I can't find much written on the subject but it seems quite reasonable to me that some incarnations are more successful than others, that some, like Allie's, don't take. That's why we use expressions like she's not all there. Though I would say she's not all here. You ought to see her eyes. She's seeing something we don't see.''

He thought of Allie's eyes, the quick lively look she gave him, lips pressed tight, after she hoisted him onto the bunk, her hands busy with him like a child bedding down a big doll.

"There is no other explanation for it, Will. If I didn't know what I know, I couldn't stand it. As it is, it is so simple, so obvious.''

For a fact, she did seem to know something. There was in her eyes just above the Mercedes seat the liveliness (so like Allie yet unlike) of someone who knows a secret you haven't caught on to. "Don't you see it, you dummy, or do I have to tell you?"

"What is it you know?"

"Allie did have another life. Unlike most of us, you and me for instance, her karma is so strong she almost remembers it. Sometimes I think she does. In fact, after one session with Ray at Virginia Beach, she did remember it."

"Ray?"

"A true mystic—and you know how hardheaded I am about such things. Well, I can tell you there was no humbug here. After trance and regression, first Ray's trance without Allie present, then Allie's regression, both wrote down what they saw. I was there, I took the papers, I read them. It's scientific proof. The particulars differ but there is enough to know what sort of life Allie had and the explanation of what she's going through now. The upshot is that our duty is to protect her and take care of her while she works it out."

"Works what out?"

"The karma of that life. Or lives."

"Lives?"

"They described two lives but essentially they were the same. Allie's version was that she had been a camp follower of the Union Army before the battle of Chancellorsville. Now here's the fascinating part. When Allie would get down on herself and crawl into her hole, she would say over and over again: I'm no good, I'm a liar, I'm the original hooker. Over and over again she would say, *I'm the original hooker.* Now, that's not Allie's style—I doubt if she ever even heard that word. But we look up the word and guess what. It turns out that the word *hooker* was first applied to camp followers of General Hooker's army who fought—guess where?—at the battle of Chancellorsville. So when she said I'm the original *hooker* she was telling the literal truth. Those that have ears—?

"What was the other version?"

"Okay. Here's what Ray had written after his trance. Allie had been not a hooker but a courtesan spy for the North in Richmond, where she was known as a great Southern belle who charmed many officers with her wit and conversation. Later we figured out that they might both be right. There had been a famous Union spy in Richmond who had been a prostitute, a hooker. Isn't that fascinating? But of course what really matters is how it explains her present life."

"How?"

"Don't you see? Then she was too much of this world, she knew too many men, talked too much, lied too much, and abused her body. So now she is not of this world, knows nobody, can't talk enough to lie, doesn't use her body at all. Or as she would put it: my body doesn't work—implying that, before, her body *worked*."

Kitty went on smoothly from Allie to herself and her karma and to him and his Scorpio tenacity: "Oh, I could have told you twenty years ago if you'd asked me, that you would have to undergo trial and exile before you finally won, like Napoleon and Lenin and Robert Bruce. Your destiny is the Return."

"Napoleon didn't win," he said.

Her belief in such matters was both absolute and perfunctory. There was a plausibility to it. Things fell into place. Mysteries were revealed. Why could he not be a believer? Who were the believers now? Everyone. Everyone believed everything. We're all from California now. Yet we believe with a kind of perfunctoriness. Even now Kitty was inattentive, eyes drifting as she talked. In the very act of uttering her ultimate truths, she was too bored to listen.

"Ah, I've got to go," he said suddenly, getting out of the car stiffly and setting one foot toward the woods.

"Where are you going?"

"Home."

"Why don't you drive?" asked Kitty, laughing.

"Right," he said, frowning and fumbling for the keys.

"Now, you're coming to see me after you've talked to Leslie?"

"Sure," he said, feeling his face. Suddenly he wanted a shave, a bath, a drink.

"Just remember. Villa number six. Dun Romin'."

"Right," he said absently. "Dun Romin'."

2

Things began to happen fast. For one thing, he noticed, the days were ending much sooner. The sun, smaller and colder, dropped quickly behind a mountain. Events speeded up. A general law

260

of acceleration prevailed. His Mercedes fairly zipped along the highway yet other cars honked and passed him.

The house was dark and silent when he stopped in the driveway. The sun seemed to be setting in the gorge. The stunted maple which looked like a post oak was nearly stripped of its leaves.

He frowned and drove into the garage. The garage was empty. Both the Rolls and Yamaiuchi's Datsun were gone. Hm.

The house above him did not tick and settle like a lived-in house cooling off. There was a sense in its silence of people having moved away. The house did not breathe. It was unlived-in. How long had he been gone?

He was standing against the inner wall of the garage watching the oblong of eastern sky. It seemed to turn violet. A small rainbow formed. There was no cloud. He shut one eye. The rainbow went away. He opened the eye. The rainbow came back. He walked to the door. There seemed to be two doors where once there was one. He walked into the wall. He closed his left eye. One door went away.

The door was unlocked. He climbed the rear stairs to his bedroom. The sun rested on the rim of the gorge like a copper plate on a shelf. The room was filled with a rosy light. He walked around, hands in pockets. The bed had been stripped. The closet was empty. No, the Greener shotgun was still there in its case. The Luger in its holster hung from a hook. Head cocked, he gazed at the room. There was something he didn't like about the light of the setting sun filling the empty room. The room seemed to have an emotion of its own. Was it the feeling of someone present or someone absent? He frowned again and turned quickly toward the bathroom. No, rooms do not have emotions. Rooms are only rooms. How he hated the fake sadness of things. As he turned, he fell. Christ, I'm weak from hunger, he thought. But it's not bad to be down here on the floor. Above him the bar of sunlight stretched out straight as a plank. Motes drifted aimlessly in and out of the light. The bar of sunlight seemed significant. He sat up and shook his head. No, things do not have significances. The laser beam was nothing more than light reflected from motes he had stirred up. It was not "stark." One place is like any other place.

A sudden sharp smell came to his nostrils. It was the smell of a Negro cabin in winter, a clean complex smell of newspapers, flour paste, coal oil, and Octagon soap. How is such a thing possible? he said, smiling, and stood up. Goodbye, Georgia.

No, the closet was not empty. A single hanger held a pair of slacks and a clean shirt he recognized and a tan cardigan sweater he did not recognize. Neatly folded on the top shelf were a T-shirt and shorts and on the shoe rack with a rolled-up sock tucked neatly in each a pair of new loafers. The gun case stood in the corner. Strange. He had never worn loafers or a cardigan sweater. Then Leslie had closed the house. She has moved me out. But she has bought me a new outfit. She has plans for me.

The bathroom was empty except for a towel, soap, comb, and his Sunbeam razor. When he saw the figure in the doorway he did not give a start but he felt his face prepare itself to address a stranger. But the stranger was his reflection in the full-length mirror fixed to the door. It was then that he saw that the expression on his face was the agreeable but slightly fearful smile one might assume with an interloper. What can I do for you? He looked like a drunk bearded mountaineer or a soldier who had fought and marched for days and slept in his clothes. The cloth of his shirt and pants felt like skin.

He ran a hot full tub. When he let himself aching and cold down into the steaming water, he groaned and laughed out loud. Oh my God, how can a simple thing like a hot bath be this good, and since it is, is happiness no more than having something you've done without for a long time and aaah does it matter?

He bathed for a long time, shaved carefully, combed his hair, and dressed. He looked at himself. He was thin, he felt weak, hungry, lightheaded, but fit enough. Something was odd, however. It was the cardigan sweater and loafers. They made him look like an agreeable youngish old man, like a young Dr. Marcus Welby. All he needed was a pipe. He found a new pipe on the dresser! And a Bible.

He went into the hall and down the front stairs and turned on the lights. It was only then that he found the two notes on the refectory table in the foyer. They were in envelopes addressed to him. One, in Leslie's hand, said *Poppy.* The other in Bertie's hand said *Willie* and below and underlined: *Urgent!*

Bertie's note read:

Please call me, Willie. Urgent.

Leslie's letter read:

Dearest Poppy:

Kitty just told me where you are. I did not want to wake you so I'm leaving this note for you, knowing you're coming here.

I've forgiven you everything. I did not mind your doing your usual number and splitting for parts unknown before the wedding, but I admit it did hurt a little to learn you had spent the past week shacked up in the woods with a little forest sprite not two miles away. But we always can have the forgiveness of sins through the riches of his grace (Eph. 1:7). Anyhow, I acted like a pill myself.

But everything is different now! My joy is fulfilled (John 3:29).

Dr. Battle told me of your whereabouts during the past week. He felt consideration for your health outweighed doctor-patient confidence.

Jack Curl and Jason and I have some wonderful ideas for the love-and-faith community you and Jack are planning. What you and your little sprite do is your business, but before you make any radical decisions, lets sit down with Lewis and Jack and finalize the Marion Peabody Foundation, which was Mother's dream.

We'll be at Jack Curl's house waiting for you. I laid out some clothes for you. Closed house. Will tell you more. Can't wait to see ya.

> Devotedly,
> Yours in the Lord,
> Leslie

Dearest? Ya? Devotedly? What's cooking here, Leslie? The slanginess was not like her. The friendliness was ominous. The "devotedly" was somewhere north of love and south of sincerely. He liked her old sour self better.

What was she up to? He felt a faint prickle of interest under the unfamiliar cashmere of the cardigan. Dr. Marcus Welby chuckled and tapped out his empty pipe. Was she afraid he was going to marry Allie and blow the Peabody millions? Then what would happen to hers and Jack Curl's love-and-faith community? Kelso would say they're out to screw you. But Kelso was crazy. He shrugged. Did it matter?

He telephoned Bertie.

"Willie, I'm delighted heh heh," said Bertie, coming as close as he could to a laugh, a hollow Hampton chortle, a whuffling sound. "Happy birthday."

"What's that?" he asked quickly. "Oh, yes. I forgot. Thank you."

"This is not just your ordinary birthday," said Bertie. Bertie's horseface, he knew, would be slanted and keen about the nostrils.

"It isn't?"

"Don't you know what this means, Willie?" Bertie's voice lowered. He sounded as if he were covering the receiver with both hands like a spy in a phone booth.

"No, what?"

"As of yesterday, you are eligible for the Seniors, a young fellow like you! They changed the rules last year."

"The Seniors," he said, musing.

"Yes. Your birthday was yesterday, which makes you eligible. First the tournament here this weekend. After that, the tour. We can do Hilton Head and Sea Island before Thanksgiving. Willie, we got them by the short and curlies heh heh hough."

"We have?"

"Figure the arithmetic. You're at least six strokes better than your new handicap of twelve which was posted last week and which was due to your slice which you can correct easily if you put your mind to it—you couldn't have planned it better, in fact. I'm ten strokes better than my twenty-five—I sneaked out yesterday and carded a ninety-four. We'll sandbag ever' sucker between here and Augusta," said Bertie, trying to talk Southern, but it still came out hollow-throat Hampton. "We'll clean up on them."

He couldn't think of anything to say.

"Willie—"

"Yes."

"Could we at least sign up for the Seniors here?"

"Why not?"

"I've been thinking about your slice."

"Yes?"

"I think I can straighten you out. Okay?"

"Sure."

"That's my boy. No, seriously. In my opinion, and Lewis

agrees, you haven't begun to realize your potential. If you put your mind to it, you could knock off Snead and Hogan."

An eighty-year-old Gene Sarazen. Why not?

Why not play golf with hale and ruddy Seniors for the next thirty years? He'd be the youngest on the tour, the Golden Bear among the old grizzlies.

When he drove the Mercedes back to town in the dark, a light flew behind the bushes at the corner of his eye as if a runner with a lantern were keeping pace. The road ran along the ridge, which fell away on both sides. He saw two roads instead of one, and thinking himself to be on an interstate, took the passing lane, until he saw headlights coming straight at him. He spun the wheel. As he was crossing the shoulder of the highway and the car which almost hit him was still blowing its horn in an outraged Doppler downbeat *eeeoooo*, he had time to wonder how shallow the ditch was and how steep the drop-off beyond it. Saplings lashed at the windows as if his car were still and a storm raged. The Mercedes, riding trees, airborne, rose and hit something hard but at an angle which bore him up even higher.

His head struck the windshield.

The car was propped at a queer angle. Though he had slid against the door and was comfortable enough, head propped against the post like a motorist taking a nap, he noticed that the window did not let onto leaves or earth as might be expected but deep empty dark. Perhaps it would be better to wait until daylight before climbing out, he thought, dozing. He thought about the Greener and the Luger he had locked in the trunk.

3

He was walking along the highway, hands in pockets. The November sun was warm on his back. Jewelweed still bloomed in the ditches. Bright yellow birds fluttered in the trees. Cars and trucks roared past him in a hurry to leave somewhere or arrive somewhere. The drivers gazed straight ahead, swerving only slightly to miss him. Their faces showed a strong sense of purpose. Most of the cars, he noticed, had North Carolina plates. North Carolina. What am I doing here? he wondered. A Mazda passed with a bumper sticker which read: YOUR GOD MAY BE DEAD BUT I TALKED TO MINE THIS MORNING.

Behind him the Mercedes was wedged securely in the crotch of a maple not high above a ravine. He had not been in danger. It was an easy matter to open a door on the high side, climb out, and drop the few feet to the soft earth.

When he thrust his hands in his pockets he found a roll of bills. He sat in the sunny dry ditch and counted them. Five hundred dollars in fifties. He smiled and nodded, put the money back in his pocket, and resumed walking. With one part of his mind he knew where the money came from. But if someone had asked him, he might not have been able to answer. Leslie has staked me, he said to himself. Leslie has a plan. He felt himself in good hands.

In the bus-station restaurant, he ate a breakfast of three fried eggs, a plate of grits and bacon, two pieces of buttered toast, and two cups of coffee. He felt fine but somewhat abstracted, like a man who is looking at something without seeing it yet cannot bring himself to tear his eyes away. A man sitting next to him at the counter began to speak to him and he nodded agreeably but didn't listen. The man was talking about Georgia.

After he paid his check, he found a tall man walking beside him. The man was talking to him. It was the same man. He looked at him. Though the tall man stood reared back, feet apart, as if he had a big belly, he did not. Actually he was thin and seemed infirm. His rimless glasses flashed. His cheeks were pale and withered but his lips curved richly as if they belonged to a hearty man.

Now they were standing more or less in line at the ticket window. The tall man was explaining something. Suddenly he made a fist of one hand and thrust it into the other open hand and pushed with all his might. The man's pale face grew red and his elbows trembled.

He began to listen.

"This is how I stay fit," said the tall man. "Even though I set at a desk ten hours a day. Sat, that is." Then, instead of pushing, he hooked his fingers together and began to pull so hard his face grew red again.

"What do you do?" he asked the tall man curiously.

"You mean what did I do?"

"Yes, what did you do?"

"I was with the Associates."

"Associates? You were associated with—?"

"No, it's a loan company. The Associates. I'm going back to settle some unfinished business. Then I'm set."

The man was returning to Georgia to sell his house. He and his wife had bought a garden home in Emerald Isle Estates. He explained the difference between a villa, a condominium, a mountain home, and a garden home. A garden home had the privacy of a villa and the maintenance services of a condominium and more land than a mountain home. Though he had lived and worked in Atlanta twenty years as an Associate, he was returning to Valdosta to sell his family home. It had once been a farm.

"Do you play golf?" he asked the tall man. Emerald Isle Estates was nothing but a raw new golf course surrounding a small new lake with eroded red banks which looked like a Georgia cattle pond.

"No, I never. But I don't have to to keep in shape. In Atlanta I walked to work twenty blocks down West Peachtree every day."

The tall man had come close and now took his arm in a freckled hand as if he were going to tell him a joke or say something about the Negroes in Atlanta, but he didn't lower his head but stood reared, head high, lips curved in a smile, rimless glasses flashing in the fluorescent light.

When he tried to move his arm, the man's grip tightened. He must have something else to say. What would the tall man do in Emerald Isle Estates if he didn't play golf? walk on the highway? watch TV? do isometrics? Who would he talk to?

"What about you?" the man said.

"What?"

"You got unfinished business in Georgia too?"

"In Georgia?"

"There's the Atlanta bus pulling in."

"Yes," he heard himself say. "I have unfinished business in Georgia." And having said it, if only to answer the man's question, he suddenly knew that he meant it. *Georgia*, the man had said, and the word came to him like a sign. Georgia! That was the place!

At any rate, it was enough to say it aloud to know what he would do.

"Whereabouts in Georgia?" asked the tall man.

"Thomasville."

"Thomasville! Well, I'll be. You selling out too?"

"No, I'm buying in."

"You going back?" the tall man asked him.

"You could say."

"What are you buying, a farm?"

"You could say."

"You retiring?"

"You might say."

"A young fellow like you? That could be a mistake."

"I don't think so."

But the tall man wasn't really listening. He was doing an exercise with his legs, resting his weight first on the ball of one foot, then the other.

"Do you know Ike Nunally's place?" the tall man asked.

"That's where I'm headed. I used to hunt there."

"Is that so? I did too. Many a time. So you going to buy a piece of the Nunally place."

"Yes."

"Which part?"

"A parcel of swamp."

"Oh, for the hunting. You must be a hunter."

"Of a sort." *But bigger game than you think.*

"You must be one of these rich Northern folks who've bought up everything around here and down there too."

"No. That is, I'm rich, but not Northern."

"But they're as nice as they can be, the ones I've met," said the tall man agreeably and inattentively, glasses flashing as he sprang gently on one foot then the other to exercise his calves.

"Yes they are."

"Now isn't that something. What a small world. We better get our tickets. You go ahead."

"After you."

"What?"

"You're catching the Georgia bus, aren't you?"

"Yes, but—"

"But what?"

But I've forgotten something. What? He felt like a man who has lost his wallet. He slapped his pocket. It was there with the five hundred dollars.

The bus swung up the ramp through sunlight and shade and onto the Blue Ridge Parkway. The two men sat side by side, hands on their knees. Will Barrett inclined his head attentively

Between them, like a silent child beckoning to them, sat the burden of the conversation to come.

"Now isn't that something," said the Associate. "Both of us going back to Georgia to make the deal of our lives. I'm selling a farm and you're buying one."

"Yes," he said, watching a low ridge which ran just above the tree line like a levee. The Associate was right. This journey would settle it for both of them. One was going back to Georgia to be rid of it forever, to get shut of the old house with its heavy Valdosta-style gable returns, and begin a new life in his garden home in Emerald Isle Estates, watch Monday-night football, do isometrics in the family room, drive to Highlands with his wife to attend Miami-style auctions. The Jews hadn't left! The other was going back to Georgia to find something he had left there, to find a place where something had happened to him. Or rather hadn't happened to him. All these years he had thought he was in luck that it didn't happen and that he had escaped with his life and a triumphant life at that. But it was something else he had escaped with, not his life. His life—or was it his death?— he had left behind in the Thomasville swamp, where it still waited for him. With a kind of sweet certainty he knew now that it was there that he would find it. Finding the post oak—he knew he could walk straight to it—and not coming out of the swamp at all was better than thrashing around these pretty mountains, playing in Scotch foursomes, crawling into caves, calling on God, Jews, and tigers. No, it was in Georgia that he would find it. And it was in Georgia that he would do it.

But as he listened to the Associate talk about his work—talk with pleasure! he enjoyed his work! he enjoyed walking twenty blocks down West Peachtree, sitting behind his desk for ten hours, making loans, good loans! good for lender and lendee, doing isometrics between appointments, he was no loan shark!— his eye traveled along the ridge and came to a notch where in the darkness of the pine and spruce there grew a single gold poplar which caught the sun like a yellow-haired girl coming out of a dark forest. Once again his heart was flooded with sweetness but a sweetness of a different sort, a sharp sweet urgency, a need to act, to run and catch. He was losing something. Something of his as solid and heavy and sweet as a pot of honey in his lap was being taken away.

"I'm not going back to Georgia," he said, rising.

"What's that?" said the Associate quickly and in a changed

voice (something was up) but making room for him with his knees.

Already at the front of the bus—how did he get there?—he was tapping the driver's shoulder, the driver a heavy uniformed man who looked like an aging airline pilot except that his fingernails were dirty and his face was sullen. His tanned neck had deep sharp hieroglyphs carved in it.

"Excuse me, driver, but I want to get out."

"What's that?"

"Stop the bus. I want to get off."

"This is an express, Mac. Next stop, Asheville."

"I said goddamn it stop the bus and let me off."

The driver went on driving the bus as if he weren't there. Angry at the beginning, his face dark with blood, the driver seemed to grow angrier still. What was he angry about? Working conditions? Life at home?

He leaned close to the driver. They both watched the pleasant road spinning under them. "If you don't stop this fucking bus right now, I'm grabbing your ass out of that seat and stopping it for you."

The driver slowed. Well, he's going to let me out, he thought. But no, it was in order to reach for a rack on the dash in front of him, and take out cards and pass them to the passengers behind him. "Please pass these along and fill them out. You are witnesses to a crime. This is a hijacking."

He looked at the four passengers on the front row of seats. They gazed straight ahead, faces like stone. Something is happening, their stricken expressions said, but it is happening too close. We do not know what to do. It was better not to look. But they took the cards dutifully and gazed at the scenery, not daring even to look at the cards.

The bus was still going slow.

"Let the man out. The man wants out." It was the Associate, standing tall and reared, glasses flashing. He was not smiling. "You heard the man. He wants out."

"I'll let him out all right," said the driver, who in his rage had gone stupid and sought now only the ultimate gesture, the last one-up face-saver, to prove himself to himself and to the passengers, who watched stone-faced holding their legal cards as dutifully as TV game players. The door opened while the bus was still moving and in the moment of his stepping down the driver slammed on the brakes, slamming him forward into metal jamb, then started up *rhhhooom*, slamming him back into the other jamb not squarely but glancingly so that he was bounced out, which would not have been serious except that the door, itself now part of the driver's stupidity and rage, was already closing and caught his foot, levering him down hard enough so that the next thing he knew, the pebbles of tar and craters of pavement were coming up at him like a moon landing fast and silent yet slow enough for him to say to himself: right, it's not going to end like this or in a Georgia swamp either because I won't stand for it and don't have to. Then the Eagle landed and the moon went dark.

4

The room was dark.

The table he was strapped to began to move. It slanted up at the foot, then slanted down, rolled over on one side, stood on end. Quick sure woman's hands moved his body, straightening it. Someone measured his head with a ruler and marked it. There was the sense of conforming his body, its warm wayward flesh and bone, to the simple cold geometry of straight metal edges. A motor went on and off. There was a hum.

When he and the table were stood on end like a mummy case, he saw stars. A window directly in front of him seemed to open into deep space. There twinkling in a thousand, a million points of light was a distant galaxy. But it was not a window, not deep space, not a galaxy, but a brain. The fore part of the brain crouched between two lobes like a sphinx.

He turned his head. The sphinx turned. He turned his head the other way. The sphinx turned the other way.

It was his own brain.

Later the same quick hands unstrapped him and led him into a brightly lit examining room. There were Leslie and Jack Curl and Vance Battle and another man, no doubt a doctor, wearing a long white coat with a rubber hammer sticking out of his pocket. Leslie and Jack were smiling at him.

"What are you grinning about?" he asked Leslie crossly. Uh oh, he thought. Something is wrong for sure. Leslie never smiles unless somebody dies or the Holy Spirit descends. What had happened to her inverted-U frown?

"Credit friend Jack here," she said, giving him a pat. Ah,

they had become friends. What was up? "There is nothing like the power of prayer."

"There you go," said Jack absently, dancing a little.

"Power of prayer to do what?" asked Will Barrett.

"To find you and get you here at Duke!" said Leslie, giving him a hug. "Oh, Poppy, you're a mess!"

Vance and the other man were holding their arms and talking, their heads down. The other man must be a doctor because he was talking to Vance both seriously and casually. He didn't have to smile. A courtesy was being extended Vance. They did not seem to be exchanging medical information as doctors do, but rather reaching an agreement, as lawyers do. They traced designs on the floor with the toes of their shoes. An agreement was reached. Both men nodded. The other doctor left.

Leslie and Jack Curl were smiling and shaking their heads. Vance winked. With so much cheerfulness—Leslie smiling and soft-eyed!—the news must be bad.

"Son, we had a time catching up with you and throwing you down," said Vance, talking more country than usual. Bad! He turned to Leslie. "What this old boy needs is some strong-arm tactics, and this little lady is just the one to do it."

"There you go," said Jack Curl, doing a turn and bumping into Leslie. There occurred between them some kind of comic Christian jostle.

He was looking down at his short hospital smock. It was tied loosely in the back. A draft blew up under the flap. There was lettering on the front. He tried to read it.

"Where am I?" he asked.

"You're at Duke, Poppy," said Leslie and sure enough took him by a strong hand. "The Duke hospital."

"Sit down, Tiger, before you fall down," said Vance.

"I feel fine," he said. He did. Except for a lightness in the head and a throbbing above one eye, he felt strong. He was hungry. "How long have I been here?"

"Twelve hours," said Vance. "And I'm here to tell you one damn thing. Out of your head you're a lot easier to get along with. You're not a bad patient. You actually hold still when I tell you."

"How did I get here from the bus?"

The three looked at each other and laughed.

Jack Curl did a turn and addressed the others, with Will Barrett as listener-in. "I don't know what friend Will here told that bus driver, but that sucker turned that bus around and delivered him straight to Linwood Hospital."

He looked at them. Their smiles and winks and jokes bore him along as skillfully as the swift hands on the X-ray table. "What am I doing here?"

Vance's eyes gazed unfocused into his. "I thought there might be a little sumpn wrong with you."

"Was there?"

"Not what I was afraid of. Actually I was right all along. It looked to me like you were having little petty-mall seizures, but when you took to falling down and acting even meaner than usual, I was afraid it might be something more serious. As it is, they even got a pill for what ails you. You won't even have to stay in a hospital. A convalescent home for a spell is all you need, long enough for me to get you regulated. Let's go back to the mountain, boy. At least I know now what was causing your slice. What a relief. I thought for a while your golf game was shot."

"Poppy," said Leslie, coming close and straightening his smock, giving it firm tugs and pats like a mother. "Vance and Dr. Ellis want to have a little powwow with you. Jack and I will be waiting in the hall. When the scientists get through with you, we want a piece of you. Jack, Vance, and I have cooked up something special for the four of us. But that can wait."

Jack Curl took his hand too and squeezed it with both of his in a special way like a fraternity grip. Jack seemed more English than before. His hair flew off unbrushed to one side. He didn't use deodorant.

They went into another room. Dr. Ellis was standing there, doing nothing, not smiling, not frowning.

When the door closed, Vance turned on the light of a shadow box, another box, then another. There was the galaxy again, not swimming in deep space now but its poor pale image, an X ray. Next to it a pelvis connected legbones to backbone as simply and comically as a Halloween skeleton. Next, a bigger woman-size pelvis had something new cradled in its womb, a puddle of white. What was hatching here?

The two doctors lined up alongside him as if he were a colleague, a man among men. The women and priests were gone and they could talk.

"Boy, you some lucky," said Vance. "You want to know what I thought you had until Dr. Ellis here talked me out of it. You know I went to Chapel Hill and we know all about Duke assholes but this is one more smart asshole."

Dr. Ellis nodded and pressed his lips together in a faint smile. Will Barrett wished Vance would not try to be funny. Dr. Ellis was not the sort of person to be called an asshole. Vance went down the bank of X rays, snapping his fingernail against the heavy celluloid. "I thought you had a prostatic growth here—" *pow* "—with metastases here—" *pow* "—here in the brain—" *pow* "I'd have given you three months. But you're some lucky. What you got I barely heard of and Dr. Ellis has written a paper about. He even invented a test for it. Frankly I think he invented the disease. And that ain't all. They can't cure it but they got a drug for it and we can control it. Ain't that right, Doctor?"

Dr. Ellis went on with his nodding and faint smile. The two doctors fell back, folded their arms, and examined the X rays as if they were a wall of Rembrandts. He saw that they were using the X rays as stage props, something to look at so they could talk to him.

"I'm afraid Dr. Battle is doing himself an injustice," said Dr. Ellis dryly, his eyes drifting along the X rays. He saw that Dr. Ellis had a way of feigning inattention which in fact allowed him to pay strict attention. "He suggested all along that you had a petit-mal epilepsy, which in fact you do, a rare form, so rare it bears the name of its discoverer. It's called Hausmann's Syndrome. It is in fact a petit-mal temporal-lobe epilepsy which is characterized by typical symptoms. It is not too well controlled by Dilantin but there's a new drug which works very well. That is to say, it clears up the symptoms. What we have to do is rule out a lesion in the temporal lobe. Dr. Battle favors that. I don't. The odd thing about the treatment is—"

"What are the symptoms?" asked Will Barrett.

Dr. Ellis shrugged. "As I recalled, Dr. Hausmann listed such items as depression, fugues, certain delusions, sexual dysfunction alternating between impotence and satyriasis, hypertension, and what he called *wahnsinnige Sehnsucht*—I rather like that. It means inappropriate longing."

It ought to be called Housmann not Hausmann, he thought, the disorder suffered by the poet who mourned dead Shropshire lads and rose-lipt maids and his own lost youth.

"As I was saying, the odd thing is that the drug is the simplest of all substances, so simple that no one would think of it—in fact, it was discovered by accident. It is nothing other than the hydrogen ion, a single nucleus of one proton, not even an electron. Isn't that intriguing? that the most complex symptoms, *wahnsinnige Sehnsucht*, inappropriate longings, depression and such, can be cured by a single proton? Apparently it all comes down to pH. I've had a series of six cases, and in each one you have petit-mal seizures plus an unstable pH which fluctuates between a mild alkalosis and acidosis. It is apparently a high sensitivity to pH changes which causes the symptoms. For instance, this morning your pH ran seven point seven. The treatment is simple but pesky. It means checking your pH every couple of hours and calibrating the medication accordingly. Anyone can pass out from alkalosis—I could put Vance out just by having him hyperventilate—but you're much more sensitive and therefore your pH must be monitored all the time. All my patients are doing well but have to be maintained under the most carefully controlled conditions.''

"What does that mean?" asked Will Barrett, taking note of the not unpleasant sensation of being caught up, diagnosed, recognized, planned for, of the prospect of one's life being ordered henceforward, like joining the army.

"I've got this one case of Hausmann's in the math department here at Duke. Instead of showing up for class he'd be found sitting in the stadium alone. Once he went to Kitty Hawk and lived in the dunes and nearly starved."

The dunes? Yes.

"Now, under treatment, he meets his classes and publishes voluminously. Except for living in our convalescent wing, he has a normal life."

"Here? He lives here in the hospital?"

"We have to monitor his blood pH every hour. One spoon of vinegar salad dressing and he's in the depths. One Alka-Seltzer and he's off for the dunes with two coeds. Heh heh. We don't know whether it's your internal governor on the blink or whether your limbic system is abnormally sensitive. Or whether you have a temporal-lobe lesion, though"—he snapped an X-ray—"I see no sign of it. Remarkable, don't you think, that a few protons, plus or minus, can cause such complicated moods? Lithium, the simplest metal, controls depression. Hydrogen, the simplest atom, controls *wahnsinnige Sehnsucht*.''

"How about that?" said Vance.

The two doctors could have been enlisting him as a colleague. Will Barrett saw that it was his, Dr. Ellis's, way of telling him good news, and a very good way it was, giving him a new lease on life as offhandedly as making an appointment. What a good fellow Dr. Ellis was!

Leslie came in, all smiles and melts, Jack Curl dancing behind her.

"Let's head for the hills, Poppy."

He looked at Dr. Ellis.

"Vance can monitor your pH as well as I. If he finds any sign of a lesion he can bring you back."

"And here's the bottom line," said Jack Curl, coming too close. "Bertie's got you signed up for the Seniors tournament next month and these two docs say you can make it. If—"

"If?"

"If you put up at my place so Vance can check your blood. You can start out on St. Mark's putting green."

He looked at Vance.

"You heard the man. Now let's get out of here, old buddy. I got sick people to tend to. I can only add one item to Dr. Ellis's diagnosis—incidentally, I concur with him now. I'll make you a press bet that the hydrogen ion will correct your slice—that may be my contribution to medical literature: the correlation of blood pH and the golf slice. Who knows?" He gave him a wink. "The hydrogen ion may even solve the Jewish question. As a matter of fact, why don't we try it for size—you're on hydrogen now, your blood pH is exactly seven point four, normal. Is Groucho Marx dead or alive?"

"Dead."

"Right. Now what happened to the Jews in North Carolina?"

"The Jews?" he said, frowning.

"Yes, the Jews."

"Why, nothing. They're going about their business as usual, I suppose."

"Right. And what about that Jewish girl in high school you were raving about last night?"

"What Jewish girl?"

"What about the Jewish exodus?"

"What exodus?"

"What about your business in Georgia?"

"What business?"

"You were talking about some unfinished business in a Georgia swamp."

"What swamp?"

"Let's head for the hills, son."

"From whence cometh our help," said Leslie.

"Okay," he said agreeably, blinking. Yes, he felt exactly as he felt when he was drafted in the army, a dazed content and a mild curiosity. His life was out of his hands.

IV

THANKSGIVING FOUND HIM COMFORTABLY INSTALLED IN ST. Mark's Convalescent Home taking pills and shots and having blood drawn every hour. Jack had put him in the penthouse suite overlooking the gorge. Leslie moved in his new clothes, cardigans, pipes, stereo, Bible, everything but the Greener and Luger. She had even retrieved the Mercedes from the maple tree, had it repaired and parked outside. With a significant look she handed the keys to him. Perhaps it was an act of faith in him.

For a long time he stood twiddling the keys and looking at the Mercedes. He opened the trunk. There lay the Greener in its case and the Luger in its holster. He stood, foot on bumper, thinking.

Vance came by twice a day to give him his "acid" and to take blood to test his pH. He came close as a lover, breath strong and sweet, sniffed at him, looked into his eyeballs. He told his patient he smelled healthy, his pressure was down, and the arteries in his eyegrounds were as supple as snakes.

Not only did Will Barrett tolerate the drug, he seemed in a queer way to prosper. A smell of pesticide hung in his nostrils. He smelled like a house sprayed for termites. A chemical exuberance took hold of him. The simplest of all atoms gave him a complex sense of well-being. If the treatment was dangerous, he felt as safe as a knife thrower's girl. Friendly knives zipped past his head, between his legs, fanned his ears, went *zoing* straight to their malignant target. A cool Carolina Salk rattling his test tubes at Duke had saved his life. How odd to be rescued,

278

salvaged, converted by the hydrogen ion! a proton as simple as a billiard ball! Did it all come down to chemistry after all? Had he fallen down in a bunker, pounded the sand with his fist in a rage of longing for Ethel Rosenblum because his pH was 7.6? A quirky energy flowed into his muscles. He couldn't sleep but didn't mind. He rose at all hours, dressed carefully, prowled the halls, explored the grounds, even drove the Mercedes. He wanted to see Allie. He forgot about Jews but not Allie. Had his longing for her been a hydrogen-ion deficiency, a *wahnsinnige Sehnsucht*? No, hydrogen or no hydrogen, he wanted to see her face. Would the protons now coursing through his brain and eyegrounds make her look different? Why hadn't she come to see him? He headed for the club, but a twisting in his head caused him to turn the Mercedes to correct the twist. Again the Mercedes took to the woods. Maybe he'd better drive around the block at first.

Then why not walk? But when he struck out through the woods, he found himself turning against the gyroscope in his head and went round in a circle. He had to stick to the sidewalks like ordinary folk.

Things increased in density and stood apart. He could see around trees. But time ran together. Was it Wednesday or Sunday? He bought a calendar Timex watch. Things increased in value. As he drove the Mercedes his attention was transfixed by the luminous turquoise of a traffic light. It glowed like a huge valuable jewel! He stopped and gazed until it turned into a great hot ruby. Surely red meant go, not stop. He went. A woman in a Dodge pickup cursed him.

He stopped driving and took up golf.

"You want to putt a round?" he asked Jack Curl.

"You got to be kidding. Get Vance or Slocum."

He got Slocum. Slocum too seemed to like him better. Everybody was relieved that he was sick not crazy, that he was being treated and was getting better. Being sick made him feel better too.

His driving and walking were peculiar, but his putting was deadly. The little hydrogen ions had odd effects. The gyroscope spinning in his head hurt his driving the Mercedes but helped his putting. All he had to do was settle over a putt, wait till the gyroscope steadied and the twisting stopped and zing, the ball flew straight for the cup like a missile locked on target.

Bertie came by. Will Barrett beat him seventeen up on eigh-

teen holes. Bertie looked left and right. "You don't have to turn
in a scorecard here, do you?" "No." "Thank God. It won't
affect your handicap." "That's right." Bertie winked. "We
missed the Seniors here but we're signed up for Hilton Head
and the whole Southern tour. We can't miss."

2

A wiry old man was watering a young pine with a bucket.

Will Barrett watched him for a while. At first the old man
appeared as part of the scenery and therefore of no particular
moment, old-man-watering-tree-in-front-of-old-folks'-home.
Then it occurred to him to wonder. Why would anyone want to
water a pine tree with a bucket?

Standing on the porch, he asked him.

The old man frowned and went on watering but presently he
replied: "They planted these seedlings too early. They should
have waited till the winter months when there is plenty of rain."

"Seedlings? Those are not seedlings. They're two years old.
I know because my wife had them planted."

"They still need water," said the old man, not raising his
eyes from the pine.

"You know about plants?"

Yes, he did. His name was Lionel Eberhart, born in Kings-
port, Tennessee. He had started out as a gardener in Asheville
with one old truck, hiring out himself and wife and two sons
and one daughter to tend lawns. They weren't afraid of work.
He started his own nursery. Before he retired he was wholesal-
ing lots of one hundred thousand rhododendron and laurel to
Sears, Roebuck.

"Why did you retire?"

"My wife died. I had three heart attacks. My two sons wanted
to put me here. My daughter wanted me to live with her but her
husband didn't. So the doctor put me here. But that's all right!
They all right! I wouldn't want to live with them! So." He went
to fill his bucket.

"Is that all you can find to do around here, water a pine tree?"

"They got a gardener. Your wife took care of everything. She
surely was a nice lady. They got ever' thing around here a fellow
would need." Still, he did not raise his eyes from the small wet
pine.

He gazed down at the old man. Quick and wiry, an East Tennessee Yankee, yes, he'd drive his wife, sons, daughter crazy with his puttering. Yes, of course he'd seen the old man before, always outside, walking with his quick stoop, raking leaves, watering trees, pestering the gardener. He'd live another thirty years.

3

Jack Curl was leaving for Hilton Head and an ecumenical meeting between a Greek Orthodox archimandrite, a Maronite patriarch, and the Episcopal bishop of North Carolina, a meeting suggested in fact by Jack Curl. Could Jack Curl reunite Christendom? He laughed, socked himself, and did a turn. Why not? Isn't it just the sort of damn fool thing God might favor? Actually Marion had conceived the idea before she died and even provided the funds.

"You mean that's the sort of thing the Peabody Trust would undertake?" he asked Jack.

"You got it, Will," said Jack, his laughter turning off like a light.

"And you want me to put Marion's money in a trust to be administered by you."

"Or Leslie. Or both."

"Well, which?"

"Take your pick. Then we'll run it up the flagpole and see who salutes it."

"What does that mean?"

Jack Curl shrugged and looked vague. "You're the lawyer. Check it out with Slocum. It comes down to naming a trustee or co-trustees. I'm glad to serve."

Jack Curl showed him around St. Mark's before he left, even though Jack must have known that he used to pilot Marion through once a week in her wheelchair. The dining room was pretty and the food good, tables for four, ladies in dresses and hairdos, gents in coats and ties, grace before meals.

"Now," said Jack, "I'm going to show you something that's going to blow your mind. Not even Marion knew about it. It's strictly off limits to the ladies. Okay. I'm going to show you a bunch of guys having a ball. I spend a little time here myself. A little, ha."

They climbed steep steps. A door opened into a spacious attic. Tracks and trains ran everywhere through a waist-high landscape. Not children's toy trains but good-sized Pennsylvania diesels, an L & N steam locomotive, a Southern Pacific freight, a Twentieth Century Limited, crossed trestles, ran through tunnels, stopped at stations, switched onto sidings, off-loaded bales of cotton, took on soybean oil. Bars came down at crossings. Bells donged. A mechanical darky on a mule doffed his cap. Lonesome whistles blew. Half a dozen men, old men, operated control panels, switches, water towers, roundhouse turnarounds. Most of the men wore railroader's caps.

"Talk about a nostalgia trip," whispered Jack Curl.

"Yes," he said and for some reason thought about Allison standing in the sunlight.

"Highball it, Shorty!" cried Jack Curl to a man wearing a railroader's cap but with a false note in his voice and Shorty did not reply. "Shorty was president of First National of Georgia," whispered Jack. "You see that guy on the roundhouse? That's Orin Henderson of Henderson Textiles. They're great guys. Come on, I'll introduce you."

"Later." He looked at his watch. What was Allie doing? It was four-thirty. The sunlight was yellow. Was she going down into herself? Was the dog worrying about her?

"Who knows, Will, you might take up railroading. You could do worse," said Jack Curl, his eyes not quite coming round to him.

"No thanks."

"Why not?"

"I'm taking up senior golf."

"All *right*!" said Jack.

"Yes."

"You remember Father Weatherbee, also a known train nut. You'll be in his hands while I'm gone. And damn good hands they are, better than Allstate. Father spent fifty years in the Philippines."

Father Weatherbee was the ancient emaciated priest whose clerical collar and lower eyelid drooped. One eye had a white rim and spun like a wheel. Smiling, he took Barrett's hand in both of his, two dry hot whispering banyan leaves. He shrugged at Jack Curl. Will Barrett saw something in his eyes.

"Father was an old highballer from Raleigh before he took to persecuting the saints," said Jack, absently socking fist into palm. "He used to ride the old Seaboard Air Line and never got over it. Right, Father?"

Father Weatherbee said something.

"What's that, Father?" asked Will Barrett, leaning toward him.

"Father Weatherbee has two unusual interests," said Jack Curl, looking at his wristwatch. "Oh my, I've got to see Leslie before—" He took Will Barrett's hand as if he meant to say goodbye. In the handshake he felt himself being steered closer to the old priest. "Father here believes in two things in this world. One is the Seaboard Air Line Railroad and the other is Apostolic Succession. Right, Padre? Frankly, it sounds more like the ancestor worship of his Mindanao tribesmen, but I don't argue with him. After all, I also get along with Leslie, who has no use for any priests, let alone a succession of priests. So what? You pays your money and you takes your choice."

"Apostolic Succession?" said Will Barrett, looking from one to the other.

"A laying on of hands which goes back to the Apostles," said Jack Curl, smiling and nodding at the highballers.

"It occurred," said Father Weatherbee in a dry hoarse voice. When he spoke, a red bleb formed at the corner of his mouth like a bubble-gum bubble.

"There you go," said Jack Curl.

Father Weatherbee said something.

"What's that?" asked Will Barrett, cocking his good ear.

"I said he reminds me of a kumongakvaikvai," said Father Weatherbee, nodding at Jack and blowing out a bleb.

"What's a kumongakvaikvai?"

"It's the dung bird of southern Mindanao. It follows herds of Kumonga cattle and eats dung like your cattle egret. Characteristically the bird perches on the backs of the beasts and utters its cry *kvai kvai*." And Father Weatherbee uttered a sound which could only have been the cry of the bird.

"Ha ha," laughed Jack Curl, giving Will Barrett the elbow. "I told you they're all characters up here."

4

"What do you think of these great John Kennedy rockers?" Jack Curl called out on the front porch. "You know I slipped a disc last year and instead of surgery I rocked. I mean really rocked. Do you know you can get a workout in one of these?''

There were at least fifty rocking chairs, damp from the fog, none occupied.

After supper he sat in a rocker and watched a cloud rise from the valley floor. To the left, where the valley narrowed, the cloud seemed to boom and echo against the sides of the gorge.

Suddenly he jumped up, remembering something he meant to ask Jack Curl, even though Jack had left hours ago. Instead, he called Vance.

''Vance, I just thought of something.''

''What's that, buddy?''

''It just occurred to me that Leslie moved all my stuff here before she found out I was sick.''

''Ahmmm.'' Vance cleared his throat. ''Well, we all knew something was wrong. You were sick. It was only a matter of diagnosis. As a matter of fact, I was the only one who didn't think you were crazy. As for what you got, we going to lick that mother, right? How're you feeling?''

''Fine. But she moved me out before I came back. What did she have in mind?''

''Let me tell you something, Will.''

''All right.''

''Leslie is much woman.''

''Yes.''

''She is some kind of woman, a fine Christian woman.''

''Right. But—''

''You know what she's going to do with St. Mark's?''

''No.''

''Well, she's transferring the convalescents to the new community Marion had planned over on Sourwood Mountain—as soon as we can get it built. And we'll use the present St. Mark's as a hospital with a new wing for radiation patients complete with a new beta cyclotron. I'm sure you'd rather live in the Peabody community. There's no reason for you to have to live in a hospital.''

''The love-and-faith community.''

''Right.''

''I see. Where is the money for all this coming from?''

Vance coughed. ''I thought you and Leslie and Slocum had worked that out. Christ, you're a lawyer.''

''You're talking about the Peabody Trust?''

"Yes."

"There is no Peabody Trust. I am Marion's sole beneficiary."

"I know, but Leslie had given me to understand that you wanted to carry out Marion's wishes in this—let alone considerations of your own health."

"What about my health?"

He could feel the shrug through the telephone. "You're going to be following a strict regime from here on out—and you're going to be fine! But let's face it. We don't know a damn thing about Hausmann's Syndrome except how to maintain a patient."

"Are you talking about maintaining me or committing me?"

"Ha ha. As long as your pH doesn't get over seven point four, you're right as rain. In fact—"

"Yes?"

"We were wondering if you might not run the Peabody community, since you're going to be out there anyway."

"We?"

"Talk to Leslie. She's another Marion."

"I see."

He went up to his room and turned on the stereo. Leslie had even popped in a tape. It was Strauss's *Vier letzte Lieder*, which used to be one of his favorites.

Earlier Jack Curl had introduced him to Warren East, formerly with Texas Instruments, who was also a music lover and had in his suite a digital sound system. "You two guys got it made," said Jack, reaching deep in his jump-suit pockets. "You can either swap tapes or get together. Warren's got everything that Victor Herbert ever composed." Again the handshake steering him against Warren East.

He looked at Warren East. Warren East did not look at him.

Leslie had put a book next to his favorite chair. It was the Bible. He picked it up. It opened to a bookmark. He read: "I will lift up mine eyes unto the hills, from whence cometh my help." Leslie had made a note in the margin: *And what lovely hills!*

Overhead in the attic the Wabash Cannonball rambled along with a rustle and a roar.

Closing the Bible, he got up fast, causing the gyroscope in his head to twist. He went by arcs down to the porch and sat in a John Kennedy rocker. It was damp. The porch was deserted. The cloud had come out of the valley. Everything beyond the banister rail was whited out. Through a window he caught sight of half of a giant TV screen in the recreation room. Lawrence Welk, still holding his baton, was dancing a waltz with a pretty young blonde.

Presently *Kojak* came on.

He felt an urge to get away from the silent white enveloping cloud and to go inside to the cheerful living room with its screen of lively sparkling colors and watch the doings of Kojak.

He rose carefully, taking care not to excite the gyroscope inside his head, then sat down with a thump.

Jesus Christ, he thought. I'm in the old folks' home.

5

The friendly atmosphere of St. Mark's was marred by two fights which occurred within the space of half an hour. He found himself embroiled in both of them. Remarkable! It had been years since he'd been in a fight or even seen a fight.

Kitty came to St. Mark's and assaulted him. Then Mr. Arnold and Mr. Ryan, his roommate for two years, got in a fistfight. Kitty must have found his suite empty and tracked him all over St. Mark's because she burst into the small room where he was visiting the two old men. It was clear when she came through the door that her rage had already carried her past caring who heard or saw her.

"You bastard," she said. Her eyes showed white all around like a wild pony's. "You—" She broke off.

"What?" he asked, noticing that he felt scared, and wondered if this natural emotion were not another sign of his return to health.

"What my butt," she said. "Now I know why—" she said and again her voice broke off, with a sob. Then with a grunt of effort as if she had to fling down a burden, she raised her woman's fists, thumbs straight along the knuckle, and, leaning across Mr. Ryan, began to beat him on the chest.

Later Mr. Ryan told him, "It looked like that lady was put out with you about something."

"Now I know why you didn't come to Dun Romin' or the summerhouse or anywhere at all, you—" Again her breath caught as she shoved past Mr. Ryan's bad knee to get at him. "You—you dirty old man!"

"Why?"

"Because you were shacked up in the woods with Allison, you—"

Mr. Arnold and Mr. Ryan were lying in bed and watching *Hollywood Squares* as if nothing unusual were going on three feet above them.

"Shacked up?"

"You—snake in the grass! Taking advantage of a psychotic girl. You—you—"

"Dirty old man?" said Mr. Ryan, looking up for the first time.

"You shut your mouth, you old asshole," said Kitty, without looking down.

"Yes ma'am," said Mr. Ryan.

"Well, I'm here to tell you one damn thing, old pal. I hope to God you're pleased with yourself. She is now hopelessly regressed. She won't say a word. And I'll tell you something else. I'm fixing it so you'll never get your filthy hands on her again, you—snake in the grass. That's exactly what you are, a snake in the grass!"

"You mean she won't talk to you?" he asked her.

"I mean she won't talk period, won't eat period, won't live period—unless I do something about it. You bastard," she said softly. "You knew where she was all along."

He had spied Mr. Arnold in the hall hopping along on his crutch. There was no mistaking that peeled-onion head and the one bright eye in his shutdown face. Then, after Kitty left, flung out, jammed her fist into her side and flounced her hip with it—it's amazing, he reflected, how trite rage is: enraged people in life act exactly like enraged people in comic books: there were stars and comets and zaps over Kitty's head—then Mr. Arnold and Mr. Ryan had a fight.

Mr. Arnold was sitting on the foot of his bed, fisted hand cradled like a baby in his good arm. Though it was his bed and his right to sit there, he was blocking Mr. Ryan's view of *Hollywood Squares*. Mr. Ryan began shifting his head back and forth in an exaggerated way to see around Mr. Arnold. He asked him to move but Mr. Arnold either didn't hear or pretended not to hear.

"You may be a pane, Erroll," he said to Mr. Arnold with an angry laugh, "but I can't see through you."

Mr. Ryan had a neat white crewcut, a youthful face, its skin smooth and pink-creased like a baby waking up. But his eye had a cast in it. One leg was gone from the hip and the other freshly amputated and bandaged below the knee. Diabetes and arteriosclerosis, he explained, watching Will with a keen and lively eye to see how he would take it, and apparently was satisfied, for he, Will, took it as he took everything else, attentively and without surprise. They had got the infection in time, Mr. Ryan said, and this time he could keep his knee. He explained, watching Will Barrett closely, that it was better to chop off a good piece the first time than nibble away as they had done with the other leg. I could have told them from the beginning, he said, that it's exactly like pruning back boxwood with the blight.

Mr. Ryan was lying on top of the bedclothes. He pulled up his hospital gown to show his stump. "Ain't that a pistol?" His thigh too had the same pink and white baby skin.

The watchful, almost angry look, he saw, was Mr. Ryan's way of asking him if he thought he would keep his knee. Is it such a bad thing, he mused chin in hand over Mr. Ryan's remaining knee, to have a knee to think about day in and day out? Even if both knees were well and all was well, what would you do here? "They going to keep chopping on me till I'll fit on a skateboard," said Mr. Ryan, watching him.

"It looks very healthy," he said. "It looks fine to me."

"Yes, it does," said Mr. Ryan instantly. "I believe they got it this time. We can't see the show, Erroll," he said to Mr. Arnold.

But Mr. Arnold didn't move.

After a while Mr. Ryan said, "Like I said, Erroll, you may be a pane but we can't see through you."

Still Mr. Arnold didn't move.

"You want to know what Erroll does?" Mr. Ryan asked Will Barrett with a smile, but his eyes were glittering.

"What?"

"He knows I can't move yet he sits his ass right there on the end of his bed between me and the TV, Erroll you shit!" said Mr. Ryan, laughing, then with a sob but still laughing lunged out between the two beds and, propping himself on the floor with one hand, grabbed Mr. Arnold's crutch with the other. When, with difficulty, veins pounding in his neck, glossy eye bulging, he got himself back in place, it appeared he meant only to steal Mr. Arnold's crutch, but no. Gripping the crutch at the small end in both hands like a baseball bat and giving himself what purchase he could by gathering his knee stump under him, he swung the crutch with all his might and caught Mr. Arnold a heavy glancing blow on his onion dome, cursing all the while.

"You no-good peckerwood son of a bitch!" he cried, his voice going suddenly hoarse.

Mr. Arnold, suddenly on the move, turned, his good eye winking at Barrett, grabbed the crossbar of the crutch with his good hand, yanked it, and kicked out at Mr. Ryan with his good leg, but fell off the bed. Mr. Ryan flew through the air like a doll and fell on top of him. Three fists rose and fell.

"You covite cocksucker," said Mr. Ryan.

"Cornholer," said Mr. Arnold clearly. He had got on top, and though he could only use one arm, the curtain of his face had been lifted by rage. His whole mouth formed curses. Cursing cures paralysis.

"Wait, hold it, okay okay," said Will Barrett, jumping clean across the bed and landing astraddle the roommates in time to catch the crutch on his shin. "Shit," he said. The two old men were grunting and embracing and cursing like lovers. "I mean for God's sake stop it!" Picking up Mr. Ryan, who, truncated, was no bigger than a chunky child, he set him in place on his pillows. Mr. Arnold was already back on his perch at the foot of the bed, once again blocking Mr. Ryan's view of *Hollywood Squares*. The fight might never have occurred. Instead of moving Mr. Arnold, Will Barrett moved the TV arm so Mr. Ryan's view could not be blocked. He looked at them. They were gazing at Paul Lynde in the middle square as if nothing had happened.

"How often does this happen?" he asked them.

"Ever' damn time they chop me down to size, Erroll sits his bony ass right where I can't see the TV," said Mr. Ryan.

"It's the onliest place I can see it good," said Mr. Arnold. "It's too little to see from back there."

"You speak very well," Will Barrett told Mr. Arnold. "The last time I saw you at my house, you didn't have much to say."

"There wasn't much to say."

"He's too damn mean to talk," said Mr. Ryan. "But knock him upside the head like a mule and he'll talk your ear off."

"How long have you been here?" Will Barrett asked Mr. Ryan.

"Two years."

"How about Mr. Arnold?"

"Ask him."

"Three years," said Mr. Arnold clearly. The curtain of his face had not yet shut down.

Strange: even during their rages they seemed to be watching him with a mute smiling appeal. They wanted to be told that no matter what happened, things would turn out well—and they believed him.

He discovered that it was possible to talk to them and even for them to talk to each other, if all three watched TV. The TV was like a fourth at bridge, the dummy partner they could all watch.

Mr. Ryan was a contractor from Charlotte who had moved to Linwood to build condominiums and villas for Mountainview Homes until diabetes and arteriosclerosis had "cut him down to size."

"Their joists are two foot on centers, the nails are cheap, and the floorboards bounce clean off in two years," said Mr. Arnold to Peter Marshall of *Hollywood Squares*. How could anger raise the curtain of his face?

"You want to know what he wants to do?" Mr. Ryan asked Jonathan Winters. "Use locust pegs and hand-split shingles for the roof. So a locust peg lasts two hundred years. He still thinks labor is thirty cents an hour."

"Are you a builder?" Will Barrett asked Mr. Arnold.

"He once built a log cabin," said Mr. Ryan. "But now by the time he finished the cabin the owners would have passed."

"Anybody can go round up a bunch of hippies and knock up a chicken shack that won't last ten years," said Mr. Arnold. "What they do is punch on their little bitty machine and figure it out so the house will fall down same time as the people."

He looked at the two old men curiously. "You can get hippies to work for you?" he asked Mr. Ryan.

"Sure you can. If you know which ones to pick. Some of them are tired of sitting around. I got me a real good gang. They work better than niggers."

"You build log cabins?" he asked Mr. Arnold.

"I can notch up a house for you," said Mr. Arnold to Rose Marie holding her rose.

"If you live long enough," said Mr. Ryan. They all watched TV in silence.

"You give me my auger," said Mr. Arnold suddenly and in a strong voice, "my ax, saw, froe, maul, mallet, and board

290

brake and I'll notch you up a house that'll be here when this whole building's fallen down—though you and your wife done real good to pay for it, otherwise we wouldn't have nothing.''

"Tell him about using hog blood and horsehair in the red-clay chinking," said Mr. Ryan.

"How much can you build a cabin for?" he asked Mr. Arnold.

"I built a four-room house with a creek-rock chimley for Roy Price down in Rabun County for two hundred and fifty dollars.''

"That was in nineteen-thirty for Christ's sake," said Mr. Ryan.

"It had overhanging dovetailing. I don't use no hogpen notch, they'll go out on you. I ain't never made a chimley that never drawed. It's all in how you make the scotch-back.''

For a long time he sat blinking between the two beds, hands stretched out to the two men as if it were still necessary to keep them apart. Then he rose suddenly, too suddenly, for his brain twisted and he almost fell down.

"Look out, potner," said Mr. Arnold, grabbing him with his good hand, which was surprisingly strong.

"You all right, Mr. Barrett?" said Mr. Ryan.

"I'm fine."

"Sure you are. You gon be out of here in no time, ain't he, Erroll?''

"Sho," said Mr. Arnold. "He's a young feller. And he's rich too.''

They both laughed loudly and looked at each other as if they had a secret.

"Yeah," he said and left.

He was in the corridor, leaning against the wall. His head was clear but there was a sharp sweet something under his heart, a sense of loss, a going away.

He smiled to himself. It no longer mattered that he couldn't remember everything.

Later that night he heard Tom Snyder ask someone: "What is your sexual preference?''

While he leaned against the wall, Kitty assaulted him again. Either she had been waiting for him, or she had left and thought of something else she had wanted to say and had come back.

"I just wanted to be sure you got one thing straight, big buddy." She swung a purse, a kind of shoulder bag with a short strap. Had she had it earlier? Did she intend to hit him with it?

"What?" he said. From nearby rooms came the soft babble of TV sets tuned to different channels.

"When Allison goes back to Valleyhead, you are not to visit her. Do—you—understand—me?" With each word she jabbed him in the ribs with two fingers. There was a conjugal familiarity between them. He felt as if they had been married and divorced.

"Yes."

"I know all about you and what's wrong with you. You ought to be grateful you're alive. But that doesn't mean you're going to get your hands on my little girl or her property. And I don't mind telling you I'm grateful they're keeping you here."

"They are?"

"Now hear this, mister. I'm making it my business to see to it that that child doesn't spend another night in that dump of a greenhouse. Alistair will be here late this afternoon. He and I are going to pick her up. If she won't go, the sheriff says all we got to do is call him and he'll deliver her to Valleyhead. And you better believe for her sake I'd do it."

"Alistair?"

"Dr. Duk."

"Oh yes. Dr. Duk."

"You know him? Isn't he wonderful?"

He was silent.

"You're going to pick her up this afternoon?" he asked her.

"You got it, buster." She blinked and, relenting a little, leaned toward him. "Now don't look so—everything's going to be fine. Now we got that straight. Now let's get you straight. Listen to me, Will."

"Okay."

"Leslie knows what she is doing, as usual. You're in the right place. You just stay here and take care of yourself, take your medicine and you'll be all right. Take care of these old folks— I understand you're going to be in charge here."

"I am?" There was the not unpleasant sense of great plans being made for him.

"You'll do just fine. And we're not exactly spring chickens ourselves." She softened and gave him a different kind of poke in the ribs. "When you feel better, come take me for a ride. No, I'll take you. We'll park at the golf course and you can hug me up, remember?"

"Remember what?"

"Hugging me up on the golf course."

"Ah—no."

He looked at his watch. If he could get away from Kitty, there was time to catch the beginning of the Morning Movie, which this morning was *King Solomon's Mines*, which was no great movie, true, but whose beginning, with Deborah Kerr and a saturnine Allan Quartermain played by Stewart Granger, he savored somewhat nevertheless. Deborah was trying to talk him into helping her find her husband in a remote unexplored country.

Strange. He had not spent a week at St. Mark's and already he was looking forward to the Morning Movie.

V

A PRINCELY BLACK WATUSI WHO LOOKED SEVEN FEET TALL stood on a rock holding a staff and gazing to the north. Somewhere beyond lay the treasures of King Solomon.

On one side of him sat Mr. Ryan, on the other Mr. Arnold. There had been time to prop Mr. Ryan in a wheelchair and push him to the game room with its forty-five-inch giant-screen Sony projector TV. He had invited Mr. Arnold to come along. Mr. Arnold had said nothing but trudged dutifully alongside Mr. Ryan's chair after tucking a blanket around him lest he topple forward.

"That's the biggest nigger I ever saw," said Mr. Ryan, gazing at the majestic Watusi. "But I can tell you one thing. That ain't no African chief. That's a blue-gum nigger from Mississippi. I'd know them anywhere. I had them working for me in crews building condos from Point Clear to Sea Island. They used to be good workers till Roosevelt ruined them."

Mr. Arnold stirred in his chair. The curtain of his face lifted a little. Leaning out and looking back, good eye winking, he spoke not to Mr. Ryan but to Barrett in the middle. "I'm here to tell you that Roosevelt was the onliest one ever done anything for us pore folks up in the hills."

The old men began to argue about Roosevelt, who had been dead for thirty-five years.

"Okay, hold it," he said and the two men subsided in good part to watch the movie.

All I have to do is tell them, he thought.

South Georgia, Alabama, Mississippi, he thought, watching

the great Watusi prince. And my father and his near death in the Georgia swamp and my near death and later his death in Mississippi and my being at his death and his wanting me to be there, his wanting me to see his brain exploded, expanding like the universe and plastering the attic with neurones like stars in the night sky. Why did he want me to be there? To show me what? Now I know. To show me the one sure sweet exodus. Yes, that's it, that's what he was first giving me in Georgia, then telling me and finally showing me, and now at last I know.

Even D'Lo knew. You po little old boy, what you going to do now? What chance you got in this world? Your daddy done kilt hisself and your mama dead and gone and here you come, po little Willie, what chance you got? She shaking her head and socking down the grits spoon, as he watched her narrow-eyed and even smiling a little, knowing she was wrong. Because he was he and they were they and here he was, free and sure and alert and sly. Nothing, no one, would ever surprise him again. Not they. They least of all. He was free of them.

His father had shot twice in the Georgia swamp, reloaded the Greener, and shot again. But the second shot was a double shot aimed at him. I thought he missed me and he did, almost, and I thought I survived and I did, almost. But now I have learned something and been surprised by it after all. Learned what? That he didn't miss me after all, that I thought I survived and I did but I've been dead of something ever since and didn't know it until now. What a surprise. They were right after all. He was right. D'Lo was right. What a surprise. But is it not also a surprise that discovering you've been dead all these years, you should now feel somewhat alive?

He killed me then and I did not know it. I even thought he had missed me. I have been living, yes, but it is a living death because I knew he wanted me dead. Am I entitled to live? I am alive by a fluke like the sole survivor of Treblinka, who lived by a fluke, but did not really feel entitled to live.

Ah, but there is a difference between feeling dead and not knowing it, and feeling dead and knowing it. Knowing it means there is a possibility of feeling alive though dead.

Very well, he was right, they were right, and I've learned at last that I am one of them. But I'm improving on them, am I not? I've found a better way than swallowing gun barrels: in short, I can shuffle off among friends and in comfort and Episcopal decorum and with good Christian folk to look after every need. Dear good Christian blacks eased me into this world, changed my diapers, and here they are again to change my diapers and ease me out, right?

Wrong.

So here is the giant-screen Sony projector TV and CBS day and night and some of the programs not half bad either, some of the programs in fact well done and amusing, yes, especially the sports and documentaries, yes? M*A*S*H ain't bad. No?

No.

There was something he had to do. Getting up so quickly that his head spun and he staggered, he found himself caught by strong hands on both sides, Mr. Arnold's good hand and both of Mr. Ryan's hands. "You all right, Will?" one asked quickly and as quickly let go and looked away. They were his friends. What delicacy and gentleness they had!

"I'm fine. I have to go now."

"You come back to visit us," Mr. Ryan said. Mr. Arnold nodded.

Stooping he looked into their faces. Who said anything about leaving for good? How did they know when he had not quite known it himself?

He stood for a moment gazing at a tarantula in Deborah Kerr's tent. Was there a whole world of meaning, of talking and listening, which took place everywhere and all the time and which no one paid attention to, at least not he?

He looked down at the new navy-blue wool dressing gown Leslie had bought for him and the Brooks Bros. pajamas and the Bean's moose-hide slippers Marion had given him one Christmas.

"Yes. I'll be back."

Thirty minutes later he had changed into street clothes, walked to his Mercedes, and was spinning down the highway. The car drove better than ever and he did not see double. Carefully yet absently, without thinking that he did so, he had dressed for the first time in months in suit, shirt, and tie, laced up the plaintoed Florsheims he hadn't worn since he left New York.

A pang struck suddenly at his heart. He had not taken his acid for twelve hours! What with the two fights and the movie, he had forgotten to go to the lab. His pH was up and the old heavy molecules were on the move again. Again the past rose to haunt him and the future rose to beckon to him. Things took on significance.

Parking at the club, he walked hands in pockets down the eighteenth fairway, feeling odd in his city clothes, kicking leaves like a businessman walking home across the Great Meadow in Central Park on a fine fall day. The soft-buttoned collar felt snug around his neck but he felt the cold through his thin socks. The fresh cold air felt good in his face.

When he came to the fence, he stretched up the top strand of wire to hear the guitar sound. He let it go slack, stretched it again harder, cocked an ear. The wire sang again, creaked, and popped against the musical bridge of the post. He let go. It sounded like a wire stretching against a fence post, no more. The near post was rotten. It broke and swayed toward him. He kicked it down and walked over the fence.

The girl and the dog were sitting on the stoop of the copper-roofed porch. The girl, holding her hand against the sun, didn't recognize him at first, but the dog did. Over he came grinning, broad tail swinging his body like an alligator. The dog grinned, swallowed, his lip caught high on a tooth embarrassing him. He looked away. The girl touched her cheek with her fingers as he looked down at her. She was thin and sallow. Perhaps it was the man's olive-drab parka she wore which looked as if it had been worn in the Aleutians in World War II.

"It's you irregardless of who," she said.

He laughed. "Irregardless of who what?"

"Of who I thought you were."

"Who did you think I was?"

"That you were an Atlantean but taller, yet I also knew you by the glancing way, you know, of your face here." She touched her temple.

"Atlantean or Atlantan?"

"Both. Atlantan businesswise with your suit, as I once saw Sarge come down the bullet in the Hyatt with attaché case and suit like that. But Atlantean also because of the way you came through the woods like you were coming from elsewhere not there."

"Not where?"

"There. The golf links and the players. You were not one of them, you never were. I mean it is a question of where you are coming from, a consideration of the reality of it."

"You mean where I actually came from this morning, don't you?" He laughed and she nodded. He laughed because he knew this was her own expression even though it sounded like local gypsy talk: like man, where are you coming from? "I came here from the hospital."

She stood up and touched his forehead like a mother checking a child for fever. "You seem fine. Are you?"

"Yes. Are you?"

"Yes. But I'm going back and down again, I think, but that's all right."

"No, it's not. I want a good look at you." He took off her Aleutian parka and stood her in the sunny warm corner of the porch.

For a while she gazed straight ahead at his necktie like a child. Then not like a child she put her head to one side in order to see his eyes from the corner of hers.

"I'm so—" she said, shaking her head. Nothing else moved about her except her hands at her side, which turned out like the beginning of a shrug.

"Yes," he said and he was kissing her mouth, she flying up at him and cleaving to him, leaving the ground surely.

"There is something I need," he told her.

"Moi aussi," she said. "Entirely apart from the needs of society and the family as a unit, or the group."

"Yes, apart from that."

"The truth is," he said when they were sitting together in the sun, "I wish to speak to you of several things. To begin with, my pH has been corrected and I feel fine. Secondly, I am in love, I think."

"Me too."

They kissed again. Her mouth was sweet and tart. His tongue went in her. Her tongue, surprised, was taken aback, then ventured forward, parting his lips shyly. Kissing her was like entering a new and happy land.

"What have you been eating?" he asked her.

"Pawpaws. They're best after a frost."

"Let me taste."

They kissed again. They were sitting now. He noticed that no matter how they kissed, standing or sitting, her body somehow fronted and flew against him.

"Kissing you is a delight but not a rounded and closed-off delight," she said.

"No?"

"No, it is an opening-out delight and a wanting. Kissing is like now fine, more is better, and what about it?"

"I know."

"Your tongue is welcome but you, that is, the salient you, would be even more so."

"I know, I know."

"Was there ever such a wanting?" she asked.

"Not that I remember."

"For true?"

"For true."

"Oh say so."

"I want you."

"Oh fine. The word is go. It is, that is, yes I'm saying."

"I understand."

"Ah ha, it is more than evident you do," she said.

"I know, I know."

"Are you fond of me besides?" she asked.

"Yes, yes. I must be sure you're all right. Are you?"

"Similarly and moreover. Do you feel a smiling ease with me as well as a sweetness for me in the deep regions?"

"Yes, in the deep regions, a sweetness, as well as the smiling ease."

"Is it possible that there is such a life?"

"As what?"

"As a life of smiling ease with someone else and the sweetness for you deep in me and play and frolic and dear sweet love the livelong day, even at four o'clock in the afternoon turning the old yellow green-glade lonesomeness into a being with you at ease not a being with you at unease?"

"Yes, it's possible."

"Could such a thing be? What a miracle, and we haven't even mentioned the nights."

"No, we haven't."

"Imagine ten hours of darkness every night!"

"Yes, imagine."

"What will we do?"

"Whatever you like."

"Then you are fond of me?"

"Yes."

"Let us not speak of love yet, I'm not sure of the word."

"No, we won't speak of love, though I feel that in the future we might."

"Similarly and moreover."

"Moreover what?"

"Moreover a continuity is beginning for the first time but it is not climbing on me."

"Me either. Something else is also clear to me."

"Over and beyond."

"Yes, over and beyond. It is this. We need each other for different things."

"What is the manifestation of the difference?"

"I need you for hoisting and you need me for interpretation."

"Say what?"

"I fall down from time to time and you are very good at hoisting. It would be pleasant to have you around to give me a hand," he said.

"The pleasure would be mine. In short, I'll do it. I am so happy about your pH."

"By the same token, I remember everything and you forget most things. I'll be your memory. Then too, your language is somewhat unusual. But I understand it. In fact, it means more than other people's. Thus, I could both remember for you and interpret for you."

"Our lapses are not due to synapses."

"No, they are as they should be."

"The implication of your consideration is that people think I'm crazy."

"That is correct. Moreover, for this very reason they are coming for you this afternoon."

"And you don't."

"Don't think you're crazy? No. Now."

"Yes?"

"Let's sit here by the dog. There are some things which I think you must do. Moreover, it is a pleasure to sit here beside you. Dear sweet Lord, what a pleasure. There are many things I don't know. But certain things have become clear to me as far as you are concerned. Therefore, I am taking it upon myself to do what I seldom do, even in the practice of law: tell somebody what to do. I also think you are ready to be told."

"The feeling is reciprocal. I am listening."

"The pawpaws are very good."

"Yes."

"However, the taste of them in your mouth is even better."

"The pleasure is mine."

"For true?"

"For true."

He kissed her again. Again she flew against him, from the side which was not possible, yet with no trouble at all.

"Now here is what you must do."

"Yes?"

"Do you wish to go back to Valleyhead?"

"No. Assuredly not. Not ever. Never."

"Very well. You don't have to. Dr. Duk and your mother and possibly the sheriff are coming for you later this afternoon, but you don't have to go."

"I don't?"

"No."

"Who says?"

"I say."

"Let's leave now." She buried her face in his shirt. "The cave! Let's go in the cave!"

He laughed. "No. We don't have to go in the cave. The cave is over and done with. We can live up here. How would you like to begin your life?"

"It is time. How would you like to begin yours?"

"I would like to."

"It's about time."

"Yes."

"Is it possible for you?"

"Yes. Now listen to me."

"I am."

"Pack a few things."

"I only have a few things."

"Don't worry, we can buy some more clothes later. There will be plenty of time but I want you to leave here within ten minutes. The sheriff's coming for you. Don't worry, this is your property and you can come back and live here if you want to. So is the island. But go get ready. I'm taking you to the Holiday Inn for a few days."

"Okay," she said. "Let me get my NATO knapsack. Do you recall how Perry Mason would stash away a client in an obscure hotel under a false name for a few days?"

"Yes."

"I read two hundred Perry Masons at Valleyhead. It was beguiling to think of the client living there with Della Street in the Beverly Arms on Sepulveda."

"Yes, but never mind that. Let's get out of here. I want to get you some hot food, a hot bath, and some clean clothes. You're too thin."

"Do I also smell bad?"

"You smell like peat moss and army clothes. I think I'll buy you a dress. Imagine you in a dress! While you take your bath, I'll get a hot plate from the Holiday Inn buffet. They close at three, so hurry up. Then while you eat, I have a short errand to run. Then I will have something to tell you."

"How about my dog?"

"Leave him here with some food. We'll come back for him. He'll discourage visitors. He knows you'll be back, doesn't he?"

"Yes. Let's go."

2

The room at the Holiday Inn was second floor rear. It was warm from the afternoon sunlight. The balcony overlooked a parking lot, a strip of grass, a chain-link fence, a meadow to the west where Holstein cows grazed, and beyond, the violet hulk of the Smokies, tall and dim enough to be a cloud.

While she bathed, he fetched two plates from the buffet, Tennessee pork sausage, sweet potatoes, butter beans, corn on the cob, ten pats of butter, corn bread, buttermilk, and apple pie. This was no ordinary Holiday Inn. When she came out of the bathroom in her pajamas, the very pajamas she had worn in her escape from Valleyhead, places were set at the round black woodlike table next to the drape, which was drawn enough to show a strip of sunlit meadow.

She began to eat. She ate fast and ate it all, gazing dry-eyed at the slot of meadow, sky, and violet mountain.

"I have an errand to run," he told her, standing and gazing down at her, hands in pockets. "I have to see Slocum about something. I'll be back in an hour."

She nodded as she finished her apple pie.

"Take a nap."

She nodded.

At the door he turned to look at her.

"I just realized something," he said. "I don't have an address. I don't live anywhere."

She smiled. "Do not trouble yourself unnecessarily. That is

not necessarily unfavorable. Many people have addresses, yet observe them.''

"Right."

"However, I should like eventually to have an address."

"Yes."

"Could we live together?" she asked.

"I think so, yes. At an address."

"What joy."

"Yes."

3

It took half an hour.

He asked only two questions, and though they were unusual, Slocum blinked only once and answered them readily, looking at him closely only when he walked in, registering his dark suit with a nod and motioning him to a chair.

They sat in a pleasant office smelling of law books and balsam. A big window let onto a view of the mountain with its skewed face and one eye out of place.

"You've left the hospital," said Slocum.

"Yeah."

"You okay?"

"I think so."

"Okay. What's up?"

Did I once practice law, he wondered, and he remembered that he had, not so much from the smell of the books as from Slocum's practiced coolness and his resolve not to be surprised. He smiled. He had been observing doctors and lawyers lately. Both were good at keeping their own counsel and seeming to know something. He hoped Slocum did.

"Two things. First thing: are you familiar with the North Carolina Revised Statutes relating to the rights of patients pursuant to involuntary admissions under the new Mental Health Law?"

"More or less, counselor." Slocum's voice took on the familiar ironic gravity of talk among lawyers and his eyes shifted slightly, lining up with his, taking in the view with him.

"I take it that no director of a treatment facility shall prohibit any mentally ill person from applying for conversion of involuntary admission status to a voluntary admission status."

"That is correct."

They both gazed at the mountain, which with its bare trees looked like a moonfaced man with a stubble.

"I wish you to prepare an application for an injunction from old Judge Jenkins enjoining said director, a Dr. Alistair Duk, from detaining the person in question whose name I shall presently give you. As a precautionary measure I wish you also to apply for a writ of habeas corpus for the same person in the event of involuntary detention, say by Dr. Duk with the assistance of the sheriff—though I think such an eventuality highly unlikely. Finally, I wish you to represent the same person in a hearing to establish her mental and legal competence. Vance will bring in a psychiatrist from Duke."

"No problem. Is that it?" Slocum asked the pied face of the mountain.

"No, that's not it."

"All right."

"As you must know, I am not a member of the North Carolina bar."

"I am aware of that. Not even an illustrious member of the New York bar can apply for a writ here. You got to use the local yokels."

"That's true. But that is not why I mentioned it."

"Why did you mention it?"

"I intend to take the North Carolina bar examination."

"Ah." Slocum's head turned but not enough for their eyes to meet. "You going to run me out of business?"

"No. I'm going to bring you in some business. How would you like the Peabody business?"

"I would like that."

"You can have it. There is something I want."

"I gathered there was."

"I want to work with you. You've often asked me to. Very well, I will, but not as a partner. I've forgotten too much. As a clerk. At first."

Now Slocum did look at him. "Why?"

"I want to."

"I see that. I had figured you figured you quit too early. But aren't you a little overqualified for this two-bit practice?"

"I'm just telling you what I want. You just tell me whether you will go with it. I shall be very pleased to trace titles, file

304

petitions, pass acts of sale, do courthouse runs. If you don't employ me, I'll open up next door and close you down.''

"I do believe you would sandbag me, just like you did in golf.''

"What do you say?''

"You want me to give you an answer now?''

"Yes.''

"Okay. My answer is that if you really do get around to taking the bar exam and—''

"—and pass?''

"And pass. And then if you feel up to it—''

"—if I'm still alive?''

"If you're still alive and kicking—''

"Yes?''

"You're on.''

"Okay.''

Slocum did not move when he rose. "You know something,'' he said to the mountain. "I always did want a Wall Street lawyer to shelve my books and do courthouse runs for me.''

"You got one.''

4

She was asleep when he returned, no sign of her but a tousle of hair and a curve of hip under the motel chenille. The sinking sun made a yellow stripe up the burlap wallpaper.

Her plate was clean. Her NATO knapsack hung from a hook in the alcove. He walked around the bed to see her. He stood looking down at her, hands in pockets. She slept like a child, face turned into the pillow, lips mashed open and making a wet spot on the cotton.

Suddenly he was tired, as tired as he had ever been in his life. Could it be that all these years he had not really slept or slept as lightly as a soldier on patrol? Could it be that not having an address, not living anywhere, meant that one was free to sleep?

Taking off his jacket, and even as he hung it up, he was, alertly he thought and casting ahead as was his wont, looking around for his suitcase, which must have his pajamas, when he realized that he had no suitcase and therefore no pajamas. Where do I go when I leave here? he wondered, yawning and turning. The gyroscope in his head resisted the turn but not unpleasantly. His pH was up. Great haunted molecules boomed around in his brain. A smell of old newspapers and flour paste and Octagon soap rose in his nostrils. Was this Georgia?

Though it was not late, the sun had already touched the top of the violet mountains. It glittered as if it had struck sparks from rock. The slot in the drapes showed a corner of the Holiday Inn property. The corner was empty, no pool, no lounges, no tables, no cars, no children's playground. Yet the grass was well trimmed up to the fence separating it from the pasture. He wondered how many people had set foot in this empty corner over the years. Perhaps none.

Yawning and moving slowly against his gyroscope, he undressed to his underwear shorts, closed the drapes on the sunset, and got into bed. Allison was in the middle of the bed and so inert and heavy with sleep that there was no ready means of making himself comfortable except by fitting himself around her.

Suddenly bethinking himself, he jumped up and turning slowly like a ship heading up in a gale found the *Do Not Disturb* sign next to the Gideon Bible and hung it outside. He hooked up the chain and shot the dead bolt.

Inert or not, she was not so unyielding that he could not put his arms around her and hold her cupped like a child in his sideways lap. Smiling in her neck, he gave her some hugs. What made him happy was the thought of her sleeping so soundly, having eaten so well, resting and digesting and fattening and restoring herself even as he held her. Already the corn bread was sticking to her ribs. Her warm breath blew regularly against his arm.

5

You packed the guns in the trunk of the car, remember?

Yes. No. Leslie did.

Go get them.

No.

Come, it's the only way, the one quick sure exit of grace and violence and beauty. Come, believe me, it's the ultimate come, not the first come which we all grow up dreaming about and which is never what we hoped, is it, but near enough to know there is something better, isn't it, the second, last and ultimate come to end all comes.

No.

Come, what else is there? What other end if you don't make the end? Make your own bright end in the darkness of this dying world, this foul and feckless place, where you know as well as I that nothing ever really works, that you were never once yourself and never will be or he himself or she herself and certainly never once we ourselves together. Come, close it out before it closes you out because believe me life does no better job with dying than with living. Close it out. At least you can do that, not only not lose but win, with one last splendid gesture defeat the whole foul feckless world. You'll do better than I, you're already in a better place, you a placeless person in a placeless place, a motel surely a better place for taking off than a swamp or an attic, yes.

No.

Go like a man, for Christ's sake, a Roman, here's your sword.

No.

Very well. Then it will close you out, since you're already impregnated with death, a slight case of sickness in the head making you crazier even than you are, smelling the past, nigger cabins, pin-oak flats, not even knowing where you are, Georgia, Alabama, Mississippi, without looking out the window to check the mountain, and from here on out nowhere to go but down.

No.

Very well, let it close you out with the drools and the shakes and your mouth fallen open, head nodding away and both hands rolling pills. But you'll never even get that far because you've got my genes and you know better.

Yes.

Then get up and go out to the car and get it and go to the empty corner of grass and fence where nobody's been. We like desert places.

All right.

It was dark.

His head as he turned to rise seemed to shift on its axis like the great world itself.

He rose and dressed in the dark, walked out to the Mercedes, unlocked the trunk, took out the leather case containing the Greener and the holster containing the Luger. It was a cold starry night. The mists of summer and fall had all blown away.

307

He walked down the highway holding the Greener like a businessman with a briefcase. When he reached the overlook the Holiday Inn looked over, he did not even pause but swung the case like a discus, the throw turning him around and heading him back. He did not hear the Greener hit bottom. As an afterthought, he pitched the Luger back over his shoulder and went away without listening.

6

It was light.

"Wake up. What's wrong? What is it?"

"What is what?" Instantly he was awake and unsurprised.

"Who were you talking to? What were you saying about Georgia? Why do you want to go to Georgia? Where did you go?"

"Outside for a walk."

She must have gotten up. The drapes were open a little. The morning light poured in. The Holsteins were grazing beyond the chain-link fence. There was something pleasant about the unused ungrazed Holiday Inn corner. Her pajamas hung in the alcove.

"Come here," he said.

"I'm here," she said. "In the bed. By you."

"Come here."

"Well, you'll have to straighten up. You were all bent over, covering your head with your arms like somebody was after you. Were they?"

"No. I don't know. Now."

"Yes. That's better. Now."

"Yes, it is." Her skin was like silk against him.

"There you are," she said.

"Yes."

"It's you."

"Yes."

"You against me, yet not really opposed."

"Yes. That is, no."

"Put your arms around me in addition."

"They are around you."

"They sure are."

When she came against him from the side, it was with the

effect of flying up to him from below like a little cave bat and clinging to him with every part of her.

They were lying on their sides facing each other.

"Come here," he said.

"I'm here."

"Now."

"Yes."

There was an angle but it did not make trouble. Entering her was like turning a corner and coming home.

"Oh my," she said.

"Yes."

"That's you for true."

"Yes."

"This was not in the book."

"What book?"

"No books, no running brooks, just you."

"Yes."

"I don't believe this," she said. "I don't, I don't."

"It's true," he said.

"Oh my, what is happening? I think I'm going to have a fit."

"Yes."

"What is going to happen?"

"You're going to have a fit."

When he woke up, she was gazing at him. "Were you having a dream?"

"I don't know."

"You were talking about—loving."

"Yes, I remember."

"Was it love like this?"

"No, not like this. I'll take this."

"Don't ever let me go," she said. "Now I know what it is I wanted. Before I only wanted."

"I won't let you go."

"Ah, do you want to know what it is?"

"What is it?"

"It is a needfulness that I didn't know until this moment that I needed. What a mystification."

"Yes, it is a mystification."

"Don't you think you better get up and close the curtain?"

"Not necessarily. The consequences of not closing the curtain are neither here nor there and in any case not direful."

"Are you making fun of me?" she said.

"Yes."

They laughed. It was the first time he had heard her laugh so, a tickled hooting laugh, the way a girl laughs with other girls.

"Oh my," she said after a while. "Perhaps that was it, after all."

"It?"

"Yes, you know, it."

"Yes."

"Would you have ever believed?" she asked someone, perhaps herself, absently.

"Yes, I would have believed," he said.

"Oh my," she said again presently. "It is now evident that whatever was wrong with me is now largely cured. Quel mystery."

"I have an idea," he said after a while.

"What?"

"Let's stay together. I do not wish to leave you again."

"Me neither. I, that is, you."

"Me too."

"Well well," she said later. Her back and legs were strong as a man's. "That was not in the book either."

"What book?"

"The pine-tree book. Or the picture book."

"What?"

"Never mind."

"I'll tell you what let's do," he said.

"What?"

"Let's get a house and live in it."

"Okay. Can we make love like that much of the time?"

"As much as you like."

"For true?"

"For true. Would you like to marry?"

"Uh, to marry might be to miscarry."

"Not necessarily. I'll practice law. You grow things in your greenhouse. We can meet after work, have supper. We can walk the Long Trail or go to the beach on your island. Then go to bed irregardless."

"Perhaps crash in a shelter?"

"What?" he said, laughing. "Crash?"

"Sure."

"Okay."

"It is a good regime. Perhaps with you to marry would not miscarry. Is it legal to do this at four o'clock in the afternoon?"

"Yes," he said.

"Now I know what was wrong with four o'clock in the afternoon."

"It would be nice to have two children and walk to school with them in the morning."

"Yes," she said.

They stayed in bed all day and all night except for meals, loving and laughing, frolicking, exchanging many a kiss and smacks on the ass while carts creaked outside and maids tapped on doors with keys. Frowning, she peered closely at his cheek and squeezed a blackhead. He straddled her thighs and rubbed her back, sore from hoisting, pressed his thumbs in the two dips at the bottom of her spine, marveling at how she was made. Each tended to the other, kneading and poking sore places. She examined him like a mother examining a child, close, stretching skin, her mouth open, grabbing hair to pull his head over to see his neck, her eyes slightly abulge with concentration, checking his cave wounds, picking at scabs. When her eyes happened to meet him, they softened and went deep. Eyes examining are different from eyes meeting eyes. As she would say, a look at a book is not a look into a look. Then she smiled and flew against him again. Her supple bent-back strength and coverage astounded him.

7

She had brought his razor from the greenhouse. It felt good to shave.

After they dressed, they ate a huge breakfast of grits and bacon and scrambled eggs in the Buccaneer Tavern, came back to the room and opened the drapes to the morning and the Smoky Mountains, which humped up like a blue whale in the clear sky. He sat her down across the round black woodlike table.

"Let's get down to business."

"Oh, look at you in your dark suit."

"Yes?"

"You look nice around the neck and head."

"Thank you. You look good all over."

"Come here," she said.

"I'm here."

"You're nice here around the ears, too."

"Thank you."

"Let's go to bed."

"But we're dressed."

"Undress."

"Okay."

Afterwards she said: "Good gosh."

"Yes."

Again at the table he said: "Now ah—"

"The business."

"Yes. Let us speak of one or two things."

"Right."

It had come to pass, for reasons which neither could have said, that he now knew what needed to be done and could say so and she could heed him, head slightly cocked, listening carefully. She looked like a survivor on the mend. Could it be that her thin face was already fuller?

"Here is what I intend to do," he told her, "and what I hope you will wish to do. If you do not wish to do so, will you tell me?"

"Assuredly."

"I propose that we marry. Wait. I don't think I am saying this right."

"No."

"Perhaps I'd better ask you."

"Very well."

"Will you marry me?"

"Yes."

"It is possible that though marriage in these times seems for some reason to be a troubled, often fatal, arrangement, we might not only survive it but revive it."

"Yes, we could survive and revive it."

"I presently have very little income of my own. I'm not counting Marion's estate, which I inherited from Marion but which I won't use. I'm not sure what I'll do with it—figure out what Marion would want—something. Therefore, I shall be working. You own valuable property. I propose that for the present we rent or buy a garden home. They are somewhat like motels but not unpleasantly so. You need to get out of that greenhouse and eat better. Garden homes are convenient and have pleasant views. We shall need a place to live until we build a house. I'll look up the Associate at Emerald Isles and give him a job making home loans. He'll be sick of isometrics and TV.''

"What's wrong with staying here?''

"Nothing. But we might need more than one room eventually.''

"That's true. Let's come back here every weekend.''

"Okay. Now you might wish to finish your greenhouse and develop your property here or on the island—perhaps build log cabins on ten- or twelve-acre plots. I have two friends, one a contractor, the other a cabin notcher, who though old and maimed can still do excellent work, I think. It would be a pleasant business.''

"Yes. I think I want to finish my greenhouse and perhaps build others against the same ridge and make use of the same warm cave air.''

"A good idea. It could be an excellent business.''

"If I could find enough men to work for me, any men who are willing, old men. But that's impossible.''

"No, I know some good men. Old men but good.''

"Do you know what a head of lettuce costs at the A & P?'' she asked him.

"No.''

"A dollar and fifty cents.''

"Is that a lot?''

She looked at him. "Yes, and three small tomatoes cost a dollar. I could make money.''

"Yes. I also have another friend who is an excellent gardener but has nothing to do but water pine trees.''

"Hire him. I have a friend at Valleyhead I would like to get out. She would be glad to work for someone who can tell her what to do. She needs that. Moreover, she's a good bookkeeper.''

"Can you tell her what to do?''

"Yes.''

"Okay. As for myself, I think I'll resume the practice of law in a small way if my health will permit it. I have an incurable mental condition but it can be controlled as long as my pH is okay.''

"How is your pH now?''

"Fine.''

Actually, his pH was up again. Fewer hydrogen ions were zipping around the heavy alkaline molecules sweet with memory and desire. Perhaps a slight case of Hausmann's Syndrome was better than none at all.

"I am sure of it. There is nothing serious wrong with you." Frowning, she leaned over and took hold of his flank in her rough hoister's hand. It was odd how she was like and unlike Kitty. "Our cases are similar. Nowadays many psychosomatic conditions can be cured. I was reading in the *National Observer* at the A & P about the supremacy of mental attitude over physical conditions."

"Yes. Whatever it is, I think it is under control. I can feel it going away."

He did feel good. The twisting in his head now felt like a scar contracting. Did he imagine it, or wasn't his brain lesion shriveling like a crab in acid? There was a faint smell of smoke high in his nostrils and the sinuses in front of his brain.

"Another thing," he said. "What do you think of our having a child and enrolling him or her in the Linwood elementary school?"

"I think well of that."

"I could drive him to school every morning and he could ride the school bus home."

"Or she, as the case may be. I thought you wanted two."

"Oh yes. I had forgotten. Could it be that now you're doing the remembering?"

"Could be."

"Now let's go to town and do some shopping. You need some clothes. I have to go to St. Mark's."

"To get your stuff?"

"Yes. Then we'll find a villa or condo or a garden home. And I need to talk to someone."

"All right. I'm going back to the greenhouse."

"Why?"

"I have to get my dog."

"Very well. I think it's safe. I don't think they will be looking for you now. We've been here for two days, haven't we?"

"Or one long night. Or both. I'm not sure."

"Very well. But don't stay long."

"All right."

She wet her thumbs with her tongue and smoothed his eyebrows. He was going to town.

* * *

8

Mr. Arnold and Mr. Ryan were lying in bed watching *Search for Tomorrow*. A curtain was drawn around the third bed. It seemed best to wait for a commercial break before putting his question. When it came, he turned down the volume and spoke fast.

"Excuse me, but this is important."

The two men gazed at him.

"You fellows want a job?"

They gazed at each other.

"I have some property and I want it developed right," he said, talking fast, so he wouldn't interfere with *Search for Tomorrow*. "I want well-built log cabins, enough land for privacy, and gardens, and at a price young couples, singles, and retired couples can afford. Not two hundred and fifty dollars maybe but less than twenty-five thousand. Mr. Ryan here has the know-how about financing, subdividing, contracting, and so forth. And he has the crew. Mr. Arnold has the building technique. What I want is for Mr. Arnold to work with Mr. Ryan's crew and teach them how to notch up a cabin, perhaps with more modern methods. I have plenty of timber, creek rocks, and flagstone. I'll handle the legal work. I figure we can build and sell cabins on ten acres of land and come out fine at twenty-five thousand." The commercial was almost over. "What do you say?"

The two old men looked at each other.

"Whereabouts we going to live?" asked Mr. Arnold.

"Wherever you like. Here. Or Mr. Arnold could notch up a cabin for the two of you."

"What, me live with that old peckerwood?" said Mr. Ryan.

"Hail fire," said Mr. Arnold.

"Look, I don't care where you live. I'm making you a proposition. This is a good deal all around. We'll incorporate—that's one thing I know how to do—and share the profits. What do you say? Mr. Ryan, can you still get a crew?"

"Slick, Tex, Tomás, and Vishnu came by to see me last week. All of them said they wished they still worked for me."

"Two of them looked like gypsies, the other two looked like women," said Mr. Arnold.

"They may look funny," said Mr. Ryan, "but they can out-work niggers. How am I going to get around?" He slapped the

315

flat sheet where his leg should have been. "I'm missing two feet and one leg."

"Any way you can. You figure it out."

"They make cars now you can drive with your hands," said Mr. Ryan, answering his own question.

"There you go. The corporation can afford one," said Will Barrett. "Mr. Arnold, are you willing to teach this crew what to do?"

"All they got to do is watch me and keep out of my way. What land we talking about?"

"The Kemp property, over by the country club."

"There's plenty of good timber there. All you got to do is keep me in logs—and somebody to pick up on one end."

"You willing to use cement chinking instead of river clay and hog blood?" Mr. Ryan asked the silent TV screen. Neither of the men seemed to notice that *Search for Tomorrow* was playing without sound.

"I chinked a house on Dog Mountain with cement. Ain't nothing wrong with cement. You just bring your boys and keep me in straight logs. We going to need some boys to get the roof up. It takes several to mortise and peg the peaks. I can't climb no roof but I can show them how to split shingles and put the sap sides together. You going to need a forty-five-degree angle on your roof and a halfway lap to keep out leaks."

"Your roof? Whose roof?" asked Mr. Ryan. "I'll show you some composition roofing that comes by the roll," Mr. Ryan told the TV, "but it looks real good. I think you'll like it. It saves labor. You're talking about splitting shingles by hand, I mean Jesus Christ."

"It sounds like tar paper but I'll look at it."

It was a good time to leave. He turned up the volume on *Search for Tomorrow*.

There was a commotion around the third bed. The curtain was pulled back. Two orderlies were trying to get an old woman onto a hospital stretcher. The woman was sitting on the edge of the bed and crying. She was no larger than a child but her ankles, clad in men's socks, were as thick as small trees. A great vessel moved in her neck in a complex out-of-sync throbbing. Her eyes were glossy and unblinking in her round heavy face. Tears ran down her cheek and caught in the dark down of her lip.

"Oh, I'm so afraid," she said loudly with a little smile and a shrug. She pronounced *afraid afred*, like ladies in Memphis and Vicksburg.

"What you scared of, honey?" asked one orderly, a giant black woman big as an old black mammy but young.

"I'm afraid I'm never going to leave the hospital. Oh, I'm so afraid."

"You be all right, honey," said the black woman, her eyes absentminded, and put a black-and-pink hand on the patient's swollen leg. "You gon be fine, bless Jesus."

Will Barrett was standing at the foot of the bed.

"Oh, hello, Will," said the patient with the same smile and shrug. "Oh, Will, I hate to leave here!"

"Yes, I know," he said. "I—" Oh Lord, I am supposed to know her. Was she an aunt? No, but she was one of ten or twelve ladies from Memphis or Mississippi he should have recognized. He made as if to give the orderlies a hand.

As he came close to her, he could hear her heart, which raced and rumbled so hard it shook her thick body.

He took her arm. It was not necessary. The other orderly, a sorrel-colored man who wore his mustache and short-sleeved smock like Sugar Ray Robinson, picked up the woman and in one swift gentle movement swung her onto the stretcher. He was an old-style dude who still wore a conk! He chewed gum like Sugar Ray. Where did he come from? Beale Street twenty years ago? After he centered the woman on the stretcher (ah, I know what that feels like, to be taken care of by strong quick sure hands at one's hips) and buckled the straps, Sugar Ray leaned close to her.

"Listen, lady, I'm gerng to tell you something." (That was the difference between them, the two orderlies, that *gerng*, his slightly self-conscious uptown correction of the black woman.) "The doctors know what they know, but I have noticed something too. I can tell about people and I'm gerng to tell you. We taking you to the hospital in Asheville and we coming to get you Tuesday and bringing you back here and that's the truth, ain't that right, Rosie?" And he smiled, a brilliant white-and-gold Sugar Ray smile, yet his eyes had not changed because they didn't have to. The patient couldn't see his eyes.

"Sho," said Rosie, her eye not quite meeting Sugar Ray's eye and not quite winking. "You gon be fine, honey."

"Ah," said the patient and, closing her eyes, slumped against the straps like a baby in its harness.

Then how does it add up in the economy of giving and getting, he wondered, that the two orderlies cared nothing (or did they?) for the old woman, that even in the very act of their offhand reassurances to her they were probably cooking up something between themselves, that they, the orderlies, who had no reason to give her anything at all, gave it because it was so little to give and so much for her to get? 2¢ = $5? How?

Does goodness come tricked out so as fakery and fondness and carrying on and is God himself as sly?

In the hall he stood gazing after the three of them. Young big black mammy, Sugar Ray, and the sick woman, the great machinery of her heart socking away so hard at her neck, it made her nod perceptibly as if she understood and agreed, yes, yes, yes.

9

Mr. Eberhart was watering small pine trees with a green plastic mop pail. He walked in a fast limping stoop from tree to tree. Standing with one leg crooked and with his long-billed cap fitting tightly on his head, he looked like a heron.

"Why are you watering these pine trees? It rained yesterday."

"It didn't rain enough. They planted these seedlings too early. The rains don't come till after Christmas."

"Didn't you used to run a nursery in Asheville?"

"Atlanta and Asheville. For forty years."

"How would you like to run a greenhouse now? Perhaps several greenhouses."

"What kind of greenhouse?" He had not yet looked up.

"An old kind. About fifty by twenty-five feet. No fans, no automatic ventilation, no thermostats."

"That's the kind I started with. You cain't build them like that now. What kind of heat? That's what put me out of business. My gas bill was nine hundred dollars a month in the winter."

"No gas bill. No electric bill. No utilities. It runs on cave air."

"Cave air," said Mr. Eberhart, watching water disappear into the sandy soil. Now he looked up.

"That's right. Cave air. A steady flow winter and summer. A steady sixty degrees. Is that too cold?"

"Cave air. I've heard of that around here."

"Is that too cold?"

"Not for lettuce, cauliflower, broccoli, or parsley. Or some orchids. What is your monthly utility cost?"

"Zero. Unless you want to live there and turn on the lights."

"Cave air." He couldn't get it through his head.

"Did you say orchids?"

"Sure." He put down the can, adjusted his cap, picked up a handful of soil. Standing alongside Barrett, he spoke quickly in an East Tennessee accent. He gave his long-billed cap a tug. They could have been a couple of umpires.

"You can grow your cymbidium cooler than that, or laelia. But you don't want to repot your cymbidium."

"Okay."

"I got my own way of growing vanda—that's what you call Hawaiian orchid. Don't nobody know about it. I've applied for a patent. You're a lawyer. You want to know what it is?"

"Sure."

Mr. Eberhart moved closer. "I use chestnut chips and a steady temperature. Most people think they got to have seventy to eighty degrees. But what vanda don't like and you got to watch is your sudden temperature change. And up here you can give them full sunlight."

"We got plenty of both, chestnut and steady temperature."

"That's where your money is."

"Where's that?" Arms folded, they gazed out over the St. Mark's putting green.

"In orchids."

"Is that right?"

"You want to know who buys orchids now?"

"Yes."

"The colored. I sold five hundred corsages to one colored-debutante ball."

"You want the job? I can get you some help."

"Sure. When do I start?"

"Next week."

"Okay." He went back to watering the pines but called after him. "I'll tell you where else the money is."

"Where?"

"Lettuce. If we got the room."

"We got the room. Do you know what a head of lettuce costs you up here?"

"No."

"A dollar and a half."

Mr. Eberhart blinked. "Did you say cave air?"

"Yes."

"I got to see that."

10

Before he found Father Weatherbee in the attic, watching trains, he was stopped by a big florid fellow wearing an L & N engineer's cap. The man had a nose like J. P. Morgan—there were noses on his nose—and wore a double-breasted blue blazer with brass buttons.

"Aren't you Will Barrett?"

"Yes sir."

"Boykin Ramsay of Winston-Salem. Reynolds Tobacco."

"Yes sir."

"You own this place."

"Yes."

"You don't charge enough."

"Is that right?"

"I understand you're going to start a Council on Aging here."

"I hadn't heard of it. It sounds like my daughter's idea—I was thinking of starting something else—farming in cave air."

"I'm eighty-five years old and I'm here to tell you I don't need any goddamn Council on Aging."

"I see."

Mr. Ramsay grabbed him around the shoulders and pulled him close. "Come here, Will," he said with a heavy but not unpleasant bourbon breath. "I want to tell you something."

"Okay. I'm here."

"I'm going to tell you the secret of getting old."

"Okay."

"Money."

"Money?"

"Making money and keeping it. If you work hard and make money and keep it, I'm here to tell you you don't need any goddamn Council on Aging or educating the public and all that shit. That's how come the Chinese were right or used to be. They kept their money and kept the respect of their families. That's the secret."

"Then why are you here?"

"Because I'm married to the sorriest damn woman in North Carolina and I got three sons who the only reason they are working is I won't support them. They're all waiting for me to die and I'm just mean enough not to. I came up here to take care of myself. Will, you be a mean old son of a bitch like me and you'll have a long happy life."

"Is that right?"

"And I'm also up here to play golf. I hear you're a real sand-bagger."

"Well—"

"Let me tell you something, Will."

"All right."

"I'm eighty-five years old and I play eighteen holes of golf every day. I line up nine mini-bottles of square Black Jack Daniel's on the tray of the golf cart when I start out and knock back one on every other tee and I break ninety. Council on Aging my ass. How you going to counsel me?"

"Well, I wasn't."

"Come on down to my room and I'll counsel you. I got some Wild Turkey."

He looked at his watch. It was three-thirty. She might still be at the greenhouse. Suppose she went back to the greenhouse and forgot about time and got becalmed by her four o'clock feeling. Suppose they came to get her. What would he do if they took her away?

"I just thought of something. I have to go out for a while."

Mr. Ramsay pulled him close. "Just remember one thing."

"Okay."

"Hang on to your money."

"Okay."

He was backing away. He had to find her. His need of her was as simple and urgent as drawing the next breath.

11

Bars of yellow sunlight broke through the clouds and leveled between the spokes of the pines. She was singing and planting avocado pits. They had sprouted, tiny spiky Mesozoic ferns.

He had heard her from a distance, standing still in the cold dripping woods, and did not recognize her. The voice was unlike her speaking voice, bell-like, lower-pitched, and plangent.

It was as if she were playing an instrument. Now as he stood close to her in the potting shed, the voice had a throaty foreign sound.

The dog watched him but she did not know he was there until he stood behind her and touched her. Unsurprised, she blushed and fell back against him, crossing her arms to touch his.

"Look!" she cried. "It's my first crop! They're already sprouting!"

"I didn't know you could do that," he said.

"Transplant?"

"No. Sing."

"I was a singer."

"What was that song?"

"It is called *Liebesbotschaft*. Love's Message."

"What does it say?"

"The lover is asking a brook to carry his message of love to a maiden."

"I never heard you sing before."

"I didn't feel like it. I stopped."

"Why did you stop?"

"Because I thought I had to sing."

"Do you think you'll sing in the future?"

"Yes."

"Why?"

"Because I don't have to. There is no reason not to. I think I can sing for people if you think it will give them pleasure. Do you?"

"Yes."

She turned to face him. "Why did you come?"

"What? Oh. I was talking to a man at St. Mark's and all of a sudden I realized it was almost four o'clock and I wanted to see you."

"You wanted to see me because you know how I feel at four o'clock in the afternoon?"

"That and more."

"What is the more?"

"I wanted badly to uh see you."

"Is that all?"

"Not quite."

She clapped her hands. "What luck."

"Luck?"

"That we both want the same, that is, the obverse of the same. The one wanting the other and vice versa. What luck. Imagine."

"Yes."

"To rule out a possible misunderstanding, what is it you want?"

"To lie down here by the Grand Crown where it is warm and put my arms around you."

"What luck. Here we are. Hold me."

"I am."

"Oh, I think you have something for me."

"Yes."

"What?"

"Love. I love you," he said. "I love you now and until the day I die."

"Oh, hold me. And tell me."

"Tell you what?"

"Is what you're saying part and parcel of what you're doing?"

"Part and parcel."

They were lying on the dog's croker sacks next to the glowing amber lights of the firebox.

"Tell me the single truth, not two or more separate truths, unless separate truths are subtruths of the single truth. Is there one truth or several separate truths?"

"Both."

"How both?"

"The single truth is I love you. The several subtruths are: I love your dearest heart. I also love your dear ass, which is the loveliest in all of Carolina. I want your ass, it and no other, and you for the rest of my life, you and no other. I also love to see you by firelight. I will always come to see you at four o'clock every afternoon if only to sit with you if it does not please you to make love—"

"It pleases me. How about now?"

"—because I love to sit by you and watch your eyes, which see everything exactly as it is. And to watch the line of your cheek. These are separate truths but are also subtruths of the single truth, I love you."

"Yes, they are and it is. I have a separate truth."

"What?"

"I love your mouth. Give it to me."

"All right."

When they sat up, he said worriedly: "I forgot to take my acid today. I wonder what my pH is."

"I don't know," she said, "but please ascertain it and maintain at the present level, high or low, whichever the case may be."

"Right," he said absently. "Is the dog ready?"

"Sure. I have packed his food. He can stay in the motel, can't he?"

"Sure." They looked at the dog. "Let's go to the car. I'll drop you and the dog at the motel. Then I have one errand to run. I'll be back in an hour."

"Very good."

The dog knew he was to go with them and followed without being called.

12

Father Weatherbee sat behind Jack Curl's mahogany desk with its collection of Russian ikons and bleeding Mexican crucifixes. Perched nervously on the edge of his chair, he looked like a timid missionary summoned by his bishop. His eyelid, lip, and collar drooped.

"Yes, Mr. Barrett?"

"Father Weatherbee, I know you're a busy man, so I'll get right to the point."

"Fine," said Father Weatherbee, who in fact seemed anxious to get back to the attic and the Seaboard Air Line.

"I intend to be married."

"Very good! My congratulations!" Father Weatherbee half rose from his chair, perhaps intending to shake hands, then changed his mind, sat down.

"I want you to perform the ceremony."

"Very good!" Father Weatherbee rose again, sat down. His lip blew a bubble. "Yes, indeed! Well! Father Curl will be back from his ecumenical council next week and I'm sure he'd be pleased to do the ah honors."

"I want you."

"Oh dear," said the old priest, leaning in his chair as if he were figuring how to get past him and out. The bleb blew up again. (Was he afraid of taking on the job just as I am afraid of taking a deposition or passing an act of sale?) "Well, let's see.

Are you a member of St. John's congregation?'' he asked, looking for a way out.

"No, not of St. John's nor of the Episcopal Church."

"Oh," said Father Weatherbee, brightening for the first time, relieved. Here was his loophole. "And your fiancée?"

"No, she's not a member of this or any church."

"Ah," said Father Weatherbee, smiling for the first time, off the hook for sure. "Perhaps the thing to do is for one or both of you to take instruction first, and Father Curl is your man for that."

"No. I am not a believer and do not wish to enter the church."

"I see." The old priest pressed the bleb back and pushed his finger up into his gum. He screwed up one bloodshot eye as if he might yet make sense of this madman. The trouble was catching on to the madness, the madness of the new church, the madness of America, and telling one from the other. "Excuse me, but I don't seem quite to—"

"The Jews may or may not be a sign," said Will Barrett earnestly, leaning halfway across the desk. His pH was rising. When his speedy hydrogen ions departed, so did the Jews. Later, Dr. Ellis would write a scientific article on the subject, entitled: "A Correlation of Plasma pH with Certain Religious Delusions in a Case of Hausmann's Syndrome."

"How's that again?" asked Father Weatherbee, cupping an ear. Did he say Jews?

"It may be true that they have not left North Carolina altogether as I had supposed. Yet their numbers are decreasing. In any event, the historical phenomenon of the Jews cannot be accounted for by historical or sociological theory. Accordingly, they may be said to be in some fashion or other a sign. Wouldn't you agree?"

"The Jews?" repeated Father Weatherbee, turning his other ear.

"My own hunch," said Will Barrett, hitching his chair even closer to the desk while Father Weatherbee rolled his chair back, "is that the Apostolic Succession involved a laying on of hands, right? This goes back to Christ himself, a Jew, a unique historical phenomenon, as unique as the Jews. Present-day Jews, whether or not they have departed North Carolina for Israel, similarly trace their origins to the same place and to kinsmen of Jesus, right? Modern historians agree there is no scientific explanation for the strange history of the Jews—"

He paused, frowning, wondering where he had gotten such an idea. Who were these "modern historians"? He couldn't think of a one. "Excuse me, Father, please bear with me a moment." (Father? Perhaps he didn't like to be called Father? Reverend? Mister? Sir?) "What I am suggesting is that though I am an unbeliever, it does not follow that your belief, the belief of the church, is untrue, that in fact it may be true, and if it is, the Jews may be the clue. Doesn't Scripture tell us that salvation comes from the Jews? At any rate, the Jews are the common denominator between us. That is to say, I am not a believer but I believe I am on the track of something. I may also tell you that I have the gift of discerning people and can tell when they know something I don't know. Accordingly, I am willing to be told whatever it is you seem to know and I will attend carefully to what you say. It is on these grounds that I ask you to perform the ceremony. In fact, I demand it—ha ha—if that is what it takes. You can't turn down a penitent, can you? We are also willing to take instructions, as long as you recognize I cannot and will not accept all of your dogmas. Unless of course you have the authority to tell me something I don't know. Do you?" Will Barrett was leaning halfway across the desk.

Father Weatherbee's chair had rolled back until it hit the wall. His white eye spun. His good bloodshot eye looked past his nose bridge at Will Barrett as if he were a cobra swaying atop his desk.

"Oh dear," he sighed. "Surely it would seem that Father Curl is your man—though of course I should be glad to be of any assistance I can."

"No, you're my man. I perceive that you seem to know something—and that by the same token Jack Curl does not."

"Oh dear," said Father Weatherbee and, sinking in his chair, appeared to be muttering to himself. He looked around vaguely and spoke so softly that Will Barrett had to cup his good ear. "It seems I understand simple foreign folk better than my own people. It seems I understand every country in the world better than my own country." He craned up his neck like a Philippine bird and looked in every direction except Will Barrett's. "How can we be the best dearest most generous people on earth, and at the same time so unhappy? How harsh everyone is here! How restless! How impatient! How worried! How sarcastic! How unhappy! How hateful! How pleasure-loving! How lascivious! Above all, how selfish! Why is it that we have more than any other people, are more generous with what we have, and yet are so selfish and unhappy? Why do we think of nothing but our own pleasure? I cannot believe my eyes at what I see on television. It makes me blush with shame. Did you know that pleasure-seeking leads to cruelty? That is why more and more people beat their children. Children interfere with pleasure. Do you hate children? Why can't we be grateful for our great blessings and thank God?'' As he gazed down at the desk, he seemed to have forgotten Will Barrett. His voice sank to a whisper. ''Why is it that Americans who are the best dearest most generous people on earth are so unhappy?'' He shook his head. ''I don't—''

''Yes! Right!'' said Will Barrett excitedly and leaned even closer. ''That is why I say it is so important to recognize a sign when you—''

But the old priest did not seem to be listening. ''There is a tiny village in Mindanao near Naga-Naga on the coast which I was able to visit only once a year. They are as poor as any people on earth, yet how kind and gentle and loving they are to each other! And happy! When I would come to the village little children would run out laughing with joy to see me, take me by the hand and lead me around the village to visit the old and the sick and the blind—and they were even happier to see me than the children! They believed me! They believed the Gospel whole and entire, and the teachings of the church. They said that if I told them, then it must be true or I would not have gone to so much trouble. During my absence betrothed couples remained continent and cheerful of their own volition.'' He sat back and looked up timidly. The bleb on his lip inflated.

''Right!'' cried Will Barrett. In his excitement he had risen from his chair and started around the desk. ''Tell me something, Father. Do you believe that Christ will come again and that in fact there are certain unmistakable signs of his coming in these very times?''

By now Father Weatherbee had also risen and had sidled past, keeping the desk between them, nodding and smiling. If only he could get back to the Atchison, Topeka and the Santa Fe and the lonesome whistle of the Seaboard Air Line, the only things in all of America he recognized.

Will Barrett stopped the old priest at the door and gazed into his face. The bad eye spun and the good eye looked back at him fearfully: What do you want of me? What do I want of him, mused Will Barrett, and suddenly realized he had gripped the old man's wrists as if he were a child. The bones were like dry sticks. He let go and fell back. For some reason the old man did not move but looked at him with a new odd expression. Will Barrett thought about Allie in her greenhouse, her wide gray eyes, her lean muscled boy's arms, her strong quick hands. His heart leapt with a secret joy. What is it I want from her and him, he wondered, not only want but must have? Is she a gift and therefore a sign of a giver? Could it be that the Lord is here, masquerading behind this simple silly holy face? Am I crazy to want both, her and Him? No, not want, must have. And will have.

About the Author

Walker Percy went to medical school and interned at Bellevue, intending to be a psychiatrist. After a bout with tuberculosis, he married and converted to Catholicism. He became a writer and his first novel, THE MOVIEGOER, won the National Book Award and has never been out of print since its publication in 1961. He and his wife live in Covington, Louisiana.

Start with a map.

Having checked into to the
Room at the Anomie
Abbey Hotel in the
beautiful seaside
community of a Acedia
Aquatics in the West Coast
of Florida, just South of Tampa
he said to himself screwed it I think the